ARDENTI

THE RANGER'S MAGI, BOOK 2

ARDENTI

ESKAY KABBA

4 Horsemen
Publications, Inc.

Published By: 4 Horsemen Publications, Inc.

4 Horsemen Publications, Inc.
PO Box 417
Sylva, NC 28779
4horsemenpublications.com
info@4horsemenpublications.com

Cover Illustration by Oxford
Cover Typography and Typesetting by Autumn Skye
Edited by Kris Cotter

Library of Congress Control Number: 2025935795

Paperback ISBN-13: 979-8-8232-0860-4
Hardcover ISBN-13: 979-8-8232-0861-1
Audiobook ISBN-13: 979-8-8232-0863-5
Ebook ISBN-13: 979-8-8232-0862-8

Content warnings: sexually explicit content, discussions of sexual grooming; incidents of violence and death

CONTENTS

CHAPTER 1

Dragon Tamer

Ciaran stopped talking for a moment and stared at the young faces in front of him sitting on the grass in the heat at dusk. Some were listening. Most were not. Instead, they stared at the yellow-eyed, blue-black dragon about ten feet in front of them. It was the closest they had ever been to a dragon.

Robetta was lying on her four legs, her eyes lazily watching the humans in front of her, her wings tucked into her side. Ciaran was to her right, between her catlike eye and batlike ear, and had just explained how important it was to not stand directly in front of a dragon unless they were familiar with the person because the beast would see it as a challenge. He told them to either stay slightly to the right or left and to keep their shoulders relaxed but their stance firm. That their tone of voice meant more to the beasts than the commands. To speak regularly, without aggression, or dragons would show aggression right back.

And that if a person showed even an ounce of fear, depending on the classification of the dragon, they would hunt and play with the person like a cat does with a mouse, which always ends up with the mouse dead. Or the dragon would charge like a cheetah hunting their dinner, which would also end in the person's demise. Or if they are lucky, the dragon would simply blow fire and end their existence in an instant.

"Any questions so far?" Ciaran asked.

No one spoke. Their eyes were wide, and some still had their pencils hanging in the air, along with their mouths, at Ciaran's warnings of death. After a long moment, a young Indian boy asked bravely, "But when do we get to ride it?" Some smiled; others chuckled.

"It will be some time, I'm afraid," Ciaran said seriously.

"It's already been fourteen months," another boy with a New Zealand accent complained.

"Right," Ciaran agreed. "And for now, this is the closest you will get to one."

There was a murmur of groans. So Ciaran decided to give them a chance. He pointed at the boy who spoke first. "You. What's your name?"

"Mohun."

"Come to me, Mohun."

All the other boys gasped in jealousy. He stood up and began walking toward Ciaran. Betta immediately raised her head and eyed him. The boy stopped walking abruptly. He looked at Ciaran, at the dragon, then back to their trainer.

"What did I tell you about fear?" Ciaran said. "Are you coming or not?"

Mohun looked at Betta once more, who was still staring at him. Then he began walking again. "We're going to be friends, you and I," he told her.

Betta watched him until he stood next to Ciaran. Then she slowly put her head back down, no longer interested. Ciaran smiled at him. "Well done."

He motioned for Mohun to go back to his spot on the grass. One by one, the six trainees between the ages of seventeen to twenty-two stood next to the dragon.

Ciaran talked a little more about how to behave around a dragon and how to gain their trust. He made them write out the major differences in attributes and personalities and how they are classified into four types: Class A being the smallest dragons, no more than ten feet in height, mostly playful, easily tamable, like Hansel, their Pigeondon. Class B were more independent, mostly loners, and appreciated their solitude. They were easily irritated and could change moods in an instant. But they generally weren't aggressive unless provoked or scared. That was Betta, the Magnetite dragon before them, and the two Irish Camouflias, Ben and Anna. They lived the longest.

Class C were usually the largest, naturally aggressive, and had more than one way of attacking their prey: Fire and venom through their teeth, claws, or body spikes. They liked the company of other dragons and found themselves in pairs and groups, especially when they hunted. Class C dragons hid in the highest mountains; their thick rubbery skin was made for colder weather, and they had long spiked tails. Hina, a Japanese dragon and the oldest on the Reserve, and the Krekardron named Malik, one of the youngest, were both Class C dragons. Hina did not have a partner anymore, but was content on the reserve around the other dragons. Malik gravitated to Betta since they were about the same age, two and three years old, respectively.

Class D dragons were the most dangerous. Their size didn't matter; it was how deadly they were. Their goal was to hunt and kill. They had the most deadly venom, the sharpest talons, and the hottest fire. Most dragons, especially Class D dragons, were extinct due to the Dragon Defunction of 1302. But every once in a while, one would appear. Their beloved London, who passed away earlier that year, was a Class D dragon.

When Ciaran was getting his degree in Dragonology, he would remember their classifications by their characteristics: A: Amiable; B: Bendable; C: Cantankerous, and D: Deadly. He ended his session that evening by giving them that same tool of remembrance.

Ciaran dismissed them, sending them back to Khalid, the trainee and dung coordinator, for their nighttime assignments. Once the trainees went back to schlepping dung, Ciaran turned his attention to the twenty-five-month-old baby dragon. "You did good there, girl," he said softly, running a hand behind her ear. Her eyes rolled around in satisfaction.

Ciaran looked to the skies. He gently ran his hand down her side until he came to her neck. Then began to climb on top. Fitting his legs snugly between her neck and shoulder, he grabbed onto two spikes and put his face in the back of her neck.

"Let's go. Hiyah!"

Betta lazily stood up on four legs and stretched them before she extended out her enormous wings. The trainees that were just with Ciaran stopped what they were doing and watched in awe. Betta turned around and trotted toward the valley. Ciaran held on as she did a nosedive straight down until her wings caught the wind, then immediately swung back up vertically, and sped up into the clouds.

Ciaran didn't direct her. He never did. They weren't horses, and it wasn't a race. They were creatures, big and dangerous, with thoughts and feelings of their own. He practiced what he taught and revered each beast with respect and admiration. It wasn't his job to control them. It was his job to help them live their best lives in safety and comfort. The Dragon Reservation of Albania was one of the oldest dragon reserves in the world, and the largest, with six dragons that frequented the valley, and a few more that never came out of the mountains. The second oldest sanctioned reservation was hidden somewhere in Siberia, and the third was in South America on a Chilean island, which Ciaran visited two years ago. Anyone who kept dragons unsanctioned by the Magi Council in their region was in violation of the Law.

Betta took him twenty thousand feet up before she plateaued and sailed across the sky. The wind was so loud in his ears he couldn't hear himself think, and his face was almost as red as his hair from the lack of oxygen from being up that high. The skyline lit up in colors of pink and orange as they flew through and around the peaks of the Verdant Mountains, as if Betta were chasing the sun. Ciaran felt another gush of wind as Malik came up from behind and then flew over them. Betta sped up to catch him, and they flew side by side. Malik flew to the nearest mountain, his strong nails digging in as he slammed into the rocks, his tail slamming even harder, causing stones to fall. Betta was more graceful, possibly because she knew she had a passenger, and landed on two feet, then four.

The dragons grunted, sniffed, and whined at each other. Ciaran lifted his head up and stared at the horizon and the setting sun. It was colder up here, at least twenty degrees lower than it was on the ground. He thought about Christopher, his partner, wishing that one day Chris would be able to experience all this with him. But Chris was Commoner, a non-magical human, who was not supposed to know about the world of magic or the Magi Community. He sighed and put his head back down.

After a while, Ciaran lifted one hand out to touch the back of her ear. "I know you want to play," he said to her gently. "But can we go home now?"

Betta understood. She gave her friend one last grunt and kicked off from her back feet into the air. The wind caught under her wings almost immediately, and she began to fly back to the valley, her home. Malik roared at her, hoping she would stay longer. She ignored him. She kept going the way she came; the sun had gone, leaving streaks of color along the horizon behind her.

Dale, the Ringmaster of the Reserve, met him at the top of the hill as Ciaran walked up from the valley where Betta landed. "You're off; Bruno is on," Dale said, getting right to it.

"Oh," Ciaran said in surprise, taking off his gloves. He looked over at the large burly man staring at the trainees suspiciously. "You're sure about that?"

"He's fine," Dale said, not turning around. "You've been on these grounds for seven days. The new dragon, Malik, is adjusting well, but he's spending more time in the mountains than down here, which makes sense. The mountains are his home, what he's familiar with. Go home in the morning. I already sent Vladimir, his Lead Tamer, home too. Bruno will take the next five days. Then we'll talk about an alternating schedule between the two of you."

Ciaran nodded. "Okay."

He looked at the time; it was just after 8 p.m. Ranger Chris Jennings wouldn't start his shift for another three hours. He went to go find his friend and Felix in the Novo and medicinal building to pass the time.

Chris could hear the loud talking and laughter as he walked up the stairs of the Tank, the forest ranger's tower and head-quarters. He opened the door and saw Ciaran laughing with Elijah, the second-shift ranger. "What did I miss?" he asked.

"Your boyfriend here was trying to explain the importance of mythical creatures in fantasy novels. We're talking Great Eagles, werewolves, and oliphants in *Lord of the Rings*," Elijah said.

Ciaran said jovially, "Could you imagine Middle Earth without it?"

They continued to argue about vampires and werewolves in *Twilight* and dragons in *A Song of Fire and Ice* while Chris was still focused on the word "boyfriend," trying to figure out if it was sarcasm or acknowledgment as he walked toward the back to his locker. Ciaran answered his thought, however. As Chris walked past Ciaran and touched his shoulder, Ciaran casually took his hand, kissed it, and then let go, all while continuing his conversation with Elijah.

Chris contained his surprise. *Well*, he thought, *Ciaran's mission to bring Malik to the Reserve must have gone better than I thought.* He went to his locker, dropped off his bag, and sat down at the table next to Ciaran.

Elijah gave his shift report and headed out ten minutes to eleven, saying, "Let me get out here and give you guys some much-needed time." He shook Ciaran's and Chris's hands and left.

Chris waited until Elijah closed the door, then turned to Ciaran. "Sooooo. You seemed pretty open about us to my coworker."

Ciaran shrugged. "Elijah saw me hanging around and knew I was waiting for you. We got to talking, and, apparently, he has known since he started, or at least suspected. It was confirmed when he saw us snogging about two weeks ago before my mission."

"I see," said Chris. "Malik is doing well?"

"He's doing remarkably well," said Ciaran. "He's still wary of the other dragons. Hansel can be annoying, and Anna and Ben are too unpredictable. But he spends his days playing and flying with Betta, and his nights sleeping in the mountains."

Chris nodded. "How is our Betta?"

"She's amazing," Ciaran said. "I was able to use her with the trainees today for the first time. She did so well, staying compliant, not scaring them off."

Chris smiled. "Wish she had some of that compliance when we first met. Instead of trying to burn me alive."

"Well, I didn't get a chance to tame her yet, innit?" said Ciaran.

"Ah, yes, my infamous dragon tamer and savior," said Chris, making Ciaran smile at him. Ciaran reached across and touched Chris's hand on the table. "You came early."

Ciaran had been coming around to patrol with him, but he had been living on the Reserve for over a week since they got back from their mission in Chad.

"Yeah. Working tonight, but I'm off for the next five days. So as long as no red sparks meet me, I won't need to go back until Monday night. Dale sent me and Vladimir home." They played with each other's fingers on the table. Ciaran continued, "So I'm going to hang around the Reserve all night, then meet you here in the morning, and go home with you."

"You don't want to go home to your flat?" Chris asked.

"No," Ciaran said. "I want to be in your space."

"I'm tempted to take off, too," Chris said.

"No, don't do that. I will be there when you leave at night and when you come home in the morning. I want to put you to sleep and wake up with you. Every day."

Chris smiled. "That was fucking romantic. More of that, please." Ciaran grinned again. Then Chris said, "Make sure you have a change of clothes, or you'll be wearing my underwear like I did at your house while you were away on mission."

Ciaran laughed. "Okay, new plan. At dawn, I will go home, get clothes, and meet you at your place by 7:30 a.m."

They sat in silence for a moment, still playing with each other's fingers. "You've been chatting about this Vlad character," Chris said, breaking the moment. "Vlad is your new best mate?"

"My new *gay* best mate," Ciaran said.

Chris's eyebrows went up, and Ciaran laughed. "Should I be worried?" Chris asked.

"Ha!" Ciaran scoffed. "He's like twenty years old and has a boyfriend. Probably a fiancé by the time he gets back."

"Well. Can't wait to hear all about him." Chris looked away, feigning jealousy.

Ciaran chuckled again. "I'm not sure if that was sarcasm or not." Chris shrugged nonchalantly. Ciaran leaned in and kissed Chris on the mouth. "No worries. I'm all yours."

"Well, show me on that bed right there," Chris tried.

Ciaran smiled at Chris's attempt to break his one rule: No fucking at work. He stood up. "Nice try. I'll see you at your place. 7:15." He kissed his forehead as he started walking out.

Chris smiled back. "It was worth a shot."

Ciaran responded by Wisp'ing in a cloud of black smoke back to the entrance of the Reserve.

CHAPTER 2

The Smell of Him

At dawn, as much as he wanted to stop by the Tank, Ciaran Wisp'd home instead. He noticed Chris had cleaned up his apartment and had done a small load of laundry, probably of Ciaran's clothes that he wore all week while there. Ciaran showered and changed into casual clothes: jeans, a t-shirt, and sneakers. He packed a bag of clothes and looked at the time. It was already 7 a.m., and he did not feel like sitting around, so he Wisp'd early to Chris's doorway.

As he sat on the top step and waited, the right door of the duplex opened and Clarissa, Chris's oldest sister, came out with her son Rudy, who saw him first.

"Ciaran!" he yelled and jumped in his arms.

"Ciaran, what a nice surprise!" she exclaimed too, in surprise.

He let Rudy go and gave her a hug with a kiss on each cheek. "Good morning. You look great," he said and meant it. Her light brown skin was glowing, and her dark curly hair shone.

"Oh! Eight months pregnant and as big as a house. I wouldn't say I look great. But that was kind of you. So you're back?"

"Yes," Ciaran said, unsure of what Chris told them about his mission.

"Well, good. Because I barely saw my brother for over a week. I'm off to work, and this one is off to school." Chris helped guide her down the steps. She turned back and asked, "Are you staying for dinner?"

"Yes."

"Good. We'll make it upstairs and bring it down to the table." She looked at him thoughtfully, then said, "Ciaran, my brother really missed you when you were away on your work trip. He really cares about you. And I'm hoping that the feeling is reciprocated."

Ciaran swallowed. "Ah... yes. The feelings are ... reciprocated." He went a little pink. "Maybe... maybe more."

She nodded, then turned to walk on. "See you at dinner," she called over her shoulder and left Ciaran with his thoughts.

Even before he and Chris became official three months ago in February, he had been in his head about his own feelings, and he never really thought about how strong Chris's feelings for him were. Sure, Chris liked him a lot, but were they as strong as Ciaran was starting to feel? He didn't know. Chris had told him many stories about people who loved him that he didn't feel the same for, but carried on with the relationship just because. The thought scared him, and Ciaran could only hope that wasn't the case for them.

Ciaran watched Chris's car drive past the house, looking for parking on the street. He walked up a few minutes later and looked Ciaran up and down. "I don't think I've ever seen you more normal-looking. You're either in your work uniform or t-shirts and boots. Not even on our date nights are you this casual."

"Well. Maybe I wanted to look nice for you." Ciaran said, and they kissed.

Chris opened the door, and Ciaran took off his shoes and dropped his bag in the entryway of the living room. Chris grabbed a plate of food and said, "Charity made me a breakfast wrap, either lamb or sheep. I can't tell." He took a bite. "Lamb."

He broke off half the sandwich and gave it to Ciaran. Ciaran was grateful to Chris's other sister for feeding them before her shift at the hospital. He took it and sat on the arm of the couch. He grabbed the remote and turned on the TV, while taking a bite, flipping through the channels. Chris watched him curiously, surprised that he wasn't trying to jump his bones after almost two weeks of not sleeping in the same bed. But Ciaran was very casually hanging around the house.

Chris quickly finished his wrap and stood behind the couch. "Is that what you want to do now? Watch the telly?"

Ciaran looked up calmly and said, "What's wrong with *NatGeo Wild*?"

Chris shook his head. "I'm going to go take a shower."

Ciaran grabbed his hand. "No wait, come sit down for a moment." Chris sat down next to Ciaran, who was still half on, half off the sofa, watching TV.

After a couple of minutes, Chris said, "I'm surprised we aren't being animals instead of just watching them. But I get it. Intimacy, right?"

Ciaran smiled a little, then muted the TV. He came off the couch and knelt between Chris's legs. He reached in and pulled Chris to a kiss, then a hug. "I have missed you," he murmured in his neck.

"Only slightly less than I've missed you," Chris replied.

Ciaran leaned up and started unbuttoning Chris's work shirt. Chris allowed him to take off his tank top, lick his nipples, then his chest, and lick down to his belly button. Ciaran opened up his belt buckle, then his zipper, but instead of pulling out his penis, he put his head down in Chris's lap and breathed deeply.

Chris laughed. "You like the smell of my funk, yeah?"

Ciaran rubbed his face back and forth on his groin area. "I love the smell of you," he said, muffled, and wrapped his arms around his back while his head lay in Chris's lap. "It does something to me, your scent. I can't explain it."

Chris took the band out of Ciaran's hair, letting his fiery red hair hang loose. "I know what you mean. Your scent does the same for me. It's not unlike anything I've ever smelled before, but it's you. It's in your clothes. It's in your Wisp. It's in that crease between your thigh and your groin. It's the scent of you. I would know it anywhere."

He massaged his scalp, giving Ciaran time to continue to breathe in his scent, and lifted up his head for a kiss. They locked eyes, neither of them saying what they really wanted to say. Then Ciaran grabbed his pants and underwear at the waist and pulled them down and all the way off. With Chris's help, Ciaran took off the freshly laundered clothes he had put on less than two hours before. He laid his naked body on top of Chris's right on the couch and kissed him.

They kissed for a while, the yearning so great between them. Ciaran moved down first, leaving hickeys on Chris's neck and collarbone, kissing and licking along the way to Chris's hairless groin. Ciaran spread Chris's legs apart and started licking inside his thighs, ignoring his weeping cock, and going for the sacks below, carefully sucking each one.

Chris started moaning loudly. So Ciaran reached down to his jeans pocket to grab his *rodulé* to do the spell to sound-proof the room. But Chris stopped him, lifting his torso up. "Don't," he said seriously. "I want the neighbors to hear us." He nudged his head to the open window. "I want the whole fucking world to hear how much I need you."

Ciaran laughed a little. "Well, let's go all out and give them a show," he said. He pushed Chris back on the couch and lifted his legs high to get a full view of his hole. "Hold these for me, will you?" Ciaran said.

Chris dutifully held himself up as Ciaran proceeded to put his tongue in and out of his anus, licked up to his testicles, and back down to his hole. Ciaran held him there, eating him out, spitting and licking it back up, not able to get enough of the smell of him. Chris moaned and groaned so loudly Ciaran was sure his wish came true and the whole neighborhood heard him.

When Chris's bottom began to tremble in his hand, he finally allowed Chris to lower his legs, but immediately licked the pre-cum sliding down his shaft to the head, and swallowed Chris's cock whole. Chris howled. Ciaran came up for air, but Chris grabbed his hair with more force than he intended and pushed Ciaran down deeper until his lips touched his groin. Ciaran gagged the second time but held on as Chris moved his head in a circular motion. He wanted to face fuck him so badly, but even more he wanted to cum inside him.

When Chris eventually let him come up, Ciaran let out a river of saliva. "Fuck," Chris whispered.

Ciaran stared into Chris's eyes. "Do it again," he commanded. He covered Chris's cock with his mouth.

Chris obliged, pushed Ciaran's head to where he was sitting in Ciaran's throat, and guided Ciaran's head in a circular motion. The simple fact was that Ciaran had his first blow job experience as the giver just a few short months ago, but he was a natural at it. And Chris loved to guide him. Ciaran stayed there a little longer than the first time until he gagged again and then Chris let him go. More spit and saliva coated Chris's cock, so much of it that it poured down his balls onto the couch.

"Guess we won't need lube today," Ciaran said breathlessly, and Chris laughed. "Maybe a little more, just in case." He looked toward the bedroom. "*Sito.*"

He licked around Chris's head as the lube floated from Chris's room and hovered over them. Chris grabbed it first. Ciaran sat up and poured a few drops on Chris's penis, which was surprising to Chris. It was like he could read his mind about what position he wanted to be in.

"I thought—"

"Don't think," Ciaran said. "Just do." He stood up and began to stroke himself, his cock rock hard with the smell of Chris still in his nose.

Chris understood. He sat up on the couch, adding more lube to himself. Ciaran turned his back to his lover and lowered himself onto Chris slowly, and they both moaned until Ciaran was sitting in Chris's lap. He sat there for a moment, trying not to put his full body weight on him, and leaned back on Chris. Chris wrapped his arms around his midsection, finding his face near his favorite place: Ciaran's armpit. He breathed in deeply, also loving the smell of him.

Ciaran began to move. Chris shuddered and began to move with him. It was so wet and slippery and tight that Chris was afraid he would cum that way too quickly. But he stayed focused as Ciaran, his alpha male boyfriend, rode him backward like a pro.

After a while, Chris tapped Ciaran's thighs, pushed Ciaran back up to a seated position, and then pushed him even farther down to the living room floor so that he was on all fours. Chris moved behind him and returned the favor, putting his face in Ciaran's ass. Ciaran let out a deep moan. Chris hawked spit three times directly into the tunnel. Then he rubbed more lube on himself, inside, outside, and all over Ciaran's freckled bottom.

Chris put one knee down and one knee up and stuffed himself deep inside of Ciaran. Ciaran let out a loud and wounded moan. Chris pulled back but only slightly and pushed in hard again. And again. Chris fucked him hard, fast, and deep, hitting Ciaran's sweet spot. Ciaran began to feel the shock waves of his orgasm. Together, they moaned in piercing octaves. As Ciaran tightened around Chris's prick, Chris couldn't stop it if he tried and spasmed deeply inside of Ciaran. He continued pumping a few moments more because it hurt so good until it really started to hurt, and he had to stop. He crashed with his back on the sofa.

"Fuck," he whispered again. He watched Ciaran lower himself to the ground, trying to catch his breath. "I wish that lasted longer."

Ciaran did not answer; instead, he lifted himself up and onto the other couch in a seated position. He looked at Chris and started stroking himself. Chris crawled over to Ciaran. He replaced Ciaran's hand with his own and began stroking, licking, and sucking Ciaran's larger-than-expected cock, making ungodly gurgling and choking sounds. His tongue traveled higher, tracking Ciaran's hard abs with his tip, grazing his teeth along his nipples, and burying his face in Ciaran's armpit. He licked him there, leaving a hickey right on the cartilage on the side as Ciaran dragged one hand through Chris's curly hair and the other jerking himself.

Chris reluctantly traveled down Ciaran's skin and sucked the head, while Ciaran pumped. As satisfying as it would be to make him cum that way, he wanted to feel Ciaran inside of him just as much as Ciaran did. So he came off and grabbed the lube off the couch where they'd left it.

Chris prepared his lover and climbed on top, knees on either side of Ciaran, and lowered himself onto Ciaran's lap, facing him. Ciaran was silent, but his mouth formed an "o" that he could not close. He leaned farther back on the couch, giving Chris a better angle, and held onto his waist as Chris began to gyrate the way he liked it. They found their rhythm and moved together as one unit. With eyes closed, they moaned liberally and expressively, and it felt so good to both of them that neither wanted it to stop. So they didn't. They stayed in the same position for a long while until Chris began to feel the waves of his orgasm.

Chris grabbed onto Ciaran's head, his elbows dug into his shoulders, and he began to bounce. Ciaran reached below and held Chris's cheek, helping him move faster. Chris held on and lost himself in his orgasm with a scream; his toes curled, and he exploded on Ciaran's chest, hands-free as he climaxed, calling out Ciaran's name. And Ciaran took the ride with Chris into orgasmic paradise, his own midsection freezing, and came inside of Chris.

Chris was still holding onto Ciaran's head, trembling, rocking, and coming down from the height of his climax. Ciaran also didn't let go. He moved his hands from Chris's butt cheeks to his back and held him, his ear right against Chris's chest, listening to his heart slow down. He waited until Chris was ready to let go first. He lifted his head, and Chris immediately brought their lips together. They kissed softly. Sweetly.

Ciaran changed positions to lie on his side, and Chris lay with him with his back turned. Ciaran draped his arm around him, and they spooned naked on the couch. Without speaking, they silently fell asleep.

Hours later they showered for over forty minutes and talked about the mission, Ciaran's newfound respect for Bruno, another Reserver who was his archenemy until they worked together in Chad, and whom Vlad chose to assign to Malik—Lucas as his Second Tamer since he worked nights, Ollivier, Lee, and Demitri as his Fixers. Ciaran confessed that he was disappointed that Mateo, another Fixer, told him after the mission he would be better suited with the Hunters, but Bruno was happy to have him. Ciaran planned to step up the group of Dungers he was currently training as Fixers since everyone that went with him that could get promoted got promoted.

Ciaran talked a lot, which was unlike him; Chris hung off his every word, giving commentary and encouragement, grateful to have Ciaran so close to him again.

Afterward, they lay in Chris's bed and touched each other until they were aroused all over again. They made love slowly and gently with Chris inside of Ciaran, facing him, taking much longer to cum. It reminded Ciaran of the dreams he used to have about Chris before they confessed their feelings to each other and wondered if it had been a premonition of some kind.

They rolled around in the bed, kissing and touching, eventually cumming one after the other. Together again, after so many days apart, they fell asleep in each other's arms, happy and content.

CHAPTER 3

Dinner with the Jennings

Charity came in around 3:30 p.m. from work and saw their clothes everywhere. She went over to Chris's room, the door wide open, and she saw them snoring away. Ciaran was on his side with his arm thrown across Chris, and Chris was on his stomach with his face in Ciaran's armpit. The blanket was covering them from the torso down, a change from the first time she had met Ciaran naked in her brother's bed. She watched them silently for another moment with a smile on her face. Then Charity silently closed the door and folded their clothes, laying them on the sofa, before going upstairs to help make dinner.

Chris woke up to the smell of cooking with Ciaran's arm still draped around him. He slowly moved him off so as not to wake him, got dressed, and came into the main area. Charity was setting the table with salad and rice.

"Hello, Chrissy," she said. "Clary will be here any minute with the food, so you may want to wake the boyfriend." Chris nodded and then looked at the clothes folded on the couch.

As he grabbed them, she teased, "Looks like you wasted no time making up for lost time."

"Shut up," he said and brought the clothes and Ciaran's bag into the room.

Ciaran was awake. He sat up and said, "Oh good. I was wondering how I was going to get my knickers."

Chris smiled at him. He bent over for a quick kiss before he pulled Ciaran out of the bed for a longer one. Ciaran's cock began to rise against him, and Chris noticed. "I could swallow you again right now," he groaned in between kisses.

Ciaran groaned, too. He stepped back and said, "Dinner. Then … maybe." Chris grinned.

By the time they got dressed and came out of the room, Clarissa was downstairs, putting the beef casserole on the table. Rudy took a seat between Ciaran and Chris, which neither of them minded, and Chris's sisters sat opposite them. They said grace, crossed themselves, and began to pass around the food. Ciaran, who was not religious, fell in line with their customs when he had dinner with them.

"How is it that everyone in this family can cook?" Ciaran asked between savory bites.

"Not everyone," said Chris. "Our dad can't cook for shite. I don't know how he's been getting on by himself all these years."

"Well, maybe if you didn't kick him out of his own home, you would know," Clarissa muttered under her breath, but loud enough for Chris to hear. He shot her a nasty look.

Charity answered Ciaran, "Ma Ami could cook with her eyes closed, and somehow it always came out perfectly. She was revered at the restaurant she worked in."

They traded stories about their late mother, remembering how she would have them in the kitchen as young as Rudy, kneading the dough for pie crusts or washing lettuce for salad. Ciaran, who could burn water, was fascinated. "The only two of us that cook are Ted because he was the eldest and hung onto my mum's skirt a lot while she was in the kitchen when he was younger so she put him to work, and Diana because Mum made her sit in the kitchen most of her childhood. Customary wifely duties and all."

They talked about Ciaran's parents being traditional, Grace being a stay-at-home mother as his father Hamish completed all his studies at a university and worked his way up as a federal official while they were growing up. Grace ran an apothecary shop now with his sister Diana in their home-town of Kingsbridge. Ciaran left out that his father was a top liaison for the Magi Council and ambassador between the Magi Community and the Commoner world. Chris's sisters had no idea of Ciaran's magical abilities or the Magi world.

As conversation died down, Clarissa turned to the couple.

"So you two are getting pretty serious," she started. Ciaran smiled, but Chris gave her a warning look. "I'm just saying I notice how much time you spend together. Practically inseparable." She threw her hands up casually.

Neither man spoke, Ciaran still smiling, Chris on the verge of a scowl. He knew his protective sister and matriarch of the family was about to start something.

"Oh, don't be shy now," Charity chimed in. "You certainly aren't shy or selfish with your bodies." She smiled and winked.

"Shut up, Sis," Chris retorted.

Their older sister ignored them both and addressed Ciaran. "I just wanted to know if it's casual or exclusive. My brother is notorious for casual."

"And if it was, it still would be my business, innit?" Chris said, annoyed.

"I'm not trying to put you on the spot, Chrissy. I am just curious about your relationship," she stated.

Charity said, "And I just want to know how good the sex is." She laughed.

"Charity, don't be crass," Clarissa scolded her.

"Don't you have a parking attendant to bone since you're so concerned about my sex life?" Chris spat at his younger sister.

"I have and I did, thank you very much. Would you like to know the details?" she said boldly back.

"Fuck off—" Chris started.

Ciaran cleared his throat loudly, and everyone looked at him. "Soooo… We're exclusive. It's not casual," he said matter-of-factly. Chris looked down at his plate and smiled.

But Clarissa had more questions. "That's good to know, Ciaran. Does your family know about him?"

"Give it a rest, Clary," Chris groaned.

"It's a valid question, Christopher," she said defensively.

They began arguing back and forth, and then Ciaran cleared his throat again and spoke the first word over them. "WELL… not yet. But I have a wedding to go to next month, and I was," he turned to Chris, "I was hoping that you would go with me. Quentin and Diana's wedding in June."

Chris was surprised. He had seen the wedding invitation on Ciaran's table, but did not think Ciaran would ask him to go. "To England? With you?"

"Ah… yeah," he said sheepishly. "If you can get the time off, it will be at least four days, a Thursday to a Sunday, or Friday to Monday."

"Oh. Um… yes. I can do that."

"Okay."

"Okay."

Rudy, in between them, said, "Okay!" They looked at him and smiled.

But Clarissa was not done. "You're sure you're ready for that, Ciaran? For Christopher to meet your family?" Chris gave her an exasperated look that she ignored. "I mean, is he going to the wedding as your friend or a date?"

"Alright, enough with the interrogation, Clary," Chris snapped. "If Ciaran isn't ready to tell his parents yet, I'm fine with it. And if I'm fine with it, then you lot can fuck off!"

"Chris…" Ciaran touched his hand and shook his head to stop him from going off. He said to his sisters, "I'm not hiding him in Albania, just so you know. I mean, I'm not going around broadcasting my private life, but I'm not denying it either. The people I work with know. The other rangers know. Our friends and my neighbors all know that we are together. So it's only a matter of time before my parents and siblings know as well. He's going to be at the wedding with me as my partner. I'm not denying how much Christopher means to me here, and I'm not going to deny him there either."

Clarissa was thoughtful. "Ciaran, I like you; I really do. You're smart, you're kind, you have a good head on your shoulders, and you are good for Chris. So I say this to you not just as Chris's sister, but as someone who cares about you, too. I want you to be sure this is what you really want for yourself. I've watched my brother pretend not to struggle with his identity for years, and it's not easy. But with the right person, who cares about you and will support you through it, it makes all the difference in the world. Other than us, he hasn't had that in his life until now. He can be that one for you. I am hopeful that you could be that one for him, too."

Chris and Ciaran were both afraid to look at each other, as Clarissa had said more about their relationship than they had discussed between themselves.

"I appreciate that, Clarissa," said Ciaran. "And the truth is, I don't know what will happen in the future with us. All I know is that right now," he looked Chris in the eyes, "I love what we have. And I'm happy with where I am."

Chris smiled at him, then turned to his sister. "Now, are we done here? Because I have to get ready for work soon."

"If Ciaran is staying, does that mean I'm sleeping upstairs again?" Charity practically whined.

"He is and will be for the rest of the week through the weekend. So yes, stay your arse upstairs," he said to his younger sister. She blew a raspberry at him. Rudy blew one back.

———

After everyone left, Ciaran waved his *dulé,* saying an incantation, and the dishes began to move from the table to the kitchen sink and wash themselves. Ciaran stood in the kitchen to supervise.

Chris came over and stood next to him. "Fucking wizards. You Magi are lazy as fuck."

"Magician," he corrected him. Ciaran smiled, watching the suds work. "Don't you wish you were one, too?"

Chris smiled back, then got serious. "Dinner was..." He sighed. "I'm really sorry about all that, Ciaran."

"Don't be," said Ciaran right away. "Obviously, Clarissa loves you. And she is just being a protective big sister. Expect Ted to do the same when you meet him."

Chris was quiet for a moment and then said, "You know, tonight was the most open you have been about us since we moved beyond friendship."

"I know," Ciaran said, turning to him. "And I'm sorry. I have been in my head a lot instead of just talking about it. I should be talking about it with you, but it's weird now talking about us with you. Not because I can't talk to you. But because I don't want you to feel like I'm not confident in us. It's more like... I don't know how I feel about me. And that's really what makes us complicated. Not because of us, but because of me. I don't know if I'm making sense. See why it's difficult for me?"

But Chris said, "I get it; I do. Which is also why I don't put any pressure on you. No pressure to tell your family. No pressure to hold hands or kiss in public. It's whatever you want to do, for as long as you'll have me."

"Well, that doesn't seem fair, innit? What about what you want?"

"I have what I want right now," Chris said. "A warm body to hold on to and a big cock to fuck me when I want." He laughed.

Ciaran shook his head. "Don't downplay it. We're so much more than that. You deserve so much more than that. You deserve—"

Chris stopped him with a hand on his chest before he said something stupid. "Ciaran, really. I'm not sitting around waiting for you to figure out if you're really straight or bi or gay or all of the above or none of the above. I'm living in the moment. And the moment calls for a hug and a kiss." He leaned in, kissed Ciaran, then pulled him in for an embrace.

Ciaran held him tight as his heart fluttered with love for Chris. "Want to shower with me again?" Chris asked softly. "You know, for intimacy purposes?" Ciaran smiled.

They showered for the second time that day, and Ciaran told Chris about how he gave Vlad relationship advice, which led to him realizing that his fellow colleagues would support his own relationship. When the Reservers returned from the last mission, word had gotten around about Ciaran's relationship with "The Ranger" as they called Chris, which resulted in playful ribbing, even from his ex-archnemesis, Bruno. Ciaran was officially dubbed "The Ranger's Magi" by the other Reservers. And Ciaran would answer to the title with a straight face in agreement with his new name. Chris rewarded his confidence with a blow job in the shower. Afterward, they rubbed lotion on each other, and Ciaran watched Chris get ready for work.

At 10:30 p.m., right before he left, Chris went into his dresser and handed Ciaran a key chain of a golden dragon and a gold key. "It's only fair that you have the key to my place while I have the key to yours. No more waiting out front for me."

Ciaran smiled. "Well, technically, I could have always entered your home, locks and all. We can open regular locked doors at will, and only another Magi's personal wards or spell can keep us out."

Chris snorted. "Fucking magicians," he said and shook his head.

Ciaran laughed. "But thank you for this. The invitation and sentiment are there, and I will use it liberally."

Chris leaned in to kiss him. He said, "Your birthday is in a couple of weeks on a Friday. Can you take the Friday overnight shift off?"

"Barring no issues, it should be fine. What do you have in mind?"

"It's a surprise. I will make all the arrangements; all you have to do is show up with an overnight bag. Now go get some sleep."

"I won't sleep," said Ciaran. "But I'll be here waiting for you in the morning. We'll sleep together."

Chris kissed him once again. "That's the best way to come home." Ciaran watched Chris walk to his car before he gently closed the door.

CHAPTER 4

The Remington Factor

Ciaran stayed with Chris for the rest of the week doing what he'd promised. He cooked—or tried to—and cleaned and spent time with Chris. They made love every day when he came home from work, slept, and fooled around every night before he left for his shift.

On Saturday, they found themselves at Nemo's, the neighborhood gay bar and Chris's favorite spot in the city. It was crowded; it was the first warm night, and summer was in the air. They noticed a couple standing around awkwardly waiting for a table and made conversation with them. They found out they were on their first date, and since Chris and Ciaran already had a table, courtesy of Chris's longstanding and personal friendship with Nemo himself, they invited them to come into their booth and share.

They were heavy in conversation when Chris looked up and saw someone that made him freeze. Ciaran noticed and looked up, too. A tall, dark-brown-skinned, handsome, bald man had entered, greeted the owner, and sat at the bar. Ciaran turned back to Chris, who was still watching the man with a stoic expression on his face. It dawned on Ciaran who it was: Chris's old flame—a child predator in Ciaran's eyes—named Rem.

Ciaran turned back to look at the man who had not noticed Chris yet. He looked at Chris and gently touched his hand that was resting on the table. Chris finally turned his gaze away to Ciaran. His expression was unreadable, which was a first for Ciaran. He had gotten pretty good at learning Chris's moods and expressions.

"Do you want to leave?" he asked quietly.

Chris shook his head, still unable to speak. He glanced once more at the bar at Rem before turning his attention back to the table and the conversation about how terrible gay dating was in Tirana. After a couple of minutes, he seemed more at ease to Ciaran.

Truthfully, Chris was a ball of emotions. Seeing Rem for the first time in a year brought back a wave of emotions that he was not prepared for—nostalgia, disgust, anger, sadness, anxiety, and a bit of fear that he would walk over and say or do something sarcastic to him about Ciaran in front of them. And he had no idea how Ciaran would react. Chris had never seen Ciaran truly angry. Irritated and annoyed, yes, but never angry. He had a feeling that Rem coming to their table would make Ciaran extremely angry.

Chris decided to ignore his thoughts and feelings and enjoy the moment with Ciaran and their tablemates, willing himself to forget Rem was in the same room as him. He did not look back up until a commotion in that direction caused a few people to glance toward the bar, including everyone at their table. A glass was pushed off the counter and shattered, and a stool fell down with a clatter as Nemo was holding onto Rem's arm tightly. He was saying a few choice words they could not hear from their distance, but they could tell by Nemo's tone that he was stern. Rem yanked his arm away and raised his palms up in surrender. He straightened out his jacket, then turned around, and looked directly at Chris.

Chris felt his heart drop in his chest. That bit of fear became an intense dread that Rem was going to walk over and all hell was going to break loose. Ciaran territorially put his hand over Chris's hand on the table without breaking his hard expression at Rem. Rem turned his attention to Ciaran, who gave him an icy glare. *Try it, I fucking dare you,* he thought to himself.

As if Rem read his mind, he chuckled, nodded, and turned around to walk out of the establishment. Nemo glanced over at them briefly, but then continued working at the bar.

"What was that about?" their tablemate asked, still looking over.

Ciaran turned and locked eyes with Chris. "I have no idea." Chris looked away and took a sip of his beer.

Ciaran kept his hand over Chris's for the next thirty minutes before making the decision for them. "Well, it's been a great night, but we have to head home," he said politely, tossing money onto the table. Chris also said his goodbyes, and Ciaran held on as they walked out of the bar. Nemo gave them both a head nod on their way out.

They walked in silence back to Chris's place, holding hands. Chris had no idea what Ciaran was thinking and was nervous about finding out. He was starting to get upset with himself for getting so emotional and transparent. Chris was afraid he had screwed everything up with just a glance at his old lover and Dominant. But he did not get the sense that Ciaran was angry. Rather, he seemed deep in thought.

When they got inside the flat, Ciaran went straight to the kitchen sink for a cup of water and stood against the counter to drink. Chris went to stand next to him. Ciaran wouldn't look at him, and he knew he needed to say something first.

"So you're angry with me?" Chris asked, even though he knew he wasn't. But he had to ask to be sure.

Ciaran paused midsip. He sighed and said, "No. I'm not angry with you."

Chris let a moment pass, wanting Ciaran to say more, but he didn't. "What then?" he practically whined.

Ciaran took another full sip before he spoke. "Frustrated. Annoyed. Dunno. And it's not like I don't get it. If my ex, Chitra, walked through that door, I might have had the same reaction. But that doesn't change how I feel."

"And how do you feel?" Chris wanted to keep him talking.

"Like I wanted to pull out my *dulé* and turn him into the weasel that he is. Or punch him in the fucking throat. Either way, it would have knocked that smug smile off his face." Ciaran took another sip, put his glass on the counter, and turned to face Chris. "So, how do you feel?"

Chris wanted to say something sarcastic, but seeing the seriousness on Ciaran's face made him not. "I feel..." He decided to go safe. "I feel lucky to have you."

Ciaran stared at him for a moment, narrowed his eyes, and went to sit on the couch in the dim living room. Chris sighed. *Of course, Ciaran would see through my bullshit.*

"Okay," Chris said, following him. "I did mean that. I am grateful for you. But also, I am grateful for Nemo for keeping Rem away from me, from us. And I feel frustrated with myself that I could let him get to me still. I gotta work on that."

Ciaran continued to look straight ahead into the dark living room. "Do you love him?" he asked softly.

"No," Chris said automatically. "And you asked me that before. The answer is unchanged."

Ciaran didn't respond. Chris sat next to him on the couch, folded up his legs, and faced him, but Ciaran was still looking ahead.

"But you're drawn to him," Ciaran said factually.

"I was, but not anymore. Not for a long time. It's hard to explain a Dom/sub relationship if you've never been in one, or never had the desire to be in something like that. But, Ciaran, I didn't feel like I wanted to be with him, if that's what you're asking. Not in any way. It was more like... I was afraid that he was going to come over and start some shit with you, with us. Because that's what we do. He makes demands of me, belittles me, and I push his buttons, and we do this dance until I give in and allow him to have control over me. But nothing, *nothing*, in me wanted that tonight. More than anything, I just didn't want him to come between us."

Ciaran wanted to say to him that it wasn't a relationship, it was grooming, but he knew it was not the right time. Not with the way he was feeling. So instead he asked, "And if I weren't there? Would the desire to push each other's buttons until someone caves be there?" Ciaran needed to hear him say the words, needed reassurance that his feelings weren't in vain.

Chris turned Ciaran's chin to him with two fingers and looked him in the eyes. "No. Because I had already decided I didn't want him in my life anymore before I met you. Not as his friend, not as his submissive, not as his anything. But more importantly, I am with you. He has never made me feel the way you do, in or out of the bedroom. Especially out of the bedroom. But in the bedroom, too."

He smiled but Ciaran didn't, so he stopped smiling and said with all seriousness. "My desire is for you, Ciaran. You and you alone. Even if I wanted to be in a dynamic like that again, it would only be with someone like you. My strong, thoughtful, caring Magus."

And Ciaran believed him. He leaned in for a kiss, and they kissed gently for a while. Ciaran then reached over and removed Chris's pants buckle, zipped down his pants, and exposed his penis. He took Chris in his mouth, first slowly, then fervently. Chris moaned appreciatively and then loudly as Ciaran kept deep-throating repeatedly without letting up. Chris lifted Ciaran off to stand up and drop his pants and underwear. He came closer and proceeded to let Ciaran work him, making small gargling noises as the head of Chris's cock continuously slid past his tonsils.

Chris grabbed his head and pushed in deeper. Ciaran hungrily accepted, sucking him hard and deep, never missing a beat. "Fuck. Ciaran. Fuck. Fuck. Ciaran. Fuck. FUCK. FUCK. FUCK!" Chris cried while slamming Ciaran's head against his skin.

Realizing he was getting loud, Ciaran pushed Chris back forcefully and pulled out his *dulé*, said, *"Arcanos susurrus,"* then dropped it on the floor as the soundproofing spell took over the room, spreading like yellow paint across the floor, up the walls, and connecting together in the ceiling.

Ciaran sat all the way back on the seat and motioned for Chris to climb up on the couch. "Come here," he commanded.

Chris did. He stood over Ciaran, feet in the cushions, knees bent, holding onto the back of the couch as Ciaran leaned his head back and continued taking Chris into his throat. Chris lost all restraint and began pounding Ciaran's face with his groin. Ciaran open up his own pants and took out his member, slowly stroking himself as he took in every inch of Chris's rock-solid cock in his mouth, listening to Chris moaning loudly with each thrust making him rock hard as well. Ciaran's only sound was the gargling noise he made as he took it all in.

When Chris finally came, he growled with intensity. He slammed his groin into Ciaran's mouth hard one more time and held it there, filling his mouth. The taste of Chris's sweet nectar was enough to make Ciaran cum as well, taking him by surprise. He moaned with Chris still in his mouth and erupted mid-stroke on his hands and his pants. He sucked as Chris removed himself slowly from his mouth, licking and swallowing along the way, making sure not one drop spilled out.

Chris groaned and fell into the seat next to him. He looked at Ciaran, who was still sitting there with his head leaned back, eyes closed, cock coated with his own cum still in hand.

Chris was still stunned. "What. The. Fuck, Ciaran? I mean... I'm not complaining, but ... are... are you okay?" He gently caressed Ciaran's red hair on the side of his head. "As much as I loved that... what was that about?"

Ciaran was silent for a long moment. He could feel the corners of his mouth bruised, his neck aching from the strain of being in one position for so long. It crossed his mind how many times Rem had Chris like that, without any care or concern for him at all. But Chris was so loving and affectionate, even in his compassion for Ciaran at that moment.

Chris was about to ask again, starting with, "Ciaran—"

But Ciaran cut him off, saying, "I'm fine."

Chris slowly got on his knees. He licked the cum off Ciaran's hand first, then licked the cum off his penis. Ciaran waited until Chris was done; then he opened his eyes. Chris stared back at him, waiting for whatever Ciaran told him to do next. But Ciaran shook his head.

"I'm not your Dom, Christopher," Ciaran said seriously. "I'm never going to treat you that way. You deserve to be cared for, physically, mentally, and emotionally in a normal, loving, stable relationship of give and take. I'm not your Dom, and you're not my sub. I can, and I will, submit to you, too."

Chris felt his heart explode with love for Ciaran. He stood up and reached for his hand. Ciaran took it and stood up. Chris wrapped his arms around his neck, and Ciaran wrapped his arms around his midsection. They silently stayed there for a long moment. Then Ciaran brought Chris to the bedroom. He took off the rest of Chris's clothes and then took off his own, pulled back the comforter, and got in the bed, pulling Chris with him. Chris turned his back to Ciaran so they could spoon. They were both awake, eyes open, deep in thought.

After a while, Chris said, "Now that we got the emotional stuff out of the way, can I tell you something?"

"Hmm?"

"I have been with a lot of people, you know this. So believe me when I say that was the best fucking blow job I have ever fucking had in my entire fucking life. I'm not kidding. Nothing even comes close. And if you're trying to make me fall in love, two more times of that and I will. You may not want a sub, but I'll be your fucking love slave for life. I mean ... *shiiiiiiit.*"

Ciaran started laughing. "Go to sleep, Chris."

CHAPTER 5

Vladimir and Alexi

Ciaran went back to work the following Monday, and Vladimir, who worked the day shift, stayed on until the night shift just to see Ciaran and tell him his story.

Vlad did what he said he was going to do. He went home to Romania and told his parents that his best friend for the past ten years had actually been his lover for the past five years and they intended to marry. As expected, his mother cried about him going to hell, and his father told him he could not step foot in their house again.

"I told them, if they were prepared to lose their only child over it, then that was on them," said Vlad with teary eyes but a firm voice. "My door will always be open. And then I left."

"I'm proud of you," Ciaran said, hoping he was as brave as the twenty-year-old man in front of him as he was poised to bring Chris to meet his family soon.

Vlad then flew to Moldova and went to Alexi's parents' house, where he knew he would be for dinner. Alexi's older brother Demetri and his family were there, and so were his older sister and little sister. His father was working late and was not expected to be home.

Vlad said, "I walked into the dining room and looked straight at him, said, 'I told my parents. Now it's time for you to tell yours.' And, Ciaran, without missing a beat, he stood up and said to his family, 'I love Vladimir. I've been in love with him since I was fifteen years old, and that's never going to change.' No one spoke, but seeing him that bold was all I needed. I walked over and got down on one knee, said, 'Will you marry me, Alexi?' And he said, 'As if you even had to ask, stupid.' He pulled me up and kissed me, and we both started crying. Then all hell broke loose."

Alexi's mother was beside herself with rage and started moving objects around the room with her *dulé* to hurl at them, screaming that he would never see one leu of their money. Then she called his father, hysterically trying to explain what had just happened. His brother was sitting there stoic, and his sister started crying, trying to calm their mother down. Only his younger sister came over and hugged them both. She told them, "Go. Now. Let me know when the wedding is." Alexi ran upstairs, threw everything he could into a suitcase, and kissed his siblings goodbye. They all cried, knowing it would be the last time they saw each other for a while.

"Alexi's father caught us at the airport while waiting for the plane back to Albania. We have no idea how he got there so fast or even got past security, but he came right up to us in the Magi transport lounge as we waited standby for our flight. He tried to keep his voice low and told Alexi that he would be cut off from his family and his money for life, and it was his last chance. And Alexi, in turn, spoke very loudly, saying, 'I choose Vladimir over anything you could ever offer me.' Ciaran, I thought my heart was going to fucking explode," Vlad said with wide eyes. "It was like all he needed was openness from me to tell the whole world how much he loves me. It was the best feeling in the world. I just grabbed his face and stuck my tongue down his throat, the first time we ever kissed in public. *Ever*. What a feeling that was."

Ciaran grinned in happiness for his young friend. Vlad told him that Alexi was staying with him in his room in Jesse's house with Lucas, Ollivier, Lee, and Mateo. They planned to marry next month, but first Alexi needed a job, and they needed to find an apartment. "Alexi worked in one of his father's banks so anything having to do with money was good, but he will take anything right now, even coming onto the Reserve as a Dunger," said Vlad.

Ciaran was thoughtful. "Let me check with Andy at the Exchange, see if they could use some hands. I can also check with Esme to see if any flats are available at the Atrium where I live."

Vlad hugged Ciaran. "I knew you would have all the answers!"

As it turned out, Andy's wife Rosemary was pregnant with their fourth child and wanted to step back from working in the Exchange, so hiring Alexi came right on time. He came in for an interview on Tuesday and started that Wednesday. Unfortunately, there were no flats available at the Atrium, but someone was moving out by the end of July, and they were welcome to the apartment if they wanted it, a one-bedroom on the first floor. So they planned their wedding for that same week and asked if they could have their wedding at the Atrium in the garden. Phoebe and Esme, who fell in love with Vladimir and Alexi's love story, were delighted to help them.

Ciaran invited them to lunch on the following Sunday so they could meet Chris and he could meet Alexi. Vlad and Alexi sat side by side awkwardly. The two young men could not have been more different. Alexi was taller than Vlad by a good three inches. He had blond, scraggly hair, was thin, and had a gentleman's charm about him, the complete opposite of Vlad's 5'8" height, dark wavy hair, scruffy beard, and rugged build. Alexi also dressed impeccably like he was an old man in the 1920s. He wore gray slacks with a vest to match, a button-down shirt, and a bow tie, with oxford shoes and a pocket watch with a gold chain hanging out. Chris joked later he was a Twink with a kink. He spoke only Russian and Moldovan although Vlad had been teaching him English daily, but he understood much of it as long as it was spoken slowly. Vlad did the translation during their lunch.

Ciaran and Chris could tell right away they were not used to being a couple, out and proud. They kept looking around and avoided any physical contact whatsoever. Chris asked, "So... how is the relationship going now that you don't have to hide anymore?"

Vlad turned pink, but he translated the question for Alexi. Alexi's cheeks also turned pink, and he responded, "*Volshebniy.*"

Vlad smiled. "He said, 'Magical.'"

That made Chris and Ciaran grin at them. Chris casually reached over and took Ciaran's hand on the table. Ciaran looked at him quizzically but said nothing else about it as he continued to ask about their relationship and plans for marriage.

"Children?" Chris asked.

"Yes, *dah*," they both said.

Vlad said, "I've always wanted siblings, and Alexi has three of them. So eventually we will adopt some wayward Magi children and raise them."

Ciaran and Chris also found out that they weren't having much intercourse. Vlad said, "At Campus, it was always hard to find the time and place, so we didn't center our relationship much around it. And then we were living apart for the last two years." Alexi nodded.

"Well, what about now? You live together, don't you?" Ciaran asked.

"Yes, but we live in a house with other men and thin walls, just like we did at Campus. They are gracious to let Alexi stay with me because they know my story, but we don't want to push it."

"What about *Arcanos susurrus*?" Chris asked.

Vlad and Alexi stared blankly. Vlad repeated the literal translation, "Secret whispers?"

"Did your parents never teach you that one?" Chris asked. "I thought all Magi learned about it."

"No," Ciaran said to Chris. "It's like talking to your parents about sex because it's really only used for one thing." Ciaran turned to Vlad. "Yes, an incantation to block out sounds escaping any room." Vlad translated for Alexi.

"*Dah, es silencio?*" he asked.

"No," Ciaran explained. "*Silencio* silences your voice, although that's a good idea, too. You do get loud, Chris."

Vlad laughed and translated, and Alexi laughed too, saying, "*V sleduyushiy raz zatkni yego pryamo pered tem, kak on zakrichit.*"

Vlad laughed and translated for Chris and Ciaran. "He said, 'Next time shut him up right before he hollers.'" They laughed.

"Yes, I'm going to try that," Ciaran said, amused. Chris nudged him with his shoulder. Ciaran nuzzled his nose against Chris's face, making him smile, and he playfully pushed Ciaran back. Vlad and Alexi smiled at their affection, turning to each other with grins.

They found out that Alexi was an advanced Magi dueler and won competitions back in Moldova. Vlad told them, "His brother is also a master dueler and taught him how to duel ever since he could hold a *rodulé*."

Alexi smiled, but it did not reach his eyes, and Vlad noticed. He absentmindedly reached over and took Alexi's hand and said a few words to him in Russian. Alexi nodded, smiled, and touched his face. Chris and Ciaran noticed their affection for each other had grown during the hour-and-a-half lunch. He secretly thanked himself for a job well done on showing the younger ones that it was okay now.

Vlad turned to the older men. "Demetri and Alexi have always been close, and it pained him that he couldn't tell his brother who he really was all this time. It pains him even more that now that he knows, he hasn't reached out to talk to him."

"So, what did you tell him?" Ciaran asked.

Vlad smiled. "Basically I said, 'Fuck your family. I'm your family now.'"

Ciaran laughed. "You've been hanging out with Mike the American too much."

Ciaran invited them upstairs to show them how the soundproofing spell worked, and they practiced the incantation while Chris took turns screaming in the bedroom for them. Other spells and incantations were bounced around, and somehow Ciaran and Alexi ended up in a friendly duel. They moved the living room furniture out of the way as Vlad and Chris sat at the kitchen table and watched.

Chris and Ciaran noticed that Vlad and Alexi were a lot more touchy-feely when it was just the four of them. Every time Alexi had the upper hand over Ciaran, Vlad would encourage and grab his hand or arm, and Alexi would lean into Vlad's neck.

Alexi really was a pro, especially in nonverbal incantations, and he caught Ciaran by surprise a few times. Ciaran's wand would fly out of his hand, or he would begin to float up and upside down with a point of Alexi's *dulé*. But then Ciaran surprised everyone with a dull shock wave without his *dulé* and only a hand gesture, knocking Alexi off his feet.

"How did you do that!?" Vlad asked, astonished.

"It's magic," Ciaran smiled, as he helped Alexi to his feet.

"That's what you did to Elder Bocari on the mission, wasn't it?" Vlad asked.

"It was," Ciaran confirmed. "Although it was much stronger; my anger fueled it."

"Fascinating," said Vlad. "I bet you and Chris do a lot of these kinds of things in here, sharing incantations and such."

But Alexi said to Vlad in Russian, "*No, Kris ne volshebnyy, dah? On tochno Commoner.*"

Ciaran heard the words "Chris" and "Commoner" in there and looked at Vlad, his heart pounding. Vlad looked at Chris puzzled, then at Ciaran, but then he turned and began talking with Alexi in fast Russian. After a few moments of conversation back and forth between the two of them, Vlad looked at Ciaran again.

"Soooo... Alexi thinks Chris is an unregistered Commoner around magic, and if he is, we don't give a shit," Vlad said in one breath.

Chris looked at Ciaran with concern, but Ciaran would not look at him. Alexi said something else in Russian to Vlad, and he smiled. "He said, 'We are familiar with keeping long-term secrets, so your secret is safe with us forever. You have our word.'"

Ciaran finally looked at Chris first and smiled reassuringly. Chris smiled back. Then Ciaran turned to Vlad and Alexi. "Let me show you how to do the *quod electrica* spell."

They talked and shared incantations, drank beer, and ordered more food from the Atrium for dinner, then drank some more. As the day grew late, they vowed to do this again, but they wanted to get back to Vlad's room and try the concealment spell. Chris wished them a happy sexing, and Ciaran walked them out.

When he came back up, Chris said, "Well, look at us, hanging out with another couple, like adults."

Ciaran sat down and pulled Chris into his lap. They kissed softly; then Ciaran said, "I want to make you climax, then shut you up right before."

Chris smiled a little and said, "You've been thinking about doing that for the last, what, seven hours or so?"

Ciaran laughed. "Yes. Now take off your clothes and get on top."

Chris obliged, and soon they were in their favorite position: Ciaran lying flat on his back while Chris was on top grinding and Ciaran was holding his cock, stroking it at the same time. Chris rode Ciaran into his first orgasm, getting louder with his moans. He felt when Chris was about to cum but waited until Chris said, "Aah, aah, going to fucking c—"

"*Silencio!*" Ciaran waved his hand and watched Chris's face scrunch up and his eyes flutter back. His mouth opened in a silent roar, and he exploded all over Ciaran's chest. When he opened his eyes, Ciaran gave Chris back his voice.

"Vis carmina omittere." He looked up and smiled. "How did that feel?"

"Intense. Like my throat locked up for a second, but it was just me straining to yell out."

"Well, turn around and cum again for me."

Chris happily obliged. Once they both came a second time, Ciaran turned on his side on the couch, and Chris turned sideways, facing him. They kissed and held each other, falling asleep naked in the living room.

CHAPTER 6

Levels

The couple drove two hours north to Tirana with overnight bags in the trunk. Ciaran only knew that they were celebrating his 28th birthday and to dress casually. They had a large dinner before they left for Tirana since Chris told him there would be lots of drinking that night.

Ciaran assumed they were going to a club of some sort, which he wasn't fond of, but he let Chris lead. And he was proven right as they pulled into a parking lot of a three-story warehouse turned nightclub with the word "Levels" written on the side.

There was a line outside, but Chris walked to the front and told the bouncer, "We're on Jax's list," and gave their names. The bouncer checked and let them right in.

At the counter, Chris told the lady the same, that they were on Jax's list, and she gave them green armbands. "This will get you into every room all night," she told them.

They entered a small vestibule with a staircase leading up and a door to the right. Partygoers were coming from all directions, but Chris led him through the door. They entered a cavernous room covered in strobe lights and loud music, with hundreds of people dancing on the dance floor. The bar ran the length of the large room on one side, catering to everyone.

Chris and Ciaran found two empty bar stools as two other people had just got up, so they were able to sit together. Chris ordered two rum and Cokes, gave the bartender his credit card, and said, "Run a tab until closing."

Ciaran noticed that everyone danced with everyone, regardless of gender, so he knew it was an LGBTQ-friendly space. There was a female couple making out near them to a Beyonce song, and he enjoyed the show.

When the song ended and the couple moved away, he turned to see that Chris was watching him. "Did you enjoy that?" he said, amused.

Ciaran smiled. "Why did you bring me here?"

Chris shrugged. "Who doesn't like to party on their birthday?"

"I don't really party," Ciaran said. "And you know this. And you also know this is not exactly my type of music."

Chris smiled slyly. "Who said we came here for the music?"

Before Ciaran could respond, a brown-haired man grabbed Chris's shoulder. "Jenna!" he yelled.

Chris turned and gave him a huge smile and a hug. "Jax!"

"I'm so glad you made it out here," Jax said, still holding onto his shoulder. "I feel like I don't get to see you; you don't come out this way anymore."

"No, I just been working, busy. Hey, meet Ciaran. Ciaran, this is one of my best friends, Jaxon."

"Ah. The new flavor of the week," Jax said playfully. But he turned to Ciaran and held out his fist for a dap. "Nice to meet you."

Chris shoved him, and he laughed. Jax gave Ciaran a dap and turned back to Chris. "Don't forget, midnight. That'll give you about an hour and a half, give or take. I won't be up there, obviously, but they know what to do. If you need me for anything, tell anyone who works here to find me."

They hugged again like brothers. "It's good to see you, Jenna. You look good. Happy." Jax winked. "Come by more; I'll always get you in."

"Thanks, brother."

As he walked on, Ciaran asked, "Jenna?"

"Yeah. It's a play off my last name. Jaxon called me that at fourteen because he said I ran like a girl and should change my name to Jenna since we already had a Chris on the team. I jabbed him, but the name stuck. You'll know who my high school friends are by them calling me Jenna or Other Chris."

He turned to the bar and ordered another round of rum and Coke while Ciaran faced forward, still people-watching.

A pretty blonde woman in a tight green dress slid in between their stools. She ordered her drink, then turned to Chris and said, "Halo."

"Hi there," responded Chris.

"*So are you going to drink all night, or are you going to dance with someone?*" she asked in Albanian. But Ciaran understood.

Ciaran watched in amusement out of his peripheral vision. Chris said back in the language, "*Maybe later.*"

The blonde said, "*Well, if you do decide, come find me.*"

She got her drink and seductively drank from it, then brushed against him as she walked away. They both watched her return to her friends a few feet away.

"I think you got competition, Ciaran," Chris said.

"Yeah? Let's hope she can suck your cock like I can," Ciaran said with a smile.

Chris turned Ciaran's stool around with his legs to face him. He kissed him on the lips, and then put his tongue in his mouth. Ciaran returned the kiss, reaching up to stroke his cheek, and they parted. Ciaran glanced at the blonde and her friends, who had a look of surprise on their faces, then started giggling. She gave him a thumbs up.

Chris, who was still looking at Ciaran, asked, "Did she see?"

"Yes," Ciaran responded.

"Good." He looked at his watch and said, "Let's go." He took Ciaran's hand and led him back out to the vestibule and up the stairs.

They entered a room not as cavernous but still large. In the center was an elevated circular stage with poles on it. Female strippers of every color, shape, and size were dancing with what little clothes they had on. Other women walked the floor serving drinks and offering lap dances. The music was different up there, less pop and techno, more rock and grunge.

Ciaran chuckled. "Where did you bring me, Christopher?"

Chris smiled and walked toward a two-seater table in the back. Ciaran followed and sat across from him. A waitress in lingerie passed them, and Chris tapped her arm and ordered six tequila shots. When they came, he moved four toward Ciaran.

He looked at it and smiled. "Are you trying to get me drunk?"

"You may want to be for what I have in store for you tonight." Chris winked at him.

Ciaran shook his head and sighed. But he took all four shots in quick succession. He started to feel warm. Chris laughed and took his first shot, then said to him, "Okay. Pick one."

"Pick one ... what?" Ciaran asked stupidly.

Chris looked at him like he was stupid. "A girl. Pick a girl, Ciaran."

"For a lap dance?"

Chris didn't answer his question. Instead, he said, "Pick the most attractive female in the room to you. I want to know what you like."

"I like you," Ciaran said.

Chris pursed his lips into a smile and said, "I know that. Now pick a woman. Anyone. Take your time." He ordered a beer instead of drinking his second shot.

Ciaran looked around. There were certainly a lot of beautiful women walking around. It took a couple of minutes, but then she appeared. She had tan skin color and the perfect hourglass shape, decent-sized breasts, a thin waist, wide hips, and a nice round derriere. And she was tall. Her long hair was pulled back in a ponytail. She wore a lavender see-through negligée with nothing but little black bows to cover her nipples, and a matching long, see-through robe over it. She walked past, barely noticing them.

Ciaran tapped Chris, harder than he intended, and Chris spilled his beer as he was mid-sip. "Sorry. Her. I want her," Ciaran said, and pointed.

Chris wiped his mouth and looked. "Ho. Lee. Shit. She is incredible. And you sure do like brown skin, don't you?" Chris teased, and Ciaran could feel himself growing pink.

"I'll be right back," Chris said and chased her down. He saw them exchange words, and he pointed at Ciaran. She nodded, and Chris handed her some money. Then she walked away. Chris came back to the table and sat down, picked up his beer, and sipped.

"What... what happened?"

"She's coming, don't worry." Then he slid his last shot over to Ciaran.

Ciaran drank it, and they waited. After ten minutes, he spotted her walking directly to their table. Ciaran straightened up his pants and sat up, ready for a lap dance.

Instead, she grabbed his hand and said, "Come with me, Ciaran."

He gasped at her calling his name. He took it and followed her, and Chris smirked at him. But surprisingly, after a few steps, she turned around and said, "You too, boyfriend." She reached out her other hand.

Chris jumped up and took it, and the two of them were led like children deeper into the room down a corridor with doors. She stopped at room number 5, and they followed her inside. The room was no bigger than a large walk-in closet. It was dimly lit with red and yellow bulbs and three plush chairs. In the center was a throne-like armchair. She closed the door, and the sounds outside the room were still loud but muffled.

"Pick a chair, birthday boy," she said to Ciaran. Ciaran sat in the throne, and Chris sat to his right on one of the plush chairs. She came closer, and Ciaran could see her eyes were light brown. In his inebriated state, she was the most beautiful woman in the world.

She said to him, "I'm Sapphire. I'm going to be your fantasy. Would you like that, Ciaran?"

He sat there and nodded. She went to the wall and pushed a button; music began to play.

Sapphire took off her see-through robe, and she danced seductively to him. She moved with fluidity and sensuality, touching herself along the way. She got closer and closer with every step. Ciaran held onto the arms of the chair and watched, feeling himself grow tight in his pants.

When she was close enough, she knelt down and rubbed her face in his crotch, and his semi-hard penis went instantly rock hard. She danced back up against him, then turned around, and sat in his lap. He inhaled sharply as her bottom rested on his center. She began to gyrate slowly, then leaned back, and moved faster. Ciaran was unsure how he was controlling his hands, probably from the shock. He had gotten a lap dance before, but not like that.

Sapphire untied one of her straps from her shoulder, and a perfect breast with a brown nipple fell out. He heard Chris gasp, but he could not turn his eyes away from it. And he was glad he didn't because the next thing she did was lift it up and put her head down, stick out her long tongue, and lick her own nipple. Chris gasped again. Sapphire turned around and straddled Ciaran, moved back and forth, dry humping him, her loose breast bouncing against Ciaran's chin.

Chris watched Ciaran and Sapphire, and it made him hard. He absentmindedly rubbed himself through his jeans and looked at Ciaran's face, his eyes wide, his mouth closed tightly, his hands gripping the arm of the chair so hard his knuckles were turning white. The song continued to play as she slid off him and turned her back to him. She danced to the floor and did a split, her thonged bottom bouncing as it hit the floor, then danced onto all fours and twerked for him. Suddenly her head was in Ciaran's lap again, and she moved with fluidity to turn around, dragging her face through his crotch again and lifted herself to stand up.

"Ho. Lee. Shit," Chris said to no one.

Sapphire was not done. She said, "Since it's your birthday, you get a special treat. Do you want to see me make myself cum, Ciaran?"

Ciaran's mouth formed a small "o" as Chris's mouth dropped into a large one. Ciaran still couldn't talk, so he just nodded.

"You promise to be a good little boy and just watch, right, no touching?" Ciaran nodded again. She turned to Chris. "You too, right?" Chris nodded as well.

Sapphire sat in the chair opposite Ciaran. They watched her take her thong off and expose her vagina. She put two fingers down there, and they watched her moan and squirm and bring herself to ecstasy. Both Chris and Ciaran were absolutely still.

Once done, she looked at Chris and said, "You have fifteen minutes." She said to Ciaran, "Happy birthday" and kissed him on the cheek, then left, closing the door behind her, leaving her thong in the center of the room.

"Chris started laughing hysterically. "I swear I did not know she was going to do all *that!*"

Ciaran still had not moved. "Why did you bring me here?" he asked quietly."

"Because I wanted you to have some fun. That shit was FUN!" Chris exclaimed.

"I... I feel like... like... like this was a test from you ... for me. And I'm not sure if I passed or failed."

"Both." Chris laughed. Ciaran finally looked over at him with a defeated look. "Oh, Ciaran," Chris said with concern. He realized he had touched a nerve.

He moved closer to the edge of his seat. "It's okay if you still find women attractive. It's okay if they make you hard or you want to fuck them. It doesn't take away how you feel about me."

"Yeah? What if I tell you that I don't want you to touch me right now?" Ciaran said seriously.

"Well, shite," Chris said sarcastically. "I would say you are human. And if I were you, I wouldn't want to be touched by anyone either, if I just got fucked with my clothes on by a beautiful goddess."

Ciaran shook his head. "I don't know what I am. Right now, I am more confused than ever."

"Then stop trying to put a fucking label on it," said Chris. "Just be. Be the guy who likes this other guy. Also be the guy who just got the craziest backroom lap dance by a beautiful woman who almost made him cream his pants. Be that guy. I like that guy."

Ciaran finally smiled. He let go of the arm of the chair and touched his aching erection. "I can't get up. I can't go out there like this."

"Well, I think she told us that we had fifteen minutes for a reason. Let me take care of that for you." He knelt in front of Ciaran and started zipping down his pants.

"Aren't there cameras in here?" Ciaran asked.

"I have no idea," Chris said before he put Ciaran's cock in his mouth.

Ciaran let out an "aaaah" as if in pain, and Chris knew this would be easy. After eight strong, deep-throating sucks, Ciaran spasmed in his mouth. He zipped Ciaran back up and stood up, his own erection visible, but he chose to ignore it.

"Are we leaving now?" asked Ciaran.

"Nope. I got a few more surprises in store for you."

"God. And now I'm worried," Ciaran deadpanned.

Chris grinned. They left hand in hand and headed for the bar.

CHAPTER 7

Birthday Wishes

Chris ordered two fireball shots, a beer for himself, and another rum and Coke for Ciaran. They sat, listened to music, and people-watched. Sapphire walked past and winked at them. Chris started laughing, making Ciaran laugh. He was definitely getting tipsy, and he was sure Ciaran was drunk by now.

At 11:40 p.m., Chris said, "Shit, we gotta go."

He took Ciaran's hand and led him back out the door they had come in, but instead of downstairs, they went up the next flight of stairs. The door opened to a room similar to the one they just came from, and the music had changed again, more techno and house music. But instead of a circular stage, there was just a circular dance floor. And instead of female strippers, there were male exotic dancers.

Ciaran couldn't help the loud laugh that escaped his lips. "Seriously!?"

Chris winked at him and pulled him to a table near the front of the dance floor that had "Reserved: Jennings" on it. He ordered four Jell-O shots, took one, and passed three to Ciaran.

Ciaran rolled his eyes at Chris, but he took them back to back. He shook his head quickly and said, "I'm canned now."

Chris laughed and took his one Jell-O shot. "These are good. I'm going to order more," said Chris, and he did.

Ciaran, who still had his rum and Coke, nursed it while they watched the show. Ciaran was watching the male bodies, and it aroused him but did not excite him. Not the way Chris did. He looked over at Chris, who was grinning. He reached over and touched his hand. "Yeah. You're canned, too."

They both laughed. Ciaran moved his hand to his leg until the show ended and the dancers cleared the stage.

A worker put a chair in the middle of the floor, and the DJ lowered the music. He said in Albanian, "<Hey, Levels family, we have a special shoutout. Somebody here is celebrating their birthday with us tonight.>"

Ciaran froze, understanding most of what was said, and looked at Chris, who would not meet his eye. The DJ called in English, "Ciaran? Ciaran Beals, please take your seat as king for the night so we can honor you."

The crowd clapped and whistled and started chanting his name. "Ciaran! Ciaran!"

Ciaran stood up and said to Chris, "Remind me to kick your arse later." Chris laughed.

He made his way to the chair, which was similar to the one he was just in, in the private room, but this one was black. He took a seat and faced the excited crowd. He could see Chris to the left of him, eager for what was about to happen next.

The DJ said, "So first things first, we need to properly wish Ciaran a happy birthday. One, two, three!" The crowd proceeded to sing "Happy Birthday," loudly, terribly, and off-key and then applauded themselves for a job well done. "And now, for your birthday present, courtesy of your boyfriend, Chris. Enjoy!"

The music started, and five male strippers came out in matching red thongs. Ciaran laughed and looked at Chris, who laughed too. They danced over him, around him, and underneath them. The crowd went wild as they gyrated their penises and asses in his face, put their faces in his crotch, and sometimes simulated fellatio. Ciaran knew if the lights were brighter, everyone would see his beet-red face and hard-on slightly forming. It was not as intense as Sapphire, more jovial and play-acting, but Ciaran was shit-faced drunk, so every touch felt good. He looked over to see Chris standing up, whistling, and hooting with the rest of the crowd and laughed again.

When it was over, the DJ said, "Aww, Ciaran was such a good sport. Give him a round of applause. Chris, come get your boy toy. We got him all ready for you!"

The crowd clapped as Ciaran stood up and adjusted his erection in an obvious way that made the crowd go wild again. He couldn't wipe the smile off his face if he wanted to. Chris came up and gave him a hug, then a peck on the lips. The crowd said, "Awwww!" and clapped again. They held hands and took their seats.

Chris ordered more drinks, and they struck up a conversation with the straight couple next to them. They were Levels regulars and talked about how lively it was every Saturday night. About thirty minutes later, the DJ announced the main event. Music came on, and a man came out in back-opened cowboy silk pants and a cowboy hat. He danced around, catching everyone's attention, and then headed Ciaran's way. As he got closer, Ciaran noticed how attractive he was. He looked to be of Middle Eastern descent, with chestnut brown hair, gray-green eyes, olive skin, and the perfect build—not too muscular but defined. He gyrated his waist and gave Ciaran full eye contact as he danced in front of him, then turned around, and sat in his lap, gyrating and grinding against him, making Ciaran's erection rise once more.

The dancer stood up and danced some more, then yanked his silk pants off to reveal his entire hairless ass with a black, silk sleeve to cover his huge cock. Ciaran stared at it with his mouth open, and the dancer took Ciaran's hand to touch it. Ciaran slowly rubbed the length of it, at least ten inches long, hard and thick, and his mouth watered. In two moves, he was on Ciaran again, straddled and facing him, looking into his eyes as he moved in a circular motion, hands around his neck.

Ciaran could not help himself this time. He found his hands on the dancer's waist and guided him. He got lost in his gray-green eyes. And for the first time ever, Ciaran found himself desiring another man besides Chris. It was surreal to him, and yet it felt like the most natural thing in the world.

Chris, who was sitting close enough to touch, watched with mixed feelings of wanting to push the dancer off his man and wanting to watch them go all the way. He watched Ciaran hold the dancer's waist like he held him. He could see and feel the desire in Ciaran, and it was incredibly sexy.

If Ciaran was straight before, Chris thought, *he definitely isn't anymore.*

The dancer leaned all the way backward to touch the ground and flipped off Ciaran, tipped his hat, and winked, then walked away, leaving Ciaran with his hands still suspended in the air where the dancer's hips were. He slowly lowered them, then touched his groin, and realized for the second time that night he was left with a hard-on, and this time nowhere to release.

Chris turned to the couple next to him. "<Who was that?>" he asked in Albanian.

"<That's American Rodeo. He always picks one person out of the crowd to basically publicly fuck. I guess it was your boyfriend's lucky day.>"

"Wow," was all Chris said. He looked at Ciaran, who had not moved. "You okay?" He touched his arm.

Ciaran looked at him for a long moment. He didn't have words to express how he felt, but he knew what he wanted. "We have to go. Now."

Chris stood up and felt he was a little tipsy. Ciaran stood up and stumbled, and Chris had to catch his arm. He laughed, and Chris smiled at him. "I got you, mate."

They walked out arm in arm down three flights of stairs into the cool night air. When they got to the car, Chris paused. "Er... my plan was to stay sober, but I guess I fucked that up. There is no way I can drive."

He started laughing, then Ciaran started laughing too, and they both leaned against the car in a fit of laughter.

When it died a little, Ciaran asked, "How far is the place?"

"Probably another fifteen minutes from here."

"Okay. Let's grab our things." They took their bags out of the trunk; then Ciaran asked, "What's the place called?"

"The Artimus." He gave him the address. "We're calling a taxi?"

"No. We're going to Wisp."

"Wha... *what?* You can do that with me!?"

Ciaran shrugged a little. "Close your eyes and think of the front entrance. Concentrate really hard and don't think about anything else. I'm going to guide us there on the count of three. Then we're going to take a step forward. You got all that?"

Chris nodded. He closed his eyes and saw the entrance. He had only been there once for a party a long time ago, but he vividly remembered what it looked like.

"Okay. One. Two. Three."

They both stepped forward. Halfway through Chris's first step, he felt lightheaded, and then he was rushing through the air, as it was knocked out of his lungs. The world went black as if he were stepping into a void, and suddenly, it was over, and his feet landed on solid ground. He opened his eyes, and he found them right in front of the lit entrance of the double doors of The Artimus.

"Ho. Lee. Shit. That was the best thing ever," he said, and Ciaran grinned. Then Chris said, "Wait, did you want to just Wisp into a well-lit area? What happened to secrecy, Ciaran?"

"Oops!" Ciaran said playfully and busted out laughing again, making Chris laugh some more.

"My God, Ciaran, you are fucked up. Let's get you inside."

They went upstairs into the one-bedroom suite and dropped their bags by the front entrance. Ciaran flopped on the couch, and Chris sat next to him. He closed his eyes and said, "Tonight was the craziest night I've ever had. Thank you, love."

Chris heard Ciaran call him "love," and it felt good to hear, even if he was drunk off his ass. He told him, "It's not over. I got one more gift for you."

"I swear if a chick with a dick pops out of the closet..." Ciaran murmured.

Chris laughed. "No. No more others. Just me tonight."

Ciaran opened his eyes and looked at him. Chris got up and went to his bag, found a small drawstring parcel, and pulled out what looked to Ciaran like a small black golf ball with a long tail and a hoop at the end. He sat in front of Ciaran on the coffee table and handed it to him.

"It's a weighted anal ball. You always give me waves of orgasms, but I don't always do it for you. Not multiple, back-to-back, mind-blowing orgasms. Let me do that for you tonight."

Ciaran held the ball in his hand. It felt heavy but soft. He guessed it was made of silicone. He said while still playing with it, "I'm starting to think this is the real reason you got me drunk tonight." He looked up at him and asked, "So. We've now entered into the introducing toys to the sexual part of our relationship?"

Chris pulled off his shirt, saying, "Well. It's the next logical step, innit? I think we've explored every position imaginable. You have the magic, but this is my way to keep the magic alive." He kissed him, then sucked his nipples. He said softly with his face in his chest, "Let me make you feel as good as you make me feel."

Ciaran lifted up his head and kissed him again. "I feel good just being with you, love."

Chris scoffed with a smile. "You're such a fucking romantic." Ciaran grinned.

Chris led Ciaran to the bedroom, grabbing the lube from his bag on the way. Once he prepared Ciaran and got him in position on his stomach with his knees in his chest, Chris pushed the weighted ball in as far as it could go. Then he stood up and lubed his own cock and slowly entered Ciaran from behind, pushing the ball farther in.

Ciaran moaned loudly again. "Fuuuuuuck, Chrisssss..."

When it was evident that it could go no farther and Chris was inside to the hilt, he lay on top of Ciaran and grinded against the ball that grinded against his prostate. Ciaran was beside himself with pleasure and kept moaning. Then Chris began to move in and out.

Ciaran's grunts became louder and more uninhibited. Between Sapphire and American Rodeo, he had more than enough foreplay than he needed for his whole body to be on fire with desire. And even with all of that, it was only Chris he thought of. And Chris's gift was sending him over the edge quicker than he ever had before. The constant pressure on his sweet spot was overwhelmingly intense. He quickly felt his orgasmic waves forming from the inside.

The waves came as soft ripples that wouldn't stop until they became ocean-wide currents. He thought he would pass out from the intensity of his climax. He clenched everything, his hands grabbing the sheets, his toes, his anus, and his eyes as tears formed.

Chris had to stop moving, or he would have cum himself. He slowly pulled back a bit, giving Ciaran a chance to catch his breath.

He asked, "Are you okay?" Ciaran couldn't talk and just nodded. Chris changed positions, turning Ciaran around to lie on his back. He leaned over him and asked, "Do you want me to stop?"

"Yes," Ciaran said breathlessly. "And fuck no."

Chris laughed. "You're drunk, so I will need clear and verbal consent here."

"Shut up and fuck me already."

Chris laughed again. "Yeah, that was verbal enough for me."

Chris entered him slowly again, and Ciaran began to moan automatically, loudly. Chris kept going until he felt his own orgasm forming, then slowed all the way down to stop it. He whispered in Ciaran's ear, "Cum again for me."

"Ooooh," Ciaran moaned. "What is this, payback?"

Chris only responded with, "I want to see your cream this time. No touching."

He sat up, put a pillow under Ciaran's waist, and entered him again with more force. Ciaran looked at Chris through his heavy-lidded eyes as Chris took control like he did the first time.

As Ciaran began to climax again, Chris felt himself clench. Chris fucked him like a rabbit in heat until Ciaran bucked his entire waist up and ejaculated. Chris lost it while watching Ciaran erupt in front of him, and he responded with his own, then collapsing on top of him.

They lay there hot, sweaty, and feeling the quickness of each other's heartbeats and trying to catch their breath. When Ciaran did, he said, "Chris?"

"Yeah?"

"If you're trying to make me fall in love, two more times of that, and I just might."

Chris busted out laughing, and Ciaran chuckled. Chris turned him around and slowly pulled out the weighted ball, then pulled the covers over them. They went to sleep almost instantly, facing each other, intoxicated, with soft grins on their faces.

CHAPTER 8

Home

Chris got the call at work two days before he was supposed to fly out to England with Ciaran for his sister's wedding. Charity told him that Clarissa was admitted to the hospital, a week before her due date, with low levels of her amniotic fluid. Chris called Ciaran immediately and told him he was leaving work and why.

"Of course," Ciaran said right away. "You have to be there."

"And..." Chris hesitated. "There is no way I can leave her, mate. I can't go with you to Kingsbridge."

"Of course not, I wouldn't have even asked," Ciaran said with concern. "You need to be there. Just keep me posted, please."

So Ciaran headed off to England alone early Friday morning. He flew into London on a plane, then Wisp'd into Kingsbridge, England. He had not been home in a year and forgot how much he missed it until he was back again. The small fisherman town was always bustling during the day. Ciaran walked the long way through the town and then through the fields that led to the back of the house.

He stopped at the large boulder under the tree where his younger brother rested in peace, about a quarter of a mile from the house.

"Hey, Shane," he started as he sat down. "I know you've been watching, but I feel like telling you, anyway."

For the next hour, he talked about Chris, how strong his feelings were for him, and his fears of what would happen when everyone found out. Somehow he knew that Shane, Sean's dead twin, was there with him. Ciaran sat quietly and thought about all the sarcastic comments Shane would make about his newfound sexuality and then how Shane would tell him to go for it, no regrets. His heart ached, but he held back tears. He started hating himself for not being there on time to save him, but then remembered his conversation with Chris about it, that everything happened the way it should have, and it brought him some relief from his grief. He knew Shane would say the same thing.

He took a couple of deep breaths and said, "I'll see you again before I head home, little brother." He kissed his fingers, placed them on the tree, and walked on.

He saw his mum and Diana in the garden before they saw him. They did not seem to be aware of his arrival, although he had magically sent his bags to the house hours ago. So Ciaran said loudly, "There's my two favorite girls!"

"Ciaran!" Grace and Diana both exclaimed.

Diana did a running jump into her brother's arms. Ciaran spun her around and kissed his little sister's head, and then took her hand, swinging it as they walked over to Grace. He gave his mother a long hug.

"It's good to see you," Grace said on his chest. "Can I give you a haircut?"

"No, Mum." He smiled at her.

She pulled apart and looked behind him. "I thought you were bringing a friend?"

"No... something came up." Ciaran chose his words carefully. He had not told his mum in the letter whether it was a male or female friend, just a very special friend of his that was going to accompany him to the wedding.

"Oh well. I hope to meet her soon," Grace said.

Ciaran did not respond. Instead, he turned to Diana. "So. It's finally happening. You're going to be a James. Part of literally the oldest Magi family in all of England, possibly Europe. Ancestral ties all the way back to Merlin. How do you feel?" They linked arms and walked to the house with Grace leading the way.

"Truth be told, I have barely seen Quentin this last year, with his Magi Commander training and all. I look forward to after the wedding humbug, and we're just living together, so I get to see more of him."

They talked about the going-ons with the other siblings and cousins while Grace cooked and served lunch for the three of them: Ted, their eldest brother, was still headquartered at the Scholarly office in London and continued to travel several times a year for missions. Alastair, their first cousin on their father's side, received a promotion to Senior Manager of International Programs of the Magi Council. He reported directly to Grandminister Graham, the head Magi in charge of the Magi Council of Europe.

Sean, Ciaran's youngest brother and the living twin, started working alongside their first cousin, Robert, on their mother's side, in the family's Magi shop. Chloé, Diana's best friend and Rob's girlfriend since their days at Campus, was working for the Magi Council in the law department, a job their father Hamish got for her. She and Rob weren't engaged yet and were still living in Quentin's house, soon to also be Diana's house. But the four of them were such good friends that no one was looking to change their living arrangements.

They talked about the wedding and tonight's rehearsal dinner. He was paired to walk down the aisle with one of her dorm mates from Campus named Shoshana. Afterward were the individual parties, and all the men were to be at the house early tomorrow to set up the chairs and tables. The wedding was set to begin at 4 p.m. right on the land the Beals owned in the same spot where Ted had married his wife Elodie six years prior.

After lunch, Grace sent Ciaran upstairs to try on his groomsman suit and rest up before tonight. Ciaran headed to the second floor to his and Ted's room, which had never changed: twin beds on opposite sides of the room with a window in between. Ciaran's side had posters of Manchester United and several dragons. Ted's side of the room had posters of Arsenal and several music artists, mostly loud grunge and punk music that Ciaran never got into.

His suit was stretched out on his bed, so he dropped his bag and tried on his suit, which fit fine. He plopped on his bed and called Ted from his cell phone.

"Hey, little brother! I kind of expected you to just show up at my door," Ted said.

"You know I had to see Mum first. Just settled into our room."

"Oh no, you aren't staying at the henhouse!"

"The what?"

"Soon that house is going to be swarming with giggly, girly bridesmaids. You do not want to be there, mate. Go to Quentin's house."

"I don't even know where Quentin's house is," said Ciaran.

"Well, go to The Magic Box Shop and hang out there until they close up. Sean and Rob will take you there. I have a couple more hours of work here myself; then I'll stop by."

Ciaran sighed. "Got it. I'm going."

He got up and changed back into his clothes, grabbed his bag and suit, and told his mother and sister the plan. Then he left the house and Wisp'd from the back porch back to London and headed to his uncle Malcolm's store.

The shop was filled with Magi of all ages, especially kids in cloaks from the nearby Campus he, too, had attended. It made him smile, watching their excitement as they talked about summer holiday plans since school was finally out. He tried to walk through without being noticed. But Sean, who had been waiting for him, shouted from the top of the stairs, "CIARAN!"

He came running down the stairs and jumped into his arms, similar to Diana's greeting earlier. Ciaran laughed and hugged his brother. After spending a year on the road with him, they had become pretty close, and he missed him a lot. Their cousin Rob, who heard Sean's yell, came from the back and gave Ciaran a hug as well.

"I was told the men are staying at Quentin's. Where do I put these for now?" He held out his bag and suit.

"Oh, yeah, sure, I got it." Rob pointed his *dulé* at Ciaran's stuff and said, *"Destinatio James domum."* It disappeared to the front entrance of Quentin's house. "So, how long are you staying?"

"Just until Sunday. I need to get back."

"Yeah, back to your special friend? Mum told us." Sean winked at him. Ciaran smiled back at him, but did not respond.

He hung around the shop until they closed an hour early. Rob grabbed Ciaran's arm, and they Wisp'd to the front steps of Quentin's house together. Before Rob could grab the knob, Quentin James popped open the door, pushing Rob and Sean aside.

"I'm so glad you could make it, mate," he greeted Ciaran happily, grabbing his hand and shaking it excitedly.

Quentin James was young and energetic. Because the James's were a rich, Generational Magi family, most of them were aristocrats and philanthropists, who spent more time arguing about politics than doing anything about it. But on his mother's side, many practiced the dark arts, including his mother. After his father died and his mother tried to persuade and then force him to join the literal dark side, Quentin ran away from home to stay with the Beals and decided to join the Magi enforcers on the war front.

After the war, instead of joining the line of the other James's in philanthropy, he pledged his life in service to the Council and Magi Enforcers, something no one in his family on either side had ever done. For that, Quentin James received all of Ciaran's respect. There was no better match for his sister than a man like him.

They sat around and drank beer, talking about life on the Reserve and Quentin's Commander training. Ted showed up with the hard stuff, scotch, and they hung out some more as they caught up on each other's lives. At 6 p.m., they got ready for the rehearsal dinner and Wisp'd together back to Kingsbridge at 7 p.m.

Ciaran saw that Ted was right; it was a henhouse. Diana had six bridesmaids, including her best friend, Chloé, and Elodie, his pregnant sister-in-law. Their aunt Elspeth was spending the night as well. More female cousins and other Mages he assumed were from their days at Campus arrived. His father, Hamish, and cousin Alastair were already there. He gave Alastair a hug, even though Alastair was not a hugger, and shook hands with his father. After salutations, Grace started sending the ladies along with Aunt Elspeth to the pub for the rehearsal dinner, and all that was left was the bridal party to do the wedding rehearsal.

Ciaran knew who Shoshana was by the way she stared at him before they were officially introduced. When it was time to pair up, she walked over to him with confidence, introduced herself, and linked arms with him. Shoshana had a mysterious beauty about her, with long wavy jet-black hair, dark blue eyes, and a curvy shape. It was obvious she wanted more from him, so Ciaran was already strategically trying to figure out how to keep his distance without offending her. Chris sending him updates via text throughout the day was a good distraction; he would simply excuse himself and spend time on his phone instead.

The wedding rehearsal went well. Quentin and Diana grinned at each other as Rob and Chloé, the best man and maid of honor, practiced the tie bind and gave each other a chaste kiss as practice. Once it concluded, they all Wisp'd to The Golden Orb, a Magi restaurant and pub in a nearby town, for dinner. As Ciaran suspected, Shoshana kept finding ways to be close to him.

Ted and Sean kept giving looks and snickering behind his back, to which he kept giving them the finger. He was grateful when Sean called for the boys to get together to head to Wanderlous, a Magi bar in London. The Beals men left and met up with four more of Quentin's and Robert's chums from Campus. They drank a lot and traded stories of their time at school before the war and during and what they had been doing since.

Ciaran was sitting next to Sean when his phone buzzed. This time, it was a photo message from Chris. He opened the picture of Charity, Chris, and Clarissa holding a baby in the bed, with the caption, *It's a Girl!*

Ciaran smiled as Sean leaned over. "And who are those beautiful people? Might one be that special someone you were supposed to be bringing?"

Ciaran pointed as he spoke. "This is Charity, Clarissa, who just had a baby, and Christopher."

"She is stunning," Sean said. "Well done, mate."

Ciaran realized he was talking about Charity and chuckled, but he did not correct him. A couple of minutes later, his phone rang, and Chris's name popped up. Sean saw and gave Ciaran a puzzled look, but Ciaran intentionally did not catch his eye. Instead, he got up to take the call outside.

"Hey, you," said Ciaran.

"Hey."

"Congratulations, Uncle Chris."

"Thanks. The last forty-eight hours were crazy."

He told Ciaran how Clarissa had to be induced because of low placenta fluid and low blood pressure and then had an emergency c-section because the baby had the cord around her neck and was losing oxygen. They were all so scared, but Chris went into the room with her and held her hand. He was the first to hold his niece.

"Clary named her Sierra, after the country where her father was born, Sierra Leone," he said. "She may never know him, but she will know where her heritage came from."

"Wow. That's amazing. I can't wait to meet her. Hug Clary for me and tell her congratulations and well done."

"I will. It was incredible, holding a newborn like that, fresh out of the womb," Chris said dreamily. "I can't wait to have my own children."

"Ah yes. The plan to populate the world with little Chris's before you're thirty," Ciaran said in amusement.

"Of course. You know I want two or three, really. Maybe four." He paused, realizing they'd never had that conversation of children together. "You don't want children, Ciaran?"

Ciaran shrugged like Chris could see him. "Dunno. I mean, I've always figured I would at some point, but I've never been one to feel like I have to have them, you know? And now that I'm..." he trailed off.

Chris laughed. "What? With a man? Men get married and start families all the time."

"I know. Sure. I guess I would leave the decision to my partner, man or woman."

"Well, I have to have them. It's a must for me. I need to be a father. And this good seed I've been just giving away has to amount to something," Chris said smugly.

Ciaran laughed. "So would you be shocked if you had kids out there that you didn't know of?"

"Actually, no, I wouldn't be shocked, and that's shameful of me, so let's not talk about that." Ciaran smiled as Chris changed the subject. "How is it going? Anyone mention my absence yet?"

"Only my mum wanted to know where my special friend was. I just said something came up. Oh, and Sean mentioned something in passing just now."

"Uh-huh, and I'm sure my gender didn't come up or the fact that I'm not a Magus?" he said, amused.

"Neither of those things came up because I didn't want to start a conversation without them meeting you first as planned," Ciaran said seriously. "We'll take another trip. Promise."

"No rush, Ciaran. I already told you, I'm good with where we are, too. No pressure to tell your family. When the time is right, it will reveal itself."

"Okay," Ciaran said softly.

Silence came between them. Chris broke it. "Sleeping alone again for a couple of days."

"Yup." Ciaran could feel Chris's melancholy through the phone. "You're going to wanker off, aren't you?" he teased.

Chris laughed. "Of course! Well, maybe not. I will be on uncle duty until Clary gets out of the hospital, and Rudy's staying downstairs with me."

"Good. You'll have no choice but to exercise self-control."

Chris said, "I'd rather you send me a dick pic so I can lose control tonight," as the door to the bar opened and Sean looked out to search for Ciaran.

Ciaran looked at his brother and said on the phone, "I gotta go. Kiss the family for me."

"So that's a no on the dick pic, then?"

Ciaran laughed again. "Goodbye, Chris," he said as Sean walked over to him.

"Hey," Sean called. "Everything okay?"

Ciaran smiled. "Yeah. Everything is great." He patted Sean on the back and went inside, leaving Sean with a puzzled look on his face again.

CHAPTER 9

Unconditional

After fighting about sleeping arrangements in Quentin's large home, Ciaran ended up sharing the third-floor bedroom with Sean. Sean pulled out a bag of marijuana saying, "Fresh from the Amazon," and coerced Ciaran into lighting up a joint with him.

Ciaran asked him, "And how are you getting on, Sean? For real?"

Sean shrugged and puffed. "Keeping busy. Haven't tried to kill myself if that's what you're asking."

"That's not what I'm asking." Ciaran snatched the joint from his hands. He hated Sean's dark humor that had developed over the last couple of years, but he understood it. "How are you keeping busy?"

"Work gives me plenty of stuff to do." He looked at Ciaran. "Really. I'm okay. The trip cleansed me a bit, gave me a clear head about all that has happened. My wombmate is dead. I've accepted it. Still practicing *Kabili*, so I'm more of a witch than a warlock now. That helps, too. I've been teaching a little of it to Diana, and she's using it to advance her skills as a Wiccan. It would be nice if people stopped asking me how I'm doing though. That would help tremendously." He took the joint back from Ciaran.

"Okay," said Ciaran. "I know you well enough to know that when you're ready to talk to me, you will. Just know I love you, and I'm here for you, unconditionally."

Sean was silent for a moment. Then said, "My *Amina* changed. It's not a penguin anymore."

"That was to be expected," said Ciaran. "You're rediscovering yourself without your other half. What is it?"

Sean didn't answer. Instead, he said, "Ainsley comes around the shop, a lot."

Ciaran's eyebrow went up. "Ainsley Addams from Campus? Your volleyball teammate?" Sean nodded. "Ainsley... Shane's girl?" Sean nodded again. "Okaaay. So... what does that mean?"

Sean fell backward on the bed. "I didn't fuck her. Quite the opposite; I kind of yelled at her last week, told her I'm not Shane, and if she was hoping I would be some kind of Shane substitute, then she's wrong."

"And what did she say?"

"She burst into tears and told me to fuck off. That she knew who I was and if I didn't want things to go further that I needed to not be a dick about it and bring up my dead brother."

Ciaran knew to read between the lines. "Go further than what? You said you didn't fuck her, but something happened." He took the joint back and puffed.

Sean paused, then said, "We went on a date about six months ago, right before she went back to Olympics training. A wonderful, fantastic date that ended with her in my bed. We kissed and cuddled, but that was it."

Ciaran nodded. "And how did that feel? Being with her?"

"It felt like…" Sean looked up at the ceiling. "Hot mint tea on a winter day. Refreshing." He looked back down at the bedspread. "But when I woke up, I felt like I was betraying him somehow. Shane and I always had a rule that we didn't share girls. I had Katie. He had Ainsley. That's the way it was supposed to be."

"But he doesn't have Ainsley anymore. No one has Ainsley anymore, innit? It's been three years."

He took the joint back, puffed, then said, "So it's my duty to covet my brother's girl?" Sean laughed.

"I didn't say that. I'm just saying, if it feels right, don't hold back. Life is short."

"Yeah. I think we all know that."

Ciaran got in the bed and put his head on the pillow. "What does she want?"

"Dunno. When she first started coming around after you and I got back, she said she just wanted to see how I was doing, and she talked about her and Shane a lot. I was her outlet. But then she slowly stopped talking about him and started telling me about herself, how playing professional volleyball in Italy gave her purpose and all, her family, her life. She asked me about things going on in my life too. And we just started connecting. That's what made me ask her out. I wanted to see if it was really something, outside of the one we loved the most dying."

"And was it? Something?" Ciaran took the joint and puffed again, then handed it back to Sean. He was done smoking.

"Pfft. I don't know anymore."

Ciaran knew that was his brother's way of shutting down, so he let him. "Well, figure it out. And when you do, don't be a dick about it. Either way. Besides being Shane's old girl, you two were friends. So treat her like a friend first. Be honest about your feelings and don't lead her on. But also, be honest about your feelings to yourself. And if it feels right, let it happen naturally."

Sean took a deep drag. "You're just full of relationship wisdom, innit?" Ciaran smiled. Then Sean asked, "So, you gonna tell me about this new bird or what?"

Ciaran hesitated. Then said, "Not yet, Sean. Let me keep this one close to me just a little while longer if that's okay."

"Yeah. Sure," he said softly.

They didn't speak again, both in their own thoughts, and quietly drifted to sleep.

***

Ted woke up Sean and Ciaran, then woke up Rob and Alastair. They went to Quentin's room and jumped on the bed, waking him up singing, "Ho, ho! Hey, hey! It's your fucking wedding day! Ho, ho! Hey, hey! It's your fucking wedding day!"

Quentin woke up alarmed, then smiling. "Oh, wow! I thought you only did this for family."

"You are family, you git," said Rob as they settled on the bed around him.

"Yeah, but you know what I mean. You all jumped on Ted's bed the same way on the day of his wedding to Elodie."

"Nope, we don't know what you mean," said Ted. "You've been family since the day Diana and Rob brought you home, like a stray puppy."

"Except we should have neutered your arse before you mounted our little sister," said Ciaran threateningly.

Quentin went bright red. "I... I ... did nothing of the sort."

Rob snorted. "Yeah, okay."

Ciaran slammed his hand hard down on Quentin's shoulder, and he winced but didn't pull away from him. "It's okay because you are making an honest woman out of her. If you weren't, then..." He gave him a knowing look.

Quentin, still red but fading, said, "Believe when I tell you, she is the one making me look good and pure here. She's the best thing that has ever happened to me. You lot are the second best." He took a deep breath.

"Thank you for always being there for me, for taking me in when my own family tried to... well... you know what they did. Despite Talindra being my aunt, you Beals have always been there for me. Ted and Ciaran, for always treating me like one of your little brothers. Sean, and Shane for that matter, for getting me into a lot of jams at Campus, but looking out for me always. Alastair, for teaching me the importance of standing on your principles, but that it's okay to change your mind. Rob, for just being the best mate ever. I'm so excited to marry Diana today, but I'm also happy that I gained a new mum and dad, three amazing brothers, and two wonderful first cousins in the process. Well, Rob, mate, you know you've always been like a brother to me. Four if you count Shane looking out for me from above. I guess what I'm saying is, this is the greatest day of my life because I'm gaining actual family that cares about me, something I didn't have before and—"

Sean cut him off. "If you don't cut this sappy shit out I'm going to sneak a jinx on your cock, and you'll have the worst honeymoon ever."

Quentin shut his mouth and smiled widely.

The wedding went off without a hitch. Diana wore a pure white lace princess-cut wedding dress, holding fresh flowers from the garden. Quentin wore a white tux with a burgundy shirt. The bridesmaids wore burgundy strapless babydoll dresses, high in the front and longer in the back, while the men wore black tuxes with a burgundy shirt. Ted and Ciaran, who had both sported ponytails, were forced into a chair right before the wedding as Grace trimmed Ted's sixteen inches of fiery red hair down to fourteen inches and Ciaran's twelve-inch hair down to ten. He was barely able to hold it in a ponytail so he shoved it behind his ears.

Quentin and Diana exchanged vows, did the magical tie-bind, and kissed. Then Quentin Wisp'd with Diana on the spot, and everyone knew their honeymoon had just started. They returned two hours later, missing the reception but just in time for dinner, happy, smiling, and holding onto each other as the Beals brothers exchanged looks.

During dinner, Ted pulled Ciaran aside and told him, "Scholarly is sending me to Somalia to investigate a possible curse that is protecting a long-lost treasure. I'm going to stop in Albania for a few days before heading on. Or I might just take you with me. We'll see how it goes."

Ciaran was excited about it. It would be a great opportunity to introduce Chris to Ted first and see how that went, before introducing him to the rest of his family. "I'll be ready."

Later on, when Ciaran was in conversation with his father, Sean, and Alastair about how the Council could do a better job of tracking illegal breeding of dragons, Chris's name brightened up the phone screen with a call. He again ignored Sean's perplexed look and excused himself, going to the far side of the garden to talk with him.

But it was not Chris's voice he heard. "I have a new baby sister!" Rudy exclaimed, excited to talk to Ciaran.

"Yeah, I heard mate, well done," Ciaran encouraged him.

"Yeah, I got to hold her and feed her, and I can't wait to play with her!"

Ciaran laughed as Chris had to explain baby safety all over again in the background. "He's just excited," Ciaran said. "I'm sure Rudy will be the most incredible big brother ever."

He could hear Rudy's smile through the phone. "I will be, promise, Ciaran!"

Chris laughed and said, "Go play with toys. Let me talk to Ciaran for a minute."

"Okay bye, Ciaran!" Rudy called and ran off.

"Blimey, that kid is cute," Ciaran said.

"Yeah? Mr. I-Don't-Want-Kids?"

"I didn't say I don't want kids. I said I will leave it to my partner to decide," Ciaran clarified. "I'm fine either way."

"Yeah, yeah, sure, sure," Chris said sarcastically. "Anyway, how is it going? Wedding went off great?"

"It was beautiful, yes. No problems at all. Oh, and my mum cut my hair so..."

Chris gasped. "How short?"

"Short."

"Ho. Lee. Shit. Ciaran, take a picture!" he pleaded.

Ciaran laughed. "No, you'll see it tomorrow."

"C'mon. I need a full-length picture too, dress tux, cloak, and all."

"Not gonna happen."

"Awww, you suck!"

"Not right now, but I will when I get back," he said seductively.

"Hmmmm, Ciaran, you are so lucky Rudy is right here, or I'd have some words for you."

Ciaran laughed again and said, "I'll be home tomorrow night. Your place then?"

"Yeah. I took a week off to play faux dad so you won't see me in the forest," Chris said.

"That's okay, you'll see me in your bed," Ciaran said seductively again.

"Hmmm... You are testing my resolve here."

Ciaran laughed for the fourth time. "I fucking miss you, mate."

"And Ieeeeee. Miiiiiiisss. Yooooou," Chris sang. They were silent for a moment. Chris broke the silence. "Well, I just wanted to check in. Sorry I missed this one. Looking forward to attending another wedding with you next month."

"Yes, Vlad and Alexi in the Atrium." The couple asked Chris and Ciaran to stand in as their witnesses to do the tie-bind, since no family would be there to attend. They readily accepted. "That should be fun."

"Yeah."

"I'll call you tonight, before bed. I'm sure Sean isn't sleeping here tonight. He has been following my bridesmaid partner Shoshana around all day. So I'll have some alone time. I'll clue you in on Ted's potential visit to Albania in a few months."

"Brilliant. I'm looking forward to that as well," said Chris. "Until tonight, lover."

Ciaran smiled. "Until then, lover."

They hung up, and Ciaran stood there a little while longer, thinking about his feelings for Chris and staring into the setting sun. He didn't notice Sean behind him until Sean came over and stood next to Ciaran.

"Hey, big brother."

"Hey, little brother."

They were silent for a brief moment; then Sean said, "That picture of your friends in Albania. I just assumed that beautiful Charity was your special friend. But all your calls all weekend have been coming from Christopher." He let the words hang in the air.

Ciaran kept looking straight ahead. "Is there something you want to ask me, Sean?"

"Nope," Sean said, shaking his head. "Because I know you well enough to know that when you want to tell me something, you will. Just know that I'll always be here for you like you've been for me. Unconditional, innit?"

Ciaran nodded. "Unconditional."

They stood staring ahead for another moment; then Ciaran turned to him and pulled Sean into a tight hug, which he returned.

"I love you, Sean."

"I love you, too, Ciaran."

He held him a bit longer, then released his little brother. Sean said, "I'm going to see Shane."

"Wait, before you go, take a picture of me. Well, two. One full length and the other a closeup of my hair."

"Oooh, somebody wants to see scruffy Ciaran all dolled up, huh?" he teased.

"Shut up and take the pictures."

Sean took Ciaran's phone and snapped two pictures, then handed it back to him before heading down the path to Shane's tree.

CHAPTER 10

High Sister

Ciaran stayed at Chris's house for the next week Wisp'ing from there to work at night and assisted in getting Rudy ready for school in the morning and taking him to school. Because Chris missed a week of work and other rangers covered for him, he generously spent the next week picking up extra shifts here and there for them. So Ciaran also did a fair amount of diaper changing and rocking during the day while Chris was working doubles and Clary slept or showered. And he found he didn't mind at all.

Chris had an overnight shift on a Saturday covering for someone, which meant he and Ciaran were in the forest at the same time and were able to leave together in the morning. When they arrived at Chris's house, Charity was walking out of his place with a man Chris had never seen before. The man greeted Chris and Ciaran, but Chris just glared at him murderously.

As soon as he left, Chris exploded on his sister. "Did you really just bring some rando into my house for a quick fuck?"

"Well, I couldn't bring him upstairs, could I?" she explained. "Not with Clary and two children there."

"So my place is the new fuck flat?" Chris growled at her. "I don't think so, Charity!"

Charity brushed him off. "As many randos that you fucked in this space, you have some nerve."

"No, Charity, I have never brought a guy I met five minutes ago into my actual living space, you fucking skank!"

"Chris…" said Ciaran quietly, but the siblings ignored him.

"Fuck off!" she yelled at Chris. "You think because you're in a relationship now you get to dictate how everyone else is getting off? Fuck you!"

"I should slap the shite out of you right now," he said coldly.

Charity ran toward him. "I fucking dare you!"

Ciaran caught her and jumped in the middle. "Okay, hold on now. Let's talk about this like adults."

Chris said, "No. If she wants to be unsafe and stupid about who she fucks, then that's on her. I don't give a shit. Just don't bring it to my flat."

"UNSAFE!" Charity was now screaming at him. "You fucking hypocrite!! You have fucked and sucked your way from Tirana to Maliq! You've fucked everybody and probably are still fucking everybody AND Ciaran raw for months. Who knows how many diseases you've passed to him by now and you're talking about me?!"

"You fucking bitch. How dare you!" Chris screamed at her back.

"All this because I'm a woman!" she screamed back. "Well, if I'm a skank, you're the biggest slut bag whore in all of Europe!"

Charity broke out of Ciaran's hold, ran to her room, and threw clothes in a bag, then stormed out without another word to either of them.

Chris called out as she reached the door, "Fucking stay out of my place and my life!" She glared at him and then slammed it hard.

He brushed past Ciaran and went into the bathroom, slamming the door. He was beyond pissed at what she did, but even more so at the things she said to him.

Ciaran sighed and went to the fridge to pull out leftovers from the night before and warmed them up while Chris showered. When Chris was done, he went straight into his room and slammed that door as well. Ciaran sighed again and went into the room, sat on the bed, and looked at him. Chris was still fuming while finding clothes to wear.

He started, "Chris—"

Chris cut him off. "No. I'm not going there with you. Drop it. All of it."

Ciaran didn't. "She didn't say anything that I don't already know or care about."

Chris glared at him. "For the record, I get tested every six months for everything, and I used protection most of the time unless I was in a relationship, obviously. I just didn't the first time with you for some reason..." he trailed off.

Ciaran said, "Well, the first time wasn't exactly planned. And we just kept going after that, no sense changing it."

Chris didn't respond at first as he got dressed. Then he said, "I've been reckless, yes, but I'm not a moron. And either way, I'm done with all that. So fuck her for even insinuating that I'm still fucking around. She has no idea how I feel..." He looked at Ciaran. "Ciaran, I'm not sleeping—"

Ciaran put his hand up to stop him. "You don't even have to say it. I'm not worried about that at all. I trust you," he said simply. "Plus, we literally spend all our time together. When would you have the time to suck and fuck your way to Tirana?" he deadpanned.

Chris groaned and laughed at the same time, putting his face in his hands. "God, Ciaran."

"Are you okay?" Ciaran touched his arm. "She said some pretty harsh things to you."

Chris sat next to him on the bed. "It's not the first time. I was just mad she went there in front of you."

"For the record, I'm not innocent either. I wasn't a virgin when we met, you know. Not in the biblical sense," Ciaran said, and Chris gave him a wide smile. "I just meant, I spent a year being reckless too. But I'm also not a moron. When Sean and I got back, I made us both get full checkups, the Magi way and the Commoner way."

Chris nodded. "We just keep having these adult conversations, don't we?" He smiled.

"Well, it's a good thing we're adults." He smiled back and leaned in for a kiss. Then Ciaran said, "Also, be gentle with your little sister." Chris groaned again and began to rise. But Ciaran held his arm. "I just mean that you could have said what you needed to say without being mean and condescending. You are worried about her being unsafe. Tell her that."

"Well, that's not going to happen anytime soon," Chris said simply. "Let's go eat."

Ciaran stayed at the flat while Chris went to work that night for another shift he had picked up. A little after midnight, Ciaran was lying on the living room couch watching TV when he heard the front door open. He got up and went into the hallway. Charity, seemingly drunk, in a super short black dress, so short he saw the bottom of her derriere, stumbled in, dropping her purse on the floor and kicking off her heels. He quickly averted his eyes.

"Hi Keeeeyyyaaaarrrooon!" she purred as she walked past him to the kitchen. She started pulling out baking pans.

"What are you doing?" he asked.

"Making brownies!" she said happily.

He sat at the table and watched her pull out the ingredients, add them to a bowl, and start mixing, talking about her night at a party from which she had just returned. Halfway through adding the cocoa powder, she pulled out a bag of cannabis and emptied at least an ounce into the mixture.

"Whoa!" Ciaran exclaimed.

Charity looked up innocently. "What?"

She mixed it all in a blender, added it to the pan, and put it in the oven. Then she sat at the table across from Ciaran and smiled seductively. "Keeeeyaaarooon," she sang his name.

Shit, Ciaran thought. He said to her, "Charity, have you been drinking tonight?"

"Yes!" she said happily again. "A lot. And now I'm going to get high."

"Aren't you a nurse? I thought medical professionals cautioned against stuff like this."

"You have the prettiest blue eyes, do you know that?" she answered him with a smile.

Bloody hell, Ciaran thought. He turned away from her and shook his head.

He let Charity ramble on about her job and one female patient she kissed when she was being discharged until the brownies were ready. She took ice cream out of the freezer, cut a slice for each of them and put a scoop on the side of the plate, then sat next to him instead of across from him. "Eat with me?" she pleaded. "Pleeeease."

Ciaran knew there was no way he was eating more than a couple of bites of the brownie, but he didn't want to upset her, so he pretended, eating more ice cream than anything else. She talked, and he watched her eat the first slice, cut another, and finish that. Then she started eating from the pan.

"So, Ciaran, do you love my brother?" she asked out of nowhere.

Ciaran did not answer; instead, he took a scoop of ice cream and smiled at her. She "hmpfed" at him. "Well, you should be careful. He is incapable of love, you know."

"I don't think that's true," he said.

Charity scoffed. "You should run."

Ciaran chuckled. "Yeah? Concerned for his happiness, innit?" he said sarcastically.

She looked up at him with her hazel eyes, then moved her chair closer to him. She rubbed her bare foot along his bare leg and said, "Unless it's only for fun you're looking for. You can get that anywhere."

Ciaran ignored her seduction. "I thought you don't share men with your brother."

"For those baby blues, I'm willing to make an exception." She leaned in to kiss him, and Ciaran stood up. As she fell over, he caught her by her shoulders.

"You're canned. You should go to bed now," he said fatherly.

She looked up again and batted her beautiful eyes. "Why don't you put me to bed?"

Ciaran started laughing. "Okay."

He helped her up, took her hand, and started leading her toward her room. Right before they got there, she reached across and grabbed his soft groin.

"Fuck, you *are* big," she purred again.

Ciaran jumped back, startled. She laughed hysterically. "You, Charity Jennings, are dangerous," he said seriously.

"And you're gorgeous." She started walking toward him, desire in her eyes.

Ciaran pulled out his *dulé* and said, *"Obex!"* A blue shield appeared in front of him, and Charity walked right into it.

"How did you do that?" she asked in astonishment.

"I'm a warlock that can do magic," he told her.

"Oh," she said, as if she understood his words. Charity reached her hand out and touched the shimmering, translucent blue wall. "What is it?" She kept touching it with both hands.

"It's a dream," Ciaran said. "This is a dream, and it's time for you to lie down so you can wake up again. *Vis carmina omittere.*"

The protection spell disappeared, and Ciaran started a new one, a star shower above her head. Charity was so high it distracted her completely from her mission to seduce her brother's boyfriend. She gasped and stared at the twinkles above her. He led the spell all the way to her bedroom, and Charity followed like a puppy. He put stars that would fade in a few minutes on her ceiling and helped her get in the bed.

He kissed her head softly and whispered, *"Somnum."*

"It's so beautiful," she said softly before the spell made her drift off to sleep.

Charity woke up and looked around. She had no recollection of how she got in her bed at Chris's house downstairs, fully dressed in her clothes from the night before. The last thing she remembered was making brownies. Her head was pounding, and her mouth was dry. She heard movement and figured either Ciaran or Chris were out there. She slowly made her way to the main area.

Ciaran had made coffee and was trying to make breakfast for Chris, burning toast in the process. He saw her and automatically handed her a cup and a piece of warm bread before it burned as well. "Good morning," he said cheerfully. "How did you sleep?"

"Ugh. I feel awful," she said. She sat at the table and put her hands on her head. "But I had the weirdest dream."

"Really?" Ciaran took a sip of his own coffee. "What was it about?"

Charity was thoughtful, trying to pull pieces of it together. "I found a blue light and followed it to a shooting star. Then rode the star all night in the skies."

Ciaran chuckled. "That sounds awesome."

"Yeah, it was—" She froze mid-sip. "Ciaran, how did I get here?"

"You came home last night, made pot brownies, and went to bed," he said matter-of-factly.

"Yes, but... there were ... other things that I did..." She put her hands to her mouth, and her eyes went wide.

Ciaran waited as the events of last night began to take shape for her. She looked horrified when she finally looked up at him. "Ciaran, did I... did we... did I try to *kiss you?*"

Ciaran kept a straight face. "No. Why?"

They stared at each other. Then Charity groaned and put her face in her hands. She reminded Ciaran of her brother when he did the same the night before, both out of embarrassment.

"Uuuugh. I'm so, so sorry. I hate the fact that you're such a great man and so loyal to him. It just makes me feel worse. My behavior was... I can't believe I even attempted to..." She looked up at him. "He can never know, okay? Never."

"Know what?" he asked innocently as he took another sip of his coffee.

Charity smiled. "You do love him, don't you?"

Ciaran smiled at her in response. Chris should know how he felt before anyone else did.

"Well, I said a lot of shit last night. Ignore all of it. Because I know my brother, and I know he feels the same about you. For what it's worth."

He smiled again. Her words were worth everything to him.

As the door opened and Chris came in, Ciaran rose from the table to greet him. Chris smiled at Ciaran, who he saw first, and Ciaran gave him a kiss. But he froze upon seeing Charity at the table. He looked back at Ciaran with a frown and said, "What is she doing here?"

Charity answered, "Just chatting with the boyfriend. He's a real keeper." She walked over to him and gave him a hug, which he did not return. "I'm sorry about yesterday. It won't happen again."

She stood on her tippy toes, kissed his cheek, and went back to her room to lie down, hoping she could recreate her calming dream.

Chris watched her walk away and rounded on his lover. "Okay. What happened?" he asked Ciaran.

Ciaran shrugged. "She loves you, mate. You have a great sister."

It was all he said. He knew he would go to his grave never telling Chris about the night before.

CHAPTER 11

Свидетели

The afternoon of Vlad and Alexi's wedding was a bright and sunny Friday. Vlad spent the night at Ciaran's house, and Alexi stayed at Jesse's house to get ready. They expected a small number of guests, but Vlad was pleasantly surprised when Alexi, Jesse, Ollivier, and Mateo Wisp'd into the Atrium with all the men from the mission, including Sarah. She had convinced Dale to give the day crew Reservers that wanted to go to the wedding an hour off to attend; then they would Wisp right back to work. When their shift was over, they would come back for the evening festivities when other friends were to appear.

Ciaran began introductions. "Hey, everyone, meet Christopher. Chris, this is Felix, Khalid, Sahid, Jesse, Bruno, Mike, Tommy, Dylan, Grayson, Lee, Jamie, Ollivier—"

Tommy interjected, "OOOOOH, you're the RANGER BOYFRIEND!" he yelled loudly. "Did you know we call him the Ranger's Magi!?"

Chris grinned and looked at Ciaran as the others snickered. Ciaran turned to his protégé. "Yes, Tommy. He's my boyfriend. And I'm the Ranger's Magi. Got all that now?"

"Oh, yeah. Sorry. Dunno why I yelled it," Tommy said sheepishly.

Felix answered, "Because you're a fucking wanker, mate. We all know it, and now Chris knows it, too." The Reservers laughed as Tommy blushed from embarrassment.

Ciaran finished introductions, and they all took their places, with Chris on one side and Ciaran on the other as their *svidetels*, or witnesses, holding onto the golden tie-bind ropes. Vlad and Alexi talked quietly in Russian on the bridge in the garden, waiting for the wedding to begin, smiling at each other. Suddenly a large puff of smoke appeared behind them. They all turned to see Lucas Wisp'd in with three people that Ciaran had never seen.

Lucas yelled to Vlad and Alexi, *"Vy ne mozhete nachat' tseremoniyu bez nikh!!"*

Vlad and Alexi were astonished. They shouted in Russian and ran to the new attendees to give hugs. Kristoff, who was standing close by, said, "Lucas said, 'You can't start the ceremony without them.' It's their family."

"Ooooh," Chris and Ciaran chorused.

They found out that Lucas had reached out to Demetri, Alexi's oldest brother, and told him about the wedding and how much his brother needed him there. Demitri brought his oldest sister Maria, and Maria reached out to Vlad's mother, Oksana. Together, they convinced her she would be miserable if she did not witness her only son's marriage. His father, however, did not know she was there.

Oksana told her son in Russian, *"I don't understand, but I didn't understand when you started using magic, either. I got used to that. I will get used to this. You will always be my son."*

Her words brought Vlad to tears, and he cried on his mother's bosom.

Demetri told his brother that it wasn't that he didn't accept him, but he was in shock. And everything happened so fast, and he did not know if Alexi wanted him to reach out. But he always thought of Vlad as part of their family. Maria said the same, and that Nina, the youngest sister, also supported them, but they implored her not to come as she was still sixteen, at Campus, and underage. Maria and Demetri were well over twenty-one and already had their inheritance. It was easier for them to defy their parents than for her. But she sent all her love and support. They all hugged and cried.

Ciaran and Chris quickly stepped out of the way as *svidetels* and allowed their family members to step in for them, handing their golden ropes to Demetri and Maria. Vlad and Alexi took their spots on the bridge in the Atrium as everyone stood and watched them exchange their vows with tears down their faces. Kristoff continued to translate the beautiful words they shared with each other for Ciaran and Chris.

Afterward, the day crew members Wisp'd back to the Reserve to return in a few hours for the reception. The ones not working went to the Atrium to help set up while Ciaran, Chris, Vlad, Alexi, and their family members toured the apartment in the Atrium that they were to move into that night. They spent time together until it was time to head to the Atrium Restaurant, which was closed for the rest of the night for the private event.

At 7 p.m., the guests started arriving, this time dressed for the party, with Dale on Sarah's one arm and Sven on the other. Russian Campus alums showed up. including the Reservers Lucas, Axel, Kristoff, and Gideon, wearing gold button-down shirts, black slacks, and black ties, their Campus colors. And Bruno came with cases of imported vodka.

Demetri wrote Phoebe a large check to cover the wedding and in anticipation of the destruction that was sure to ensue. Sure enough, almost everyone became ridiculously drunk, including Vlad and Alexi, and the Campus alum broke many glasses on purpose to celebrate the occasion and danced on tables singing their school songs.

Chris and Ciaran, who were not drunk, sat at the counter and resumed their typical role of people-watching. Chris pointed out, "Hey, one of the Campus alums has red hair like yours."

But Ciaran nodded. "I already talked with him. His great-great-grandmother was a Beals."

"You're joking," Chris said as his mouth dropped.

"Nope. I told you: Throw a stone on any country, and you'll hit a Beals." That made Chris laugh out loud.

As the night went on, they thought they lost the newlyweds, but Chris spotted them in the corner in a heavy make-out session, hands on each other's bottoms without a care in the world who saw them.

"I guess they aren't shy about their love anymore," Chris said, amused.

Ciaran laughed. "Yeah. It's good though; they deserve to be happy. They are so in love."

He smiled at Chris, and Chris smiled back. Phoebe slid over to them from the other side of the counter.

"So, when is the big day for the two of you?" she teased.

They both scoffed. Ciaran said, "Phoebe, they are light years ahead of us."

"And this is small potatoes for a romantic like Ciaran," said Chris with laughter. "He's going to need a fanfare proposal before he agrees to marry someone like me."

Ciaran feigned being shocked. "What does that mean? I'm a simple guy."

"Yeah, okay, mate. You'll want a proposal in the city of love or something like that."

Ciaran grinned. "Paris, France. At the top of the Eiffel Tower with Manchester United spelling out the words, 'Will You Marry Me' below us." Chris and Phoebe both laughed. "What?" said Ciaran innocently. "I've only been to France once and never to the Eiffel Tower."

"See?" said Chris. "You aren't as simple as you think!"

"No, that's just because you're too simple. You don't think big enough. We would be patrolling or sitting right here eating breakfast, and you'd turn to me and say, 'Hey, Ciaran, marry me, okay?' And I would say 'Fuck off, ask me again in Paris.'"

The three laughed again. Phoebe said, "Sounds like you guys aren't as far off as you think." She winked and touched both of their shoulders as she walked on.

"I've always wanted to go to France," Chris said casually. "To speak French in France was Ma Ami's dream, that she made mine. It was to be my graduation present, just the two of us." Chris tried not to be solemn about it and quickly took a sip of his drink.

"Well," said Ciaran, just as casually, "My sister-in-law's family has a chateau there. Maybe we'll make it to France one day, and we'll live out your mother's dream together. You'll have to be my guide, though. I understand little, and I speak it even less."

"*Je serai ton compagnon partout, mon amour,*" said Chris seriously. "*Je te suivrai jusqu'au bout du monde si tu me le demandes. Je ferais n'importe quoi pour toi.*"

Ciaran only caught a few words, but he understood. They stared at each other; then the connection was broken by the commotion in front of them as another plate shattered in celebration.

CHAPTER 12

Motus Willow

A few weeks later, after patrol, Chris and Ciaran were lying around the Tank talking about the pockets of the woods that had yet to be explored.

"The Northwestern part of the woods is where the Hunters go for food for the dragons. Wild animals roam that denser part. Actually, you should be thanking the Hunters. They've been taking care of your wildcat problem for decades," Ciaran said.

"Hmmm... I'm starting to think that's where my tree is," Chris said thoughtfully.

"What tree?" Ciaran asked.

"There's this tree that we used to play under as kids," explained Chris. "Ma Ami used to take us there. Sis would splash in the river, and Clary would lie on the grass with Mum talking about whatever boy trouble she was having at the moment, and I would play clubhouse under the leaves. I loved that tree. We were always so happy there. It's like a cross between a weeping willow and a Japanese cherry blossom, but so much bigger, and it blooms all year round. There is no other tree like it in all of Verdant."

Ciaran's eyebrows turned in. "Chris..." he said softly.

Chris didn't hear him, lost in his own thoughts. "When I started working in the woods, I tried to find it again, but either I was looking in the wrong place or someone cut it down or maybe it died. I know I should let it go, but I just can't. There was something really special about that tree."

Ciaran sat up and looked at him. "It's near a river, you say? Where the Berzanta River meets the bottom of the mountain? Huge boulders all around?"

Chris looked up at him. "Yeah. Have you seen it? You know where it is?"

"Of course. It's near the Reserve. And it's one of ours, a Motus Willow."

Chris slowly sat up, too. "Are you serious, Ciaran?"

"Yes!" said Ciaran excitedly. "I pass it all the time. It's probably half a kilometer north of the Reserve entrance."

"It can't be," Chris said. "I've looked all around there. It's not there."

"Yes..." Ciaran was thoughtful. "But if you looked for it when you first got here, the wards would have stopped you from getting too close. Because the river leads to an entrance into the mountains that will bring you right into the valley of the Reserve."

"What spell?"

"There's an aversion spell around the Reserve. I believe Scholarly had it expanded that way about ten years ago because any person could follow the river and have it take them into dragon territory. So that makes sense that you played there as a child, but you couldn't find it as an adult. But I blocked that spell from you ages ago. There is nothing to stop you from going there now."

Chris stared at Ciaran. Ciaran could almost read his mind. He wanted to go right now.

"C'mon, mate," he said. "Let's go see your tree."

They started walking as if they were going to the Reserve, but then Ciaran kept going farther north to the small wooden bridge over the creek that led to the river. They crossed it and went down a small slope. Chris remembered the slope vividly and started walking faster ahead of Ciaran, like on autopilot. He gasped when he saw the leaves at first. They were pink as they usually were in the summer, white in the winter.

The closer he got, the more emotional he felt, hyperventilating, his chest tightening. By the time he pushed the long leaves aside and stepped under the Motus Willow, Chris was flooded with emotions and was crying. He remembered playing hide-and-seek with Charity, his mother making a lei out of the leaves and wrapping them in it, playing with his toy soldiers along the side of the tree and the roots, and the day Clary said, "Let's take pictures so we'll never forget the best time of our lives," but most importantly, he remembered his mother.

By the time Ciaran caught up, Chris was laughing and crying as memory after memory overwhelmed him. "This is it, Ciaran! This is my tree!" he cried.

He hugged and kissed him, then ran around the tree a few times like a young child. Ciaran, who was also feeling emotional, tried not to let it overwhelm him, as he knew it was the tree expounding on emotions that were already there. Chris suddenly came around to the side of the tree, dropped to his knees, and started digging between two roots with his bare hands. Ciaran watched Chris pull out a metal tin Superman lunchbox. He let out a moan and started crying even more.

"Ciaran, look! It's still here!" he cried.

He opened the box, and there were some rocks, a game of jacks, toy soldiers that looked like they had been preserved for twenty years, and two pictures. Chris let out a sound that was a cross between joy and pain. He stood up and pushed the tin box for Ciaran to hold and held both pictures to his chest. He stood against the tree, closed his eyes, and cried openly, speaking in French.

"*Ma mere, mère, mère pourquoi m'as-tu laissé derrière, pourquoi ne m'as-tu pas emmené avec toi? je suis si perdu sans toi, si perdu si perdu...*"

Chris was speaking so fast that Ciaran only made out one word: *ma mere,* my mother. He did not need to know the words to know that Chris was grieving and talking to her. And suddenly Chris's grief overwhelmed him. Before he could catch himself, his own eyes welled up with tears, and he brushed them away. He touched Chris's shoulder and let him grieve.

Suddenly Chris opened his eyes and looked up into the leaves. "She's here, Ciaran," he implored. "Can you feel her? I can. I can *feel* her. I can hear her laugh. I can..." He looked at his arms, and the hair on them was rising. "She's here. It's like she never left me."

Ciaran grabbed Chris's other hand and held it tightly, brushing more tears from his eyes. "Because she has never left you, Christopher. She's always with you. But, yes, if this was her favorite place, then her essence may still be here."

Chris looked at Ciaran. "I wish you would have met her. She would have loved you." He gave him a sad smile and wiped Ciaran's tears as well. Then he showed Ciaran the pictures.

The first was a picture of Chris at six years old, smiling with all his teeth and a woman kneeling next to him, kissing his cheek. The picture was taken where they were now, except they had on heavy coats and the leaves were white. The second was a full-length picture of his mother, not quite as young as the picture of her and her husband on Chris's mantle, but still fairly young. She was standing in front of Chris's house with a soft smile and kind eyes.

"She is so beautiful," Ciaran said, and he meant it.

"The most beautiful woman in the world. No one could ever compare." Chris sniffed. "She took a single picture with all of us that day. Both of my sisters have theirs, but I buried mine here along with this one of her, thinking I would never lose it. When she died, I went crazy trying to find this tree and this picture. I figured because of my grief, I couldn't think straight to remember where it was. But now I know. And now I have her back."

He let a few more tears drop as he looked at the picture. "Ma Ami," Chris said softly. Ciaran wiped his own tears again, then reached over to wipe Chris's. "You don't know what you've done for me, Ciaran. You've given her back to me. Thank you," Chris said sincerely.

"Of course," Ciaran said just as softly. "But this was nothing. I would do anything for you too, you know. Anything." He wiped Chris's tears again, ignoring the trail of his own down his cheek. "I'd follow you to the ends of the earth too. That's what you said to me in French, right?"

Chris looked into his eyes, and again he was flooded with emotions, but this time they were all for Ciaran. He kissed him passionately, pushing the box out of Ciaran's hands and pulling at his work uniform. Ciaran kissed him back, unable to stop himself. Chris got the top half of his work jumper off his shoulders to his waist. He licked Ciaran's neck and bit his nipples through his shirt, then kissed him again.

As Chris grabbed his crotch, Ciaran found a small bit of resolve. "Chris... Chris wait..." he tried.

"Shut up, Ciaran." Chris stopped pawing at him and looked into his eyes. "Shut the fuck up."

Ciaran stared back at him and knew he had lost the battle the moment he stepped under the tree of emotions with his lover. He grabbed Chris's neck and put his tongue in his mouth.

Chris yanked the rest of Ciaran's uniform to his ankles with his clothes and fell to his knees, taking Ciaran in his mouth with one motion. Ciaran moaned louder than he intended and held Chris's head as he deep-throated him easily in six quick sessions. Chris came up with a loud popping sound, then licked and sucked his balls, licked back up to the head, and then deep-throated again.

Ciaran could not stop moaning and barely noticed as Chris zipped down his own zipper and opened his pants. Chris knew he had no lube on him, so he made himself gag a few times and spit on his cock. He kept gagging, pulling Ciaran to the edge of ejaculating. But instead Chris stood up and turned Ciaran around, and Ciaran did not resist. He held onto the trunk of the tree and braced for impact. Chris spit a few more times on himself until he was dripping in saliva and pre-cum, then thrusted inside.

Ciaran grunted, but didn't stop him. Instead, he did the opposite, made himself malleable, and let Chris dominate him. Chris held onto Ciaran's waist, thrusting into him as if he were trying to put his whole body inside of him. Ciaran could feel Chris's intense desire and need as if they were his own, and it overwhelmed him again. He took one of Chris's hands off his waist and pulled it toward his chest so he could lace their fingers. He tried not to make any noises himself because he wanted to feel and hear all of how Chris felt about him in that moment.

Chris was there, and then he wasn't. It was an out-of-body experience for him, and he felt euphoric. He could feel how tightly Ciaran held him, as if he would never let him go. He could hear the sounds of him thrusting into Ciaran. And although his eyes were closed, he could see them against the tree—his tree—becoming one, the leaves gently swaying around them, encouraging them. When he finally came, he moaned the whole time. He felt light and thought he was going to fly away with how amazing it felt to empty out and fill Ciaran up.

And before he could stop the words from tumbling out of his mouth, Chris collapsed against Ciaran's back and said, "I love you." Then he gasped.

Chris felt Ciaran freeze, so he froze as well. No one spoke. Then Chris slowly eased out of Ciaran. He took a few steps back, tripping over his pants that were still around his ankles, and fell to the ground with a thump. Ciaran turned around and sat down at the base of the tree, his face unreadable, neutral. Chris averted his eyes and started pulling up his pants.

Ciaran stopped him. "No, don't. Come here," he said. Then Ciaran removed one pant leg and boot.

He motioned with his fingers for Chris to come closer. Chris removed both boots and his pants silently and crawled over. Still avoiding Ciaran's eyes, he deep-throated Ciaran a few more times, creating more saliva. When it was glistening in spit and pre-cum, he straddled him and lowered himself down slowly. Ciaran held onto Chris's waist as Chris began to move with his hands in Ciaran's hair.

When Chris finally looked at him, they locked eyes, as intently as they did the first time they met, and neither could turn from the other. Somehow, Chris heard him. It was like a whisper in the back of his head, but he heard Ciaran think, *<Cum for me, Chris.>* And he didn't question how or why that was possible. He just did what he was told.

Chris rode Ciaran like he always did, moving circularly, then back and forth, bringing himself to orgasm. But something felt different that time, almost spiritual, as they became one once more under the tree whose leaves were still swaying, despite the humidity in the air. They moved together rhythmically, and Chris started moaning as the waves came. Ciaran reached down and grabbed hold of Chris, stroking. And Chris heard him again, *<Cum for me.>*

Chris put both hands around Ciaran's neck and managed to close his eyes despite Ciaran's intense gaze. And when he finally came, the climax was the most intense Chris ever felt. Wave upon wave of orgasmic pleasure brought him to tears, and he let out a holler like he never had before. At the height of Chris's orgasm, Ciaran released with a low "hmmmm" and warmed Chris up on the inside, as Chris exploded simultaneously on Ciaran's chest.

When Chris stopped moving, he heard Ciaran say out loud, "I love you, too."

Chris opened his eyes and looked at Ciaran, who was still staring at him intently. He avoided his gaze and adjusted to sit on Ciaran's lap, resting his legs on either side of him.

"You love me..." Chris trailed off in a whisper.

Ciaran wrapped his arms around his back to pull him closer. "I think I've known for a while now," Ciaran said quietly. "A few weeks. Maybe months." He let his words sink in for Chris as he held him, and they did.

"You love me," Chris whispered again. He looked down at Ciaran's chest.

"I do. How could I not?" Ciaran said with a clear voice as his own tears finally fell again. "You're the most incredible person I have ever known. Everything about you is incredible. I love your passion for everything. I love how brave and strong you are. I love that you make me laugh, even during the most inappropriate times. I love your serious face and your excited face. I love how intelligent you are and how empathetic you are. I love how silly and immature you get when I make you act like an adult." Chris laughed a little.

"I am in love with you, Christopher Jennings," Ciaran continued. "I don't know what I was doing before you came into my life, but you are my whole life. I can't imagine any future that doesn't involve me loving you as much as I do right now. You are my future." Chris's tears started flowing again, and Ciaran touched his face. "I'm going to love you forever, Chris."

"You know, Ciaran?" Chris started. He looked into Ciaran's eyes through his tears. "I'm going to love you forever too, and then three days after that, I'm going to marry you and give you Chris-looking children with C names and we're going to settle right here in Albania and be a fat, happy gay couple. Or we won't have any kids at all, and we'll travel the world and visit all the countries in Africa that have Magi villages and learn how to do unconventional magic with our feet." Ciaran laughed. "Whatever you want to do, as long as I get to love you and be with you while doing it. Because I'm going to love you forever, Ciaran. I really, really am."

Ciaran said, "Why not both? Why don't we have Chris-looking children with C names and travel through Africa with them? So we both get what we want."

"I want that so badly with you," said Chris.

They kissed passionately. Then Chris said, "So what do we do now?"

"Well, first, we get our arses off this grass. Then we go to your place and make love again."

"No, yours," Chris said. "No distractions." They kissed again.

"Then I stop playing around and tell my family," Ciaran said. "Starting with Ted, who will be here in two days."

"Okay," Chris said.

He tapped Chris's leg so he could get off him, and they started putting on their clothes. When dressed, Ciaran picked up the lunchbox. "Do you want to keep this?" he asked.

"No. Let's bury it again. I have what I needed." He put the pictures in his pocket and buried the lunchbox where it was.

Chris then stood up and said, "Say it again."

Ciaran smiled. "I love you."

Chris came closer and kissed his face. "Say it again."

Ciaran laughed. "Why do I have to be the one to keep saying it?"

"Because I said it first and you'll never let me live that down, so now you have to say it more times than me."

"Fair enough." Ciaran laughed. "I am ridiculously, unequivocally, unreasonably, in love with you, Chris Jennings." Chris grinned, then kissed his cheek again.

As they walked back to the Tank hand in hand, Ciaran explained what a Motus Willow does. "It enhances your emotions, so whatever you are feeling, it expounds on it ten times more. The leaves are a key ingredient in love potions. Which is also why love potions are dangerous because emotions can be very intense, but also fickle."

"So that's why I couldn't stop crying," Chris deduced.

"Right. Your happiness about finding the tree was elation, but your sadness about your mother brought full-on tremendous grief like it happened yesterday."

"And then I felt immense passion for you." He smiled.

Ciaran smiled back. "Enough passion to tell me you love me. First," he teased him.

Chris shoved him with his shoulder. "I didn't stand a chance." Ciaran laughed. "Also, Ciaran, I heard you. I heard you in my head tell me to cum."

Ciaran looked at him skeptically. "That's impossible."

"But I did," Chris said earnestly. "Something about that tree brought us closer than ever before."

"Can you hear my thoughts now?" Ciaran asked.

Chris tried, but it was nothing. "No."

"Huh," Ciaran said. "Interesting. There was definitely an intensity that I have never felt before. Not even when we're playing around with my sister's concoctions for lasting lovemaking."

"So was it lust or love?" Chris asked. "Was it all real or just what we felt in that moment?"

They had reached the parking lot, and Ciaran pulled Chris under the lamppost where they first kissed six months ago. He took both of Chris's hands.

"I meant every word of what I said under that tree," Ciaran told him. "If I could remember it all verbatim, I would say it again, right here where it all started. But this is especially true: I am in love with you, Chris. That is real."

Chris smiled. "Well, I remember everything I said, and I could tell you verbatim, but I'd rather show you."

He put his hands on Ciaran's neck and said, "I'm going to love you forever, Ciaran Beals, my amazing Magus, and three days after that. You're my best friend, my lover, and my everything."

And they kissed slow and long under the lamppost.

CHAPTER 13

Ted Beals

Chris went with Ciaran to his flat in the morning to prepare for Ted's arrival that afternoon. However, as they entered the apartment after work, they were surprised to see Ted's duffle bag in the middle of the living room.

Ciaran's heart started beating fast. "He must have come early and went to the Atrium." They looked at each other.

"You're ready?" Chris asked.

Ciaran nodded, even though he was nervous. "Let's go."

They dropped off their bags and went through the residential entrance into the Atrium from the back. Ciaran spotted Ted sitting at a center table talking with Lewis, the cook and Phoebe's youngest brother. He wore a black Beatles t-shirt, black ripped jeans with two silver chains hanging off them, one for his wallet and one for his pocket watch his dad gave him when he turned of age, and gray timberland boots. His hair, the same color as Ciaran's, was pulled back in a ponytail, but much longer. He had fewer freckles than Ciaran, mostly bunched up on his high cheekbones, and he was thinner and at least an inch taller. But where Ciaran had an easygoing, quieter nature, Ted was louder and owned the room with his confidence, Chris could tell.

Chris turned to Ciaran after a glance at Ted and said, "Ciaran, you are not the cutest Beals, are you?"

"Don't flirt with my brother," he said, rolling his eyes.

"I make no promises." He winked at his lover.

Ted saw Ciaran coming toward him and said, "Hey, little brother!" He stood up to hug him.

After the hug, Ciaran stepped back and introduced them. "This is Chris. Chris, my brother, Ted."

"Oh, a friend of Ciaran's, hey!" He greeted Chris cheerfully with a handshake.

Ciaran started to say something, but Chris said loudly, cutting him off, "Yup, that's me, friend of Ciaran's. It's nice to meet you, Ted. I've heard great things."

"Well, I'm Ted so that's all you would hear," he said cockily. Chris laughed. "Irish, innit? I could hear the lucky charms in your accent."

Chris laughed again as they sat at the table, with Ciaran sliding next to him. He immediately liked Ted. "Born and bred through my Irish father. But I lived in Albania my entire life."

"Oh, so you're a Reserver, then?" Ted asked Chris.

"No, I'm actually a forest ranger," Chris told him.

"Oh, wow. I didn't know the Albanian division had a Magi in that position. It's kind of mundane Commoner work."

"Well, they do have us Magi in the best places to ensure our livelihood," said Chris casually. "Arslan as a detective, me as a ranger, you know."

Ciaran's eyes double-blinked at the conversation that was happening, and he slowly turned to Chris. Chris avoided his eyes and took a sip of water.

"Oh, you know Arslan then?" Ted asked. "What's he been up to lately?"

Chris said nonchalantly, "Oh, you know Arslan, sarcastic little fucker, innit?"

Ted laughed and said, "That he is!"

Ciaran blinked at Chris three times. He could not believe how Chris was letting Ted believe he was a Magus. Not just letting him believe it, but building upon it. But he said nothing to correct him.

Phoebe came over and hugged Ted from behind. "I heard you were here."

"Hello, lovely," Ted said, and patted her hand.

Phoebe looked at Chris and Ciaran, too. "Well, if it isn't all my favorite boys in one place. What can I get for you?" She held out her pen and pad to take their order.

Ciaran said, "Same."

Chris said, "Same."

Ted said, "Well, I don't know what 'same' is, but I guess I'm having that too."

Phoebe told him, "Goat meat and couscous with egg on top or on the side."

"I like mine on top," Chris said and caressed Ciaran's leg under the table.

Ciaran closed his eyes, and when he opened them, he looked over at Chris, who was still avoiding his gaze. Ted gave his order, "On top then."

Ciaran needed to take control of this conversation. "So, tell me about this mission."

"Right," Ted began. "So a few months ago, the Council got a message from the African Coalition regarding a cursed cavern that they couldn't figure out, and it was killing any Magi that went close to it. They needed help. The Council sent it to Scholarly to investigate since it wasn't a law issue.

So here was the report: A village in Somalia was digging to expand its water supply and came across an underground cave. The first couple of AMC expeditioners went in and did not come out. After a week, the second group did not go all the way in, but they explained that there were eerie sounds the farther in they went, and they did not like the way it made them feel, so they retreated. They sent two experienced Magi from the village in next, with an ear-muffling spell on.

"Three days later, one came out carrying his dead cousin. He explained he saw the bodies of the first group, and it looked like they took some time to die, as if they were put in some kind of sleeping curse that they couldn't wake up from, and they just wasted away. They got all the way into the tunnel to a large opening, and there was a fucking talking chimera in there! When his cousin tried to pass it, it attacked and killed him. But then it moved away and allowed him to take the body back. It's bloody bonkers!"

Ciaran and Chris were both stunned. Ted continued, "This all happened a week ago, so now they are calling in the expert. Me." He smiled triumphantly. "I've already figured out it's saying some kind of riddle, and it's guarding something. Now I just need to figure out how to solve it without going crazy, or you know, dying. If it's a talking chimera, we might be able to read its lips. But I need a second. You up for it, Ciaran?"

"Seriously? I thought you were joking when you said it before."

Ted shook his head. "AMC are sending me in with an Elfsten. I need someone I can trust by my side."

"Elfsten?" Chris asked softly.

"Half man, half elf," Ciaran responded in a murmur. To Ted, he said, "I would love to, but I don't think I can get the time off. Dale sort of just gave me a promotion."

"You didn't tell me that," Chris said quietly.

"Congrats, little brother! What kind?" Ted said excitedly. Ciaran looked at Chris a little long, then caught himself, and looked at Ted.

"Well, Jesse just received his DE credentials, Dragon Excellence, so he is officially a dragonologist. Dale wants to bump him up to Assistant Trainer, where I am now, and make me Senior Managing Tamer and basically manage all of the Tamers and Fixers. Ollivier, Lucas, and Vlad are studying to also get their degrees, so that would make more dragonologists and leaders on the reservation. And you know Lucy, Dale's actual boss, is all for that. Bruno is also getting bumped up to Senior Managing Hunters and Trainees, giving him more responsibility during the day. Dale told me a while ago that the idea is for Bruno and I to take over for Dale and Sven someday, so they are basically grooming us now." He looked at Chris again, who gave him a small smile.

"Wow, that is fantastic, little brother; you deserve it." Ted gave him a fist bump across the table.

"I'm really proud of you," said Chris. He gave his leg a squeeze under the table.

"Thanks, mates. But one caveat is that if I'm managing all the Tamers and Fixers, they should be seeing me during the day as well." He looked at Chris again.

"Well, that's easy," Ted said. "Pick a Friday or Saturday or both for a day shift. You work overnight Wednesday to Thursday, you're off the rest of Thursday and go in on Friday morning, and possibly Saturday mornings. So now your weekend nights are free again. If you're making more money, you can work five days instead of six."

Chris nodded. "That's actually a good idea."

Ciaran, too, liked that idea; it meant more weekend nights with Chris. "Yeah, I'll figure it out soon."

"Well, if you want to go with me on my newest adventure, leave Dale to me. I will talk to him when I go to the Reserve tomorrow," Ted said.

"Wait!" Chris said, shocked. "Why are you allowed to be on the Reserve grounds? I thought no one was allowed but Reservers." He looked at Ciaran.

"Because I'm Ted Beals. Haven't you heard, mate?" He winked at Chris.

Ciaran rolled his eyes and answered, "Because Ted is also a Senior Certified Dragonologist, along with his many other degrees, and has had encounters with dragons in his line of work. Dale respects Ted's ability to handle himself around them. He's allowed to come on grounds but not into the valley. He stays up in the field or at the top and watches. He can't touch, and he certainly cannot ride a dragon, no matter how much he begs."

Ted laughed loudly. "Dale's a pisshead. They let me ride them in Siberia." Chris chuckled as Ciaran rolled his eyes with a smile.

As they ate, they talked about Ted's experiences with dragons, and Chris chimed in with his dragon knowledge that even impressed Ciaran. He could tell Ted liked Chris, and that made him happy.

Afterward, Ted said, "Chris, are you hanging around a bit? Or do you have a nice, warm bed with a lady waiting for you?" He winked at him.

Chris smiled. "My bed is currently empty of women right now. Plus, I took a nap at the Tank for an hour or so, so I'm not tired just yet." He turned to Ciaran and said innocently, "Is it okay if I crash at your place today, hang out with you and your brother for a while?"

Ciaran's eyes narrowed, and he looked at Chris like he wanted to tell him to stop it. Ted answered for him, grabbing Chris's shoulder. "Of course it's okay! Let's go."

As they started walking toward the back entrance, Chris noticed Phoebe, Elsie, and Lewis behind the counter watching them, smiling. Elsie mouthed, "Good luck" to him. Chris put up two crossed fingers and grinned at them.

Once upstairs, Ciaran went to make tea while Ted sat on the couch. Chris took two books from his bag and returned them to Ciaran's bookshelf. Ted noticed they were Campus textbooks and thought it odd for an adult Magus to be reading them.

"Witch or warlock?" Ted asked.

"Huh?" Chris said, turning around.

"Where do you fall? More witchy? Spells, potions, and such? Or more warlock: Duels, incantations, *Vis* strengthening?"

"Oh," Chris turned back to the bookshelf. "I don't believe in labels."

"So, where did you go to Campus, Chris?" he asked.

"I didn't," Chris said casually. "I was homeschooled on the ways of magic."

"Yeah? That's interesting. Who did you learn the most from?" Ted asked, getting even more curious.

"My mother taught me everything I know," he said, still facing the bookshelf.

"Really? So you were brought up as Commoner then?"

"Yes, I am very much a Commoner in a lot of ways," Chris said.

Ciaran rolled his eyes from the kitchen. He heard Ted say, "How so?"

"Well, I don't practice the *Vis*. I just like to read about it." He was still searching the shelf, mostly to avoid Ted's eyes.

"So you're an *Absentem Magi*?" Ted deduced.

Ciaran didn't know if Chris even knew what that was and quickly came into the living room to Chris saying, "No, I'm just not interested in magic in that way."

"Wow. That's ... interesting. Do you own a *rodulé?*" Ted said. Disbelief surrounded him. Something was off, but he couldn't put his finger on it.

"No. I do not own a *dulé*," Chris said.

Before Ted could ask another question, Ciaran said, "Hey Ted, what about Barton being out for the rest of the season? Hard luck for Arsenal, huh?"

Ted's attention turned to Ciaran. "We haven't lost him. It's a shoulder injury, and he will be back."

"Doubt it." Ciaran laughed. And they went on a rant about their football clubs.

Chris took that time to go into Ciaran's room to change, putting on Ciaran's gray sweatpants and a black t-shirt from his drawer.

When he came out, Ted asked him, "Who do you follow, Chris?"

"Oh, I think Ciaran has convinced me to go with Manchester now, but my heart was previously with West Ham." Ciaran stared at Chris in disbelief; Chris didn't follow any football teams, especially not English ones. He didn't even know that Chris knew who West Ham was. Chris winked at him before continuing to talk about their goalie stats blocking goals.

"Ah, West Ham! People like the idea of them, but not their actual skill," Ted quipped.

"Hold on now," and then Chris proceeded to talk about other players that had impressed him. Ciaran sat there listening, trying very hard not to blow his cover, astonished by how much Chris knew about the game. He sat down and relaxed a bit as they talked sports, moving on to Spanish football leagues and other topics.

Before they knew it, noon rolled around, and Ciaran said, "I'm going to go downstairs and get us some food."

"Oh, don't bother. Mum sent her shepherd's pies." He pulled out four small round cupcake-size containers from his bag, took out his *dulé*, and pointed it at them. The pies immediately expanded to serving sizes, wrapped in clear plastic. He handed them to Ciaran.

"Sweet! Thanks, Mum!" he said excitedly. He went to the kitchen to warm them up. Chris was sitting at the desk under the bookshelf, and it reminded Ted of the conversation earlier.

"So, Chris, what kind of magic do you know?" Ted asked.

Chris smiled. "That's a weird way to phrase it. What do you actually want to know about me?"

"I'm just asking about the kind of magic that your mum taught you since she taught you everything you know." He smiled back.

"My mum taught me the magic of a kind heart, a winning smile, and to never back down from a challenge." He held his smile.

Ted laughed. "So no real defensive magic, then. Wasn't part of the war efforts a few years ago, innit?"

"Why, do you want to challenge me to a duel?" He raised his eyebrow.

"C'mon. You couldn't handle me. You don't even own a *dulé*; you said so yourself."

"Wands are a European invention," Chris said matter-of-factly. "Africans, Asians, and South Americans have been creating and using magic without wands since the beginning of time, while you Brit boys were still writing your names with dung on your cave walls."

"Oh ho! Look who knows a little history," Ted chided. "A *rodulé* is still a tool, one that you don't have. Can you even call yourself a real Magus if you don't have one?"

"I can take you on without one," Chris said seriously and shrugged.

Ted scoffed and stood up. "I don't think so. You're more like a below-average Magi or a less-than-average Commoner."

"Was that an insult?" Chris scoffed. "A weak one at that."

"No, it's a fact," Ted said. "And you'll know when I'm being insulting. Didn't you hear? I'm Ted Beals."

Chris also stood up. "Yes, the great and powerful Ted Beals. Who still needs to hide behind his *dulé* to create any real magic."

"No, I don't hide behind my *dulé*; I use it to harness my *Vis*. But you wouldn't know anything about that, would you? Not being accepted into any Campus, yeah?" Ted winked. "Now it's an insult."

"You know you're really proud of that tool, aren't you? You gonna whip it out next and smack me across the face with it?" Chris said defensively.

Ted laughed. "Oh, you definitely couldn't handle that, mate. The size would just scare you away." He winked again and adjusted his groin area.

"Oh, I'm sure whatever you got can't compare to mine," Chris said, adjusting his own groin, knowing they weren't talking about wands anymore. "In fact, I can guarantee mine is bigger and more powerful." He took a step toward Ted.

Ted smirked. "You think you're a big man, don't you?" He took a step toward Chris.

Ciaran, who had heard enough from the kitchen, quickly got in the middle of his brother and boyfriend, who were about to square up. "Whoa, what's going on here?"

He put a hand on Ted's chest and glared at him; then he turned around and glared at Chris even more. Chris backed up, put his palms up, and walked away. Ted crossed his arms over his chest and watched Chris.

"On second thought," Chris said, "I think I am going to go. I have to work tonight, so I should get some rest." He grabbed his bag and started walking out without looking back.

Ciaran sighed and said to Ted, "I'm going to walk him out." He followed Chris out the door while Ted watched them both quizzically.

Chris continued to walk about two paces in front of Ciaran, down the stairs, and across the corridor into the Atrium. When Ciaran passed through the Atrium doors into the garden, Chris turned around. Before Ciaran could say something, Chris kissed him on the mouth and pulled him close, then smiled.

Ciaran shook his head. "You're a crazy shithead, you know that?" Chris laughed. "What the fuck was all that?"

Chris shrugged. "Oh, I was just fucking with him. I thought I was smug and conceited, but Ted beat me there." Chris chuckled. "I would never actually challenge him, though."

"No, not that part. The part where you pretended to be a Magus."

"Oh, that." Chris laughed. "I don't know. It was just something to do. Anyway, I figured it would make it easier for you."

"How? Because I do plan on telling him, and now, it's like we lied to him or something."

Chris looked at him seriously. "Honestly, do or don't tell him. It doesn't matter to me. It changes nothing about us."

Ciaran put his hands in his jeans pockets and looked away from Chris, who did not understand the gravity of the situation. Chris held him tighter and asked, "Are you really thinking about going with him next week?"

"I'm thinking about it," he said without looking at Chris.

"Leaving me all over again?" Chris said, turning his face and putting their foreheads together.

"It's not like that. If you don't want me to go, I won't."

"And take you away from Tiny Dick Ted? I wouldn't dream of it."

Ciaran smiled and looked at him, shaking his head. "I can't believe you two."

Chris played with the soft hairs on Ciaran's arm. "I'll be fine. Go spend some time with your brother next week."

Ciaran leaned his head on Chris's shoulder. "Will I see you tomorrow?" he asked softly.

"Only if you want to." He reached up and touched Ciaran's hair. "I'm glad it's growing back in long. I need something to grab onto."

Ciaran shook his head, still on Chris's shoulder. "I love you."

"I know. And three days after that," Chris replied. "Go back upstairs. I'll call you later."

Ciaran picked his head up for a kiss, and Chris gave him a slow and sweet one. He let go of Ciaran first; he backed away and then smiled.

"Love you," Chris called out.

Ciaran watched him leave, then headed upstairs.

CHAPTER 14

Brotherly Love

Ted was sitting on the arm of the couch with his feet in the cushions and his arms crossed when Ciaran came in. He sat on the opposite side of the couch and looked at Ted.

Ted started with, "Soooo... that bloke is a Commoner."

Ciaran shook his head. "That obvious, huh?"

"Actually, no, and that's what was so fascinating!" Ted exclaimed. "He really had me going there for a moment. He's a funny guy." He chuckled.

"That he is."

"So someone in his family is a Magi, then?" Ted asked.

Ciaran inhaled, then exhaled. "No. No, they are all Commoners."

"But he knows so much. Where did he learn it all?" Ciaran didn't answer; he turned away from Ted's gaze. Ted's smile changed to a frown. "Ciaran? *Ciaran?* Where did he learn it all, Ciaran?" He waited. "Ciaran, tell me you didn't?" He started shaking his head furiously.

"Didn't what, Ted?" Ciaran asked.

Ted's voice rose, "Tell me you didn't confess the deepest secrets of our Magi Community to some run-of-the-mill Commoner!"

"He's not some average Commoner," Ciaran said quietly.

But Ted wasn't listening; he started yelling and throwing his hands around. "YOU!! I can't believe you did that! Do you know how much trouble you just got yourself into? Are you fucking mad!?"

Ciaran also raised his voice. "It's not like I planned it!"

"Well, explain it to me then," Ted said plainly, crossing his arms again. "Explain it to me like I'm an idiot."

So Ciaran did. He described their first encounter with Betta and then the dark warlock and how they patrolled almost every night since. Ted listened and then said, "I still don't understand why you didn't *abscondo* him in the beginning."

"At the time, I didn't know either. I just trusted him right away. I still trust him. I trust him with my life." He looked Ted in the eyes.

Ted was still shaking his head. "Bloody hell, Ciaran, this is mad. The only people who do shit like this are people who are in love or in a relationship that they are trying to..." He trailed off.

Ciaran watched Ted's face as the truth dawned on him. He looked at Ciaran with his mouth agape and held his gaze as he slowly slid onto the couch. They stared at each other for another moment. Ted then took a deep breath and blew it out in a whistle.

He turned to sit cross-legged and faced Ciaran with his hands in his lap. "Okay, little brother. Start talking."

Ciaran turned to Ted with one knee on the couch and his other leg on the floor. "What do you want to know?"

"Everything. How long?"

"How long what?"

Ted scoffed. "Okay. Let's start with something simple. How long have you two been in a relationship?"

"A little over six months," Ciaran stated.

"Six months!?" Ted yelled at him. "You've been in a relationship for six bloody months, and you didn't tell me!?" He swung out and punched Ciaran on the arm hard.

"Oy!" Ciaran rubbed his shoulder. "I didn't know how to tell you, how to tell anyone."

"I'm not anyone. I'm your big brother. And this is a major change for you. How could you not tell me?"

"I don't know," Ciaran said. "I barely knew how to tell myself."

Ted ran his hands through his hair and touched his knees. "What a mind fuck you must have been going through. Am I gay, am I straight, am bi, am I still kind of straight but I like this gay bloke, am I bi and still like boys and girls, have I always liked boys and just didn't know, do I still like girls... *shit!*"

Ciaran smiled. "I forget how well you know how I think."

"Yeah, fucker, that's why you should have called me!" He punched his arm again.

"Oy, stop! Alright, I should have told you." Ciaran rubbed his arm again.

Ted then said, "So. How goes it? How is the relationship?"

"It's going ... pretty ... great actually," Ciaran said, smiling to himself. "Really great. Scary how easy it all is with him. He's a bit of me, in so many ways. We became fast friends then it just became something more before either of us knew what hit us. He's kind and smart and so funny. And he's secure in who he is, in his manhood, but he's also not afraid to show his emotions."

"Ha! Mr. My-Cock-Is-Bigger-Than-Yours shows emotions!" He laughed. "Can't imagine it."

"Yeah, well, he's also a little arrogant and immature," Ciaran said. "Sometimes a lot immature as you just witnessed and likes to push buttons for shits and giggles, not unlike you."

"Obviously!" Ted grinned.

"But Ted, he's an all-round solid guy. The most incredible person I've ever met. He lights up every room he's in and just knows how to put people at ease around him. I saw that when we were just mates. And now we're bonded in this way that's indescribable. He brings parts of me out that I didn't know I was capable of. And I'm bringing out parts of him that he's buried from everyone. It's like..." Ciaran trailed off.

Ted read between the lines. "You're in love with him," he said factually.

"I am," Ciaran said with a nod.

Ted smiled. "And obviously he loves you, too. It's funny, if I didn't know, I wouldn't have seen it, but now that I know, I *definitely* see it. It's obvious. The way you are around each other. You move like a couple, finish each other's sentences, side glances, and communicate with how you look at each other. Awww. Little Ciaran is in love!" He reached over and touched his face.

"Shut up," Ciaran said and smacked his hand away.

Ted chuckled, then said, "Okay, tell me the rest of it. How is it?"

Ciaran looked at him, confused. "How is what?"

"C'mon, you gonna make me say it? The *sex!* You guys weren't talking football and dragons in here for the last six months." He smiled knowingly. "C'mon. Top or Bottom? Or both?" His eyebrows went up twice.

Ciaran lowered his head and said, "Absolutely not."

"Oh, c'mon!" Ted cried. "If he were a woman, you wouldn't hesitate to tell me all about it, so don't hesitate now."

Ciaran nodded and smiled. He had never loved his brother as much as he did in that moment.

"The sex is fucking fantastic," he said simply. Ted let out a cackle, and Ciaran laughed as well. "I'm not kidding," he continued. "I have experienced a whole new level of sex I didn't even know was possible. We make love almost every day, sometimes twice a day, and every single time it's amazing. Both, by the way. But mostly Top."

Ted let out another loud cackle and slapped Ciaran's legs. "Ciaran, Ciaran my boy!" He laughed. "But the first time couldn't have been amazing. That shit must have hurt like hell."

"Actually, it wasn't terrible. I mean, yes, there was pain at first, but mostly pleasure, and lots of it. I am probably lucky that I had him." He smiled to himself, thinking about it. Ted noticed.

"Well, don't hold back on me now!" he said. Ciaran shook his head again, looked up at the ceiling, and smiled. Ted leaned over and touched Ciaran's knee. "Ciaran, you have been carrying around six months of feelings in uncharted territory. Now, if you're fine and don't need to talk, then I'll let it go. But if there is ever a time to let it out, now's the time. Plus, I'm bloody nosy!"

Ciaran laughed. "Okay."

He told Ted about the first time, starting with the kiss under the lamppost. Ted had commentary all throughout and did not balk or cringe at the explicit parts. Ciaran told him how Dale basically told him to stop being a pussy and go for it. Ted exclaimed, "Ha! Good on Dale!" He told him about the intense blow job that literally made his knees weak, ["Holy Merlin's balls, that sounds amazing!"] when he first entered Chris, ["Shit Ciaran, no real lubricant? He must have really loved you back then because there is no way a man would ever..."] Chris's full body massage and how he broke Ciaran in, ["Ah, got you in the mood, he used lube, lots of patience, good man"] and how he came, and then came again hands-free for the first time in his life. ["Wait! You mean to tell me that for your first time with him, you came three times in the span of what, three to four hours, give or take? Fucking A, I would have fell in love with him too!"]

Ciaran was admittedly relieved to talk to someone about his relationship. He regretted not talking to him earlier but was glad he did it now; it was the right time.

When he told Ted about them under the Motus Willow a few days prior and how they could feel each other's emotions, Ted gasped. "So he's your *Ardenti*."

"My what?" Ciaran asked in confusion.

"*Ardenti*. Your soulmate, your heat, your *passion*. You set each other's souls on fire. And it's going to burn together until it fuses into one."

Ciaran stared at him. "What are you on?"

Ted chuckled, but said, "I'm serious. Elodie explained it to me: When your heart, mind, and soul are fused with another, that's *Ardenti*. It happens when there is some kind of life-or-death situation. The two souls cling to each other and never let go. Tell me you don't feel intense passion and love for him. Almost from the moment you met him."

"We..." Ciaran was thoughtful. "It was definitely intense. I felt every single thing he felt for me, and I know he felt the same about me. That's when we confessed our love for the first time. And he said he heard my words to him, the thought in my head."

"What thought was that?"

Ciaran hesitated, then said, "I told him to cum for me."

Ted fell backward and laughed loudly. "And did he?"

Ciaran turned bright red and looked at the ceiling again with a smile. "He did."

"Well, a Motus will do that, won't it?" Ted said with another laugh, "but the *Ardenti* made it possible for him to feel you."

"I don't know if I believe all this," Ciaran said skeptically.

Ted shrugged. "Only time will tell. Tell your *Ardenti* to come out with us tomorrow night, so I can meet Chris, your lover, instead of Chris, the pretend magician."

Ciaran chuckled. He pulled out his phone and sent Chris a simple text,

[Told Ted everything. Everything. Come out with us tomorrow night.]

Chris didn't send a text back right away. "I guess Chris really did fall asleep when he got home," he said, more to himself.

"We're going out tonight, so you get some rest, too," Ted told him.

"Ugh. What hole in the wall are you dragging me to?" Ciaran asked.

"New place called Dracs in Durrës."

"Fucking hell, I've heard of that place. It's crawling with humans who want to be vampires and actual daywalkers."

"Aren't you glad I didn't invite your boy? They would have literally smelled the Commoner on him."

Ciaran rolled his eyes. "Two hours, tops. Then I'm coming home." He stood up to walk to his room.

Ted stood up, too. "Ciaran," he called. Ciaran turned around and looked at his brother, who smiled at him. Ciaran walked back over and gave him a hug.

"Thank you," Ciaran whispered. Ted patted his back, then let him go, so he could take a nap.

Chris, who had indeed fallen asleep, woke up hours later, read his text, and smiled. He called Ciaran immediately.

Ciaran and Ted were in the bedroom getting dressed when his phone went off. Ted grabbed it off the dresser first upon seeing Chris's name come up. He answered, "Hey, Cocky Cocksucking Chris, how's it going?"

"Bloody hell," Ciaran groaned and glared at him.

But Chris laughed. "Hey Tiny Dick Ted! Kindly put my boyfriend on the phone, please."

Ciaran came over to take the phone from Ted, but he slapped Ciaran's hand away and jumped forward out of his range. "In a minute." He told Chris, "I'm taking him out tonight, so don't get jealous."

"No worries at all. I trust him with my heart and my life."

"Funny, he said the same thing about you."

"Yeah? That is something, isn't it?" Chris smiled.

"It is," Ted said. "Chris, come out with us tomorrow night so my brother can introduce you to me proper, yeah."

"Yes, of course. I'm looking forward to it."

Ted handed Ciaran the phone, saying loudly, "Hey Ciaran! Your BOYFRIEND is on the phone!" Then he cackled.

Ciaran shook his head and said to Chris, "I promise he handled it with a lot more maturity than he is displaying right now."

Chris smiled. "How do you feel?"

"Honestly, I feel great. I should have told Ted ages ago. Should have known he would more than just accept it. He would full-on embrace it. Embrace me."

"Well, it's always good to have one person in your corner."

"Well, now I have two," Ciaran said, making Chris smile again. "So you're coming out with us tomorrow night, yeah?"

Chris said, "Let me choose the place, please?"

"Not Nemo's," Ciaran said.

"What's a Nemo?" Ted asked, eavesdropping on their conversation.

"Why the hell would I take your brother to a very gay bar?" Chris asked in astonishment.

"I don't know, shock value?"

"Yeah, let's not expose your brother to everything just yet." They both laughed. "No, Ted is a music guy like me, right?"

Ted asked louder, "What's a Nemo?"

"Yeah, why?" Ciaran asked, ignoring his brother.

"I got the perfect place. We have to get there by 7 p.m., though, to get on the list."

"Hello?? Nemo??" Ted called.

"Okay, we can do that. You'll drive? Ted knows how to drive but—"

Ted bellowed, "CAN SOMEBODY PLEASE TELL ME WHAT THE FUCK IS A NEMO!?"

"Put me on speaker, love," Chris said. Ciaran pressed the speakerphone button.

Chris said, "Hey Teddy-Boy, Nemo's is a bar where mates get their cocks sucked or fucked up the arse by other men in the loo. Still wanna go?"

Ted's face went from amusement to shock, then recovered. "Tempting offer. But I'll pass this time." Chris and Ciaran both laughed. He took Chris off speakerphone.

"Call me on patrol tonight," Ciaran said.

"Will do," said Chris. Ciaran hesitated to say it, and Chris heard it in his pause. "Did you tell him that you love me, Ciaran?"

"I did."

"Then that's all that matters. I love you too. Until then," Chris said. Ciaran smiled and hung up.

CHAPTER 15

Karaoke Night

The next night, Chris met Ciaran and Ted in the Atrium Restaurant. He came in and walked up to Ciaran, kissing him on the cheek and touching his back, then lifted his hand to shake Ted's and greet him. "Ted. Good night, innit?"

"Good night, indeed, Christopher," Ted said with a grin. He shook his hand and said, "And that's Big Dick Ted to you, sir." They all laughed.

"Let's get going," Chris said.

Chris drove about twenty minutes south and parked in front of a lounge. When they got closer to the sign, they saw that it said, "Karaoke Night. Bring your A-game and win free drinks all night."

Ciaran groaned. "Oh, fuck no."

Ted laughed. "Oh, hell yes!"

Chris laughed as well and opened the door for them to go inside. They found a table on the right side near the bar, but close enough to the stage. Chris added all three of their names to the karaoke list despite Ciaran's constant refusal.

"No way, no fucking way I'm going up there," Ciaran said plainly.

"Yes, you are," said Chris.

"C'mon, it will be fun," Ted encouraged. Ciaran kept shaking his head.

Chris ordered nine firebomb shots for them. "You'll feel better when you're less sober, Ciaran." Ted laughed and took his three shots.

They both taunted Ciaran until he caved by saying, "Why do I hate you both right now?" He took his three shots, and Chris took his. Chris ordered more shots as the competition got underway.

After a few people went on stage, Chris got up and sang a U2 song that everyone loved. Ted was excited, commentating, "The boyfriend can sing! We just might win this shit!"

Ted sang a rock song kind of badly, but he flirted with all the women in the crowd, and they gave him a standing ovation. Ted and Chris later did a Beatles song together, and the crowd went wild. When it was their turn again, they sang a White Stripes song that again got people on their feet, mostly due to Chris's singing and Ted's gyrating for the women again.

Finally, Chris found a song that he knew Ciaran would sing. Ted was surprised at the selection, but Chris said Ciaran knew all the words and would belt it out every time it would come on the radio. Chris grew to love it.

Ciaran looked at the selection and smiled. "No."

"OH, COME ON!!" Chris yelled at him. "We'll go on stage with you. We'll be your backup dancers. You won't even have to move. Just stand there and sing."

They waited as Ciaran continued to smile at them, then shook his head in defeat, and stood up. Chris and Ted both got excited and hugged him, then dragged him on the stage. They gave him the microphone and stood on either side of him and waited until the first couple of beats were heard. And Ciaran started to sing "Magic" by Coldplay in perfect pitch.

Ted and Chris danced behind him, first uncoordinated, then they finally got a two-step, three-move pattern, and joined him in the chorus. By the end, the crowd was on their feet and singing along. With Ciaran hitting the high notes at the end, they won the night's contest.

Their waitress started them off with a pitcher of beer and explained the rules. "Nothing top shelf. Here's the list you can order off, and drinks are free at this table all night, just for the three of you." Then she said to Ciaran, "You were cute tonight." She winked at him.

Chris watched her walk away, and Ted took notice. "So, you're into the ladies, too?" he asked.

Chris turned his attention to Ted. "Oh yeah, I'm into everything. I'm pansexual. I am naturally and physically attracted to people, regardless of gender. I just happen to be in love with a man right now."

"In love, you say?" Ted teased.

"Yes," Chris said. "I am in love with your brother."

Ted smiled. "*Félicitations!*" he said in French. He clanged his glass against Chris's, who laughed.

"But just because I'm in love doesn't mean I stopped noticing beautiful women. I know Ciaran hasn't." He winked at him, and Ciaran groaned.

"Really?" Ted leaned into the table. "Tell me more."

Ciaran rolled his eyes. "Chris took me to a club with exotic dancers for my birthday. Female and male strippers."

"And both equally excited him," Chris finished for him. "I think he surprised himself with that."

"That shouldn't have surprised you," he said to Ciaran. "You've been dating women your whole life; I doubt that switch is turned off."

"It's not, and I don't think he should worry about whether it does or doesn't go off, and just live in the moment," Chris said.

"Agreed!" said Ted. "I'm married and deeply in love with my wife, but I'm also around beautiful women all the time. I can't turn it off. I can't help if my cock stands at attention without my consent." They laughed. "But then again, I don't have true *Ardenti* with Elodie, like you two."

Chris asked, *"Ardenti?"*

Ciaran chuckled. "He thinks soulmates," he said to Chris.

"No. I'm telling you, it's more than that," said Ted. "Chris, do you know the term, 'ardent love?'"

"Yeah," said Chris. "It's like having a passionate kind of love." He looked at Ciaran. "We have that."

"So think about it like this," said Ted. "When two Magi feel *Ardenti* for each other, their souls combine like two pieces of wax melting together until it's just one soul. Not just soulmates. It's stronger than a marital tie-bind. I believe you felt this infusion from the moment you met; you just didn't know it."

"That's so fascinating," said Chris in awe. He looked at Ciaran, who smiled at him.

"When you meet Elodie, she'll explain it to you better. The French are all about love and passion," Ted said. "Back to you and this being open to all genders. What's your type, Chris? Female leaning, of course; I know your type of male." He winked at him.

Chris laughed. "I don't know if I have a type. I just like what I like."

"Well, pick a feminine one. Let me see your interest."

"Ted, are you really about to troll for women with my partner right now?" Ciaran asked. But Chris was already looking around.

"Let's see… that one." Chris gestured toward a tall, brown-haired woman with skinny jeans showing off her long legs and shapely bottom, and small breasts in a tank top with a bra. "She's beautiful, but her sexiness is in the way she carries herself. Self-assured but not conceited."

Ted nodded. "Good choice." He looked around. "I like … her." He secretly pointed to a thin blonde with a short gray dress and wide hips. "The sex appeal is strong with that one."

"Seriously, Ted?" Ciaran scolded as Chris busted out laughing.

"What?" Ted said innocently and smiled. "What's your choice, Ciaran?"

"No, I'm not playing this game." Ciaran shook his head.

But Chris said, "I can pick one out for him."

"Yeah, let's do that," Ted said. "Don't worry, Ciaran, attraction changes nothing about your ardent love with Chris." Chris chuckled at that.

"You both are arseholes," said Ciaran dryly. His boyfriend and brother ignored him and continued to look around.

"There!" Ted said first. He pointed to a dark-haired woman in leggings, high heels, and a see-through black tank top with an obvious pink bra. "Ciaran likes a bit of mystery."

Ciaran turned to see who Ted was referring to and turned back to the table, smiling into his drink and turning pink, making Ted laugh. "Got you!"

"That's a good choice," Chris acknowledged, "but I would say … her."

Chris nodded toward a woman in the middle of her friends, a short, brown-skinned, East Asian woman with slick black hair, in a short yellow dress that crisscrossed her chest holding up her large breasts. Ciaran looked behind him to see the other woman, looked at Chris, smiled again, turned pink, and looked away.

"You like her better, don't you?" Chris taunted him.

"Arseholes," Ciaran said again.

"No, it's my girl for sure," said Ted. "She's perfect for you."

"Maybe, but Ciaran has a fetish for brown-skinned people," Chris said in amusement.

Ted's eyes went wide. "Whaaat!?" He started cackling.

"Fuck off, I do not," Ciaran said in astonishment.

"Oh, yes, you do. I see you notice women when we're out, Ciaran. I see who catches your eye. Also, before me, your last girlfriend was what, Filipino? Pakistani?"

"Indian."

"Exactly. And Sapphire? And American Rodeo?"

"Who are these *people!?*" Ted asked, still laughing.

"The female stripper he picked out and the male stripper that almost made him cum on himself," Chris said. Ted started laughing louder.

"Okay, listen," Ciaran started, throwing up a hand. "It's not a fetish. That makes me sound pervy and a bit racist. It's more like... I'm very pale, and my skin just looks better against someone not as pale as me. Especially in bed." Chris grinned at him.

"Yeah, I can see that," Ted said. "Seeing how your first real sexual experience was with brown-skinned women. It was probably because of the twins."

Chris almost spit out his drink. "Twins!?? *What??*"

"You never told him that?" Ted asked.

Ciaran sighed and looked up at the ceiling. "No, and thanks for that."

Chris asked, "Wait, you had a threesome with twins and never told me!?"

"It wasn't a threesome," Ciaran denied.

"It was as good as!" Ted said.

Ted told the story of how Ciaran visited him in Ethiopia when he was on a job. They met identical twin sisters, beautiful, long-haired, brown-skinned women who took them back to their flat, and they each took one to their bed.

"All I know is somewhere in the middle of the night, my twin left me and was in bed with him," said Ted.

Chris's mouth was open. "Ho. Lee. Shit. Ciaran, what did you *do!?*"

"I didn't do anything, really. I was seventeen and inexperienced," he said innocently.

"Well, you must have done something right because I woke up alone and you had two grown, very naked women in the bed with you!" Ted laughed, and Ciaran blushed.

"Well, out with it," Chris said. "What happened?"

Ciaran just shook his head and drank from his glass. Ted said, "Oh, Ciaran doesn't kiss and tell… Unless I drag it out of him kicking and screaming."

"Of all the sexual escapades I've told you about, and you deny me this one important fact about you?" Chris teased him. That made them all laugh.

The woman in the yellow dress had walked over and tried to find an opening at the bar, ending up right near their table. She ordered her drink and turned around, catching Ciaran eyeing her. She smiled. *"Alo."*

Ciaran raised his glass. *"Përshëndetje."*

Chris and Ted stared at each other, trying not to laugh. She turned around to retrieve her drink and glanced at Ciaran again with a smile, before heading back to her friends, with Ciaran watching her the whole time. When she was a good distance away, Ted and Chris started laughing.

"Fuck, you are so right, Christopher," Ted said, still laughing.

"Fuck off," Ciaran said, leaning back and taking a sip of his beer.

Chris reached over to stroke the hair on the nape of Ciaran's neck and smiled at him smugly. Ciaran went pink again. "I don't have a fetish," he mumbled, making them laugh again.

They continued to get free drinks and talk about things. By midnight Ted was a little tipsy, but Ciaran and Chris were very drunk. They walked to the car, and Chris said, "Shit. I did it again. There is no way I'm driving."

"We'll just Wisp again," Ciaran said.

"Right," Chris said happily.

But Ted grabbed his brother's arm. "Are you out of your fucking mind!? You can't *Wisp* with a Commoner!"

"Well, technically you can, and we have," Ciaran said, amused, and Chris snickered.

Ted looked at both of them in disbelief. "This is *not* happening. I'm going to drive. You're going to put the directions in my phone's GPS, and we're getting home the legal way. Got it?" They both nodded like children.

Chris and Ciaran got in the backseat while Ted drove north. Chris started it; he brushed his hand on Ciaran's genitals. Ciaran looked at him and stuck his tongue in Chris's mouth. They started making out furiously. And Ted would not have minded if they hadn't started moaning and pawing at their clothes. He drew the line there and started banging on the dashboard.

"Oy! Oy! I'm not your fucking taxi driver, yeah. Cut that shit out. All the way out!"

They stopped and laughed. Chris put his head on Ciaran's shoulder and his hand on Ciaran's leg. Then he put his hand down Ciaran's pants and started sucking on his neck. Ciaran closed his eyes and moaned as low as he could while Chris worked him.

Ted looked at them through the rearview mirror. "It's like I got two horny teenagers in the back. Guess I'm sleeping on the couch tonight. And make sure you muffle the shite out of that room. Not one sigh or moan I hear, or both of you are getting jinxed."

Chris said, "Yes, Papa," from inside Ciaran's neck, making him laugh.

"Fuck, now I'm horny," Ted said to no one. "Too many beautiful women and alcohol. Guess I'm sending Elodie a dick pic tonight."

"You are not," Ciaran said. "It's after midnight, and she's pregnant. Don't wake her up with your foolishness."

"So? If I can't send dick pics to my wife whenever I want to, then who can I send them to? That's why you get married, to send dick pics to your wife—or husband—whenever you feel like it." Chris and Ciaran laughed.

When they reached Ciaran's place, Chris and Ciaran went straight to the bedroom and used the spell to block out sounds while they made love for the next hour, and Ted talked with Elodie on the phone, missing her.

CHAPTER 16

The Plan

The next morning, Chris and Ciaran were awakened by a loud banging on the bedroom door. "Get up, boys!"

Ciaran groaned; his head was pounding. Chris moved his head from one side to the next. Ted banged on the door again and yelled, "You've got ten minutes, or I'm sending a post about the two of you to Mum!"

Twenty minutes later they sat at a booth in the Atrium Restaurant, Ciaran and Chris on one side wearing tank tops and sweatpants, Ted on the other in a t-shirt and jeans. He watched the couple for a while as they played with each other's fingers on the table and leaned into each other, sharing glances and sly smiles. Now that Ted knew, there was no reason to pretend they weren't as close as two lovers could get.

Elsie came over to take their order. Ted asked her, "So, Elsie, am I the last one to know about these two sitting across the table?"

"Probably," she said, smiling. "They've been an item for a year now."

Ted's eyes widened. "Oh? A year, you say?"

"It wasn't like this in the beginning. We were…" Ciaran looked at Chris for answers.

Chris looked at him but talked to Ted. "Not like now. We were close, yes. I think we both wanted something to happen, but…"

"We weren't sure. For different reasons," Ciaran finished.

"Although now I think we both wish we just went for it earlier? Yeah?" Chris looked at Ciaran.

"Yeah," Ciaran said softly. "Six months of dallying around…" He moved closer to Chris's shoulder and kissed it. Chris leaned into him. They seemed to forget others were with them.

Elsie said to them, "I remember the day you two first walked in here and I asked Ciaran afterward to introduce me to his cute friend, and you never did. Mum was the one who told me to leave it alone, that something else was happening between the two of you that did not involve anyone else. So we all watched and waited for months, me, Mum, Lewis, Andy. Even Rosemary had her say, 'This hasn't happened yet?'" She laughed.

"So when did you know for sure?" Chris asked her, with Ciaran still leaning into his neck.

"Oh, that kiss you did at the counter. Everybody found out that day, didn't we?"

Ted was shocked. "What? Ciaran doing full PDA? I don't believe it."

Elsie sat down next to Ted. "Well, believe it. It was dreamy."

"When was this?" asked Ted.

"Honestly, I don't remember," said Chris.

"It was two weeks after I came back from the mission in Chad," Ciaran answered. They all looked at him. "We were sitting at the counter waiting for our food to take it upstairs and people watching."

Chris remembered. "Yeah. I made some sort of joke, and you just kissed me. I don't even remember what I said."

Ciaran did. He lifted his head and looked at Chris. "You said, 'All these Commoners in here and they don't even know who you really are.' And I knew you were talking about me being a Magus, but it hit me a bit harder, you know. I had just told a young bloke to stop being scared of who he was and who he loved, and here I was doing the same thing, whether consciously or unconsciously. I needed to stop hiding."

"I knew you were going to kiss me, you know," Chris said, staring into his eyes. "You had that look in your eyes that you save for me when we're alone. And I thought, *Okay, first public peck.*"

Elsie finished the story. "Oh, no honey, this was no peck! It was a hot and heavy like no one was watching kind of kiss. And it went on and on. Gets me all hot just thinking about it." She pretended to fan herself. "No one really noticed. It was crowded. But I did. And so did Mum."

Chris smiled. "I remember Phoebe came up silently to the counter with our food, smiling so hard, and said, 'Have a good day, gentlemen.'" They all laughed, except Ted.

"My neighbor Charlotte noticed," Ciaran said. "She said something a few days later, 'That sweet and handsome man you got there, don't screw it up.'" They laughed again without Ted. "So yeah, first public kiss. No regrets."

Chris took Ciaran's hand softly on the table and entwined their fingers. Ciaran lifted it to kiss the back of his hand; then Chris leaned in for a soft kiss on the lips. They stared at each other.

"Don't you just love them together?" Elsie gushed. "Let me put your orders in."

When she left, Ted knew it was time to have "the talk" with them. He clasped his hands and put them on the table, folding them. "Okay, gentlemen. What's the plan?"

They both looked at him. "The plan for what?" Ciaran asked. "To tell Mum and Dad?"

Ted scoffed at him and rolled his eyes at his brother. He looked at Chris. "Chris, did Ciaran explain to you how dangerous this whole thing is?" Ciaran sat up straighter and glared at his brother, who ignored him. "How he broke one of our most sacred Magi laws? How much trouble he could be in if anyone went to The Magi Council about how much you know?"

"I know, Ted. I know," Ciaran mumbled. Ted ignored him again, addressing Chris.

Chris said confidently, "I know the importance of Magi secrecy since the thirteenth century."

"Oh good. You're well-read," he deadpanned. "Now tell me what the punishment is for someone who breaks our Magi laws, especially the one about secrecy?" He raised an eyebrow.

Chris opened his mouth, then closed it. He looked at Ciaran, who was still glaring at Ted. "Er... a fine?"

"No," said Ted. "Worst-case scenario is that they throw Ciaran in Claustra for ten years and *abscondo* your memory so you'll never remember him or us again. Maybe *abscondo* Ciaran's memory, too, for good measure, to ensure you'll never find each other again."

Chris's mouth dropped open in shock. He looked at Ciaran. "Is... is that *true?*"

Ciaran addressed his brother. "That's for a serious breach; Ted; this is more of an infraction."

"Which could still lead to some prison time for you and *abscondo* for him. Really, Ciaran, what the fuck were you thinking!?" he scolded him.

"Clearly I wasn't," said Ciaran, getting upset.

"Clearly neither of you were thinking!" he yelled in a whispering tone. "I'm absolutely sure everyone here knows he's a Commoner. And they're just pretending not to know if he's registered or not. What if someone reports it to the Albanian Magi Division, or what if someone at the Reserve reports it? You're fucked! And you're fucked, too!" He wagged a finger at both of them, still whispering angrily. "I mean, you two are just sitting in Magi spaces without a care in the world like none of this could happen, thinking with your little heads instead of your big ones. What the bloody fuck!?"

Chris looked at Ciaran, who had turned his face toward the window at Ted's scolding. He turned back to Ted. "So what do we do?" Chris asked.

Ted addressed Ciaran. "You have to tell Mum and Dad. Dad especially. He can talk directly to Graham and see what he can do to get the least possible punishment. I mean, half our family works for the Council or Scholarly, Ciaran, so it should be okay, but you can't let this go on too much longer."

Ciaran turned to Ted. "I just didn't want to do it like that, to introduce him like, 'Hey, everyone, I did a huge fucking thing, and, oh, I need your help to get out of it.'"

Ted softened. "I get that, little brother, but you will need help. I'm on your side here. And I do support you and this relationship. But it will end tragically if we don't put the steps in place now."

Ciaran nodded. "I'll write to Mum and Dad tonight. I'll ease them into who Chris is. Maybe by Christmas, I can give it to them fully. Then we can start the year off fresh."

Ted nodded. He said to Chris, "Will you come home for Christmas with Ciaran? That way, you can meet everyone and have a sit down with our parents."

Before Chris could respond, Ciaran said, "No, he needs to be with his family for Christmas."

But Chris touched his arm. "Ciaran, you are the most important thing to me right now. We are important, and I am prioritizing us over everything else." He turned to Ted. "I'll be there. I will put in my two weeks now so we can stay through New Year's. I'll meet the family, talk to your parents, and go down to the Council office together if need be, to sort this whole thing out. We have to make it right because I can't lose him, Ted."

"I can't lose him either, so thank you," Ted said. "You're a good man, Christopher. Ciaran is lucky to have you."

Ciaran looked at Chris and nodded. Chris mouthed, *love you.* Ciaran put his head back on Chris's shoulder, and they locked hands on the table. Chris said to Ted, "Come for dinner tonight, and meet my sisters, Ted."

"I would love to meet them," Ted said; then his eyes narrowed. "Do they know?"

"Not a thing. I would never break Ciaran's confidence, even before we got together. I made that promise to him on the day we met, and I meant it. No one will ever know about the Magi Community from me."

Ted nodded. "And I believe you."

Their food came, and they ate as Ted continued to lecture them on all the ways they had been reckless and could have been caught. "And Wisp'ing with a Commoner too. It's like you're asking for it!"

"You're starting to sound like my older sister with all this scolding. I'm going to regret having you both in the same room, aren't I?" Chris said miserably. Ciaran sat there silently taking it.

After they ate, Chris said, "I'm going to go home and tell my sisters we're having guests and help cook dinner. What are you going to do today?"

Ciaran answered, "We're going to the Reserve for a bit so Ted can continue to convince Dale to give me a week off so I can go curse-breaking with him."

Chris nodded. "Okay. Dinner's at 6 p.m.. Don't be late." He kissed Ciaran, then leaned into his ear, and said, "And three days after that," making Ciaran smile.

CHAPTER 17

Fight or Flight

At first, Dale told Ted to fuck off, but then agreed to let Ciaran go for a week. After hanging out on the Reserve for the day, they went back to Ciaran's house to get ready for dinner, then Wisp'd to Chris's doorstep, and Ciaran let himself in. Chris was setting up the table on their arrival and asked Ciaran to give him a hand bringing down the food from upstairs, which he agreed to.

When they left, Ted went to use the bathroom. He did not hear the front door open and close.

Charity rushed in from work, having to pee badly. She ran into the bathroom and opened the door to see Ted standing there. His eyes widened, but he did not move since he was already midstream.

Charity's eyes also widened, and she exclaimed, "OH!"

Out of habit, her eyes traveled downward for a long moment, then looked up. Ted smiled at the young woman, who could have been Chris's twin, except for her hazel eyes. He finished, flushed the toilet, and went to wash his hands.

Charity spoke first. "You are not Ciaran."

"No, I am not. I'm his brother Ted." He dried his hands on a towel and reached out to shake hers.

She gave him her hand and said, *"Au chante."*

Ted responded, *"Oui, comme je devrais ente."* He kissed her hand.

Charity was beside herself. *"Tu parles Français!"*

"Oui, my wife is French." He smiled.

She snatched her hand back and mocked, *"Oh l'horreir!* And here I thought I could make you mine. *Pitie."*

Ted laughed. "You are cute and funny, just like your brother."

"Oh trust me, I am better than him in every way," she said seductively, licked her lips, and stared at him with her hazel eyes intensely. "Now kindly exit the bathroom so I can relieve myself."

He chuckled and quickly got out of her way and vowed to avoid any one-on-one interactions with her, possibly forever.

Chris and Ciaran came back with a pan of lamb chops with mint and basil sauce and a pot of couscous, then went back upstairs for the Mediterranean pasta and Greek salad. Clarissa followed them back down, baby-wearing three-month-old Sierra and holding Rudy's hand.

"Wow, you're handsome," Clarissa commented on Ted after introducing herself.

"And you are stunning," Ted said back. "You all are, really."

"Including me?" Chris asked, amused.

"Grow a pair of tits, and then I'll answer that one," Ted said, making them all laugh.

At dinner, Clarissa asked about Ted's profession, and he told them he was an archaeologist and explorer for a museum in England. When Rudy asked what an explorer was, Ted told him, "I search and uncover things that were buried long ago."

"Really??" Rudy asked excitedly. "Like dinosaur bones?"

"I've never actually found dinosaur bones, but I did find a dragon bone once," he said and winked at Clarissa, who smiled at his jest. Chris grinned, too.

"You're kidding!" Rudy said.

"Okay, no dragon bones," Ted said, in faux sadness. "But I did find gold one time."

"So you hunt for buried treasure, too?" Rudy was in awe of Ted's job and wanted to do the same when he grew up.

"That's exactly what I do," he said. "I'm actually going on an expedition next week and taking Ciaran with me." Chris frowned at Ciaran, who returned with a look of apology.

"Oh God, Chrissy did not like that at all," Charity told Ted. "Chris is going to be moping around here like his pet fish died." Chris gave her the middle finger.

"So what do you think about all this, Ted? Your brother and mine together, romantically?" Clarissa asked.

"I think they make a good couple," he said simply.

"Yes. But what will the rest of your family think? I'm sure your parents aren't going to expect Ciaran to bring home someone so different from what they've envisioned for their son."

"Honestly, I don't think my parents will have a problem with it at all. Nor my siblings, with him being a man, if that's what you're asking." He left it open, and Clarissa caught it.

"So, what will they have a problem with? The fact that he's not white?" Clarissa asked plainly.

Ted paused, then said, "What if I said that our family, the Beals, wouldn't have a problem with any of it, but our community back home might have a problem with a huge difference like that?"

The table got very quiet. Clarissa said coldly, "Well, I would say that your community is prejudiced, and I don't want my brother a part of that."

"But clearly it's too late for that, innit?" Ted said, folding his hands together on the table, like he did at breakfast. "They're in love, and it's glaringly evident they aren't coming apart any time soon, if ever. You can't just tell two people in love that they can't be together because of things about themselves that they cannot change."

"Chrissy, you're in love?" Charity said softly.

"I am, so what of it?" he said, waiting for her to mock him somehow.

"Nothing. I'm not surprised. I told Ciaran you were." She smiled at him.

Clarissa redirected the conversation. "That's neither here nor there. If your community won't accept this relationship, then maybe Ciaran needs to make the sacrifice and remove himself from the community."

Ted said, "You don't know what you're asking," at the same time Chris said, "That's not possible."

But Ciaran said, "Actually, it's not so farfetched, and it's not impossible." Ted and Chris both looked at him. "Uncle Harrison, Alastair's father, did it. He simply left, and no one in the Community has seen or heard from him since."

"Harrison was a selfish prick and con artist who left his wife and son because he couldn't hack it at Scholarly," Ted said, almost angrily.

"Okay, but my point is it's been done," Ciaran countered. "People simply stop participating in the rituals. And live a normal, *common* life."

"What... what are you *saying?*" Chris said, stunned. "That you would give it all up for me? You love..." He almost said "magic," but caught himself. "You love who you are and the community you belong to."

"Yes, and I will always be who I am because I can't change my DNA," said Ciaran. "But I can change being a part of that world. As I've said, plenty of people have done it; I wouldn't be the first."

Ted was also stunned. "Really, little brother. I can't believe you just said that."

Ciaran turned to Ted. "I would do anything for Chris. Have you got all that now?"

Chris touched his shoulder for him to turn back to him. "And I love you enough to never ask you to do that for me. No, we will find another way. Even if it means running and hiding."

Clarissa and Charity were confused. "What are you talking about? Running away from what?" Clarissa asked.

Ted answered, "There are some officials in our community that would frown upon how they came together and their current relationship. And because of that, they would attempt to see them separated forever."

"Because he's African?" Charity asked incredulously.

"Because he's … different than us," Ted said evasively.

"Well, this is shite," said Clarissa, annoyed. "No one is running. You either stay and fight, or you leave the community and make it on your own. Remember, Ma Ami had to do the same. She stayed and fought for as long as she could with Papa's family that hated her, offended by her African dark skin and beauty. And when she couldn't anymore, they came here and created their family, and they made their own way. So if you really want to be together, then decide together how you are going to approach this prejudice. But you're not running and hiding."

"So, what will it be?" Ted asked them. "Will you stay and fight or denounce the community and create your own way?"

Chris answered, "We stay and fight. Right, Ciaran?"

Ciaran took Chris's hand. "We stay and fight then."

But Clarissa was not done. "Just know that when shit hits the fan, you'll always have this house to come back to, just like Ma Ami had. She passed it on to her children for this very reason."

"What if I told you that you'd have to fight with him?" Ted asked her. "You too, Charity? And you too one day, Rudy?"

"I can fight!" Rudy said proudly.

"Okay, now you're just not making sense, Ted," Charity said.

"Well, in our community, family is everything. And if one person in the family is a part of the community, you all are. You have accepted Ciaran without knowing all this about him, and I thank you for that, on behalf of myself and my parents. And mark my words, we will absolutely do the same for Chris. But Chris will need his family with him to head down the rabbit hole, no matter how deep it goes. Would you be willing to do that for him, for Chris and Ciaran? Do you believe that strongly in their relationship? In their ardent love?"

Charity answered automatically, "Yes, absolutely. If it's Ciaran that Chris loves, then I want that for him, too."

But Clarissa was uneasy. "I... I don't know. I want to say yes, but I don't really know what we're talking about here. I feel like we're dancing around a topic that I am unaware of. Also, I don't want my brother to get hurt fighting a losing battle."

Ciaran spoke up. "I would never hurt Chris or let anyone in my community do so. Not ever. I would literally die first," he said seriously. He squeezed Chris's hand. Chris squeezed back.

"Wow," Charity said softly. Clarissa agreed. She believed Ciaran would protect her brother at all costs.

She said to Ted, "Okay. We definitely support this relationship, and we're willing to fight for them to be together if Chris wants it." She gave her brother a worrying look. "Are you sure, Chrissy?"

"I have never been more sure of something or someone my entire life. I'm staying with Ciaran, and we're fighting."

"And if we do end up running," Ciaran said, looking at Chris, "I already know a few African communities that would take us in." Chris nudged him with a grin.

"I don't get the joke," Clarissa said. "Unless you're talking about Ma Ami's family still in Senegal?" They smiled at each other and didn't answer. "Okay, fine, keep your secrets."

Clarissa turned to Ted again. "When my brother goes home to your family in December, I need you to promise to protect him. I know Ciaran will. But you are coming here telling us this is borderline dangerous for them to be together, so I need to know you will take care of my only brother."

Ted put his hand over his heart. "You have my word. I won't let any harm come to him."

"Hey, I need your word, too, that you will bring my Ciaran back to me in one piece next week," Chris said seriously.

Ted laughed. "On my life, I will keep Ciaran as far from danger as possible."

CHAPTER 18

Caves and Riddles

Chris spent the night at Ciaran's house and planned to stay there all week. Ciaran made him promise to go to work every day. They said their passionate goodbyes the night before and in the morning. Then the Beals men transported to the airport in Tirana and flew to Somalia.

The heat hit the men first, before they stepped out of the Magi transport station at Berbera International Airport to the rain falling in Hargeisa. Dirk, the Elfsten, who was annoyed that the Magi-African United Coalition—MAUC— had sent him there to monitor the situation, greeted them dismissively and steered them to a car. The short, bald-headed African man talked much as he drove, mostly to complain about the dry heat and how he could have been enjoying an ice-cold beer in his air-conditioned flat instead of driving them to a Magi village called Qarsoon. It was set up very much like the other Magi villages Ciaran and Sean had visited during their year traveling the world, spending half of their time right on the continent. Lots of one-room bungalows made of stone, cement, and sand, but upon entering them, they transformed into beautiful multifamily compounds.

They met with some of the locals before a man named Nokundu approached them, letting him know that he would be their guide and translator. Nokundu let them know that he was the one that had brought his dead cousin back from the last expedition and was nervous about going back into the cave. But he was happy to help in any way he could to solve the mystery of the chimera.

"Can you *Ja'wana?*" he asked.

Ciaran and Ted looked at each other, then back at Nokundu. "Describe it," said Ted.

"Travel through air," he explained.

"Oooh," both men said in recognition. "We call it Wisp'ing," said Ted. "And yes, we can. Coordinates are fine. Or you can guide us."

"I can do both," he said. He gave them the coordinates and then looped arms with them both. "Now we *Ja'wana*," Nokundu said and stepped forward, taking Ciaran and Ted with him.

They Wisp'd through the void and ended up in the middle of a desert with a mountain in the distance. There was one 10'-by-10' hut next to them, and Nokundu ushered them inside. As expected, the room was five times more than that, with compartments along the side to separate living quarters.

Nokundu introduced Ted and Ciaran to the six Magi who had been trying to uncover the secrets of the cave. Two of the six spoke English. There was also a witch doctor, and medium, who manifested all genders. They told Ted that he and Ciaran would save them all, but there would be a sacrifice they all would have to live with. But Nokundu said that the witch doctor had been saying that for a few months by that point, so the others did not take their predictions too seriously.

Ted got right to it, not needing to rest and wanting to get right to work. "Today is just an observation day," said Ted. "We go in with a deaf ear spell to get a sense of what's going on. No one approaches the chimera; keep a good ten feet distance at all times. We observe; we search around; we take pictures; that's it."

"Then I don't think we all should go," Nokundu said. "We may make it nervous, and it would want to attack us to defend itself. That's what happened to the first group. And to us."

Ted sensed it. "I would want you to be there, Nokundu. But if you aren't up to it, that's perfectly fine. I understand if you need to grieve your loss."

The oldest Magi, Elder Abu, started speaking, and Nokundu translated: "We do not grieve what is now gone; there is no purpose in that. We grieve the dying, and we honor the dead. But they have gone on to the new world, and their *Vis* is passed onto another soul in this world. There is no grief in that."

So Ciaran said, "Four is enough." Ted nodded.

"Oh good. You don't need me to go then," Dirk said in relief. Ted rolled his eyes, and Ciaran snickered.

***

It was getting dark, and no one wanted to go into the cave at night, so they decided to leave at first light. Ciaran sent Chris an *Amina* message:

"*Hi, love. We made it safely, a plan is formed, and we are heading to the cave tomorrow morning. You know, the last time I did one of these things, I think I loved you then, and I was afraid to end with how I was feeling because I didn't know how you felt. How freeing it is now to tell you how incredible it feels to be in love with you and to be loved by you. Sleep well tonight and tomorrow night, knowing that."*

Ted caught the tail end of his message before Ciaran sent his dragon on. He walked up to Ciaran, shaking his head with a smile. "I still can't believe you have been in a relationship for over six months and didn't tell me."

"Well, you know now. You know way too much now, in fact," Ciaran said.

"It's better than you keeping it inside and going through it alone," Ted said with a shrug.

"You're really okay with it?" Ciaran asked him. "All of it?"

"What, that my brother likes sucking *cooooock?*" Ted said and then started laughing.

Ciaran took a swing at him and chased him in the desert. When he caught him, they started slap boxing, before falling into a brotherly hug onto the sand.

"No, Ciaran, I don't have a problem with any of it," Ted answered him seriously when the laughter died. "But I have to be honest. I am a bit worried about what will happen when it's revealed how much he knows. The Council is changing for the better under Graham's leadership. But the same old cronies are there that were under Savannah Brickenhouse, who we all know was in league with her cousin Talindra, even if we can't prove it. They have an agenda, and it's still brewing underneath. The Grandminister is trying to root them out one by one instead of causing mass hysteria and suspicion, but Savannah is still there. So we have to be careful, tread lightly, and hope for understanding."

Ciaran nodded. "I sent my letter to Mum last night, telling her I'm in a relationship with a man and that I am going to bring him home for Christmas."

Ted patted his back. "Good on you. And thanks for telling me because when she harasses the shit out of me, and you know she will, I will know how much to tell her and how much to leave out."

Ciaran smiled. "Thanks, Ted."

———

Ciaran, Ted, Nokundu, and Mosi, who did not speak English, set off at first light. The cave was a couple of kilometers from the campsite, and they saw the entrance right away. As they approached the opening at the bottom of the mountain, Ted pointed his *rodulé* at each of them and called, *"Surdi,"* the spell to make one deaf, before putting it on himself. They went in single file with their wands lit and Ted leading the way. It was a hole large enough for a man to walk upright through, and it sloped downward.

A mile in, they entered a large opening. Mosi formed fire on the far side of the cave, and it lit the whole room up. They heard the rustling and saw the chimera immediately. It had a human face with a mane like a lion, the body of a goat, and a dragon's tail. It had been watching them from the moment they entered and rose up when the room was made brighter. And it was definitely saying something.

Ted motioned for everyone to spread out and keep away from the chimera. Ciaran took out his notebook and drew out the writings on the cave walls. Ted checked for magical tracks, and the two villagers looked around the chimera to see what it was guarding, still keeping a fair distance. The chimera was talking, trailing them with its eyes, but thanks to Ted's charm, they could hear nothing. After a couple of hours, they came back together and decided to head back to the camp for lunch and compare notes.

Nokundu said, "It definitely is trying to tell us something, but it's not Arabic or Somali."

Ciaran handed them his drawings of the symbols around the cave. "This is what I got. I tried to be as precise as possible."

"And Mosi saw what it was guarding. There is a hole close to the ground just a few feet behind it. That has to be it."

Mosi spoke, and Nokundo translated, "Ah, this is an ancient language and dialect. I do not know this, but Abu might. He studied under the original Busaras, and they spoke Cushitic languages."

So Mosi went to grab their elder, waking him from his midday nap. A few others followed him, including his son Aadan, who was also somewhat familiar with ancient languages. Abu read the markings on the cave from Ciaran's drawings and nodded. "It predates Somali," he said. He told Nokundo what was written. "The one will sacrifice for the many to hear the message for the plenty."

"So it's a poem," Ted deduced.

"A riddle that we need to solve to get her to move," Ciaran said. "Which would mean that one of us will need to actually hear the riddle to solve it."

The Magi began to argue among themselves who would be foolish enough to do it as Ciaran and Ted listened. Eventually, Ted said, "No one is sacrificing themselves, despite what your medium said. This is an ancient cave, and we are modern Magus men. Surely we can figure out how to do this without another one among you dying."

They spent the rest of the day discussing tactics and agreed to go back tomorrow to try again. Before bed, Ciaran sent Chris another message.

Chris was sitting on the steps of the Tank on the warm September night, and the sky was so clear he could see the stars. He reminisced about camping with his friends in high school, laying out under the stars, drinking beer, and talking about girls, all to keep his mind off of Ciaran. But while looking up, he saw the outline of the silvery dragon flying toward him, and he smiled. It landed on the catwalk right behind him, and he turned around to hear Ciaran's message.

"Hello, my love. So. We still have no idea what the fuck we're doing, but the food is amazing. [Chris laughed] You haven't had fresh goat meat until it's killed, skinned, and roasted right in front of you. So if we do need to run, the Qarsoon village in Somalia is where we're starting out, deal?" ["Deal." Chris said.] "Shit, Chris, I miss you. Charity is right. We do not like being away from each other. It's borderline torture, not having your body heat next to me, your leg in between mine. Maybe Ted is onto something with this Ardenti thing. You should just move in for real. Or maybe I'll give up my apartment and move into the house, since you own it and I'm just renting. Or maybe that's not what you want. Maybe it's fine the way it is, in case you need space. Or maybe I should stop talking right now... Be safe tonight. Love you."

The dragon stretched its wings and flew upward into the sky, disintegrating into the stars, leaving Chris wide-eyed, surprised, and smiling. The only reason he hadn't moved in fully with Ciaran was because Clarissa needed him there. But he liked Ciaran keeping his apartment because when he needed a break from it all that was where he went. It was his sanctuary, and Ciaran was the effigy he revered in that space.

He made a note to reassure him their living arrangements had nothing to do with him needing his space from him, and getting closer was all he'd ever wanted.

CHAPTER 19

Sacrifice

Ted, Ciaran, Nokundu, Mosi, and this time Aadan set out again, deafening spell on, into the cave in the morning. The chimera was up and waiting for them, watching them curiously. They stood in front of her, and she began talking. The plan was to read her lips as much as possible and see if they could piece together the riddle.

Again, they were there for hours and left in the afternoon for lunch. What they could agree on so far was that the poem was eight lines repeated in twenty-five-second intervals. But they were split on what language it was speaking. So Elder Abu accompanied them back to the cave in the afternoon with their notebooks and studied the chimera's tongue movements. In the evening, the six of them, along with the Elder Yared, who had stayed back with Dirk, met to put together what they had learned.

Abu, through Nokundu's translation told them, "It is a mixture of the old and the new. Tell me what you think was being said, and I will try to translate it."

After a few more hours of this, and barely agreeing on the words they could understand, they only interpreted "gift," "desire," "a," "the," and "winds." Thus began another argument about who was going to be the "one" to sacrifice themselves for the "many." Ted and Ciaran sat back and listened as they each made an impassioned defense about why they should be the one. But in the end, Abu said definitively, "It will be me. I am ninety-eight years old, and this will be my time. I am ready."

He knew that whatever the chimera did would put him in a deep sleep, and he would most likely die before they could travel the mile back outside the cave, so he was willing to stay until they figured it out and broke the curse. Ted tried to talk him out of it, but Nokundu told him to stop. Their way was that when a person determined the day and hour of their death, everyone was to respect it. So Ted and Ciaran stayed quiet.

That night, the village did a grieving ritual for his ultimate death, full of magic and awe, celebrating his life. Abu passed along his title of Elder to his oldest son Aadan. The ceremony went late into the night, so Ciaran did not get a chance to send a full message to Chris, but he knew Chris needed his company.

The dragon *Amina* met Chris at Marker 1, and Chris laughed. "Ah, I know what this is."

Indeed, Ciaran's voice said, *"Let's patrol."*

The *Amina* followed Chris on foot as he went to each marker, and after Marker 15, the last one, it followed him to the Tank and curled up on the bed. Chris asked him, "So how long are you going to be here with me this time?"

The dragon did not answer. Instead, it watched Chris with intense eyes. At 3 a.m., the same time Ciaran would have left to head back to the Reserve, the dragon stood up and stretched its wings.

"Thanks for keeping me company, little one," he said, as it flew through the closest wall. Even from far away, Ciaran always knew how to make him feel special, loved, and comforted.

<hr>

The team set out at first light again: Ted, Ciaran, Nodunku, Mosi, and now Abu. Aadan decided not to come; he did not want to see his father's death. The plan was to have Ted remove Abu's deafening spell in front of the chimera to hear the riddle and write the words in the air so they could all see it. Ted would translate it to English right then and there and try to solve the riddle in the cave. Abu needed to resist enough to get the full message out before his slumber hit, enough time to give them the words and the answers that they sought.

And at first, it worked. When they were all inside and lined up, Ted pointed his *dulé* at Elder Abu and said, "*Vis carmina omittere.*"

Abu's eyes went wide, and he immediately put his hands to his ears, screaming. Nokundu ran to him, but Abu held out one hand to stop him. The old man started using one finger to write out the words in the air. The words got larger, and he was able to write out the first five lines before he passed out. They all ran to him except Ciaran, who used his *rodulé* and translated it into English:

Dying for thirsting

A desire of us all
Dry winds crying
What made us all
The element of life—

Ciaran looked over as they rallied around Elder Abu. He knew there was only one option; he needed the last three lines to understand the riddle. He took a deep breath and pointed the *dulé* to his ear and said, *"Vis carmina omittere."*

Immediately, he felt a rushing in his ears, like he was trapped in a river of rapid waters, while simultaneously going down in an airplane. His ears burned with pressure, and he grabbed them, yelling in pain. Ted turned around and saw Ciaran, and his heart immediately dropped in his chest.

"Ciaran!! Ciaran, no!" He started running toward his brother.

Ciaran held his hand up to stop him as the elder had done, and he fought through the pain. He listened through the rushing water sound in his ear. The words came clear as day and in English. He used his *dulé* to write them in the air.

**The liquid divine
An unreachable gift
Bring me mine**

After he wrote the last line, Ciaran had an epiphany, and he understood what needed to be done. He smiled at Ted. Then his eyes rolled back, and he fainted.

"NOOOOO!" Ted screamed. He was close enough to catch him before Ciaran's head hit the solid, rocky ground.

Ciaran was heavy, but Ted was determined. He half carried, had dragged Ciaran up the cave. He tried to Wisp with no use; he tried to use his wand to make them fly, *"Avifors!"* to go faster, *"Citius!"* but no magic was working.

As he pulled Ciaran along, he resulted to praying to a higher power he didn't believe in. "God, please, please, please, don't let him die, please, God, please!"

He almost cried when he saw the light from the mouth of the cave, which gave him strength and motivation to go faster. At the entrance, he dropped himself and Ciaran right outside of it.

"Ciaran! Ciaran! Answer me, damn it!" Ted screamed his name and shook him over and over again.

Ciaran did not move.

***

Chris was jolted out of sleep. He sat up and was sweating profusely, like he was in a closed humid room. He had a bad dream, he thought, but didn't remember what he was dreaming about. His heart was racing, and his ears felt slightly clogged, as if he were underwater. Chris looked over at the time. It was about four in the afternoon. Chris rose from his bed and immediately felt lightheaded and faint. He sat back down.

"What the fuck," he said to himself.

He sat there until his heartbeat slowed down and slowly stood up. Once he was sure he wasn't going to faint, he began walking gingerly to the bathroom. He felt weak, like he wanted to go back to sleep, but knew he couldn't. He would need to relieve Clarissa and babysit Sierra and Rudy soon to give her a break before he started his shift. He stood in the shower, making the water lukewarm to shake off his tiredness. It helped a little, but not by much. He still felt sluggish. *Something is wrong*, his body screamed at him.

His soul screamed at him.

"Ciaran!" he said out loud.

Chris jumped out of the shower and ran to his bedroom, sliding across the wooden floor, and grabbed his cell phone. He called Ciaran's phone, but it immediately went to voicemail, filling him with intense dread. But he tried to keep his voice light as he left a message.

"Hi. When you get this message, call me. I felt… I don't know. Ciaran, I really need to hear your voice right now. Call me, okay?"

Chris ended the call and stood there for a moment. The phone buzzed in his hand, and he fumbled, trying to read the message. But it was Clarissa asking him when he was coming upstairs.

Chris sighed and put on clothes. He went to babysit his niece and nephew before work, trying not to be worried.

CHAPTER 20

Dying for Thirsting

Ted was screaming for help, tears stinging his eyes. His ears were still muffled, so he didn't hear when the two elders, Yared and Aadan, came behind him. He felt them pull him away, and they lifted Ciaran up, carrying him back to the bungalow.

Ted followed them wordlessly with Dirk by his side as they laid Ciaran on the nearest bed. The medicine person moved their hands over him to check for his vitals. They started talking to Ted, but he could not make out what they were saying. Ted realized he still had the spell on him and quickly pointed his *dulé* to his head and ended it. As the medicine person worked, Nodunku and Mosi came in, holding Abu's lifeless body. Aadan choked up at seeing his father, but held back tears, as it was not their way to cry over a body after a life has left it.

Nokundu translated for Ted what their Novo was saying. "He is alive, but between two worlds. We don't know which way he will go. But we have a potion we could give him that may bring him back to consciousness on our side."

"Will it work?" said Ted.

"We believe so. He is not far gone, just beneath the surface. We need to keep him awake for as long as possible when he opens his eyes. And our Novo will pray to the ancestors to assist us."

Ted nodded. "Please do all you can. I don't know what I would do if—" He stopped talking; he couldn't even formulate the words. "Please, just help him."

Nodunku held his shoulder. "We will do everything possible to save him, keep him on this side with us."

The witch doctor gave Ciaran the tonic by forcing his mouth and throat open with a tube and sending it down into his esophagus. They waited. After a full minute and a half, Ciaran's eyes fluttered, and he started to stir. He opened one eye slowly, then the other, still in slits.

His ears were pressurized like he had been on a bad plane ride, muffled and in pain, but he managed to ask hoarsely, "Did we get it?"

Ted kneeled down next to him and took his hand. "Yes, you crazy son of a bitch!" he growled at his brother.

Ciaran gave a small nod and started to close his eyes again. Ted yelled, "NO! Don't go back there. Stay with us, Ciaran, please, stay with me!" Ted felt his tears well up again.

Ciaran squeezed his hand and gave a small nod. "Need ... water," he groaned.

The medicine person came to bring Ciaran a cup to sip, but Ciaran shook his head. He said again, "Water." Then he closed his eyes. He was so tired.

Ted shook him. "Ciaran!" Ciaran reached up and took Ted's hand. He squeezed it, but did not open his eyes. Ted squeezed it again, and Ciaran squeezed back.

Ted whispered, "Stay on this side, okay, Ciaran? Okay, little brother? Please? Stay on this side with me, okay? For me? For Chris?"

He squeezed Ciaran's hand again. Ciaran slowly nodded and gave him a weak squeeze back.

***

By 6 a.m. Chris was beyond worried. Chris knew something was wrong with Ciaran. Every cell in his body told him that.

He paced the catwalk at the Tank and kept looking up at the sky for the *Amina*. But, instead, all he saw was the sun come up. He called Ciaran's cell phone for the fortieth time, which kept going to voicemail. He tried to keep his voice even again.

"Hey love, I am starting to think you're avoiding me. At any point, if you want to send your little silvery guy, I will be here waiting. I... I love you, Ciaran."

He went inside the Tank and paced until Miche arrived at 6:45 a.m. for his shift. Chris asked him, "Do you mind if I take off a bit early? I have a family emergency."

"Sure, whatever," the other ranger replied.

Chris drove a bit too fast to the Atrium and let himself into Ciaran's flat. All was quiet, except for a faint tapping he heard coming from the kitchen. He went over and saw that there was a pigeon right outside the window. Chris opened the window, and the pigeon flew inside, then landed on the table, and lifted its leg. There was a letter attached with a tiny package.

Chris grabbed both, and the package grew in his hands so quickly, he dropped it on the table in surprise. He watched it become a 12"x10"x10" cube box. The pigeon squawked at him and left out the window. Since the letter was still in his hand, he opened it, thinking it was from Ciaran. Instead, he saw unfamiliar writing. After reading through it once, he realized it was from Ciaran's mother, Grace. He read it again, slowly.

My Dear Ciaran,

How thrilled I was to receive your letter. A post from you is always a special surprise. And I am over the moon to find out why, that you are in love! How wonderful! I can't wait to meet the man that has stolen your heart. Of course, we will welcome him with open arms for Christmas! If he has family, then invite them too, the more the merrier.

I've also sent a pigeon along to your home with minced meat pies because I didn't want it to spoil while you were in Somalia. Say hello to the Wyndfield family for me at the Atrium, Dale, and the rest of your brothers at the Reserve. And give Christopher a hug from me. If you love him, then I love him, too.

Eat veggies, not just steaks all the time. Wear your socks with your boots, and not the black socks, they give you bunions. Try white cotton ones for air. And please consider switching to daytime again, so that you can get some proper sleep.

Love always,
your dear Mum

Apparently, Ciaran had done what he said he was going to do and told her about their relationship and that he was in love with him. And she responded with such motherly love and enthusiasm that Chris's eyes welled up with tears. He sniffed, wiped his eyes, and took a deep breath. He opened the box and put the pies in the fridge. Then he went back downstairs to the restaurant portion of the Atrium to speak to Phoebe.

"Hey, did Ciaran or Ted call, or check in?" he asked her.

"No, honey. Is everything okay?" Phoebe asked concernedly.

"Yeah, yeah. I just wanted to make sure; my phone is not working great, so I thought maybe he called down here or something." He lied and mumbled his way through the conversation. She nodded, but she was unconvinced. He tried to sound more confident.

"Also, Ted doesn't have my number, so he wouldn't know to call me, but he knows I'm upstairs, so you know."

Phoebe nodded again. "Well leave your number down here with me so if they do call, I will have them call you upstairs."

"Yeah, that's a great idea."

Chris gave Phoebe his number. She gave him a small smile, and he smiled back, then went back upstairs. Chris lay on Ciaran's bed with his phone on his chest, staring at the ceiling until exhaustion took over and he dozed off.

Ted sat by Ciaran's bedside for the rest of the day into the night and never let go of his hand. Every so often he would squeeze tightly until Ciaran squeezed back. The medicine person gave Ciaran the potion every hour and planned to until he could stay awake for longer periods of time. They also prayed over Ciaran in intervals. Ciaran would become lucid at times, averaging about five to ten minutes, and ask for water before he needed to rest again.

Nokundu, Mosi, Yared, Aadan, and Dirk sat in the room with Ted and Ciaran to discuss what they had learned so far. Ted was mildly paying attention; nothing was more important at that moment than his brother. He already planned that as soon as Ciaran was well enough, they were leaving, with or without breaking the curse in the cave.

Nodunku said, "'Dying for thirsting, a desire of us all'? Thirsting after desire? Desire for what? Love? Life?"

Aadan said, "It is the liquid divine. Something the gods or ancestors consider divine. I would say love, but how do you show a bloodthirsty chimera love?"

"Let's hug it. Who wants to go first?" Dirk said.

"Be serious," Yared said. "We need to look at it as a whole: 'Dying for thirsting, a desire of us all. Dry winds crying, what made us all...'"

As they continued to talk and Ted quietly listened, Ciaran squeezed his hand without Ted squeezing it first. Ted ignored it at first, grateful that he was still with him. But Ciaran kept squeezing Ted's hand. Ted looked down at Ciaran quizzically, thinking Ciaran wanted water again. And suddenly Ciaran's continued request made absolute sense.

"WATER!!" Ted yelled. They all turned to look at him. He said to Ciaran, "You're a fucking genius, little brother!" Ted said to the rest of them, "The message, the riddle, it's about water. Think about it: 'Dying for thirsting ... dry winds crying ... the element of life ... the liquid divine!' Give the damn beast some water!"

"Is it really that simple? Water?" Aadan said what everyone else was thinking.

"YES!" said Ted excitedly as Ciaran squeezed his hand again. "It's that fucking simple. If you give the chimera water, she will let you pass." They all still looked skeptical. He answered their question out loud, "I've never been so sure of something in my life." He paused as Ciaran squeezed his hand again. "And Ciaran agrees with me. Give it water."

"Well, it doesn't hurt to try it," Nokundu said. "There is a water source behind it that we are trying to get to so maybe it has been trying to get to water, too. Maybe that's the poetry behind it. Dying for thirsting, a desire of us all… Yes. It is making more sense the more I say it. Yes. We will do so, now."

Ted stayed with Ciaran while Dirk followed the four men back into the cave, muffling spell on, with a bowl of water from the river near them. Nodunku came back to report to Ted what happened.

Aadan was the one who approached the chimera, quoting the riddle back to her as he walked slowly. She stood up, but she did not attack. He stopped two feet in front of her, bowed, and placed the bowl down, then stepped back slowly as she approached. They watched the chimera bend over and lap up the water, and waited until she had her fill. Then she stood up, walked to the right of the cave, and lay down. They waited a bit more to see if she was going to move, but they soon heard light snoring, and they realized they had done it.

"It was incredible, Ted," he said. "We cannot thank you or Ciaran enough for this. And there was treasure down there, lots of it, and a crypt. Mosi believes it is the tomb of Hiwot Maji, a very powerful priestess from many centuries ago. Water was her strength. When it was time for her to die, she went into the desert and never returned."

Ted nodded as Nokundu continued, "The Elfsten said he will harvest thirty percent of the treasure for the MAUC. Aadan made him make sure that a significant amount goes to you and your brother for your sacrifice. 'The one will sacrifice for the many,' the chimera said. Well, we had two sacrifices, and you should be honored for it."

"I appreciate it; I really do, thank you," Ted said. "But all I want in this world is for Ciaran to wake up fully so I can take him home."

Nodunku touched his shoulder and left. Ted leaned back in the chair and closed his eyes.

"Water. For me this time," Ciaran croaked in a hoarse whisper.

Ted's eyes snapped open. "Ciaran! Ciaran, are you awake?"

"Yes." He swallowed and whispered, "And thirsting is my greatest desire."

Ted yelled for the medicine person who came over and held Ciaran's head up as he drank water. "Are you really awake this time? No more slipping to the other side?"

"I am. I'm here, on the living side." Ciaran then said, "Call Chris, please. He's afraid. He's so afraid. I can feel him."

"Okay, I will," Ted assured him.

"Now," Ciaran said. "He's going out of his mind with worry. Please..."

"Okay, Ciaran, relax," Ted said again. "I will call him now."

"Tell him I'm okay. Tell him, 'Forever, and three days after that.'"

"Okay. What does that mean?"

"Just tell him," Ciaran begged, thoroughly exhausted again. "Tell him I'm alive."

"Okay, little brother," he said as he pulled out his phone. "Just close your eyes and rest. I'll tell him right now." He got up and left the tent.

Chris was startled by his phone ringing on his chest and jumped. A number he didn't recognize was on it. "Ciaran!" he yelled.

"No, it's Ted. Hey."

"Ted." Chris paused. "Where's Ciaran, Ted?"

"He's ... okay."

"I didn't ask *how* he is, I can *feel* how he is," Chris snapped. "I asked *where* he is. And why wouldn't he be okay? What happened?"

"It's a long story, but that's why I started with Ciaran's okay. He just can't talk right now."

Chris lost it. "Damn it, Ted! I asked for one thing, to bring him back to me in one piece!"

Ted also lost it, the emotional toll of the last couple of days hitting him hard. "Well FUCK, I don't think your boyfriend got the bloody memo because nobody told him to be the fucking hero and risk his life!"

Chris let out all the air in his chest. "Oh God... He's so weak ... dehydrated ... His ears are bad; his headaches ... I can feel him."

"And he can feel you too apparently," said Ted. "And he wanted me to let you know that he is alive, to ease your fears."

"Just alive or..." He didn't want to know, but he needed to know.

"He's sleeping," Ted said. "In and out of consciousness, but he is getting stronger every hour, more awake than sleeping moments. He might have a ruptured eardrum, but we won't know until we get him home. But because his ears are still pressurized we aren't getting on a plane, so we're traveling little by little like Commoners, which will be a longer trip but safer for him." Chris was still quiet, so Ted continued, "I have our first leg of the trip scheduled for 5 p.m. tomorrow so we should be back by 5 a.m. Saturday morning. He's okay, Christopher. I'm bringing him back to you in one piece, just like I promised."

"Please have him call me when he wakes up next. Just let me hear his voice, Ted," Chris said quietly.

"Yeah, I can do that. His phone died, and Mr. Hero forgot to charge it, but mine is ready to go so save this number. And go to work tonight; Ciaran doesn't like you missing days for him. Also, he said to tell you, 'Forever and three days after that.'"

Chris smiled. "Okay. Let him tell me himself though. Before you start traveling."

"Will do."

———————◆———————

Ciaran opened his eyes fully for the first time in almost two days. He had been hearing things around him albeit somewhat muffled. His throat was dry again, as if he couldn't get enough water in his system. His ears were still in pain, but they were the clearest they had been since the cave. And he had a splitting headache. He groaned, and Ted appeared by his side almost instantly.

"Ciaran? You awake?"

"Yeah," he whispered. "Water."

Ted left and came back with a cup of water and a straw. Ciaran drank slowly and long until the cup was done. "More." Ted left and came back with a bigger cup. Ciaran drank that as well. "I'm tired," he said. "But I am awake now, fully."

"Can you sit up?" Ted asked.

Ciaran tried, but his head felt like it was made of boulders, and it was pounding. He shook his head slowly.

"Okay, well just lie down. Can you talk?"

"Yeah," he croaked.

"Good. Call your boyfriend before he kicks my bloody balls in."

Ciaran smiled. "How many days have I been out?"

"About a day and a half. It's Friday afternoon, and we leave in three hours. Also, we're forty thousand pounds richer. It would have been fifty thousand pounds, but I had to arrange transport."

"So we got it then? It's done? I thought I dreamed that."

"Yes. Congratulations, you broke the curse. And if you ever do something like that again, I will kill you myself," his brother said seriously. "Do you know how many people I would have had to answer to if something happened to you? Chris? Mum and Dad? All of our siblings? Hell, even Dale would be upset, losing his new Managing Tamer."

Ciaran tried to laugh, but it hurt a bit. "Oh ow! I'm sorry. I won't do it again. I'm going back to my nice, boring life of dragon taming, leaving the exploring to you."

Ted smiled and put the phone in Ciaran's hand. "Chris is waiting for your call."

CHAPTER 21

Chitra

By the time Ciaran made it back to Albania his ears had returned to normal, but the fatigue was still there. He spent the week resting while Chris waited on him, hand and foot at Ciaran's. And Ciaran went back to work as good as could be by the following Monday.

When he came onto the Reserve, Dale handed him a rolled-up document. "I know your ears are shit now, but do your eyes still work?" he teased with a straight face.

Ciaran rolled his eyes and opened it. It was official, signed by Lucinda Chesterfield, Scholarly Senior Director of Magi Anime and Wildlife in Europe (MAWE), that Ciaran was the Dragon Reservation of Albania's Senior Manager. Ciaran smiled and told Dale his new schedule: He would work overnights on Monday, Tuesday, and Wednesday, have Thursday off, go in on Friday and Saturday mornings, and be off on Sundays. Dale grumbled about him working five days instead of six, but he agreed.

Ciaran immediately walked over to Tommy and gave Tommy the Lead Tamer position on Betta. Tommy was ecstatically jumping around until Betta swiped her paw at him, sending him to the ground. Tommy scowled and cursed at her, but she was unperturbed. Ciaran chuckled and left the boy and his dragon alone, heading to his office next to Sven's which already had his name and title embossed in gold on the door. He walked in, sat down, and put his feet on his new desk.

Bruno pushed open his door. "Got your invitation to the prom, Mr. Senior Manager?"

Ciaran grinned. "Sure did. I assume you did, too?"

"Office is right next to yours," he said, nudging his head toward the right.

"Will you be my date?" Ciaran asked. "I like blue corsages."

"Fuck off, Ciaran," Bruno said and walked farther down the hall. Ciaran grinned. "Rehoboth's back," Ciaran heard Bruno say in the hallway.

"What?" Ciaran said in surprise and walked out into the hall, following Bruno to his office.

"She showed up with a hatchling, too," said Bruno, who also sat at his desk and put his feet up.

Ciaran leaned on the door. "I wonder what made her come down. She's been up in the mountains for years."

"Five years," Bruno said. "Since the days of the war."

Ciaran was thoughtful. "So she got knocked up, hatched a little one, and plans to drop it off with us?"

"Well, Amphiteries aren't known to be family-orientated," Bruno said with a yawn. "Lee named her Dory. He's taken to caring for her. I figured we should just give him the Tamer job full-time. He can handle a two-month-old dragon by himself." He rubbed his eyes.

Ciaran chuckled. "Not used to the overnight shift yet, innit?"

"Didn't I tell you to fuck off?" Bruno said with another yawn.

Ciaran chuckled and did the opposite. He sat in front of Bruno's desk and discussed splitting their supervisory duties. Since they would be in charge of the work and schedules of all the Tamers and Fixers, they planned to alternate their days and nights but made sure their weekends overlapped, like Sven and Dale did.

One Saturday a few weeks later, Ciaran helped Bruno train the Dungers on how to protect themselves against dragons by putting them in pairs and having one throw an *ignitus* spell and the other put up an ash burner protection. He and Bruno walked through the four pairs, perfecting their incantation and countering their stance. Ciaran happened to turn his head and watched Dale come up the hill with a beautiful Indian woman wearing a colorful sari.

Chitra, he said in his head as he stared at her. She took his breath away as she always did.

Bruno looked at Ciaran's reaction and laughed in a way he had never heard Bruno laugh before. "Fuck off, Bruno," Ciaran said under his breath as they walked closer to them.

"I'm sorry," he said, still laughing. "But your face is fucking priceless."

"Ciaran!" she called to him before he could respond to Bruno. "You're here! During the day! On a Saturday! How things have changed."

She gave him a soft hug, and he held onto her. She smelled as she always did, like citrus oranges, bringing back nostalgia for him.

"What are you doing here?" he asked, letting her go, but still holding her hands.

"You're not coming back, right?" Bruno said to her.

"No, Bruno." She chuckled. "My brother joined the Reserve about a year ago, so I wanted to come check on him. Mohun!" she called out.

Chitra looked over at the Indian boy who had stopped practicing, eager to hug his sister but knew he could not. Ciaran nodded the okay to him, and he ran to his sister. They began talking in Punjabi to each other.

Dale snapped at her, "Did you come here to disturb my men? You were always a distraction, and you still are. Mohun, get your arse back in formation, or you'll be sitting in dung for the next month!"

The boy let go of his sister and ran back to his place as she shook her head.

Then Dale barked at his new managers. "Ciaran! Bruno! Don't you have shit to do!?"

Chitra rolled her eyes but smiled at him. "You're still a ray of sunshine on a rainy day aren't you, Dale?"

"And you're still a shit Tamer and an even shittier employee!" he told her.

She laughed and turned to Ciaran. "How much more time do you have here?"

Bruno answered for him, "He'll be done in an hour." Ciaran side glared at him.

She smiled and reached for another hug to Ciaran, which he gave her. "I'm going to see Sarah. Come find me when you're done."

Chitra called to Mohun again and said some words that made him smile, then walked on with Dale.

"Sooo..." Bruno started.

"Fuck. Off," Ciaran muttered and walked away. Bruno chuckled again.

◆

Ciaran met Chitra in the garden with Sarah after his training session. She stood up immediately. "I heard Rehoboth is back. Take me to her."

She linked her arm around him as if saying no was not an option. Ciaran, still enamored by her wide, brown eyes, wouldn't have refused anyway. At one point, he looked down and saw a ring on her left hand, but did not say anything.

They walked into the valley and talked, first about what she had been up to since she left the Reserve, six months before the last battle over three years ago. She had two brothers at Campus, another at the Scholarly building, and she felt her family was unsafe in London. So they all moved back to Punjab, India. Her brothers finished their Magi education at the much smaller Pundhi School of Magic, which wasn't associated with any Magi Campus. She was grateful they had made the decision to go after seeing the destruction of Scholarly and the deaths of the Council members.

"My brothers would have stayed and fought and probably died, and it would have broke my heart." Then she remembered and said with wide eyes, "Oh, Ciaran, I didn't mean to say that. I'm so, so sorry for your loss."

"Thank you. And you are right. Lots of good Magi died that day. You were right to get them out before. Never feel guilty about that," Ciaran told her.

She told him that the oldest one was back in London working for Scholarly again; the middle one was Mohun, who had always wanted to join the Reserve; and the last one was still at Pundhi. Chitra was in Punjab.

"With my husband," she said without looking at him. "Arranged by my parents, who told me I was too old to be without a husband. But he is nice, and we're opening up SVE, School for *Vis* Excellence in Mumbai, for those who want to learn advanced magic outside of their regular studies, but do not want to work for Scholarly."

"So do you love him?" Ciaran asked.

Chitra smiled at him. "I love him enough." He smiled back at her.

"Speaking of love," she continued. "There's a rumor going on around here that you may want to clarify for me."

Ciaran chuckled. "Really? What is the rumor?"

Chitra chuckled as well. "You're going to make me work for this information? Fine. First question, are you dating someone?"

"Yes. I am."

"Okay, we're getting closer." They laughed. "Now, pop quiz: Man or woman?"

Ciaran laughed again. "His name is Christopher."

"My stars, Ciaran!" she exclaimed. "Did I hurt you so badly that you officially went to the other side?"

Ciaran kept laughing. "Life just happened that way for me. And I'm happy."

"You look happy," she said sincerely. "So do you love him?"

Ciaran smiled. "I love him ... *more* than enough."

She squeezed his arm. "I would love to meet him someday. The ranger."

"Well, if you hang around, you just might. We're meeting up at 3 p.m. at the ranger's station."

Chitra almost squealed. "Delightful! Give him a heads up though. It would be awkward for me if the shoe was on the other foot."

Her attention turned to Rehoboth as they had arrived in the valley. She was licking her daughter Dory clean. Chitra whistled in a tune she had used when she was Rehoboth's Tamer. The dragon looked up sharply. Rehoboth resembled a legless alligator with triple the size wings, a long snout, and small, but sharp, teeth. Chitra pulled out her *rodulé* and made dragon bubbles, the same she used to do for Rehoboth when she was a young dragon. Rehoboth let out a cry and slithered over to Chitra as Dory tried to eat the bubbles. Chitra ran to the female dragon, and they greeted each other as old friends. When Rehoboth lay her head down, Chitra hiked up her sari and climbed on top. Rehoboth slid to the edge of the cliff and stretched her wings, and they took off to the skies. Baby Dory took a moment to realize her mother had left and clumsily flew off after her, her wings bigger than her 4' body.

Ciaran watched them in the sky for a moment before he called Chris. "Pop quiz: Would you rather go go-cart racing like we planned or meet my ex-girlfriend Chitra?"

"*What!?* We're absolutely doing both!" Chris said excitedly.

Ciaran laughed. "She's here, and she wants to meet you."

"And who am I to disappoint her?" Chris said smugly. "You're still off at 3 p.m.?"

"Yes. I'll meet you at the Tank, in the parking lot."

"Wonderful. Hey, Ciaran, pretend we are still just best friends for a moment. Does she look just as good as you remember?"

Ciaran smiled. "She looks and smells fucking fantastic. You'll see."

Chris cackled. "Ho. Lee. Shit. This is going to be amazing."

Ciaran came up to the parking lot alone. He saw Chris's car, but Chris was not there. He figured where Chris went, so he went upstairs into the Tank. Chris was sitting at the table talking to Natasha, a newer weekend ranger who was being trained by Miche. They were laughing about academy teachers when Ciaran walked in, watching her shamelessly flirt with him.

"Hope I'm not interrupting," Ciaran said.

"Hey," Chris said with a grin and stood up. He walked to Ciaran and kissed him on the lips, then turned back to the female ranger. "I'll see you around, Natasha."

She did not seem phased by the kiss at all. Instead, she ignored Ciaran completely and said to Chris seductively, "I can't wait."

Ciaran smiled and took Chris's hand to walk him out. "I think Natasha wants to rock your world."

"Jealous much? While I am moments away from meeting your hot ex-girlfriend? Where is she?" Chris asked as they stood against the rail.

"She got pulled into a conversation with Sarah and Felix, and she said she would be along in a minute." They waited. "So Ted told me Mum came to see him at the flat, pretending to check on Elodie but really fishing for info about you."

"Did she really?" Chris said wide-eyed.

Ciaran nodded. "I didn't tell him that I didn't tell her that you're a Commoner, and he figured that out by her line of questioning. He reamed me out for leaving out a very important part. But I told him that information is better in person; then we'll tell them all of it."

Chris nodded as Chitra Wisp'd at the edge of the woods, black smoke catching his attention. An Indian woman in a bright sari was standing there. She looked around, then up at the Tank. They both stared down at her for a moment. She smiled and started walking toward them.

"Speaking of in-person... Ho. Lee. Shit, Ciaran," Chris said quietly. "Um... Best friend mode activated: Ciaran, she is ... gorgeous. Stunning. Her body is like ... perfect. I can see her shiny, glistening hair from here. How the hell did you let that get away? And why aren't you trying to fuck her now?"

Ciaran looked at Chris and smiled. "Don't flirt with my ex-girlfriend, please."

Chris winked. "I make no promises," he said, and he started walking down the stairs, pulling Ciaran with him by his hand. Ciaran sighed and followed.

They met in the parking lot, and Chitra spoke first. "You must be Christopher. The Ranger."

"That I am," he told her with a bright smile.

"You're so tall and handsome," she exclaimed. She reached up and gave him a soft hug.

"Oh, you're a hugger!" Chris let go of Ciaran's hand to return the hug and sniffed. Then lifted her up and spun her around, winking at Ciaran who looked amused.

Chitra cried, "Oh!" and they laughed as he put her back down. "I'm so happy to meet you. Do you know what they call Ciaran on the Reserve?"

Chris grinned. "Yes. The Ranger's Magi."

She grinned too. "Indeed. He is yours."

"And I am all his," he said sincerely. "And Ciaran had nothing but great things to say about you, Chitra," he said.

"Well, I hope so. Though, I have to say I wasn't the best partner to him," she said.

"Really? How so?" Chris asked.

Chitra glanced at Ciaran first. "Well. Ciaran is all stoic on the outside, but on the inside, he loves the idea of love. And I just ... didn't. I'm naturally a little more reserved in my feelings. But you seem open with your feelings. And you're fun. I like that."

"Yes, our Ciaran is a bit of a romantic, isn't he. Truthfully, I was more like you, resistant to it at first, but I have to admit, it felt good to let him in this stiff heart of mine."

"And that's exactly what he needed," Chitra said. "Someone who he could let in, too, and it gets reciprocated. And I was not ready for that. It's nice that you are."

"You know, I am right here," said Ciaran.

"Hush, love, the grownups are talking," Chris said. He put his arm around Chitra, and they started walking toward his car, with Ciaran sheepishly following. "So would you say he was more of a serious boyfriend than a good time?" Chris asked.

"Oh, yes. Ciaran is very serious. Not that we didn't have some fun, but work was always the priority, and it left little time for other things. He can also be a bit broody and in his head, so watch for those moments."

"Yes, we have had those moments. I'm typically able to snap him out of it, pushing his buttons a bit."

"And see, I never pushed. I would just leave him in his head, and then we'd have a nice good fuck, and it would bring him back to his senses," Chitra said, amused.

Chris's eyes widened as he looked back at Ciaran. "Really? And when I use sex to push him I'm being immature, isn't that right, Ciaran?" he called out from over his shoulder. Ciaran's eyes narrowed.

"Oh, don't let that fool you," said Chitra. "Sex is a great way to get Ciaran out of a funk. Come to think of it, I'm not surprised he ended up with a man. There was nothing Ciaran liked more than an exceptional blow job."

Chris snorted out a laugh as Ciaran said, "Hey! Enough already you two." Chitra and Chris laughed together.

"You really are fun," Chitra said. "I can see why Ciaran loves you, Chris."

"Is it obvious?" Chris winked at her as they stopped at his car.

She looked at Ciaran and walked up to give him a hug. Holding on to him, she said, "Keep him close to your heart. You deserve to be happy."

"I'm going to try with all my might," he told her.

She hugged him again and then kissed him softly on the lips which he returned before he realized what he was doing. She pulled away and turned to Chris and gave him a hug; then she took his face in her soft hands and kissed him on the lips as well.

"I'll see you boys around." She walked on a little way then Wisp'd, leaving them both staring at the spot where she just was, her citrusy scent in the air.

Chris said after a moment, "Best friend mode activated again: I can feel how she makes you feel."

Ciaran let air out his lungs. "Is that right?"

"Yeah. You miss her."

"A little, yes," said Ciaran quietly.

"She's wonderful," Chris said. "I met her for five minutes, and I miss her already."

Ciaran smiled and turned to Chris, pulling him into his arms and kissing him passionately. "I love you."

Chris responded with, "I wonder if she does threesomes."

Ciaran laughed and shoved him.

CHAPTER 22

Under the Stars

November came around, and it was warmer than expected. Chris's 27th birthday fell on a Wednesday, so they agreed to celebrate the whole weekend, with Ciaran taking Friday and Saturday off. Ciaran told Chris, "Pack a bag for the weekend; we're leaving right after your shift first thing in the morning." And Chris agreed.

On Friday morning Ciaran Wisp'd to the Tank with his own duffle bag and met Chris at his car. "Drive to Vlore," he told him.

Chris's eyes narrowed. "We aren't going to see my father, right?"

Ciaran looked at him like he was crazy. "What? Why the hell would I take you to see your dad for your birthday weekend? I didn't even remember that he lived there."

"Yeah, he does. A boathouse on the bay."

"Well, we are going toward the bay, but that's not part of my plan."

Chris nodded; then he got excited. "We're going boating, Ciaran, aren't we!?"

Ciaran smiled. "Yes, you horse's arse, now drive. It's a little over three hours to get there, and we're on a schedule. I would Wisp us, but we might need the car. And Ted told us not to do that anymore."

Chris scoffed. "Ted worries too much." He put the car in drive and headed off.

They drove and chatted and listened to music. It was a little after 10 a.m. when they arrived at the pier. Chris was tired, and Ciaran was hungry. They went down to the private boats and stopped at one named *Zona e Magjistarit*, The Magician's Lair. A tall, middle-aged man met them on the dock wearing all white, with a shorter man behind him wearing all black.

"I am Jetmir," he said. "I will be your captain, and Artoran is the first mate and your chef. Other than the two of us, you are left to your own devices. We will be in the Mediterranean Sea for the next 24 hours. If you would like to dock for dinner either Saturday or Sunday night, please let me know in advance. Otherwise, we will be at The Bluest Eye by tomorrow afternoon. Any questions?"

They both shook their heads no. Ciaran took Chris's hand and followed Jetmir aboard the luxury yacht, which was at least eighty-five feet long and two levels. Chris was in awe. They walked into the lower level first, which had a common room with couches, chairs, and a stocked bar. They chose the biggest bedroom in the front to drop off their bags, then headed to the top deck where their brunch was waiting for them: Wine, cheese, scrambled eggs, sausages, Greek salad, fresh fruit, smoked meats, hummus, and warm pita bread. Artoran reintroduced himself as the chef and quietly walked away.

They drank the whole bottle of Bellini champagne and ate until their bellies were full. Chris asked him, "Okay, out with it. How could you afford this, Ciaran? I know Dale's raise wasn't that good."

Ciaran smiled. "No, but I did get a small windfall from my mission with Ted."

"I hope you didn't spend it all on me, did you?"

"No, not all of it. But enough. You're worth it," Ciaran said seriously. Chris smiled. "Oh and my brother Sean wrote to me, saying congrats on my relationship—he used more uncouth words—and he sent me this as a present." He pulled out a clear sandwich bag with an ounce of marijuana and put it on the table. "Homegrown with seeds from the Amazon in South America."

Chris was stunned. "What. The. Fuck, Ciaran. Why did I not know in the year and a half we've known each other and nine months we've been coupling that you partake!?"

"Because I don't. At least, not regularly. I'm not a novice, but it's not my thing. Sean on the other hand is a connoisseur of sorts and started growing his own strains when we got home from our trip, mixing it with our Magi herbs. He sells it to Commoners too, in the UK and in the States, right out of the shop."

Chris opened it and smelled how potent it was. "This is sweet. I haven't smoked since college, so thank you, brother Sean." He closed it up and put it aside. "I will save it for later. Right now I just want to sleep. But not indoors, outdoors."

"On a lounge chair?" Ciaran asked.

"I guess, yeah, under the awning though. I mean, if I could bring the bed out there I would." Chris chuckled at that.

Ciaran was thoughtful. "Well, why not? We'll just take the bed from the other room and lay it out on the deck under the awning."

Chris smiled slowly. "I knew I really liked you." Ciaran smiled.

They took the full-size bed from the middle room with the bedclothes and placed it on the lower level deck in the shade. They stripped down to their underwear and got under the covers, facing each other.

Chris said, "I really want you, but I am so tired." His eyes blinked in sleepiness.

"Get some sleep. We have three full days," Ciaran said. He touched his face lovingly, and Chris closed his eyes. The sound of the motor and the waves quickly put him to sleep as well.

Ciaran woke up first right at dusk and watched the setting sun for a while. The boat had stopped somewhere in the Adriatic Sea. He leaned over and touched Chris who stirred a bit, then pulled back the covers. Chris was lying on his side still. Ciaran reached into his boxer briefs and started rubbing his genitals. As his erection grew, Chris stirred again and made a small moan. Ciaran leaned all the way over and put Chris in his mouth, sucking the head gently.

Chris let out an audible sound and turned all the way onto his back, but did not open his eyes. Ciaran sucked, licked, and stroked Chris into ejaculating into his mouth. After Chris came, he opened his eyes and watched Ciaran.

"Fuck me," Chris said. Not waiting for a response, he sat up, pushed Ciaran down, and got on top of him.

Ciaran laughed. "Wait!" He held his hand toward the doorway and said, "*Cedo.*" In seconds, the bottle of flavored lubricant came into Ciaran's hand. He quietly put Chris onto all fours, prepared him, and penetrated.

They moaned and grunted loud and free, staying in that position until Chris's rectum squeezed and his body began to tremble. Ciaran slowed all the way down, rubbed his back, kissed his neck, then started all over again, slow thrusts, gradually picking up the pace. Chris hit his orgasmic peak again, moaning louder than the last time. His insides wrapped so tightly around Ciaran that Ciaran pulled all the way out to keep from cumming.

Chris moaned, "What the fuck did you do that for?"

Ciaran did not answer. He wrapped both arms around Chris's midsection and put his head on his back listening to his fast heartbeat. When it slowed, Ciaran kissed his neck and shoulders, then down his back, all the way to his bottom, then kissed and licked his hole with a hard and fast tongue, sucked his balls, then back to his hole.

Chris moaned again. "I'm going to die at twenty-seven, a slow and happy death right now."

When Ciaran couldn't take it anymore, his own horniness consuming him, he resumed the position behind Chris and was not slow and steady anymore. He slammed into Chris hard and fast until he came, and groaned out of pleasure. He fell backward on the bed; Chris lowered himself on his stomach. The sky was dark and full of stars, but neither noticed as they lay there without touching and stared at each other for a while.

<*I love you,*> Ciaran thought.

Chris said out loud, "I love you, too."

Ciaran stared at him. <*You can hear my thoughts again?*>

"Very, very faintly," Chris said out loud. "Like a conscious thought in the back of my head, but in your voice." <*Can you hear mine?*> Chris asked back in his head.

"It's not something that happens regularly, not even in a marriage tie-bind," said Ciaran. "Ted learned telepathy, but he only does it with Elodie."

"So you didn't hear my thoughts just now?" Chris asked.

Ciaran shook his head. "No. But you're not a Magus. So you wouldn't have been able to reciprocate that kind of *Vis.*" <*But I can send you my thoughts,*> he said in his head.

"And your feelings," Chris said out loud. "I knew the moment you fainted in the cave. I felt it, like it was happening to me. And I feel how strongly you feel for me every single day. That's why it's hard when we're apart, I realize that now. It's like a part of me is missing."

"A part of your soul, perhaps," Ciaran said with a smile.

Chris smiled back. "Between sharing thoughts and feelings, maybe your brother was onto something with this *Ardenti* stuff."

<Yeah,> Ciaran said in his head. <Maybe.> Chris grinned. <Does it scare you? Our souls becoming one? Not just soulmates. Actually becoming one soul.>

Chris stared at Ciaran for a long moment. "No. It means we'll always be together." Ciaran grinned at him and touched his face. He moved closer for a kiss.

An announcement came over the speaker, and they heard Jetmir say, "Dinner is served on the top deck."

They got up and dressed, then moved to the top deck for dinner. After dinner, Chris pulled out the Ziplock bag, and he started rolling a joint while Ciaran watched. He lit it with the candle on the table and took two puffs and passed it to Ciaran. He said, "This time last year we were playing that card game, *Flama Arca*. That's how we passed the time, playing card games. And look at us now."

Ciaran passed it back to him after one puff and said, "This time last year I was trying to figure out why you talked about sex so damn much. And here we are." He passed it to Chris as he laughed and smoked.

"This time last year I wasn't thinking about you in this way. I mean, maybe like a little crush, but not in an actual we're going to get together kind of way. Just something to wanker off to when I got lonely," Chris said.

"This time last year I wasn't thinking about you this way either. Not even in my wildest dreams did I see this coming. Not until you massaged me about a month later, and I realized how much I wanted to fuck you. Like, right then and there if I was bold enough." Ciaran held his hand out, and Chris gave him the joint.

"That massage, huh? I could tell I was making you uncomfortable, but that's why I kept going. I liked to make you uncomfortable and watch you turn red. I still do." He smiled.

Ciaran looked at him intently. "No, you weren't making me uncomfortable. You were making me hard. I was horny as fuck. And that's what made me uncomfortable. You, Chris Jennings, have never made me feel uncomfortable. You brought out feelings in me that I didn't understand. But you being you made this the easiest decision ever." He took a long drag and passed it back to Chris.

Chris puffed in silence, looking up at the stars. "You make this easy, Ciaran. I am along for this ride of committed love that you are taking me on, the highs and lows of it all."

"Lows?" Ciaran asked curiously.

"Yes. You know the times you just go away and almost get yourself killed? Those are ultimate lows for me. I've figured something out, Ciaran." He passed the joint to Ciaran and leaned into the table. "I realize that I'm cured. Whether it's the *Ardenti* or not, you have officially cured me of my commitment issues. Because the God's honest truth is I cannot live without you. After what happened to you, to us, while you were in Somalia proved it to me. If something were to ever happen to you, please believe me when I tell you, I am following you to the grave. I refused to be on this earth without you, or in any dimension that you aren't on."

Ciaran looked at him for a moment, the seriousness and darkness of what he said concerned him a bit. He puffed and then said, "You know, there is a middle ground between 'Relationships scare the shit out of me so I just try not to do them' and 'If you die, I die.'"

Chris shrugged. "Not for me. I've never given my all to anyone before. Call it soul-infused, binding, magical, ardent love. Call it what you want. All I know is that I am just as much the Magi's ranger as you are my Magi. We're already one."

Ciaran smiled. He passed the joint back to Chris. "I'll never take that for granted. I promise to take care of your heart, body, and soul for the rest of your days on earth. And three days after that."

Chris looked at him and said, "Those sound like vows, Ciaran. Is that also part of this weekend plan?" He winked.

Ciaran grinned. "No. And if you fucking propose right now, I'm going to kick you off this ship."

They both laughed. They were quiet for a minute before Chris spoke again.

"On New Year's Day, you asked me what I wanted. I told you I wanted someone to take me sailing and to make love under the stars." He puffed and tried to pass it to Ciaran who refused. "And you did just that."

"I remember everything you said that night," Ciaran said seriously.

"Do you really?" Chris said, amused.

"You wanted someone that knows about your past, accepts it, never brings it up, and wants to fuck you anyway," said Ciaran. Chris laughed heartily.

But Ciaran continued, "You want someone that you could cook for, give back massages to, and it gets reciprocated. You want someone that makes you laugh when you're sad, calms you down when you're mad. A love that gives you a reason to get out of bed in the morning. You want to be able to love freely, unconditionally, and to know that person will take care of you, completely."

Chris was no longer laughing. Between the weed and Ciaran actually remembering the words he barely remembered, he was getting very emotional. "And yes, someone to take you sailing and to make love under the stars," Ciaran concluded.

"Wow," was all Chris could get out. Then he said, "You never told me what you wanted, you know."

"Because I didn't know exactly. But whatever I would have said then would never compare to what I actually have now. Falling in love with my best friend. I don't know if *Ardenti* is real or not. I just know that we being able to combine our hearts, our minds, our souls together is all I'll want and need in this world."

Chris finished the joint and put it out on his plate. He stood up and held out his hand. "No more talking."

He led Ciaran inside to their bedroom, and they made love again to the sounds of the waves.

———

Ciaran rose earlier than Chris and woke him up to go to the top deck to watch the sunrise and take pictures. They went to the second level to a breakfast of eggs and sausage, baguettes, crepes, croissants, fruits, and a screwdriver for drinks. Then they sat in the hot tub on the top deck and watched the yacht sail to the Karaburun Peninsula and dock.

Jetmir came up and said to them, "You will need to take the motorboat into the Bay of Crama if you would like to explore the caves. Beach gear is already on the boat, and Artoran will pack a lunch basket if you so choose. Stay as long as you like. I will not pull off until you are safely back on the vessel."

The men gathered their swimsuits and made their way to the boat, then traveled the few yards to the shore. There were no other boats since it was not the time of year people would normally visit there, and they knew they would be alone. They explored the caves and the blue lagoon inside, then went back to the beach to set up their blanket.

As they were eating lunch, Chris told him, "Soooo, I've never had sex on the beach."

Ciaran smiled at him. "Are you asking?"

"I'm just throwing it out there. In case you wanted to make another fantasy of mine come true."

Ciaran did not respond, but a few moments later he conjured another spell to warm the temperature where they were a bit more, then he stood up, stripped naked, and jumped into the ocean, to Chris's amusement. After a couple of laps, he came back and lay face down on the blanket, still wet, and closed his eyes. Chris smiled, removed his clothing, grabbed the lube Ciaran made sure that they brought along with them for this very purpose, and mounted him. And Chris made love to him, bending Ciaran into various positions until he was satisfied. They fell asleep on the sand, still naked.

Chris woke up to the setting sun. Somehow his face ended up at Ciaran's tailbone, not that he minded at all. He went for a night swim, then came back to Ciaran still sleeping. Chris lay down next to him and caressed his back gently until Ciaran woke up.

"Hey, love," Ciaran said.

"Let's not go back to the boat tonight. Let's stay here," Chris said.

"Anything you want to do, we'll do it," Ciaran told him.

He turned over and pulled Chris close to him. They lay there together, again staring at the stars in the sky. Eventually, they put on their clothes, and Chris lit another joint while Ciaran conjured a fire. They ate the rest of their food, talking and laughing about childhood stories.

After a while, Chris said, "I want to go dancing tomorrow."

Ciaran puffed. "You're really pushing this whole 'I'll do anything for you' thing, aren't you?"

Chris laughed. He picked up his cell phone and called his friend Other Chris who lived in the area, who instructed him on where to go in Vlore tomorrow night, and some of their friends would be there. Other Chris would not be, because his wife was pregnant, and he wanted to stay home with her.

Ciaran agreed, but said, "But don't expect me to dance. Dance with who you want, flirt with who you want, just make sure they know you're coming home with me." Chris chuckled but agreed.

The next day, Jetmir headed back to Vlore, and they exited the boat that evening to drive to the address his friend had given him. It was exactly what Ciaran expected—loud techno music, which he detested, and people high and drunk all around him with no consideration for others. But he did not voice his disdain; after all, it was Chris's birthday weekend. Instead, he sat at the bar and drank a lot while Chris flirted and danced with girl after girl after girl. Chris came over to Ciaran briefly to introduce three of his friends from his days at university: Nevena, Ariza, and Constantine. Then they all went back to the dance floor.

As the night went on, Ciaran was drinking enough alcohol to make him hot with jealousy, watching women and men come onto his lover. Intoxicated, he pushed through the crowd and met Chris out on the dance floor. Chris watched Ciaran lumber toward him with a grin, able to feel Ciaran's jealousy. Before he could say something cheeky, Ciaran grabbed him and kissed him passionately. The dancers around them went wild and started cheering. Although the music was fast, Chris held onto Ciaran's neck, and they danced slow, grinding their erections together as everyone jumped around them.

He leaned into Ciaran's ear and whispered, "You always allow me to be me. I love that about you, Ciaran."

Ciaran whispered back, "Say it again."

Chris leaned his head back and yelled into the noise, "I LOVE YOU, CIARAN BEALS!"

The people around them cheered again. Ciaran laughed and held him tighter. Chris whispered in his ear again, "I'm ready to make love again."

Ciaran grinned. "Let's go."

They headed back to the docks and the boat and told Jetmir to head out into the peninsula again. The couple found their outside bed since it was a clear night again. Chris lubed up Ciaran's penis and got on top. He moved back and forth in the motion that Ciaran liked, bringing himself to orgasm. When Ciaran knew he was close, he grabbed Chris's member and jerked him until he ejaculated first, then thrusted upward until he too came.

Chris collapsed on top of Ciaran's chest, which was milked with his cum, and said, "Thank you. This has been one of the best weekends of my life."

<Me too,> he said in Chris's head. He played with Chris's curls in a soothing way.

Chris stared at the twinkling lights in the sky until he fell asleep.

CHAPTER 23

Papa

The boat docked at 9 a.m. on Monday morning. When they got to the car, Chris said, "Do you mind if we make a quick stop before heading home?"

"No, not at all. Where do you want to go?"

Chris didn't answer. They pulled out of the parking lot and headed north along the shoreline for another twenty minutes before he stopped at a private marina. They walked down the boardwalk; then Chris approached a small boathouse on the water. He knocked, but no one answered. He started banging on the door.

Then they heard from farther down the pier a gruff voice with a heavy Irish accent yell out, "Who da fuck is banging on my door?"

Chris turned to face Ciaran. "You ready to meet my papa?" Then, without waiting for an answer, he turned around and started walking toward the end of the pier.

The man was wearing a Hawaiian shirt, board shorts, long socks, and boots, with a fishing hat on, and was standing up with a fishing pole in the water. He didn't turn around until Chris said, "It's your favorite son," dripping with sarcasm.

He looked at him and then turned back to the water. "Yeah, that's strange. Because I thought I had two daughters and a whoring, flaming fruitcake son that never came to see me."

Ciaran's mouth opened slightly in shock. Chris took a deep breath and said, "I've got company, so keep the dickishness to a minimum, yeah?"

Chris's father turned around again and this time looked at Ciaran. Then he looked at Chris and said, "The new catch of the day? He's a fucking ginger; throw him back."

Chris ignored his comment and said, "This is my boyfriend, Ciaran. Ciaran, this is my father, Collum Jennings."

Ciaran found his bearings and stepped forward to hold out his hand for a shake. "How do you do?" he said politely.

Collum shook it back a little roughly, looked him in the eyes, and said, "You don't look wimpy." He let his hand go.

"That's because I'm not wimpy," Ciaran said steadily. "And neither is Chris, for the record. Nor a whore. Nor a flaming fruitcake."

Chris held back a smile as Collum grunted. "You must really like him. Word of advice: a whore cannot be kept. Best to move along before he breaks you down, like all the others in his past."

Chris's almost-smile quickly turned into a scowl. "Okay, enough of that shite. We were in the neighborhood, and I thought I would stop by and say hi. But clearly that was a mistake, so goodbye and fuck off." He turned around and touched Ciaran's arm to drag him away.

Collum called out, "How are my girls?"

Chris turned back around. "Clary had the baby in June. It's November. You should go see her."

Collum growled. "You, fucker, you. You know I'm not going anywhere near that house."

Chris shrugged. "Suit yourself. But Sierra looks just like Ma Ami, same complexion, and everything, with your eyes. So it may be worth the trip and your pride."

His father grunted again. "What are you doing out this way, anyway?"

"Ciaran took me on a boat ride for my birthday," he said proudly. Then said, "You do remember it was my birthday last Wednesday, yeah?"

"Oy!" He laughed. "*Snagged tú féin fuck balbh saibhir an uair seo*, yeah? Now you're a gold digging whore?"

Ciaran crossed his arms in annoyance, getting tired of this banter. He didn't need to know Irish Gaelic to know that Collum was throwing insults at his son.

"Better a gold digging whore than a piece of shite father, I always say," said Chris in English. He turned to leave again, but Collum called out again.

"Oy! You didn't tell me about my Chary."

Chris turned around a second time. "Sis is well. Working long hours at the hospital and helping Clary with the kids. They will all be here next month for the gathering, but I won't. I'm going to London with Ciaran to meet and spend time with his family."

"Well, well, well, aren't you a world traveler. Stop in Ireland to see your family, then."

Chris rolled his eyes. "Goodbye, Papa."

He turned a third time to leave, and a third time Collum stopped him. "Wait! Go to Logoreci Grocers; you know you were on your way there next, anyway. Pick me up four steaks, instant mash, cheese, and a pack of fags." Then he laughed as Chris stared at him blankly. "Oy. Actual fags, the smoking kind."

"You're gonna give me money this time?" Chris's eyes narrowed.

"*Fuck níl!* Ask your ginger-haired boyfriend."

Ciaran was about to retort, but Chris quickly grabbed his arm and turned him around to start walking. Collum called after them, "And don't forget my fags like last time!"

They walked back up the boardwalk and Chris was fuming. "I fucking hate that sonofabitch," he grumbled.

"I've never seen a dynamic so volatile between a father and son before," Ciaran said. "He makes Dale look like Father of the Year."

Chris was still mumbling some words in Gaelic with clenched fists as they made their way back to the parking lot. But instead of turning right toward the car, Chris made a left and started walking up the hill. "Where are we going?" Ciaran asked.

"To get him his fucking groceries," Chris said angrily.

"Why?" Ciaran said, before he could stop himself.

Chris did not answer. They stopped at a small market on the corner, and Chris walked in first. A woman was at the counter reading a magazine. She had light brown hair and delicate, beautiful features. Chris smiled a smile that Ciaran noticed.

He said quietly, "Emiranda."

She looked up with her round brown eyes, and she smiled that same gentle smile back at him. "Well. Look who clawed their way out of hell to visit me," she said in a heavy Eastern European accent. "Hello, Other Chris!"

She came around the counter, reached up to his neck, and gave him a hug. He closed his eyes and hugged her back tightly; then they kissed each other's cheek at the same time, then hugged again, holding onto each other a bit longer.

They heard a voice from the back yell, "Did you say Other Chris!? The fucker actually showed up!?"

Emiranda said to Chris, "I haven't seen you in almost a year. What kept you away?"

"Work. And well..." He turned around. "Meet Ciaran. The boyfriend."

She smiled at Ciaran, walked up, and wrapped her arms around his midsection like they were old friends. "It's nice to meet you, Ciaran, finally. Chris thinks the world of you." She reached up and kissed him on the cheek.

Before he could respond, Other Chris had come up the stairs. "Did I hear you say..." He looked at Chris and yelled, "Other fucking Chris!"

They ran up and gave each other a brotherly hug. Other Chris was the same stocky build as Ciaran, with ash-blond hair and dark blue eyes.

"I know, it's been a while," Chris said, holding onto his shoulders.

"Well, yeah! I know you don't like the old man, but I thought you liked us!" he teased.

"Oh, he had a good reason to ignore us," Emi said. She pointed at Ciaran in an obvious way that made Chris laugh.

"Ciaran," Chris said. "These are my best friends, Cristobal and Emiranda. Other Chris, this is my boyfriend Ciaran."

"Whoa! Boyfriend alert!" Other Chris teased again. "How you doing, man?" He also greeted Ciaran like an old friend with a slap handshake and pulled him into a half hug.

"I'm well. How about yourself?" Ciaran said.

"Oh, you know, keeping it tight and close to the balls," Cristobal said with a grin.

Chris laughed, and so did Ciaran. Chris said to him, "Something is seriously wrong with you."

"So, did you see the old man?" Other Chris asked.

"Yeah, I saw that fucker. He sent me up here with a grocery list." He scowled again.

"Oh, we'll take care of that for you," said Emi. "C'mon, let's go get what he needs."

She took his arm and moved him farther into the store. They watched them disappear. Other Chris turned to Ciaran to say, "Obviously, they're talking about you." He winked at him before moving behind the counter.

"Obviously." Ciaran chuckled.

"Other Chris must be serious about you to bring you around us. Especially using the B word. That's shit like ... once every other blue moon. You must be something special to him." He looked at Ciaran intently.

Ciaran understood. "And he's something special to me, too," he told him confidently.

Other Chris smiled. "Good. He's been through a lot, I'm sure you know. So the last thing I would want is for him to get into a situation that will further hurt him, you know? He's been my brother since we were children. I love that man." He looked at Ciaran and waited.

Ciaran did not hesitate with his words. "I love him, too. Believe that."

Other Chris nodded. "Good." He changed the subject. "So how's the old man? Still a rotten sonofabitch to his only son?"

Ciaran nodded slowly. "Why is their relationship so bad?"

Other Chris's eyes widened. "Ooooh, he hasn't told you yet. Well, he'll get around to it. But you may need to pry it out of him; he doesn't like to talk about the incident. It was one of the worst days of his life, to be honest."

"Incident?" Ciaran said, confused.

"I've already said too much. He'll tell you when he's ready."

Other Chris moved to stock shelves to his left as a finality of the conversation, leaving Ciaran to wonder about the "Incident." Chris came back giggling with Emi and a bag of groceries. Other Chris reached down to the shelf below him and put a pack of cigarettes on the counter.

"Don't forget the smokes. He was cursing you out for a week that last time. In English and Irish."

"Fuck him and these fags," he said, but he took them and added them to the bag. "What do I owe you?" he asked, taking out his wallet.

"Shut the fuck up and get out of here with that bag," Other Chris said, and Chris grinned. He then said, "You know he's going to want you to stay for dinner."

"And I'm going to politely decline," Chris said with a straight face.

"No, stay!" Emiranda pleaded. "If you do, we'll come over too, and it won't be that bad."

"Emi, girl, I love you, but no. I've had all I can take right now. I just had an amazing weekend, and I would like to keep it that way. Plus, we both have to work tonight."

"Well, don't stay away too long," Other Chris said. "Ciaran, I'm counting on you to bring him back."

"Will do," Ciaran promised. "Nice meeting you both."

They gave their hugs and handshakes, and again Emi held on to Chris a bit long, even with Other Chris right there, who seemed used to their affection for each other.

As they walked back to the marina, Chris said happily, "Best friends in the world, those two."

When they got to the boathouse, Chris dropped the bag at the front door, then called down, "Oy! Come get your shit. I'm not walking down there again."

Collum scowled and walked up, picked up the bag without a thank you. Instead he said, "You're such a sorry sack of shite, aren't you?"

"You taught me everything I know," retorted Chris. He turned around to leave.

"Wait, stay for dinner. I'll grill fish."

Chris whirled around so fast and said viscerally, "*Fuck nil!* So you can call me a sissy and wimpy and a fruitcake and a whore eight more times and insult my ginger-haired boyfriend? Are you fucking mad!?"

Collum lost his temper too and yelled, "Well then, fuck off then! Go! Get the fuck out of here!" He started yelling some words in Irish Gaelic, which, again, Ciaran didn't have to understand to know they were more insults.

Chris turned around and called sarcastically over his shoulder, "Love you, too, Papa."

Ciaran followed Chris in silence to the car. Chris drove for about twenty minutes before Ciaran asked quietly, "What happened between you and your father? What was 'the Incident?'"

Chris was silent for another minute, then grumbled, "Fucking Other Chris talks too fucking much."

"He didn't tell me anything. He said you would tell me when you were ready."

"It's a long story."

"We have a three-hour drive," Ciaran reminded him.

Chris sighed heavily and was quiet for a moment before he spoke. "You have to understand that our relationship was always … testy. He's always had this disdain for me, and I never measured up to the son he always wanted, like his brother's sons. I was too emo, too into music, and dance. Even track and field wasn't sporty enough for him. It was my mum who played the mediator between us. So when she died…" Chris sighed. But Ciaran was quiet and allowed him to continue.

"I started junior year at Uni the following fall after my mum died. I was still on a scholarship for track and field, and I was with Natalis, but also still seeing Rem. In one of our first school meets, there were Olympic scouts there, and that was what I had been working toward literally since I was fourteen years old, to be scouted for the national team. Collum found out from my sisters, Charity most likely, that I was sleeping with Rem since I was sixteen. So, I was on the field running a 400 meter when Collum showed up. He just went straight for Rem, punched him in the face and kept punching him when he was down."

"Whoa," Ciaran said.

"Yeah," Chris said with a sigh. "When it dawned on me that someone was beating up Rem in the middle of the field, I ran off track and tried to help. I got there and realized it was my own father. He was going at him like he wanted to kill him, and I had to stop him. But when I intervened, he turned on me, started beating me right in the middle of the field, too. It took other players to get him off me. He's calling Rem all kinds of names, a fag, a cocksucker, a whore that was fucking a teenager, essentially outing our relationship. My father was arrested, but then when it all came out, they fired Rem from the university, and they suspended me from track and field for the rest of the season, ultimately ending my scholarship and any chance I had at the Olympics."

"Oh. Wow." Ciaran shook his head.

Chris nodded. "I didn't speak to that sonofabitch for the next couple of months until I had to go home for Christmas, the first without Ma Ami. Of course, we got into a huge fight over the 'Incident' where he threw some more homophobic comments at me. And then he told me, 'No son of mine is living under my roof thinking it's okay to be a fag.' Those were his words to me. So I kindly reminded him that the house that was in Ma Ami's family was left to her adult children, not her husband, so actually it was my house, and he could he get the fuck out. He laughed at me and thought I was joking.

"The next day was Christmas. I called the police and had him arrested for trespassing and had his belongings packed up and sitting on the sidewalk when he returned from jail. That was seven years ago, and he hasn't stepped foot in the house since. The first two years we didn't speak to each other at all. And he didn't come to my college graduation. On the fourth anniversary of Ma Ami's death, my sisters managed to get us both in the same room, and it wasn't great but it wasn't terrible either. Without my mum to mediate, our relationship has dissolved into what it is now. We're on speaking terms, but it's kind of disastrous, so we both just avoid it altogether if we can."

Ciaran did not speak at first, taking all Chris had said. "So now you've met the worst father on the face of the planet." Ciaran opened his mouth, then closed it abruptly. "I saw that," Chris said while his eyes were on the road. "Say what you were going to say."

"Hmmmm... I don't think you're going to like what I have to say."

Chris's eyes narrowed. "Don't tell me you are in agreement with anything that he has done, Ciaran!" he yelled.

"Listen, I think that he handled the situation in the worst possible way that a father ever could have handled it."

"But...?"

Ciaran sighed. "But... He wasn't wrong in his reason why."

"What the fuck, Ciaran!?" Chris yelled again. "So it was okay for him to beat the shit out of my boyfriend, then beat the shit out of me because he found out I'm not straight!? What the absolute fuck, Ciaran!?"

Ciaran said calmly, "First, stop yelling at me. Second, that's not what I said. You assume he went after Rem because of your sexuality, but I don't think so. I think he went after Rem because he's a child predator."

Chris's mouth dropped wide open in shock. He looked at Ciaran, then back at the road. "Ciaran, Rem didn't rape me. I wanted to be with him. And I told you about the D/s dynamic we had, which I fully consented to every time."

Ciaran shook his head almost angrily. "Chris, you were a 16-year-old impressionable boy with a crush. Whether you were attracted to him or not, he was, in fact, a grown man having sex with a *teenager*. And not that it mattered, it could have been the most loving thing you've ever experienced, but to add insult to injury, he abused the shit out of you and continued to do so for *years!* Him calling it a D/s dynamic was to cover the fact that he abused you, mentally, emotionally, and yes, sexually!"

"Ciaran—" Chris started in shock.

But Ciaran continued, getting everything off his chest that he wanted to say from the night Chris first told him about Remington. "You didn't consent, Christopher! You were groomed into it. This is a man your parents trusted to train you and mentor you, not to *screw* you. Ask yourself, Christopher, honestly, if you found out that your 16-year-old son or *daughter* was sleeping with his or her 22-year-old coach whom you trusted, tell me you wouldn't want to kick his fucking teeth out before sending him six feet under!"

Chris took a moment to pick his jaw off his lap, then said, "I was an adult by the time Collum found out. I was nineteen, almost twenty by then."

"Okay. Ask yourself, would that have mattered to you? Would that have changed the fact that he fucked your son when he still was a *child?*" Ciaran challenged him.

Ciaran waited. Chris was silent for the next couple of moments, then yelled, "FUCK!" He hit the steering wheel hard with the palm of his hand.

Ciaran continued, "I think the problem is you've never actually talked about the incident, hashed it out. So you've been believing your father is just a homophobic nob, which really he probably is that, too, but also maybe a solid dad a bit who lost his shit when he discovered what Rem did to you. And he's been thinking you're an ungrateful, disrespectful arsehole who chose his child molester over him. So there's that."

Chris was silent for a few minutes, and Ciaran let him be. "He really hurt me, the things he said. I will never forget it."

"Yes, that was fucked up. And then you threw him out of his house, the house he raised his three children and watched the love of his life die in. That was fucked up, too. So you've both been really awful to each other."

Chris kept driving in silence. But Ciaran could feel Chris fuming, and it was because he knew Ciaran was right. "Fuck!" he said again.

Eventually, Chris pulled over and leaned his seat back. Ciaran did, too. After a bit of silence, Chris asked, "So what do I do now?"

"You don't have to do anything, really. He's still the father in this situation, so the onus is on him to want to fix it, not you as the son. But ... if you want to, you could start a conversation with him at some point about this. Or not talk about the incident but just, you know, try harder. Model positive dialogue for him, see if he catches on and starts to talk to you with some respect."

"When I'm ready, will you be there with me?" Chris asked vulnerably.

"Absolutely. I will be right there by your side." He kissed Chris on his shoulder.

Chris sat all the way up and said, "How is it so easy to talk with you about these things?"

Ciaran sat up as well. "Because I'm your best friend, mate. Just because we fucked like rabbits all weekend doesn't change that."

Chris chuckled. They kissed again and went home.

CHAPTER 24

Angst and Awe

December rolled around with bitter cold winds and trepidation for Ciaran and Chris. They didn't talk about it much as time got closer, but they were both nervous and anxious about Christmas with the Beals. They decided not to outright lie and pretend that Chris was a Magus like he did with Ted, but to be extremely evasive about his background and his ability to do magic until the holidays passed and they could discuss it with his parents openly. They knew Ted would not tell.

Ciaran reminded Chris of his immediate and extended family: They would be staying with Diana and her husband Quentin, who were hosting Christmas dinner at their home in London. Chris already knew Ted, who was bringing his pregnant wife Elodie and their children, and he would meet Sean, too, but they were not sure if Sean was staying at Diana's house. Their cousins, Robert from his mother's side of the family, and Alastair, from his father's side, would also be spending Christmas with them. Alastair's mother, his aunt Elspeth, was most likely to be with them too, since her brother-in-law Hamish was the only one able to tolerate her whip tongue. Rob and his long-term girlfriend, Chloé, were also living in the home with Diana and Quentin, all schoolmates from their time at Campus. Chloé, who was from a Commoner family but started showing magical capabilities around eight years old, and Diana were best friends growing up in Kingsbridge together. It was Ciaran's parents who went with Diana to talk to Chloé's parents and explain what was happening to their daughter.

Ciaran made the arrangements to fly out of Tirana to London on an early morning flight on Christmas Eve so that Chris could spend the day before with his family on the anniversary of his mother's death. The day after Christmas they would travel to Kingsbridge and have a sit down with Hamish and Grace and tell them about Chris's Commoner status so they could help Ciaran figure out the next steps. They continued to verbally assure one another that it would all work out fine, although they could feel the worry from the other.

Chris and Ciaran met with Charity, Clarissa, Rudy, and six-month-old Sierra at one of Ma Ami's favorite restaurants in the city. Ciaran held Sierra, who had taken very much to being carried around by him and pulling on his red hair. They were both surprised when Collum showed up thirty minutes after their arrival, wearing dress pants and a button-down shirt. Ciaran noticed that he had a full head of wavy salt and pepper hair. He was clean shaven and handsome, especially when he smiled at seeing his daughters. Ciaran saw just how much Chris looked like his dad.

"Papa tu es là, je suis si heureux!" Charity exclaimed and jumped up to hug him.

Clarissa rose as well. *"Papa, je savais que tu ne nous décevrais pas, tu as l'air bien."*

He spoke back to them in English. "Well, I couldn't disappoint me little girls." He kissed them both on the cheek.

Chris did not rise, but he said politely, *"C'est bon de te voir père."*

Collum looked around, and his response was, "Really, the ginger is still here?"

Chris's eyes narrowed, and he said, "The ginger's name is Ciaran. And yes, he's still here, with me, where he will always be. He's my partner. Show some respect, please."

Ciaran smiled. He stood up and went over to Collum. "Would you like to hold your granddaughter, Collum?"

He looked suspiciously at him, but reached out as Ciaran handed him the baby. Sierra looked at him curiously, then reached out to touch his face. Collum swallowed and choked up a bit. "Christ. It's like looking at a mini version of my Ami."

Charity's eyes welled up, and Clarissa grinned. Collum sat down to dinner with his family.

They ate and traded stories about their mother as Ciaran listened. Clarissa said, "Ciaran, *ma mere* would have really liked you. You are everything she could have ever wanted for Christopher."

Collum snorted in disgust. Chris, who had been keeping it together, couldn't help himself. "What's your problem with Ciaran?"

"Chris, no," Ciaran said under his breath, but he was ignored.

"Nothing. Just that what Ma Ami would have wanted was for her son to be with a woman."

"No, that's what *you* want," Chris said. "Mum knew who I was since I was fifteen years old. She wouldn't be surprised in the slightest." Collum snorted again. "What the fuck is your problem with me?" Chris said more heatedly. Ciaran touched his arm, and he shrugged him off. "No, stop. Are you really this homophobic that you can't just be happy that your son is happy, whether with a man or woman?"

Collum's eyes narrowed, and Ciaran saw again just how much Chris looked like his dad. "Well, I would have to give a shite about you in general before I gave a shite about your love life," he said nastily.

"Papa!" Clarissa scolded.

"Papa! *C'était cruel!*" Charity chastised him right behind her sister. Ciaran was also visibly angry at Collum.

"You know what, Papa?" Chris said calmly. "You're right. It was completely foolish of me to think that for one moment in your miserable life you would care enough about me to be happy for me. But once again, you've shown me exactly who you are. Maybe one day you will see me as your son. But until then, I will no longer put myself through this torture. I'm done. For good this time." He motioned to Ciaran to go, and he also stood up.

"Oh, Chris, you've always been such a sensitive lass. Sit down, you sissy," Collum said dismissively.

Chris ignored his father and kissed and hugged his sisters goodbye, along with his niece and nephew, and Ciaran did the same. "Good luck with Ciaran's parents!" they called after them. Ciaran and Chris held hands and left the restaurant.

Ciaran wanted to talk in the car, make sure he was okay, but Chris clearly did not, as he put on rock music on repeat and deafeningly loud. After the second song, Ciaran grabbed Chris's hand. He felt him try to pull away, but Ciaran pulled it back and held it tightly until Chris finally relaxed in his hand.

When they got to their hotel room by the airport, Chris went to lie on the bed, clothes on, looking up at the ceiling. Ciaran started to talk to him, "Chris—"

Chris cut him off. "Don't start Ciaran, please," he said, defeated. "I tried, and he hates me. So fuck him." He felt his tears well up, and he quickly brushed them away.

Ciaran lay next to him on his side to face him. "I was going to say I think you handled it incredibly well. And I'm so proud of you for that. And even prouder to be the man in your life." He moved in close to drape his arm across Chris's belly.

Chris did not respond except to put his hand over Ciaran's hand. They fell asleep in this manner and woke up at 4 a.m. to catch their flight.

Diana was in the kitchen Christmas Eve morning making tea when she heard the pop by the front door. Two large suitcases appeared, and she knew her brother was on his way with his boyfriend, Chris.

Grace had told them a few months ago that Ciaran had a special male friend that he was bringing to Christmas with him, and they were all to be cordial to him and respectful of their relationship. Not that she needed to say it to them. Of course, they would welcome Ciaran's partner. Diana was surprised, but it quickly turned to excitement to meet him. She got an even bigger surprise when she received a message from him a month ago, requesting they stay at their home instead of in Kingsbridge since Chris had never been to London and they wanted to spend the day sightseeing. Of course, she and Quentin agreed, grateful for the opportunity to spend time with the brother she rarely saw and to get to know them as a couple.

Diana pointed her *dulé* and said, *"Dimittunt situm."* The luggage disappeared from the entrance and appeared in their room on the third floor.

An hour later, there was a knock at the door. She opened it wide and jumped into her brother's arms like she always did, yelling his name. "Ciaran!"

Ciaran caught her midjump, knowing it would never get old for him. He kissed her forehead and put her down gently.

"You're a woman now, Diana, not a little girl," he teased.

"But you'll always be here to catch me," she quipped back. She turned to a tall, handsome, brown-skinned man. "You must be Chris," she said, and she wrapped her arms around his midsection, as she was at least a full foot smaller than him.

"Lovely to meet you, Diana," he said, hugging the small woman with strawberry-blonde hair and bright blue eyes.

"Come inside," she told them and led them into the kitchen. They made small talk about the flight and the weather as she served them tea. Chris noted that Diana looked like a smaller, feminine version of Ciaran, especially when she smiled or laughed.

"Did you want to rest first?" she asked them.

Ciaran looked at Chris, then said, "No. We're going to run around London a bit and end up at The Magic Box Shop."

"Very well. We're having a smaller dinner tonight, just the six of us, and Mum is going to stop by. I'm not sure if Dad will join us; he may have to work late so he can have the rest of the week off. Of course you will meet everyone tomorrow."

"Thanks, Diana. We'll be back by dinner, promise," Ciaran said.

They headed back out into the cold, with their collars turned up, leather gloves on, and scarfs tight around their necks. They walked the streets, with Chris taking pictures on his phone in Trafalgar Square, at Big Ben, the Palace of Westminster, Queen Victoria's Garden, and Hyde Park.

As they got closer to a white stone building in the heart of West London, Ciaran turned to him. "Okay, Chris. Try very hard not to look around in awe everywhere. Blend in. You ready?" Chris nodded, unsure what was going to happen. "I'm serious. Try not to look like a complete Commoner and tourist."

Chris rolled his eyes. "I'll be fine."

"Okay. Here we go."

They stepped up to the front entrance and waited for someone to pass them, smiling politely. Ciaran walked through the revolving doors with Chris next to him. But he didn't come out on the other side. They rotated three times and then stepped back out the front entrance. Only it was not the street of London they had been on.

As soon as they walked through, Chris's eyes did go wide, and he tried really hard to control himself. "Where are we?" Chris breathed out.

"Still London," Ciaran said. "Just hidden. This area is called Myrddin, which is the actual name of—"

"Merlin," Chris finished for him.

"Correct," Ciaran said with a smile. "It is rumored that where Scholarly stands is where Merlin's original home was located."

"Wow."

Chris couldn't help but to stare at everything. There was magic in the air, literally. Wands casting spells, charms, and jinxes all around him, pigeons and other kinds of birds flying around with letters or packages tied to their legs, all manner of doors, windows, and items seemingly opening, closing, and moving about by themselves. The streets were full as Magi shopped for holiday gifts or stood around talking.

Some were in wizard-looking clothing, men in pointy hats to sparkling shoes or women wearing all black as if they came right out of a Grimm fairy tale. Chris took note that the younger the Magus or Mage was, the more they were inclined to wear regular modern clothing, aside from a cloak here and there. It was truly fascinating.

Ciaran looked at Chris, struggling to hold in his excitement, but his wide eyes betrayed him. Ciaran laughed and made Chris laugh as well. "Okay there, mate?" Ciaran teased.

"Fuck off, Ciaran," he muttered, embarrassed.

Ciaran held him by his waist with one hand and ran his hands through his curly hair with his other hand. "All this around, and you're the most magical person I see."

He kissed him full on the lips in the middle of the street, softly at first, then licked the inside of his mouth.

"Wow, Ciaran," Chris said breathlessly, "That was romantic and sexy." They kissed again, softly; then Ciaran took his hand.

They went into every shop and explored together. Alexi assisted Chris in exchanging Euros before he left so he had enough Sagems—Magi money made from the oldest Magi tree dating back over 10,000 years—to buy souvenirs. He was able to sneak into a store and secretly buy Ciaran a present when he ran into an old friend from Campus and started a conversation. They visited a Magi bookstore and Ciaran picked up a few books, then a cloak shop where Chris bought himself an authentic Magi black cloak with a yellow silk lining. Ciaran showed him where Ted worked, the Scholarly building, but they did not go inside, knowing that they would see Ted and his family tomorrow. They turned another corner, and Chris saw the huge flashy sign before Ciaran pointed it out: "The Magic Box Shop."

"Wow," Chris murmured.

"Yeah, it's my Uncle Malcolm's shop. That's Rob's dad, my mum's brother. It's a hodgepodge of magical items. It's always been the place to be for the younger crowd," he explained as he opened the doors. "He's an experimental witch, always creating new inventions, spells, and potions."

They went inside the shop of two floors. It was full of patrons who had come to buy presents the day before Christmas. They squeezed through the crowd and started looking around, trying not to get separated. While looking at a disappearing mirror, Ciaran felt someone pinch his butt. He turned around with a scowl and faced Sean.

"I heard you like that kind of thing now," Sean said with a grin.

"Wanker!" Ciaran said with a laugh. He gave his brother a hug. He then pulled Chris over and said above the crowd, "This is Chris. Chris, this is Sean."

"Sean, my favorite little brother, how are you?" Chris said, shaking his hand.

"Chris, my brother's lover, good to meet you," Sean said back, and they both laughed. Sean was about as tall as Ciaran at 6', but much skinnier, like their oldest brother Ted. Sean's hair was more copper colored and closely cropped, and he had fewer freckles on his face.

Rob walked over absentmindedly. "Hey, Sean, do we have anymore Snakeberry... Ciaran!"

"Hey, Rob!" They hugged as well; then Ciaran said, "This is Chris. Chris, Rob."

"Oh, hey, mate." He shook his hand politely. "Aunt Grace said we're supposed to be nice to you or something." He turned back to Sean. "Jolene is asking for these Snakeberries, but I really think she just wants you."

Sean winked at Ciaran and Chris. "I'm sure she does want me. Excuse me, gentlemen."

Ciaran shook his head, and Chris laughed. "Okay, that kid is definitely the cutest Beals."

Rob, who was still standing there, said, "Hey! I'm cute!"

Chris chuckled, and Ciaran rolled his eyes. "You're a Livingston, not a Beals. Or did you forget?"

"Shut up," said Rob. "I'm as good as!"

Ciaran smiled. "What time are you closing up tonight?"

"Dunno," Rob said. "It was supposed to be 5 p.m., but with this crowd, it will probably be a bit later. Apologize to Diana for me missing dinner. Chloé, too, if you see her, although I suspect she'll be working late, too." A customer tapped his arm, and he turned away.

Chris and Ciaran continued to explore the shop. Chris picked up a Fallen Fifty Foto Frame. It was those who died in the last battle right in the streets of Myrddin. Moving images would appear one by one with their names, ages, and professions, or Campus scrolling across the bottom. He stood there and went through all of them. He had never seen a picture of Darragh as an adult, so he was curious. When she appeared, he saw a woman not classically beautiful, but by the way she shifted her sparkling gray eyes and gave a mysterious smile in the photo, he liked her immediately. He was almost sad when her picture dissolved into someone else, a child no older than thirteen.

Shane's image came a couple of photos later. He was the spitting image of the young man he just met, but his eyes were much brighter, happier, he realized. His smile was wide and genuine, and Chris knew he would not have been able to tell them apart if he were alive. The photo again faded before he was ready, and it showed an adult female Mage who looked fierce, always ready for battle.

He heard Ciaran's voice behind him. "I don't have one of these. I couldn't imagine staring at dead people all day long. C'mon, let's go."

CHAPTER 25

Meet the Beals

Diana opened the door and whispered, "Mum is here." Ciaran and Chris looked at each other and smiled nervously. They walked to the kitchen where Grace was at the stove and Quentin was wiping down the counters, or rather monitoring the counters getting wiped by themselves.

Grace threw her arms around Ciaran and kissed both his cheeks. "So good to see you, my son," she said. She touched his hair that had lengthened since she last cut it six months ago.

Grace Beals was average height for a woman, which still made her shorter than all her sons. Her hair was light brown, and she kept it short in a pixie cut. But Ciaran's wide blue eyes were from his mother.

Before she asked, he said, "No, Mum, I'm not cutting it; don't ask." He took her hand from his hair and turned her around. "Mum, this is…"

But Grace had already pulled Chris in for a big hug. As he bent down, she also landed two kisses on his cheeks.

"Christopher, of course! I'm so glad you can join us for Christmas. It's lovely to meet you, dear."

"Thank you for welcoming me, Mrs. Beals," Chris said. "Ciaran talks about you so often I feel like I already know you."

Grace beamed. "Does he!? How wonderful to hear. I wish I could say the same, but Ciaran only recently told us about you."

"Oh, you know Ciaran, he likes to be hush hush when it comes to matters of the heart. I would like to think I have brought it out of him a bit."

"It seems you have," she said with a warm smile. "Come, I was just setting the table for dinner." She took his hand and led him farther into the galley kitchen where the long table was, leaving Ciaran to follow.

But they were paused as Quentin wiped his hands on a dishcloth and came over to shake Chris's hand happily. "Good to meet you, Chris. I'm Quentin."

Chris shook his hand and said, "Oh, I know who you are. I don't think there is a Magi on earth that doesn't know the famous James name, a Generational Magi. But I'm looking forward to getting to know just the man Quentin."

Quentin smiled. "I appreciate that." He gave him a friendly pat on the back, then went to shake Ciaran's hand. "Alright there, Ciaran?"

Ciaran pulled him into a brotherly hug. "It's good to be home."

"Can I help with anything?" Chris asked. "I know my way around the kitchen."

"Really?" Grace said. "It's always nice to hear when a man can cook."

"Especially since Ciaran can't boil water," Diana said, and they laughed.

"I'm not that bad," Ciaran tried to defend himself as he sat at the table.

"When I met Ciaran," Chris said, also having a seat, "he was living off your meat pies, Mrs. Beals, and Phoebe's steaks in the Atrium. I've been getting some more veggies into his diet. But, of course, we both can't get enough of your cooking, so keep those coming."

Grace blushed. "Oh, you!"

Diana looked over at Ciaran and mouthed, *He's charming.* Ciaran nodded and smiled. Grace asked him, "What kind of dishes do you make?"

"Senegalese, French, and Mediterranean food, mostly. I can whip up a quick ratatouille if you are interested."

"I'm interested!" Diana said excitedly. "Come to the garden. Let's see if we have all the ingredients. And if not, we'll conjure something up."

Ciaran gave Chris a hard look, but Chris just smiled at him reassuringly and went to the garden with Diana. As soon as the door closed, Grace turned to Ciaran, "Oh, I like him."

Ciaran smiled. "As I knew you would."

"So he comes from a Commoner family?" she deduced. "I can tell he's not from Magi stock, but has raw talent. What are his parents like?"

"Actually," Ciaran said, "If it's okay with you all, can we not ask about his family this week? His mum died about eight years ago, two days before Christmas, and it's hard for him this time of year. He and his dad are estranged, as not having her around to mediate their past fights has put a real dent in their relationship. I just want him to have a good time with our family. There'll be plenty of time to talk about his background and family when we come to Kingsbridge."

Grace had clapped both hands over her mouth as Ciaran talked. "I... I had no idea. That poor sweet boy. Yes, we'll spread the word. No family talk with Chris, won't we, Quentin?"

Quentin nodded. "We definitely will. It's no fun talking about dead parents, especially at the holidays." Quentin's father passed away, also seven years ago, during the war. And he and his mother, a known dark Mage, were also estranged.

Chris and Diana came back in with a handful of vegetables and laughing. She helped Chris with the ratatouille as Quentin helped Grace with baking fresh bread. Ciaran sat at the table and watched. Conversation was light and fun, mostly discussing the enclosed garden and how it needed deweeding. Chris offered to help, mostly because he was fascinated with a fully bloomed garden in the middle of winter, but he kept that part to himself.

When the food was ready, Ciaran set the table, his contribution to the family dinner. As they started passing around the beef stew, fresh bread, and ratatouille, the door opened, and Rob and Sean walked in.

"Oh good! We made it!" Sean called out.

They sat down at the long table and joined in the conversation, talking about food, cooking, and cuisine, with Sean and Ciaran talking about all the good food they ate while traveling the world. An hour and a half later, the door opened again. They expected to see Chloé, but instead Ted came through like he had just stepped out of a biker magazine with his leather jacket and biker boots.

"Oh ho! Any left for me!?" he called out.

"What are you doing here? Leaving poor, pregnant Elodie home by herself with two children on Christmas Eve?" Grace scolded.

"Relax, Mum, she knew I was stopping by here to see how things are going. Hey, I know that guy!" he said as he pointed to Chris.

Chris stood up, and they gave each other a handshake. Then Ted pulled out a chair and instead of sitting in it, he sat at the top of the chair with his feet in the seat. Grace and Diana both gave him deadly stares, which he ignored.

"Soooo. What are we talking about?" Ted reached over and grabbed a piece of bread and dipped it into the ratatouille. "Mmmm, who made this?"

Sean said, "We're just finding out how Chris knows every song in the world and likes dancing, clubbing, and having fun, literally the opposite of Ciaran." The family laughed.

"Yeah," Ted said with a nod. "Chris took us to karaoke night at a bar, and we had to get Ciaran pissed and put on a song he knew all the words to before he got up there."

Rob and Sean's mouths dropped. Rob said, "Seriously, you got Ciaran to *sing*?" as Grace said, "What do you mean 'pissed?' You know I don't like you boys drinking excessively."

"Relax, Mum, we were fine," Ted said dismissively. He dipped his bread again and said, "Seriously, Diana, your cooking just went up ten notches. Elodie would be impressed with your ratatouille."

Diana rolled her eyes. "I didn't make it; Chris did."

"Well, you helped, added the spices and all," Chris complimented.

"Yes, when you told me too," she said back.

"Ah yes, you're a bit of a Frenchman. *Merveilleux*. My Elodie is going to love having someone else to talk to in French."

"Is that where your family is from? France?" Sean asked.

"Hush, we don't need to talk about Chris's family right now." Grace tried to shut it down.

"No, it's okay," Chris said. "My mum was born in Senegal, West Africa, a francophone country. And my dad is Irish, born and raised. He moved to Albania with my mum after I was born. So I was born in Ireland, raised in Albania, and grew up speaking French, English, Albanian, and Irish Gaelic."

"Wow," Rob said, "I barely speak English."

"So is that where you get your *Vis* from?" Sean asked. "The African side of you, most likely."

Ciaran held his breath as Chris responded. "My mum died before I got the chance to ask her about any magical lineage." Everyone got quiet.

"I'm so sorry. I didn't know," Sean said quietly. He put his head down.

Chris said lightheartedly, "Of course you didn't. No need to be sorry, Sean." Sean looked up. Chris turned to the table. "To be honest, this is the first Christmas Eve I've had in years that I haven't been completely depressed. Quite the opposite, really, I've just been enjoying myself here with you amazing people. I hope to spend many more Christmases with your family." He turned to Ciaran, who smiled at him.

"Here, here!" Ted said as he raised his bread, breaking the tension, and everyone else chuckled.

Grace changed the subject. "So, did everyone finish their Christmas shopping? Because I will need help tomorrow getting this place ready."

"Yes, Mum," they all mumbled.

"Good. Don't forget to label your presents so the house knows where to put them."

"Yes, Mum," they mumbled again.

Chris said, "Good, now I get to see which one of your family members send you those hideous, cartoon-like Christmas sweaters." He laughed as Ciaran's eyes went wide.

Everyone went quiet. Chris knew he had said something wrong but didn't know how bad until Grace said plainly, "I am the one that gives my children Christmas sweaters every year."

Chris's eyes went wide, and he started stuttering, "Oh... Mrs. Beals... I ... didn't... didn't mean... I ... was just ... saying... I... I didn't mean..."

Ted busted out laughing loudly. Others at the table began to laugh heartily, except Chris, who turned red with embarrassment, and Grace, who smiled a bit. "My apologies," he said quietly.

"Holy crap, that was amazing!" said Ted, still laughing, tears in his eyes.

"Watch your tongue, young man," Grace said sternly to Ted.

"Sorry, Mum," he said, still laughing, wiping his eyes. He got off the chair. "Okay, ladies and gents. I will see you for dinner tomorrow, 6 p.m. sharp. Happy Christmas." He gave his mother and sister kisses on their cheeks and left.

The conversation moved to changes within the Magi Council that affected businesses like The Magic Box Shop and the Beals Apothecary, more restrictive of who they could sell to. After 9 p.m., the door opened again, and Hamish and Chloé showed up.

"Sorry," Hamish said, "We were doing some last-minute tasks for Graham." He walked up to Chris. "Hello, Christopher Jennings."

Chris immediately stood up and held out his hand. "Hello, Mr. Beals. Good to meet you, sir."

"Call me Hamish," Ciaran's father said kindly. Hamish was tall like his sons, more lanky like Ted and Sean, and had the same fiery red hair that Diana, Ted, and Ciaran had.

Chloé also said polite hellos to Chris and Ciaran, then slid in next to Rob, and gave him a quick peck on the lips as he set up her plate. She looked thoroughly exhausted. They started talking quietly as Hamish asked the table how their day had been while they ate.

When Hamish had his fill, Grace said they needed to get going. "I'll be back in the morning to help cook and clean. Be ready," she told the men in the house.

"I'll be heading out, too," Sean said. "I'm picking up Alastair and Aunt Elspeth and bringing them over tomorrow."

Ciaran watched Sean point his *rodulé* at the table, and without saying a word, a bowl was conjured, and leftovers were coming together, falling into it. As he walked out, he gave Ciaran a thumbs up behind Chris's back and nodded. Ciaran smiled and nodded back. Sean's bowl followed behind him out the front door.

Ciaran said, "Well, we're going to bed now too. It's been a long day. We'll see you all in the morning." Chris started walking out behind Ciaran, then turned around.

"I just want to say again, Diana, Quentin, thank you for inviting me into your home. I'm already having the best time here."

Diana said, "You're welcome," and Quentin said, "Happy to have you, mate."

Chris followed Ciaran upstairs in silence to the third floor, and Ciaran closed the door behind Chris. Chris started to say, "I think that went pretty—" But he was silenced by Ciaran's passionate kiss. Chris returned his passion, wrapping his arms around his shoulders, rubbing the nape of his neck.

Ciaran broke off first. "You're amazing, you know that?"

Chris shrugged smugly. "I've been told that a time or two."

Ciaran kissed him again. "Show me how amazing you are."

He pulled out his dulé to silence the room and lock the door. They made love in their favorite position, with Ciaran lying on his back and Chris riding him on top, cumming and climaxing together loudly, although no one in the house was the wiser.

CHAPTER 26

Happy Christmas

Icy rain instead of snow fell on Christmas morning. Every room's fireplace was roaring and cozy when Chris woke up with Ciaran wrapped around him. He slid out of the bed and pulled back the curtains to watch the pellets fall to the ground, creating a sheer glow on the London sidewalk. He grabbed his phone and called Clarissa and Rudy to wish them a Happy Christmas in a quiet tone and told them where their presents were located since he had hidden them in their flat upstairs. He had bought toys for Rudy and Sierra and identical heart-shaped white gold necklaces that said "Big Sis" and "Lil Sis," respectively for his sisters. He called Charity next, but she did not pick up, so he left her a message. Then he turned to see Ciaran still asleep, lying on his back, so he decided to wake him up with kisses on his face and licks in his armpits. It quickly turned into kisses along his torso, then farther down.

Ciaran groaned and chuckled, reaching one hand up and running his hands through Chris's hair. "Good morning, love."

Chris did not answer, not until he had made Ciaran rise and brought him over the edge with a climax and ejaculation.

"Now that's a way to wake up on Christmas morning," he said with his eyes still closed.

"Good morning," Chris said, rising from below until they were face-to-face. "Happy Christmas." Ciaran smiled. "And thank you."

"Thank you for what?"

"For coming into my life. Loving me the way you do. Introducing me to your family. All of it. More. I'm really happy today."

Ciaran pulled him in for a kiss. "I'm happy, too. Happy Christmas." They kissed again.

Then Chris said excitedly, "Okay, on to presents!" He pointed to the dresser where there was a stack of gifts.

"You don't want me to—"

"No!" Chris yelled, throwing wrapped gifts on the bed. "Presents!"

Some were individual gifts, and others were joint gifts for the two of them. Ted's gifts were labeled individually, but it was matching Magi robes; Chris's was light blue with silver stars, and Ciaran's was dark blue with black stars. Chris was so excited to have his very own Magi robe that he put it on right away. Sean's present was labeled with both their names on it, a box of several items from their store. They discovered a trick bottom where underneath it was about 3 ounces of what he called Beals Weeds. Diana got Ciaran and Chris a box of potions she made herself, everything from enhanced sexual pleasure to easing anxiety. And Quentin put Chris's name on a box of a brand new Magi chess set, with a note to him saying, "I hear you're the one to beat."

Chloé sent Ciaran a collection of books of dendrology and botany. He gave them to Chris, saying, "These are for you. I asked her to pick up a book of Magi trees. The Motus Willow is in here. The other talks about their healing properties and what the leaves and roots are used for."

"So I too can become a witch?" he deadpanned.

But Ciaran shrugged. "You don't need the *Vis* to create potions. You just need Magi wildlife. Diana is actually a certified wiccan, and everyone in Kingsbridge knows it. They just don't know how true it is."

"Fascinating," Chris said, picking up another box.

Rob's gift also had both their names on it, filled with Magi treats and sweets. As Chris started going through the candy, Ciaran pulled out a small box.

He got on one knee and handed it to Chris. "This is yours," he said with amusement.

"You're fucking crazy if that's a ring," Chris said.

Ciaran laughed. He put it in Chris's hand and stood up. "Hold it with two hands," he instructed. Chris did. Ciaran took out his *dulé* and pointed it at the box, saying, *"Dilato."*

The box grew to twenty times its size into a large round container. Chris opened it, and inside was a premium wool authentic park ranger fedora. He was speechless. He had mentioned to Ciaran when they first started hanging out the regular cotton ones weren't as good and someday he would get an authentic one.

"Ciaran, you're like the best boyfriend ever. Seriously, if there was ever a boyfriend contest, I would enter you, and you would win," Chris gushed.

Chris put the box on the bed and put on the hat. "It looks great, but it's clashing with the robe." He took off the attire until he was back in his black boxer briefs. "That's better!" He posed in front of the dresser mirror.

Ciaran took out his phone and took pictures of Chris in his hat and underwear. "This is going to be your ID picture, for sure."

Chris kissed his face a few more times and then said, "This is so awesome." He kissed his lips. "Seriously. Best boyfriend ever." They kissed some more; then Chris said, "Okay, your turn. And I hope you like it. It's definitely not as exciting, but I waited because I wanted to get you something from your world so..."

He pulled out two packages from the bags of gifts they put in the corner and gave them to him. Ciaran sat on the edge of the bed and opened up the first one. It was a plastic wand case with a jelly-like substance inside. Chris explained, "It's a *Rodulé* Retractor. First, you need to put your *dulé* inside so it recognizes yours only: then you pull it out, so it recognizes your hands as well. And then no matter where your *dulé* is, it will always find its way back to you. The guy at the wand shop said you are guaranteed never to lose it. Try it."

Ciaran picked his *dulé* off the bed and placed it inside. As soon as he touched the jelly, it glowed purple, then pink, then back to clear. He pulled his wand out, expecting it to be cold, but it was warm to the touch. He then tossed it across the room. After a few moments, the stick floated back to its gel casing, still in his hand.

Ciaran smiled. "That's so fucking cool."

Chris was happy. "Yeah, you really like it? Mopsanthus said it's for young Magi who are always losing their *dulés* around Campus and such. I know we sometimes get a little drunk or sex focused like last night and you leave it wherever. This way, you always know where it is. You can leave it on your nightstand."

"But what if I'm at your place?" Ciaran asked.

"That's why you have two." He handed Ciaran the second package with the same jelly substance, but this time it was in a different case than the plastic one the first one was in. "The gel is inside, but the box I had made in Albania. It's for your other *rodulé*."

Ciaran smiled mysteriously. "What other *dulé*?" he asked innocently.

Chris smiled back. "The *dulé* you keep hidden at the top of your bookshelf that you don't want anyone to know you have." Ciaran laughed. "From time in Uganda or South Africa?"

"Yes. Uganda. They don't use *rodulés* there, but they made one for both of us, from the bark of a jackfruit tree and the feather of a blue Turano. It's really powerful. I haven't touched it since I got back."

"Yes, it is. It vibrated in my hand," Chris said.

"That's impossible. You aren't a Magus," Ciaran said factually.

"That's what I thought," Chris said. "I've touched your *dulé* dozens of times, and it feels like a regular stick to me. But that one... I don't know. It's like it wanted me to know something. I got a little scared and put it back. But the box was made for it so you can stop using it as a bookend. The carvings on the side of the case say in Ugandan 'White Warrior.' For what they used to call you and Sean."

Ciaran smiled. "What amazing and thoughtful gifts. Thank you." They kissed, and Ciaran said, "I love you."

Chris said it back, "And I love you forever. And three days after that."

They kissed again and opened up the last present from Grace, matching Christmas sweaters, which made Ciaran laugh remembering Chris's blunder the night before. Ciaran's sweater was black with a large white C on it with small white dragons along the border of a starry night sky. Chris's sweater was white with a large black C on it with little black trees along the border and an open sky and clouds. Ironically, they heard Grace's voice boom from downstairs.

"RISE AND SHINE! TIME TO GET MOVING!" she called loudly.

Ciaran smiled. "Ready to really meet my real mum?"

<hr>

They took showers individually and went downstairs to help prepare for the Christmas dinner. Chris spent the day with Diana in the kitchen, mostly because Chloé snuck out earlier in the day to go into the office and she needed assistance. Ciaran, Rob, and Quentin were being directed by Grace on what to clean and how to rearrange the living room. At 4:45 p.m., Diana sent everyone upstairs to clean up, change, and not to come back down until 6 p.m. sharp for dinner. Chris and Ciaran opted to wear their new Grace-made sweaters instead of their outfits, mostly Chris's idea so he could show how much he appreciated it. That made Ciaran laugh at Chris's faux pas all over again.

At six, they were the first down and were greeted at the bottom of the stairs by Diana, who wore a burgundy dress with a black ribbon with white stars in her hair that twinkled. She walked them to the parlor where Quentin, in a shirt of the same burgundy fabric as Diana and a black tie with white, twinkling stars, met them and escorted them to their seats. The kitchen table was enlarged to seat at least twenty guests and placed in the center of the parlor where all the furniture had vanished. It had a burgundy runner and three black candle centerpieces. White, black, and burgundy candles floated above the table, providing enough light.

There was already a guest there, an older woman with curly black hair pulled into a loose bun. Chris was wondering why her gray eyes and sly smile were so familiar when Ciaran yelled out her name.

"Mrs. Downs, hello," Ciaran said in surprise, walking right to her. "I don't know if you remember me…"

She smiled warmly. "Ciaran, of course. You were one of Darragh's closest and dearest friends." She stood up and kissed both his cheeks. "Your mum invited me to spend Christmas with you all."

Ciaran said, "I would like you to meet Christopher Jennings, my partner. Chris, this is Davina Downs, Darragh's mother."

"It's so nice to meet you," Davina said.

"Likewise," Chris said politely and also kissed both cheeks.

The front door opened, and they all turned to the hallway. Ted walked in with Elodie, his son Teddy, and daughter Victoré in his arms. Elodie wore a forest green sweetheart chiffon lace three-quarter length maternity dress, and two-year-old Victoré wore a matching babydoll dress. Elodie's white-blonde hair was parted down the middle and lay straight down to her waistline. Ted wore a black dress shirt, black pants, and a forest green dinner jacket, and five-year-old Teddy looked like a miniature version of his father.

As they came into the parlor, Chris turned to Ciaran and whispered, "Best friend mode fucking activated! Whoa. Your sister-in-law is… *whoa*."

Ciaran whispered back, "Do. Not. Flirt. With. Her."

Chris whispered, "No promises." He walked ahead to greet them.

Chris held out his hand to greet Elodie first in French. *"Madame Elodie, quelle joie de vous rencontrer!"* He bowed his head and kissed her hand.

Elodie beamed. *"Un français charmant, comme c'est mag-nifique!"* She said some other words in fast French, which he responded to in equally fast French, and they both smiled and laughed.

"Okay, okay, enough of the charming my wife," Ted said. "Back off, mate." He gave Chris a playful shove and then a hug.

Ciaran greeted Elodie with a kiss on the cheek. "Hello, Elodie. Beautiful as always."

"*Merci.* It will be nice to have you around," she said in her heavy French accent. "Okay, stand together," she demanded of Ciaran and Chris, which they did. She touched her heart. "Ah, *mon coeur.* So handsome and beautiful you two are together. *Ardenti* looks good on you. You wear it so well," she purred. They looked at each other and smiled.

The door opened again, and Alastair walked in. "Apologies for my tardiness."

Ted rolled his eyes. "It's 6:03. I think you're forgiven."

Alastair Beals was tall and thin and had the face of a Beals, but his hair and eyes were brown. He wore a gray suit with a black cloak and stylish glasses. He walked up to Chris and gave him a stiff handshake. "Commoner Ranger Christopher Jennings. Very nice to meet you. I am Minister Alastair Beals. How do you do?"

Chris mimicked his seriousness and shook his hand firmly. "Very well, Minister, and yourself?"

"Good, good." Alastair turned to Ted and said, "Happy Christmas," and tried to shake his hand. Ted slapped it away and gave him a hug. Ciaran came over and also gave Alastair a hug right on top of him and Ted. Alastair looked uncomfortable, but he reached his arms up and returned the three-way hug with two pats, then dropped his arms. "Right," he mumbled.

"I thought you were coming with Sean and your mum," Ciaran said.

"I had some last-minute Magi business to attend to," he said evasively. Then he moved away to greet everyone else in the room.

Chris said to the Beals brothers, "You didn't tell me you had a cousin with a perpetual stick up his bum. He's going to be fun to fuck with." Ted and Ciaran laughed.

The door opened again, and Hamish and Sean entered with an older heavyset woman holding a cane and wearing a gray dress to match her mostly gray hair with some red strands. She went for the first seat at the table and turned to the room.

"Well. C'mon, greet your aunt," she said in a demanding voice.

Diana, Quentin, Ted, Elodie, and Ciaran got in line, and Chris joined to stand next to Ciaran. Hamish took that time to go upstairs and find Grace while Sean took Victoré from Ted and went to play with the kids. One by one, Aunt Elspeth greeted them with a snarky comment: "Diana, you're too thin; eat something. And why aren't you with child yet?"; "Mr. James, lovely home. When are you going to start filling up my niece so you can fill these walls with children?"; "The punk phase is over, Theodore. Cut your hair and put on a suit, for God's sakes."; "Elodie, your beauty shines brighter every time I see you. Don't lose it, or you'll be fat and old like me."

When it was Ciaran's turn, he kissed his aunt and then turned to introduce Chris. "Aunt Elspeth, this is—"

She cut him off. "Yes, yes, the boyfriend, I heard. Well. Stand up straight. Let me look at you."

She put the glasses that were around her neck on her face and looked Chris up and down before he had a chance to talk. "Well," Elspeth started. "You're certainly handsome enough. Give me your hand," she demanded, and he did. "Oh good, strong hands. Calluses mean you aren't afraid to get your hands dirty. You're definitely a man if I ever met one."

"Um, yes, yes I am. It is a pleasure to meet you, Aunt Elspeth," Chris said.

"Hmpf." She let his hand go, put her hands in her lap, and peered at him over the top of her glasses. "How is Ciaran treating you?"

"Very well, ma'am. I couldn't ask for anything better."

"Good. Make sure you return the favor. Beals men are libidinous in the bedroom, so you make sure you can keep up," she said sternly.

Chris kept a straight face while Ciaran smiled, and everyone else around him stifled a laugh. "I will do my best, ma'am."

"Good, good." She turned to Ciaran. "He's alright. Good choice."

Ciaran said, "Thank you, Aunt Elspeth. It means a lot coming from you." He hugged her again.

"Oh, go on," she chided, but secretly Ciaran was her favorite Beals.

Rob and Chloé had walked into the parlor at that moment, and Aunt Elspeth called after them, "Oy! The unmarried couple. Still living in sin, are you?" she chastised them. Rob reluctantly made his way over to greet her with Chloé at his side.

Chris and Ciaran took that opportunity to slowly move away to the middle of the room to where Ted, Sean, Diana, and Quentin were still laughing at their aunt's comments.

"Shut up," Ciaran told them, and they started laughing harder, including Chris.

Mr. and Mrs. Beals came into the room. They wore silver together, Grace in a silver evening gown and Hamish in a silver Magi robes with a matching hat. Diana moved to the front of the room and rang the dinner bell. They all took their places, with Quentin at one end of the table and Mr. Beals at the other. Quentin and Diana stood up.

Quentin said, "We want to thank you all for celebrating our first Christmas as the James family in our home. It has been a tough few years, but there is so much to celebrate, so much good news at the table, so let us hold on to these precious moments. Cheers to us."

Everyone followed Quentin in raising their glasses and said, "Cheers!"

Diana then said, "And now we present your dinner." She clapped her hands once, and the food appeared on the table. Chris flinched, and his eyes went wide, and Chloé noticed.

Diana walked to the other side of the table to her father and handed him the carving knife. Hamish in turn walked all the way back up to Quentin and handed it to him. "It's your house. It's your first carve, son."

Quentin smiled and began to carve the turkey while they exchanged sides of roast potatoes, stuffing, Yorkshire pudding, cottage pie, roasted veggies, and a crab casserole that Chris made. Everyone morphed into side conversations with Chris and Ciaran sitting next to Davina on Quentin's side of the table, across from Diana, Chloé, Rob, and Sean.

Davina asked, "So when was the last time you've seen Selma and Andres?"

"It's been a while, over a year now, but we're going to hang out with them this weekend in Brighton," said Ciaran.

"That's wonderful," she said. "It's so nice when they are in town. They come to visit, which is nice."

"Ciaran, I didn't realize you and Darragh were close," Quentin said. "She was my commander and trained me in the military."

"Yeah, we were schoolmates of the same year and shared the same circle of friends."

"That's interesting," Chloé said. "For a while, we thought it was Ted who fancied Darragh."

Ted heard his name from the other end of the table. "Me and Darragh? Nah. She was an amazing girl, but she was too busy causing mischief with Selma and Magna to worry about me."

"Did you say Magna? As in Magna Keystone?" Diana asked curiously.

"The very same," Ted said. "They were the biggest pranksters at Campus before Shane and Sean got there."

Diana and Chloé exchanged looks of shock. "I don't believe it. She is a stickler for the rules."

"Yeah, I've had one encounter with Magna the Maleficent, and she is scary." Quentin shuddered.

Alastair chimed in, "I supposed she gave it all up when she left Campus and wanted to be taken seriously. That's what you do, anyway. Darragh did the same, becoming a disciplined *Veneficus*, despite her colorful days at Campus."

"Darragh was always going to become a Magi Enforcer," Ciaran said defensively. "That didn't change her sense of humor one bit, nor was it marred by her colorful Campus days."

"Well, you would say that; you fancied her," Ted said to Ciaran, amused.

"Oh my God!" exclaimed Diana.

Chris turned to Ciaran with a smile. "Really?"

"Who did he fancy? Darragh?" Grace asked from the other end of the table as Davina giggled.

"Okay, firstly," Ciaran said loudly. "We were friends. Mostly."

"Come to think of it, I did catch you two snogging in a classroom in my last year," Alastair said, happy to contribute some gossip.

"OH MY GOD!" Diana exclaimed again.

Rob's mouth dropped. "You snogged Darragh!??"

"Is that true?" Grace asked.

"Alright, alright, settle down." Ciaran used his stern voice. "We... sort of... went together as fifteen-year-olds very briefly. Extremely briefly." The table went crazy with surprise, shock, and laughter.

Chris shook his head with a smile. "Ciaran, you've been keeping secrets, haven't you?"

"I told you, Ciaran doesn't kiss and tell unless you drag it out of him," Ted said.

"Alright already, you can all stop now," said Ciaran at the continued noises of surprise. "Obviously, it didn't go any-where. It really started out as a joke; she was trying to hook Selma and Andres up, and she asked me to go with her to spy on their first outing together but to pretend we were on a date as well. They got on great, but, of course, Darragh being Darragh giggled the whole time, and we got kicked out." Everyone laughed, remembering how silly Darragh was. "So on the way back we got to talking about how everyone around us is hooking up, and we should just hook up too so we don't feel left out and I agreed." Ciaran started going pink.

"So how did it end?" Sean asked. "Because literally, you could have been Mrs. Down's son-in-law. No offense, Chris." Davina had a large smile.

"No offense taken. I'm quite enjoying these parts of my Ciaran's life I had no idea of," said Chris. "So how did it end, Ciaran?"

"Well, it kind of fizzled out on its own months later. Truthfully, it might have been more me. After coming face-to-face with my first dragon, I began to be obsessed with them, even more obsessed than before, if that was possible. The school year ended, and we didn't talk all holiday. We got back to Campus, and we resumed a friendship like it never happened."

"Wait, what dragon?" Rob asked.

"Oh right, you thought you were the only ones having adventures at Campus, innit?" Ted said smugly.

Chloé answered, "I do know there were several mysterious transport stations at our Campus unknown by Magi officials. And I know Ted, Alastair, Magna, and Darragh had a hand in closing some of them, which was how you got special recognition from Scholarly. It's all in the books at the Council."

Ted corrected her. "No, Darragh had a hand in closing them. I just went along for the ride. But it did propel me into my current career. I realized how much I liked solving mysteries."

"Why did I not know about any of this?" Grace said. "Campus was not that exciting when Hamish and I attended."

"It was," Hamish countered. "You were just a stickler for the rules. And a nerd." Grace's mouth dropped in shock as her children giggled. She playfully hit her husband, who kissed her on the cheek.

Chris asked, "So did you date Selma too, your other best friend?"

"No," Ciaran said flatly.

"Ha!" Ted exclaimed. "Not for lack of trying!" Davina giggled again.

"How could I when she was enamored by the great Ted Beals?" Ciaran retorted.

Ted laughed. "She was not."

"Are you kidding? If Darragh hadn't turned Selma's attention to Andres, your children would be brown instead of white and blonde!"

They all laughed except Elodie. "Well, it's a good thing she did because he is my perfect mate," she said jealously and held onto his arm.

Chris leaned over to her and said something in French, which made her giggle, and she responded in French, which made him blush. She then said in English, "I would love to visit you in Albania."

Ted laughed. "Oh really! You've never shown any interest in going to Albania with me in the past."

"That's because you go for the dragons. I'm going to spend time with Christopher," she said simply.

Elodie let go of Ted's arm and held onto Chris's, who smiled and said to her. "*Je serais honoré.* Ciaran and I would love to have you there."

"So, do you guys live together?" Sean asked.

Chris said, "No, not technically."

He looked at Ciaran, who said, "We might as well; we're at each other's flat every day."

"We've exchanged keys, so his place is mine and mine is his," Chris said.

"Why would you need to exchange keys if you both are Magus?" Chloé asked.

But her question was ignored by Chris and Ciaran, and not heard by anyone else, as Quentin asked a question. "Why not just get a place together?"

They looked at each other. Chris said, "It's an option that has come up before. But Ciaran really wants to build a home right near or in the woods, and I work in the same forest that

I spent my whole life in, so it doesn't sound as appealing to me. Except for the quiet."

"And Chris lives in a duplex with his sisters, nephew, and young niece, and they all rely on him for so much. I don't really want to take him from all that."

"Sounds like you both need to make some sacrifices to make it work," Davina said. They nodded and looked at each other again.

"Just make sure you get a two-bedroom, two-bath flat. The last thing you want is a place with one bathroom," Rob said seriously.

Ciaran looked at Rob quizzically. "Why would we need two bedrooms?"

"To spread out, of course. Or if one of you is okay with turning the living room into a bedroom for the other. But that would be awkward." He laughed at his joke.

Chris said, "But we would share the one bedroom."

"Well, that's stupid. You're a little too old for bunk beds, innit?" He laughed again.

"Are you really this dense?" Sean said incredulously.

"What?" Rob asked in confusion.

Chloé half whispered to him, "They're together, Rob."

"Yeah, I can see that. They came together," he whispered back.

She tried again. "No, sweetheart. They are *together*, together. Partners. A couple." She gave him a look.

Rob laughed her off, then looked at Ciaran and Chris, who stared at him seriously. His smile waned quickly, and he looked at Sean to the left of him, who raised both eyebrows and nodded. Rob's face fell to a shock, and he quickly drank water, then choked on it. Sean and Chloé both tapped his back until his coughing subsided.

He was completely red when he looked at them and said, "Guess you'll only need one bedroom then. But still... two bathrooms..."

Ciaran smiled. "Thanks, Robert, that's good advice. Chris does have more hair products than I do." They laughed.

Rob leaned over to Chloé and tried to whisper, "Was I the only one who didn't know?"

Chloé, Chris, Ciaran, Sean, Diana, and Quentin said in unison, "YES."

"Oh," Rob said sheepishly and went red again. He drank his cup of water but more slowly.

Davina snorted a laugh. "Oh my stars, I just adore this family." She started laughing harder, which made them all laugh, including Rob.

Aunt Elspeth called from down the table, "What's the joke down there? I like a good joke too." Which only made them laugh harder.

CHAPTER 27

Unregistered Commoner

Diana, who noted everyone was done with dinner, clapped her hands. The plates vanished, and dessert appeared on the table—lemon meringue pie that Elodie brought, chocolate mousse that Chris made last minute, cherry pie that Grace made, peach cobbler that Aunt Elspeth brought along, white frosted cake that Diana made, and homemade baklava that Clarissa sent along with them. Chris's eyes went wide again at the appearing, disappearing, and reappearing food, but then he quickly recovered.

Chloé noticed again and was deeply suspicious. "So, Chris, are either of your parents Magi?"

"No, they were not," he said simply.

"Oh, so you're like me then: a Commoner born, Magi discovered?" she asked.

Ted intervened. "Hey, Chris, why don't you get on that piano over there and sing something?"

Chris smiled thankfully at Ted and stood up to go over to the piano. He played with the keys a bit, then started playing "The Scientist" by Coldplay.

Sean slapped his own forehead playfully. "Ooooh, now I get it. You like Coldplay. No wonder Ciaran likes you. Because you are literally the opposite of him in every single way except that."

His brothers and Diana laughed. Ciaran went to stand by the piano and put his hands on his shoulders as he played the tune, then Diana and Elodie did as well, each sitting on opposite sides of him on the bench. He started singing the first verse, and the ladies joined him in the chorus.

When it was done, others in the room clapped. But Ted said, "Um… yeah, okay, but I meant Christmas carols, you dung head."

"Don't use that kind of language, Ted," Grace said disapprovingly. "Chris, dear, play what you want. It was lovely."

Chris played a couple of Christmas songs, and they all went over to the piano to join in except Aunt Elspeth who had refused to move her seat since she came in and Chloé who was thoughtful. When Quentin walked past her to use the bathroom, she took her chance and followed him out of the parlor.

She waited for him to come out and grabbed his arm in the hallway. "Can I talk to you for a moment?" she whispered and half dragged him farther down the hall, closer to the kitchen, without waiting for a response.

"Ow owww! What!?" he said in annoyance.

Chloé took a deep breath. "Chris is a Commoner. And no, not a Commoner with the *Vis* discovered in his bloodline like me. Just a regular Commoner."

"Come off it, Chloé," he said skeptically.

He tried to walk away, but she grabbed his arm back. "I'm serious. I've been watching him all day. He's nervous and jittery around magic, like it's all new to him. He won't answer any questions about his background—"

Quentin cut her off. "We told you his mother died around this time, and he doesn't want to talk about it."

"Okay, but he doesn't act like a Magi at all; just someone who has been around Magi. And maybe studied them."

"Maybe he's just an *Absentem Magi*," Quentin said.

"Quentin, an *Absentem Magi* is someone from a Magi family who has the *Vis* in their DNA, but for whatever reason is unable to do magic," she said impatiently. "Do you know what we call non-magical people who grew up in non-magical families? Commoners!"

Quentin opened his mouth and then closed it. He looked at her for a moment, then said, "And you don't think the Council knows."

She shook her head. "No, I don't. I would have remembered his name on the registry at the office. And I never thought to look for it because we all assumed he was a Magi. Which means..." She breathed out air.

"Chloé..." Quentin warned.

"Do you know how much trouble any of our families could get into if anyone found out? My family and yours? The Beals? The Livingstons? Davina!" she blurted out in a harsh whisper. "You're a mercenary Commander in training. Your wife is a secret Magi Enforcer. I mean, your father-in-law is a top Council official, and Alastair is the Council's senior coordinator. And you're hosting an unregistered Commoner and using the *Vis* in front of him. At best, we could all be stripped of our titles, at worst, thrown into Claustra!"

Quentin held up his hand. He was used to Chloé's hysteria. "Okay. We don't know for sure, so don't go making a scene in front of everyone. No more questions to Chris. When everyone leaves, I will ask them what his status is point blank, and whatever he says, we believe them, and we move on."

"And if he is a Commoner?" Chloé asked.

"Then we deal with it as a family," Quentin said definitively.

Rob walked over to them in the hallway. "I was looking for you, Clo. What's up?" He looked back and forth between the two of them.

"Nothing," Quentin said and walked away.

He looked at Chloé, who mumbled, "work stuff" and led him back into the parlor. She sat back as everyone enjoyed the rest of the night, watching. Waiting.

When Teddy and Victoré fell asleep under the piano, Ted said, "Well, it's way past Teddy's bedtime, so we're going to head out." He lifted him up to hold him as he slept and gave one armed hugs to everyone. Elodie picked up Victoré, too.

Ted walked over to Chris and Ciaran. "You'll be in Kingsbridge soon, then?" he asked them knowingly.

"Yes," answered Ciaran. "I told Dad we were spending the next couple of days with them before we head to Brighton on New Year's Day."

Ted nodded. "Call me if you need me to come over for support." He gave them both hugs and said goodbyes to everyone else.

After Ted's family and Davina left, Grace and Diana went into the kitchen to clean up while Hamish, Quentin, Rob, Alastair, Sean, Chris, and Ciaran got into a heated debate about FIFA. Chloé sat quietly in the corner, biting her lip.

As the men got louder, Aunt Elspeth slammed her cane on the floor, and a *Silencio* spell hit everyone at once for the next thirty seconds. "Enough! You would have thought you had investments tied to it. Shut up already. Now, who is going to take me home? Not that troublesome son of mine, of course."

Alastair tried not to roll his eyes, always the picture of decorum. "Are you ready, Mum?"

"My dear, I've been ready since the last of the cherry pie. Grab the crab bake, and let's go." Alastair followed instructions and escorted his mother out.

Sean looked at his watch. "Well, this party is over. Guess it's time to find another one." He winked at Ciaran, who shook his head and smiled. They all knew Sean was going to end up at a bar in Myrddin to pick up a Mage.

Hamish said, "Yes, it is nearly midnight. I'll grab Grace." He went into the kitchen to find his wife as Sean gave hugs and left.

Grace came out of the kitchen. "Diana is going to finish up." She hugged Quentin. "This was simply divine. Thank you for hosting Christmas this year. I'm so happy to have you as my son now."

Quentin smiled, thinking about how hard it was to convince her to agree that he and Diana could do it and not screw it up. "Thanks for coming, Mum." She hugged him tighter.

Grace went around and hugged Rob and Ciaran, then hugged Chris. "It was lovely to finally meet you. Ciaran says you're coming by the house to stay for a few days, yes?"

"Absolutely looking forward to it." Chris kissed both her cheeks and hugged her again.

After the parents left, Rob, Quentin, Chris, and Ciaran opened a bottle of whiskey and mingled around the piano, talking. Chloé was trying to catch Quentin's eye, but he purposely ignored her. After a while, she stood up and went into the hallway and called, "Diana, can you come here a moment?"

When Diana came into the room, she took her hand and led her to stand in front of the men. "Quentin, it's time," she said. He gave her an exasperated look.

"Time for what?" Rob asked.

Everyone looked from Quentin to Chloé. Quentin took a deep breath and sat up, looking at Ciaran. "So. Chloé has a theory that she brought to my attention earlier, and if you don't want to talk about it right now, which I completely understand, it's important to know that no matter what, we support—"

Chloé cut him off. "Oh, for god's sake, Quentin! Ciaran, is Chris a Commoner or not!?"

No one spoke as Ciaran's heart dropped. Diana's eyes went wide, and she looked at Chloé instead of at Ciaran. Ciaran looked over at Chris, who stared back.

After a few moments, Ciaran said, without breaking eye contact with his lover, "Yes."

Diana put both hands to her mouth and turned her back to the room.

"Oh Ciaran. Ciaran," Chloé groaned. She ran her fingers through her hair furiously. Quentin sat there stoic, not sure what to say or think.

"I don't get it," Rob said. "We all know he comes from a Commoner family. So do you." He pointed at Chloé.

"No, Robert," Chloé said, "Chris is not a Magus at all. Chris is an unregistered Commoner. Which means Ciaran broke Magi law, broke the law of secrecy, knowingly. And we all broke it unknowingly by Ciaran bringing him among us, since we were using our *Vis* around him. This is bad, Rob, really, really bad."

Rob shook his head. "Well, we just won't tell, right? It stays right here in this room, okay?"

Quentin spoke. "No, that can't happen, can it, Chloé? You made sure of that, bringing Diana in on it." He looked at her sadly.

Ciaran broke his gaze from Chris and looked at Diana. She slowly turned around, her hands still on her mouth and her eyes wide. She kept shaking her head vigorously.

"What does Diana have to do with it?" Rob asked. "She doesn't work for the Council."

Diana let out a moan through her hands, and her eyes welled up in tears. She knelt down to the floor in a crouch. Quentin was still looking at Chloé, who avoided his gaze.

Rob was still confused at all the looks around him. "WHAT!?" he bellowed.

Then it dawned on Ciaran. "Oh." He gave his sister a sad smile. "You're pledged to the Magi Secrecy Unit. I see."

Diana looked at him as her tears fell, then nodded. Ciaran nodded back. She sat on the floor completely and covered her face with her hands. Ciaran got up and walked to the nearest window and stared out of it, whiskey still in his hand.

Rob was still confused. "So what does that mean? She doesn't *have* to tell, right, Diana?"

Diana let out another moan through her hands. Quentin answered for her. "She is bound by her *Vis*, Rob. If she hears it, she is obligated and mandated to tell no matter what. And Chloé made sure she was in the room to hear the infraction. So now that Diana knows, she has twenty-four hours from this moment to report it on her own, or the psychosis will begin. And she will descend into madness."

Chris's mouth dropped along with Rob's. "Ho. Lee. Shit."

He drank the rest of his whiskey in one gulp and walked over to stand next to Ciaran to stare out the window as well, watching the rain continue to fall out of the dark sky.

Rob was shocked and angry. "But ... how could ... why'd ... How the fuck could you do that, Chloé!?"

Ciaran turned from the window. "Don't, Robert. It's not her fault. It's no one's fault but my own." He looked at his sister. "Diana, do what you need to do."

Diana got off the floor and came over to him. "We'll go together, okay? We'll go directly to Grandminister Graham and talk to him. It's your first ever infraction; it should be fine." She reached up to touch his face. "I won't let anything happen to you."

Ciaran touched his little sister too. "And I won't let anything happen to you, either. Tomorrow morning, first thing, we go. And we should tell Dad; he should be there."

"We'll call him in the morning and tell him to meet us there. Not Mum, though, she won't like this at all," Diana said. Ciaran nodded, and they hugged, her small body wrapped around his.

When she let go, Ciaran turned to Chris and saw the worry on his face. He touched his neck and kissed him for the first time in front of his family. He took his hand and entwined their fingers and led him from the parlor as everyone's eyes were on them.

At the doorway, Chris turned around. "I'm so sorry if I caused anyone issues or if my presence here has gotten anyone in trouble. I want you all to know, Ciaran did not throw his life away on a whim or fleeting romance. I am in love with him. And whatever happens to him, happens to me, too."

He turned to Ciaran and said, "We stay and fight."

Ciaran nodded. He gave one last look to the room, who were all watching them, then took Chris upstairs without speaking. They lay on the bed fully clothed, holding onto each other, listening to the fight that exploded without them.

CHAPTER 28

Ciaran's Little Problem

As soon as Chris and Ciaran left the parlor, Rob yelled, "How could you do that, Chloé!? How *could* you!?"

"Rob, I don't think you understand how bad this is," she started, running her hands through her hair again. "I work for the Council, in the law division, and so does half your family. Quentin is Magi royalty and a NV commander-in-training. We could all be thrown into Claustra just for all the magic we performed in the last forty-eight hours in front of him, forget losing our jobs!"

"Oh, okay, so it's better that just Ciaran end up in Claustra, innit?" said Rob heatedly.

"That's not fair! I did not break the law," Chloé stated.

Quentin interjected, "And I told you I was going to handle it."

"No, what you were going to do was let them get away with it a little while longer until they were ready to come forward," she said to him.

"And why would that be so bad!?" Quentin said, also raising his voice in anger.

"Exactly!" Rob yelled. "And I heard Aunt Grace say they were going over there soon. I bet they were going to tell them then."

"We couldn't take that risk," Chloé said simply.

Rob got louder. "No, YOU couldn't take that risk because YOU always have to be in the right!"

"What is that supposed to mean?" she cried.

"That everything is not black or white, good or bad. There is a lot of gray in this world, and sometimes you just have to be okay in the gray," Quentin said.

"I can't believe you two are ganging up on me like this! I did nothing wrong!" Chloé turned to Diana. "You know I did nothing wrong, don't you, Diana?"

Diana looked away with tears falling from her eyes and her arms crossed, furious at her best friend, too, for setting her up that way.

"No, Chloé," Rob said angrily. "You did *everything* wrong. You forced my cousin to choose between the love for her brother and her own sanity! You put Quentin in the most compromising position; then you took the decision out of his hands. You keep talking about how bad this is for us, but what you really mean is how bad this is for *you*, and your ambition with the Magi Council." Her mouth dropped at his words as he continued, "You were selfish, uncaring, inconsiderate, a pompous, little know-it-all witch and I'm sick of this shit. It never changes with you! It doesn't matter who gets hurt in the process, does it? As long as you get to be right. Well, I'll tell you right now, if anything, ANYTHING happens to either of my cousins because of your actions here tonight, just know you've lost me, too, for good!"

He stormed out of the room and out the front door, Wisp'ing on the top step, leaving Chloé stunned and frozen in place.

Quentin walked closer to her. "He didn't mean it. Just give him a moment to cool off."

Tears fell from her eyes, and she quickly wiped them away. Then she went upstairs and closed her bedroom door.

Quentin walked over to Diana, who was still sitting near the window. He pulled her to stand and hugged her. She said on his shoulder, "I've changed my mind. We have to let Dad know, now. Maybe Ted, too. Something tells me he knows already."

He nodded. "I'll take care of it. You go upstairs and get some rest." He kissed her forehead and said, "Hey, did I tell you how exquisitely beautiful you looked tonight?" He smiled at her, and she smiled through her tears. They kissed lips, and then she went upstairs.

When Quentin was alone, he conjured his hawk *Amina* with a message to Ted:

"We have a little problem. Meet me outside your flat in two minutes."

He waited a moment, grabbed his coat, then Wisp'd to the doorstep, just as Ted opened the door. "Get in here; it's freezing!" Ted commanded.

Quentin came inside and told Ted what had just happened. Ted started pacing in his living room, thoughtful. Quentin had to ask, "Did you know?"

Ted stopped pacing and looked at him. "Are you asking me as a Magi military official or as my brother?" Quentin cocked his head to the side and gave him a "come off it" look. Ted started pacing again. "Of course, I knew. But I wasn't turning my brother in. Plus, I like Chris. I get why Ciaran did what he did. I mean, you saw him, got to know him. He's a great guy."

He stopped pacing. "Let's go to Kingsbridge." Not waiting for a response from Quentin, he conjured his Barnaby lion *Amina* with the message:

"Dad, meet Quentin and me at the backdoor in five minutes. It's urgent. Don't tell Mum."

It was enough time for Ted to tell Elodie he'd be right back, put on shoes, and grab a jacket. Then he and Quentin Wisp'd, ending up in the garden together. The backdoor was open, and they ran inside to get out of the cold rain.

Hamish was sitting at the kitchen table. "It's a good thing she went straight to bed, and I was downstairs having a cuppa. What's wrong?" he asked.

Quentin again explained what had happened at the house. Hamish didn't say anything, looking solemn. When he ended with Rob storming off, Hamish turned to his eldest son. "Ted, you've spent a couple of days with them. Is it real between them? Lasting?"

He nodded. "It's as real as me and Elodie, as Quentin and Diana. The real deal, Dad."

Hamish sighed, then stood up. "Go home and get some rest, the both of you. Graham gets in sometime between 6 a.m. and 6:30 a.m., but we'll show up at 7 a.m. to give him some time to settle in. He'll do what he can to keep Ciaran out of Claustra, I'm sure of it. Not a word of this to your mother."

They shook hands and Wisp'd back to London to their respective homes.

When Quentin returned to his home, all was quiet. As Quentin began up the stairs and turned onto the second landing to go to his room, he heard a voice at the top of the third-floor landing.

"Quentin," Ciaran called.

Quentin looked up at him. "Hey."

"Where did you go?"

He raised his chin up, hoping it wouldn't make Ciaran upset. "I went to talk to Ted, and then we talked with your dad."

But Ciaran nodded. "Is my father angry with me?"

"More concerned than anything else," Quentin said. Ciaran nodded again. "He said he will meet us at the Council office at 7 a.m. to talk to the Grandminister. We're all going to be there to support you, Diana and myself, Rob, Ted, and I suspect Chloé will want to come as well."

Ciaran was thoughtful. "Can you do me a favor? Can you stay here with Chris instead? I don't want him here by himself, waiting. And if it doesn't turn out as planned, well, between you, Sean, and Rob, I think you'll have a more level head about it."

Quentin understood. "Sure, Ciaran. I can do that."

He sighed. "I'm so sorry I put you in this position, endangering your livelihood, your family, your career."

Quentin shrugged. "I'm sorry that I put you and Lucy in the position to smuggle me and an illegal dragon out of the country to the Reserve to get away from my mother at fourteen years old."

Ciaran chuckled. "Did I tell you Rehoboth had a daughter? She left for the mountains for like five years and came back with a baby dragon. We named her Dory. She's like a lost fish floundering around."

Quentin smiled. "Awesome. I'm happy to hear that she's doing well, despite her disappearing acts."

"We think she'll stay this time. She has something to live for."

"I think we all know what that's like, innit?" he said to Ciaran, and they nodded.

Ciaran stood up. "Thanks, again." They went to their rooms.

Chris was still lying on the bed with his clothes on when Ciaran came in. "Was that Quentin or Rob?" Chris asked.

"Quentin," Ciaran said, as he gently closed the door behind him. "He saw Ted and told my dad who is going to meet me at the Council office in the morning. Rob probably went to go find Sean. So everyone knows now."

Chris caught how he said "Me" and not "Us", and immediately sat up. "I'm coming with you," he said defensively.

"No, you are not," Ciaran stated. "For one, I don't think you are physically able to get past the guards seeing how you are, in fact, an unregistered Commoner. And two, if you do, they will immediately detain and *abscondo* you. So no, you're staying here."

Chris ignored his concerns. "I'm going with you, Ciaran. Even if that means standing outside and waiting, I'm going with you. Don't try to stop me."

Ciaran opened his mouth, then closed it. He said, "Okay."

Chris was ready to continue arguing and was thrown off by Ciaran's response. "I mean it!"

"Okay."

"Don't try anything on me. I'm going."

"Okay."

Chris lay back down on the bed. "Take off your clothes," Ciaran demanded.

Chris smiled. "Need to expel some nervous energy, huh?"

Ciaran took off his sweater and shirt. "No. I don't have any nervous energy. I just want to make love to you."

Chris watched Ciaran get completely naked first, his erection pointing straight ahead. Then he stood up, took off all his clothes, and sat down on the edge of the bed. Ciaran stood between his legs and kissed him.

As Ciaran grabbed Chris's cock, Chris said, "You forgot to say the incantation."

Ciaran kissed him hard and said, "Fuck 'em."

He stretched across Chris's body, using his knees to pull his thighs apart, calling for the lube to float over.

Quentin got dressed for bed while telling Diana about the conversation with Ted, with Hamish, and then with Ciaran just a few minutes ago.

"So you're going to stay here with Chris while the rest of us go?" she asked.

"Yes. I'll keep him as occupied as I can until you all get back."

"And if we all don't come back?" Diana asked quietly.

Quentin didn't answer. He got into the bed and wrapped his arms around her. After a few moments, she said, "Where do you think Rob went?"

"Probably to Sean's."

She nodded. "He said some harsh words to Chloé tonight. But he's not wrong. You explained it perfectly. Sometimes we just have to live within the gray."

"Well, Chloé doesn't know how to do that—"

"Shhhh!!!" Diana cried. "What... what is *that*?"

They listened to someone crying, or sounding like they were in pain, deep groaning. Quentin was about to get out of bed to check it out when Diana grabbed his arm and started giggling.

"It's them, Quentin. It's Ciaran and Chris!"

Quentin listened again ,and then he realized what he was hearing was them having sex. "Oh no oh no oh God!" He closed his hands over his ears, and Diana laughed harder.

"It's quite passionate if you listen closely," she said, smiling.

"As if we have a choice not to listen!" he exclaimed.

Quentin lay back down with Diana, and they looked at each other as the moans got louder, then started laughing.

Rob opened the door, already knowing he was sleeping in the room on the second floor and not with Chloé. He was still pissed. He found Sean at Wanderlous and told him what had happened. Sean told him, "I'll meet you at home at daybreak. Ciaran's not walking in there without me."

Rob was distracted upon entering the home, but as soon as he started up the stairs, he heard them. He stopped mid-stairway and paused; his mouth opened. He had never heard two people have sex before—Magi were quiet about that sort of thing—but knew that's what they were doing, and doing it loudly. At the door to the room directly below them, he paused again. Quentin's room door opened, and he peered out. They looked at each other and started snickering.

Quentin said, "A part of me wants to tell them to quit it, but a bigger part of me, sadly, is considering it could be the last time for a while, so let them have at it."

Rob nodded. "Plus, it's probably driving Chloé bonkers being next door, hearing it all firsthand. They can have at it all night, just to spite her."

Quentin laughed. "Where were you?"

"With Sean," Rob replied over the ah ah ah's that were happening and the thumping of the headboard against the wall above them. "He's equally pissed, but more concerned about Ciaran's well-being. He's going with us tomorrow."

"That's good because—" Quentin was cut off by a long and loud roar. There was a brief pause, and the thumping continued.

"Bloody fucking hell," Quentin said as they both looked up. "We're silencing our ears tonight."

Rob shook his head and looked at Quentin. "On second thought, I think I will sleep on the sitting room floor."

He magicked the pillows and blanket from the room and had it follow him downstairs while Quentin closed his room door.

<hr>

Chris and Ciaran barely slept. They kept waking up and looking at each other, afraid that one would disappear suddenly. Around 6 a.m. Chris dozed off, and Ciaran slowly got out the bed and dressed in the dark. He went to kiss Chris goodbye and Chris immediately opened his eyes.

"Ciaran, I'm coming," he said drowsily. He began to rise from the bed.

Ciaran took his face in both hands, pulled his bottom lip between his two, and put his tongue in Chris's mouth. Chris let out a soft whimper and melted against him. Ciaran pulled back slightly and breathed on his lips, "*Somnum.*"

Chris immediately became lax in his arms and fell backward onto the bed, falling into a deep sleep. Ciaran kissed his lips one last time and closed the door. His heart had already begun to ache.

On the second floor, Diana and Quentin were waiting for him. She led the way to the bottom floor where Rob, Sean, and Ted were waiting at the front door.

"What are you all doing here?" asked Ciaran, seriously.

Ted answered, "There was no way you were walking into Council without us, little brother." He patted him on the shoulder.

Ciaran was overwhelmed and felt his tears well up. He quickly blinked them away and took a deep breath. "Okay. Let's go." He turned to give Quentin a handshake and half hug. "Thank you. Keep him calm, occupied. Don't let him flip out. Tell him... tell him I'll be back soon."

Quentin nodded. Ciaran resisted the urge to look up toward the third floor as his heart continued to ache. The Magi men and Diana grabbed their coats and headed out into the cold air and dawning sun together and Wisp'd.

CHAPTER 29

The Infraction

It was all quiet, as it was the Thursday morning after Christmas, and most workers were still on holiday. Hamish and Alastair came walking toward them in the large, bright entryway. Hamish reached his son and embraced him with a hand on each shoulder. "Ciaran."

"Dad. I'm so sorry." Ciaran hung his head low.

Hamish lifted his chin up and said, "We'll make it right." His eyes swept over all his children and nephew before he turned around. They followed him to the front desk. "Jamey, Happy Christmas."

"Happy Christmas, Minister Beals," the guard named Jamey said. "Bringing in the family for a tour of some sort?"

"No. We are here to see the Grandminister. Is he in?"

"Yes, he arrived at a quarter past. Is he expecting you?"

"No, but I have some news that I think he will want to hear from me first."

Officer Jamey nodded and picked up a small, blue memo pad, and said to it, "Good morning, Grandminister Graham,

Hamish Beals, Alastair Beals, and," he counted, "five of their family members are here to see you."

The words appeared on the pad of paper. He blew on it, and the entire paper disappeared. Less than a minute later, a paper appeared on his desk with the words, *"Send them all up."*

He nodded at them and said, "You're free to enter. Non-Council officials, please present your *rodulés* for admittance."

Ted, Sean, Ciaran, and Rob presented their wands and were logged in. Diana lifted her right wrist instead. Officer Jamey waved his *dulé* over it as her invisible tattoo shone and nodded. They traveled on the lift together to the top floor in silence, entering a large, carpeted corridor where there were a few desks with Council assistants working. Hamish knocked on the heavy double wooden doors at the end of the hall.

"Come in," Graham called.

Graham was at his desk writing, but stood up when they entered. As a heavy English man of African descent, he easily intimidated others, but to the Beals, he was family. He stretched his arms wide.

"The Beals clan, how wonderful to see you all." He came around to shake hands, leaving Hamish for last. "So, to what do I owe this visit?"

Hamish said, as he connected one hand and touched Graham's arm with the other, "Unfortunately, it's not a social call, Graham. There is a serious matter that needs your attention, your empathy, and, hopefully, your support."

"Of course," he said seriously. Graham motioned for them all to sit as he sat back behind his desk. Hamish and Ciaran took the leather seats directly in front of him while the others sat in chairs and couches around the expansive room. Graham waited.

Ciaran took a deep breath and started. "I broke Magi law."

Graham glanced at Diana, who inhaled sharply and touched her chest, then exhaled as if a weight had been lifted off her. He turned his eyes back to Ciaran. "Go on."

Ciaran told Graham everything, from the moment he met Chris and the escaped dragon, patrolling, the fight with the CV, his mixed-up feelings, the kiss, falling in love, bringing him home for Christmas, Chloé's accusation and his confession, Diana's confession and coming there. Graham had leaned back halfway through Ciaran's explaining, with his eyes closed, face unreadable.

Ciaran ended with, "I swear, we had every intention of coming forward. I just wanted an opportunity to have him meet my family first, so they can understand why I couldn't *abscondo* his memory then and why I love him so now." Ciaran sniffed, letting the tears flow as he talked. "If I were here in England, maybe I would have handled it more realistically, properly. It would have been easy to pop over and say, 'Hey Dad, I think I like this one, let's bring him in,' you know? I typically handle things properly like that. But I just... I..." Ciaran was lost for words and put his head in his hands.

Graham opened his eyes and leaned forward, clasping his hands together on his desk. "Ciaran. I understand what you went through and what you are still going through. Believe it or not, you aren't the first young man who has slipped up for reciprocal love. Each infraction is handled on a case-by-case basis, depending on the length of time, severity, and whether the other wants to come in, be inducted into our world. So the first question is, is he willing to do that? Take The Oath and become part of our community, officially?"

"Yes, absolutely," Ciaran said automatically, lifting his head up.

"Okay, then. Let's talk about the specifics of the infraction." He took out a fresh piece of parchment, and it floated its way to Alastair, who immediately grabbed it, knowing his role before Graham said, "Alastair, take notes."

"Yes, Grandminister," said Alastair and moved to stand next to the desk.

Graham began by asking, "So approximately how long has he known? You said since last summer?"

"Yes, last summer as in last year though, not this past one," Ciaran admitted.

Graham raised his eyebrow. "So, about a year and a half?"

"Almost. About sixteen months."

"And you are absolutely sure he has not told anyone else?"

"Not a soul. He has two sisters that he is very close to, and they know nothing about me except that I am a conservationist that works in the forest," Ciaran said.

Ted spoke up. "I can confirm that. I met them in September, and they know nothing."

Graham held his hand up for Alastair to stop writing, and he did. "Theodore," he started slowly, "Did you know that your brother broke Magi law?"

Ted did not respond, but gave Graham a defiant look.

"Okay. Let me rephrase the question. Did all of you in this room find out about Ciaran's infraction in the last twelve hours?" Graham asked.

"Yes, Minister," Diana spoke for them. "We found out last night. Myself, Robert, Quentin, and Chloé were there when Ciaran confessed without prompting. That was 11:53 p.m."

"Rob came to me and told me after midnight," Sean said.

"Quentin came to me also after midnight, and we went to tell Dad," Ted said.

Hamish said, "Yes, the boys came and told me about a quarter to 1 a.m. about Ciaran's confession."

"Alastair, did you get all that? Exactly as they stated it," Graham said.

Alastair nodded. "Yes, sir, I recorded it exactly as it was stated. By the way, Minister, full disclosure, I found out at exactly 6:38 a.m. when my uncle unexpectedly came to my place of residence."

"Thank you, Alastair." He turned back to Ciaran. "So for sixteen months, give or take, you have been confiding in your Commoner partner our Magi world secrets as it pertains to you and you only, correct?" Ciaran nodded. "I need a vocal affirmative here."

Ciaran spoke. "Yes, Minister."

"Okay. Have you been consistently performing magic around him?"

"Um... yes, but very minimal," Ciaran said.

Graham nodded. "Yes, I assume so. Very rarely has someone in your situation broken only one law, it is usually the two: the law of secrecy and the use of magic in front of a Commoner. How minimal are the spells?"

"Ah... opening and closing doors, bringing items to me or sending them back in their place, cleaning charms, silencing incantations, soundproofing we use almost daily—"

Rob snorted and said, "Not last night, you didn't!" Everyone turned to look at him. "Sorry," he mumbled and went pink.

Graham asked, "Anything else? Jinxing for fun? Blood magic spells? Transformations and turning him into a cat? Broom flying?"

"No, sir. And people do that?" Ciaran asked in surprise. "Turn others into cats?"

"You'd be surprised," he said dryly. "And what else has he seen? A dragon? Just one?"

Ciaran confirmed. "Yes, just the one."

"Pigeons delivering packages? Anything else?" Graham kept asking.

"Yes. And we have Emmth at the Atrium, a couple of fairies and gnomes. And there is a stunted kraken in the water, but I don't think he's actually ever paid attention to him."

"Okay," said Graham. "Where is he now?" Then he held up his hand as Ciaran was about to answer, "No, scratch that question from the record. What I want to ask is, would he be able to come in and get this settled, preferably today, with an interview?"

Ciaran said, "Yes, I can arrange that."

"Good. We can make the arrangements to meet in a mutual location. Now, I will need to pull together a committee to discuss these two infractions and decide on an appropriate disciplinary action. How long are you in town?"

"Until next week," Ciaran answered.

"Well, you may have to stay a bit longer, until we have completed a thorough investigation, starting in Albania. People will be interviewed at your place of employment and his, the Atrium where you live, and everyone at Christmas dinner. And of course your partner's interview. Once we have completed the investigation and if it all checks out, we will induct him. Then we will look to see whether his family needs to be inducted as well. Do you think they will take The Oath?"

"I don't know. I would certainly want them to, and I know he would; he is really close to his sisters."

Ted said, "They will. Remember, I inadvertently asked the question. Charity immediately said, 'Yes.' Clarissa hesitated, but eventually came around. She will want to be there for her brother."

Graham turned to Ciaran's siblings. "You are all here as witness to their relationship. Do you support this union?"

They all affirmed "yes," in their own way.

"And you, Hamish?" Graham turned to him. "Any objections?"

Hamish shook his head. "None. I support my son, and I trust his judgment. Chris is a fine young man."

Graham looked at Alastair, who was busy writing. "Alastair, what say you? You are part of this family, too."

Alastair looked up, surprised. "Oh! Well, yes, he is a fine young man. Respectable enough for a Commoner. I didn't really see a serious side to him, but it was a holiday, so I think hanging around the right sort, someone who can guide him like Ciaran and myself, he would fit right in with other registered Commoners."

Ciaran smiled at his posh cousin.

"Okay," Graham said. He turned back to Ciaran. "Nothing that you have told me is out of the ordinary. The length of time may be a complication, but if we can confirm he has kept it to himself, then it should be fine. Most likely probation of some kind."

Ciaran said, "I need your word, Grandminister, sir, that you won't *abscondo* him. You can't erase the last year and a half of his life, of our lives together. It's been the most important thing to me. He is the most important thing to me."

"You are not really in a position to make demands, son," Graham said sternly. "I will follow the recommendations of the committee, based on the outcome of the investigation. However, for your peace of mind, *abscondo* will not be part of my recommendation for him or for you, no. But I need you to promise me something in return. If he is currently in a Magi household, get him out now, or at the very least, no more magic displayed in front of him. Straight and narrow until the investigation is complete. You both will be living as Commoners for now. Do I need to confiscate your *dulé* to ensure that happens?"

Ciaran shook his head. "No, sir. No more magic at all. Got it. And we'll move him to a hotel immediately."

Graham turned to Alastair again. "Send a message to the Albanian division of the Council, and get a detective to open up the investigation. We might as well start today. I will have you sign some papers, Ciaran, and then you can go home and live your Commoner life."

"So I'm free to leave?" He almost couldn't believe it.

Graham raised his hand again for Alastair to pause writing. "Ciaran, your father is one of my oldest and closest friends. So no, I am not detaining his son in Claustra because he fell in love with a Commoner."

Ciaran nodded. He felt like running around the room in joy. He was going home to Chris.

Chris mumbled Ciaran's name, then woke up alarmed. He looked around the room and screamed, "CIARAN!"

He ran down two flights of stairs, calling his name. At the bottom, he yanked open the door and was met with an icy blast of wind, and realized he was only in his underwear. He quickly shut the door and turned around. Quentin was standing in the hallway outside the kitchen.

"What time is it?" Chris asked him.

Quentin looked at his watch. "Ten minutes to nine."

"Fuck!" Chris exclaimed. He leaned against the nearest wall.

"Why don't you get dressed and wait with me in the kitchen?" Quentin said calmly. "Got a nice cuppa for you."

Chris narrowed his eyes at him. "So what, are you my nanny now?"

Quentin shrugged. "I can be that. Or I can be a friend, also worried about the outcome. We can encourage each other."

Chris stood there a little while longer against the wall, cursing Ciaran in his mind, wishing he could hear him, and Quentin waited. After a minute, he silently went back upstairs.

Quentin made two cups of tea and sat at the table in the kitchen. Chris came back downstairs in Ciaran's blue Dragon Reservation of Albania t-shirt and a pair of sweatpants. Quentin wordlessly passed him the cup as he sat down, and they waited.

<hr>

"Okay," Alastair said, putting down the phone. "I just spoke with Detective Arslan, who is familiar with you, Ciaran. He wanted me to say, and I quote, 'I'm going to kick your arse for this.' Not my words, Grandminister." Ciaran resisted the urge to smile.

"It's fine, no worries, Alastair," Graham said.

Alastair continued, "Yes, well, he said it's a skeleton crew because of the holiday, but they will send two agents to the Reserve today to begin the interviews."

Graham nodded his approval. "Okay. Draw up the sanction that will include a thirty-day probationary tracking for Ciaran. That's to ensure you aren't doing any magic. Call Officer Decampo up here to administer the tracking. Then we'll get him set up and on his way."

This time Ciaran did smile.

Savannah Brickenhouse reorganized the papers on her desk for the second time that morning. As Department Manager of Magi Enforcement, she didn't need to be in, but honestly she had nowhere else to go for the holidays. She had no family since she was shunned for her connection to the evil Mage Talindra who had started the civil war that almost destroyed the Magi world. Work was her only refuge.

She debated leaving when a memo appeared in her inbox pile:

To: The Department Managers of Magi Enforcement

From: Office of the Magi Council Grandminister, Headquarters

Re: Magi Law Infractions

Open Investigation for one Magus, Ciaran Archibald Beals, Dragonologist and Senior Manager at the Dragon Reservation of Albania. Home Country: Albania

Offense: Two Infractions:

1: Knowingly and willingly broke the Magi Law of Secrecy and Concealment by revealing himself as a Magus to a Commoner with no apparent ties to the Magi World and Community.

2: Knowingly and willingly use of his Vis in front of same unregistered Commoner on multiple occasions.

Status: Pending. A committee will be formed after the investigation is complete to decide on the severity of the breach and appropriate consequences.

Current Sanction: Vis magicis vestigium—30 days

Current Whereabouts: London, England

8:56 a.m., 26 December

Her mouth went from shock at the name Beals coming across her desk, and then her lips formed a curved smile. She had been after the Grandminister's position for the last decade, and this may be what she needed to move up and to destroy the Beals family all at once.

She yelled for her assistant. "Fritz!"

Her assistant came running in. "Yes, Mistress Brickenhouse."

"Find me Ciaran Beals, now!" she demanded.

"Yes, ma'am, right away." He pulled out his *dulé* and conjured a map. It began beeping instantly. "Ma'am. He's ... here."

Savannah stood up. "Here, where?"

"He's ... in the building. His *rodulé* was submitted for admittance just under two hours ago, no exit."

Savannah turned to her mirror on the wall and tapped it with her *dulé*. Immediately Officer Jamey from downstairs appeared. "Mistress?" he called.

She asked him, "Is Ciaran Beals still in the building?"

"Yes, Mistress. He is upstairs in the Grandminister's office with his family."

"Thank you." She waved her *dulé*, and Jamey disappeared. She turned to Fritz and smiled.

"Find me Officers Prinston and Maris; have them meet me on the top floor. And call Claustra. They are getting a new prisoner today."

CHAPTER 30

He's Gone

Officer Decampo did not come to the Minister's office. After thirty minutes of waiting, they decided to travel down to the floor that housed the Council officers and find him or another one to put the tracking on Ciaran. They talked amiably as they walked toward the lifts, Ciaran, Ted, and Sean leading them, Graham and Hamish in the rear.

As the lifts opened, Savannah and her three officers stepped out. They did not notice her until she said loudly, "Ah, Minister, I was just coming to see you. And thank you for bringing Mr. Beals to me. I will take it from here."

She waved her *dulé*, and Ciaran's wand flew out of his pocket into hers while simultaneously his wrists were instantly bounded and shackled behind his back in invisible chains. Before anyone could react, the three officers waved their *dulés*. Ciaran was lifted off his feet a few inches and sent hurling through the air toward them.

Ted and Sean instantly took out their *dulés*, but Grandminister Graham ran ahead to stand in front of them.

"Savannah!" Graham barked. "What are you doing?"

"My job, Grandminister. See, it has come to my attention that Mr. Beals has broken Magi law, and since magical law infractions are in my area, I am perfectly within my rights to detain the suspect until a hearing can be performed. And, given the nature of the holidays, it appears there won't be a hearing until, let's say, some time in January!" she said gleefully.

Everyone but Ciaran began yelling and protesting as the Council officials paused their work to watch what was happening. Graham raised his hand to quiet them down. "You don't have to do this, Savannah," Graham said. "I was handling it."

She turned on him. "Really? The Grandminister of the Magi Council of all of Europe has braced himself to handle minor duties of a magical law infraction issue? Surely, you have more important matters to attend? Or are you seeking favoritism for a friend?" She glanced at Hamish and looked at Graham, folding her hands in front of her.

"Better than seeking revenge on an entire family!" Chloé called out as she turned the corner. Everyone was shocked to see her there, but she was not looking at them. She had her eyes for the mean Mage in front of her.

"Don't do this, Mistress Savannah. You don't even know Ciaran. He's the one Beals that would probably see your side in all this and understand that you are just following protocol because he's the most law-abiding citizen you'll ever meet. Ciaran—"

"Hold your tongue and save it for the trial, little witch," Savannah cut her off nastily. She smiled at the rest of the Beals. "That's right, not a committee meeting. A hearing. And until then, Ciaran will be in Claustra. You all have a great day."

As she turned around Sean said loudly, "You really are a too right royal bitch."

She turned back sharply and slowly walked toward him. "Ah. Sean is it? Or Shane, I can't always remember. Oh, right, Shane is the one that got himself blown up, didn't he?"

Sean went from anger to rage in a second. The *dulé*, still in his hand, was shaking in fury as she continued to taunt him.

Savannah gave him a nasty smile. "I meant to send my condolences, really, but it just got away from me. So allow me to give them to you now: How utterly awful it must be to have lost your other, possibly better, half. Tell me, dear, does it hurt often when you think about him dying? Were you even there? Did you actually see your brother's life drain from his eyes? Tsk tsk. Poor Sean. Might I suggest an Emmth to take his place. He might be more useful—"

"That's enough!" Hamish barked. She turned to him but did not dare taunt the older man at the loss of his son. Hamish touched Sean's shoulder. Sean lowered his *dulé*, but he was still shaking in anger. "You shut your filthy mouth right now, or you deal with me."

Graham said calmly, "Savannah, take Ciaran and go."

She smiled at him, turned around, and started walking down the hall again. The assistants was horrified by what she said to him and began to whisper amongst themselves.

But then Alastair spoke up. "No, Savannah, Sean was not with him in the moment, but I was," he said proudly. She stopped in her tracks but did not turn around. "And do you know what I saw? I saw the bravest man I have ever known, my cousin, give his life to save the lives of others that day. And what were you doing that day, Savannah? Kowtowing to the devil herself, Talindra? Sucking at her tit like you did the entire five years before she tried to take over Scholarly and the Council? Because while others like me were stupidly coerced into serving her, you followed your cousin willingly. And everyone knows it, and no one respects you for it. Not even your own family. So do us all a favor, keel over and die, will you?"

Ted and Ciaran looked at their cousin, open-mouthed. Alastair, their respectable and dignified cousin, had never spoken to anyone that way before. The crowd of Council employees had gathered as Alastair talked, nodding in agreement and giving Savannah dirty looks. She was furious, her face was beet red, and she stormed off, her officers pulling Ciaran behind her.

When the lift doors opened, Ciaran looked over his shoulder and yelled, "Ted! Chris—"

Ted called back, "Don't worry, we got it, Ciaran. Hang in there, you'll be out soon."

Ciaran was pushed into the lift doors, and he stood straight up, his face like stone. Savannah, who was still beet red and fuming, said, "Don't be so sure about that. I will make sure you never see your family again." They heard a loud boom as the lift rose to the main floor.

Ciaran did not react or respond, but inside he was terrified. All he could think of was Chris's face right before he sent him to sleep. *I'm sorry, Christopher*, he said in his head. But he knew the message would not get to him. The *Ardenti* wasn't strong enough yet.

Sean had exploded. He started screaming and firing off spells from his *dulé* in the direction of the lifts until Ted wrestled it out of his hand. Ted tried to hug him, but Sean somehow was able to throw a stunning spell at him without his *dulé* or words, and Ted flipped in the air, falling backward. Sean kicked the closest chair to him, then picked up another chair, and threw it into a nearby wall, sending the workers scrambling. Ted regained himself again and ran to grab Sean by pinning both his arms at his side and pulling him down to the ground. Sean continued to scream and fight Ted off him, so Rob and Hamish went over to help him contain Sean's rage. Diana ran to Chloé, and they held each other and cried.

Alastair was also going to help Sean, but Graham grabbed his arm. "Alastair, I need you to go down to Valerie in scheduling and get Ciaran the closest available hearing date. It won't be tomorrow, but if we're lucky, early next week. Then start to rally ten Council officials for the hearing, starting with Magna. I know they are old friends. Lucy, too. Those two can help." Alastair nodded and hurried off.

Graham turned to Chloé. "You brought it to light. You know what you have to do now."

She nodded, and said to Diana, "I'm going to save him. I promise." Before any more words could be exchanged, she ran off behind Alastair.

Graham walked over to Ted, Sean, and Hamish, all on the floor. Sean had stopped screaming and dissolved to sobbing in his brother's arms while his father and cousin tried to give him encouraging words. Others started coming around as well, encouraging the Beals and disparaging Brickenhouse and her behavior.

Graham knelt down and said to Hamish, "I understand if you want to be here for your son. But I would like to have a few words with you before you head out to talk with Grace."

"Go ahead, Dad, we got Sean," Ted said. Hamish stood up and followed the Grandminister back to his office.

After a couple of minutes, Sean quieted down. Rob asked, "What do we do now, Ted?"

Ted sighed. "We tell Chris. He's going to flip, so be ready for it, but we have to keep him calm. Ciaran says he doesn't do well when they are apart, so he's going to need all of us. A lot of support around him. A family."

They were quiet for a few more minutes. Then Diana said, "Do we wait for Dad?"

"I don't know," Ted said. "What time is it?"

"9:38 a.m.," Rob told him.

Ted sighed again. "We have to get going. Chris is going to want to know what happened to Ciaran." He said softly to Sean, "Can you walk, little brother?"

Sean nodded and stood up on his own. He started walking to the elevators, and the rest of them followed him. Ted handed him back his *dulé*.

As soon as the doors closed, Sean gripped it tightly and said darkly, "Somebody should have killed that evil bitch."

No one disagreed with him.

Chris and Quentin were talking about Quentin's family, having evil witches and warlocks on his mother's side, and his father's side of Scholarly Magi that could be traced back to the original Magi in England. Some at Scholarly claim the James line could be traced back to Merlin himself. After his father died when he was ten, everything changed for his mother, and she dove deeper into the dark. Quentin was describing how it felt to be possessed by a dark curse set upon him by his own mother when he was fourteen.

"That was her way to try to make me come back to the dark side. It made me confused, sad, angry at everything and everyone. Graham was the only person that recognized what was happening to me. He had seen it before. Once it was removed, I was done with the lot of them after that. I turned my back on my family, joined the Magi military, and never looked back. He's a good man, and a fair leader."

"Hm. I hope so," said Chris. "So, do you feel different now? Less ... murdery?"

Quentin laughed. "I don't think I ever felt ... murdery. But sometimes I feel like it's still in me, like it's always there waiting for me. So I'm careful with my temper and stay positive. The Beals all know it, and they love me anyway. Especially Diana."

That made Chris smile. "I have one of those," Chris admitted. "I call it my dark cloud. It has always been there, ever since I was a child. I had to learn how to keep it at bay, too."

"What does it feel like?" Quentin asked.

"It feels like ... darkness surrounding me and encouraging me to give up. Hopeless, helpless. It used to be bad, but it hasn't gotten that bad in a long time. If I feel it starting to pull me under, I usually tell it to shut the fuck up and do something that makes me happy."

"Does Ciaran know?"

"He knows that I get sad sometimes. Especially when I think about my mum. But really, since Ciaran has come into my life, it's so much easier to turn it around. His love is ... magical to me."

"Well, maybe you have an evil hex attaching itself to you somewhere, too," Quentin said seriously. "Could be ancestral."

Chris smiled. "Yeah? You think it's where I get my magical abilities from?" he joked.

They laughed as the front door opened, startling them. They both stood up in anticipation and went to the kitchen doorway. Ted came in first, followed by Sean, Diana, and

Rob. Chris's heart fell into his chest as he looked at their faces as they passed him.

He swallowed first. "Where's Ciaran?" he asked calmly.

Diana went to Quentin and sat down with him at the table. She gave him a sad look; he held her in comfort. Rob sat in the chair closest to Chris, and Sean went all the way to the other end of the kitchen table and put his head down.

Ted stood at the front of the rectangular table and said, "Have a seat, Christopher."

Chris became angry and walked up to him, getting in Ted's face. "No! Tell me what happened to Ciaran!"

Ted said again, calmly but sternly, "Sit down, Christopher."

They stood nose to nose for a few seconds, unblinking. Ted waited. Chris resigned and went to take a seat. Ted remained standing. He explained what happened in the meeting with Graham and how everything was fine, and then the encounter with Savannah Brickenhouse, the Senior Manager of the Magi Enforcement Department which led to Ciaran's arrest on the spot. Quentin flinched at the sound of his aunt's name. Diana squeezed his hand in comfort.

Ted concluded, "So Alastair and Chloé are working on getting him the quickest court date and going to have Ciaran's friends assist in stacking the jury, I assume, with as many people that know Ciaran as possible. We have a real shot to get him out of there; we just need to wait this whole thing out."

Chris was stunned. He could barely think. He heard all that Ted said, but all that stuck out to him was that Ciaran was arrested, taken away, and was sitting in Magi prison. Because of him. When Ted stopped talking, Chris stood up and attempted to walk, but couldn't really move his feet, so instead he turned and put his head on the hutch behind him.

With his eyes closed, he said, "I need someone to say it out loud. Because when I say it in my head, it doesn't sound real; like this is just some waking nightmare that I'm in." He turned around and leaned his back on the hutch, eyes still closed. "Somebody say ... that I may never see Ciaran again."

No one spoke. Sean lifted his head briefly to look at Chris, but then put his head back down.

Chris whispered, "Somebody just say it."

Ted opened his mouth to speak, but the words caught in his throat. It dawned on him that in being strong for everyone else, he had been neglecting his own fear, that he could lose his brother, his very first best friend. He closed his mouth and turned his back on everyone as his own tears welled up. Chris likewise let his tears fall down his face, eyes still closed.

Diana stood up, walked over to him, and hugged his midsection, leaning her head on his chest. "It could be a really long time before you see Ciaran again. Before any of us see him again. And if that happens, we will get through this together. As a family."

Chris patted her back and nodded. After a moment, Quentin stood up. "I'm going to go see him. In Claustra."

Diana turned around to face him. "How?"

"Well. I'm a *Nigri Veneficus*, innit? So I have access. And I'm Quentin James. If there was ever a time to use my royalty status, it's now." He turned to Chris, who was looking at him. "I'll let you know how he's doing and pass along any messages."

Chris nodded. "Thanks, mate."

Quentin went upstairs to get changed, and Diana went with him. Chris sat on the opposite side of Sean and put his head down on the table as Sean had done. Without looking up, Sean found Chris's hand across from him and grabbed it. They clasped tightly and squeezed simultaneously, then continued to hold on to each other, heads on the table, eyes closed. Ted stayed standing. No one spoke.

Quentin came back downstairs with a black sweater with a black leather patch of a fist holding a *rodulé* and put on a black cloak. "Is there anything you want me to tell him, Chris?"

Chris lifted his head. Before he could respond, a silvery rabbit came through the nearest wall and stopped in front of him. "It's Chloé!" Rob said.

The rabbit spoke in Chloé's voice. "*We have a date for Ciaran's hearing, Monday the 30th of December at 8 a.m. Magna is on board, and she is actually taking the lead in gathering the jurors. She says she knows what she is doing. I have appointed myself his Councilor; that's his lawyer. Alastair is going to help me work on my defense for the next couple of days until the hearing, so you won't see me. I'm... I'm so sorry, Christopher. I didn't mean... I'm going to bring Ciaran home to you. I promise,*" she said definitively. Her rabbit hopped away out of the next wall.

Sean lifted his head and said, "If it's anyone that has a shot, it's her and Alastair."

Ted nodded. "Yeah, I would put my money on Alastair any day of the week. And Chloé is brilliant."

Quentin agreed. "Same. Chloé can do this. She will do it." Diana nodded at him. Rob didn't say anything.

Chris was overwhelmed. "Thank you. All of you. Quentin, I don't know what to say to Ciaran right now. Except let him know I am right here. I'm not going anywhere. We promised each other we would stay and fight. So that's what we're going to do."

Quentin nodded, kissed Diana, and said, "I'll be back in a few hours." He left the house.

Diana stood up. "I'm going to make some food and calming elixir. We could all use some right now."

CHAPTER 31

Claustra

Quentin Wisp'd to the Isles of Scilly where the gneiss stone building stood, hidden on one of the uninhabited islands. There were no doors or windows, just a big stone structure, but Quentin knew where to go. He walked to the far right side and held up his *dulé*. The section of stone glowed for him ,and he was able to walk into the cold, stone entryway. Quentin heard her voice before he approached.

Mrs. Beals was yelling at the front desk officers. "I don't understand why I can't just go up and see my son. He's MY SON!"

The first guard at the desk said, "I'm sorry, ma'am, you can't just go see him. He isn't allowed visitors. Now Minister Beals is a Council official and can go up, but you cannot, Mistress."

Grace was fuming. "What is this rubbish!? I'm his MOTHER. I'm not a visitor. I'm not some stranger coming in for a quick chat. I need to make sure he is okay in this god-forsaken place, that he is going to be eating well and treated well. He doesn't belong here!"

"Mistress Beals, this isn't a nursery!" Guard Number Two said harshly. "This is a place for dangerous *Veneficus*. Whether he belongs here, whether he stays, is not for us to decide. But as long as he is here, he will be treated like everyone else."

"But you could decide to let her up," Quentin interjected as he walked up.

Grace and Hamish turned around. "Oh, Quentin!" Grace exclaimed. She ran into his arms, sobbing.

He resisted the urge to call her Mum and instead said politely, "There, there, Mrs. Beals." He walked her back over to the front desk. "I actually am also here to see Ciaran Beals. I have an important message for him."

Guard Number One was becoming frustrated. "What is this, upside down day? No unauthorized person is going to see Ciaran Beals. It's Claustra regulations!"

The third guard said to him, "Yeah, but he's Quentin James."

"I know who he is!" Guard Number One snapped.

Quentin said, "Then you should know that I would never do anything to jeopardize the integrity of this facility." He tapped the leather CV on his sweater. It glowed yellow, then went back to black. "So, if it's okay with you, I would like to escort Minister and Mistress Beals upstairs for a brief moment and escort them back out. And you have my word there will be no more incidents such as this."

Guard Number One looked like he wanted to say no again, but then changed his mind. "Williams!" he barked. "Escort the three to Beals's cell. They have three minutes."

Guard Number Three, now known as Williams, led the way up the stone steps to the fourth floor. They walked down a dark, stone corridor until he stopped in the middle of the hallway. The guard tapped his *dulé* on a stone, and an iron door revealed itself. Willams touched the knob and pulled the door back, and another set of iron bars was there. Williams did not open the gate.

Ciaran was sitting cross-legged on the flimsy cot, rubbing his wrists. There were two-inch black bands tattooed around them to subdue his magic, and he could feel the effect it had on him. He looked up when he heard the first door open and was shocked to see his parents there.

"Ciaran!" Grace yelled. She stretched her whole arm through the bar.

Ciaran ran up and grabbed it. "Mother! Dad!" he cried, then, "Quentin!" He held his mother's hand tight and said, "How is Chris, Quentin?"

"He's... He took the news as expected," Quentin responded. "But we're all rallying around him. He says he's not going anywhere, and he's going to stay and fight like you agreed."

Ciaran shook his head profusely. "Quentin, no. I changed my mind. Tell Chris he has to go, and go now. Leave..." He looked over at the guard, who was clearly listening. "Leave the place he is currently in and go home. They don't know his last name or anything about him. If this goes bad, if I get convicted, the first thing Savannah will do is find him and *abscondo* his memory. I can't let that happen. Whenever I get out, I will find him, wherever he is. Tell him that."

Grace sighed. "Oh, Ciaran, that could be years! You don't even know if you will feel—"

"And if it's years, then I will find him, Mother!" Ciaran snapped. "And we will be together. He means everything to me! Don't you understand?"

Grace was shocked at his tone. Ciaran had never raised his voice to her in all his years on earth.

"Now, now, we'll have a talk with Chris, okay?" Hamish said gently. "Don't get worked up."

Ciaran turned to his father and said, "Dad, you have to convince him to go. He's going to be stubborn, but it's the best thing for us right now. If they take me from him, I can't let them take the memory of me from him."

Hamish reached in and patted his shoulder. Williams said, "One minute left."

Quentin remembered. "Right, I have some news. Your hearing is set for Monday at 8 a.m. So you just need to hang on for the next four days. Chloé is your Councilor. They already started working on your defense, her and Alastair."

"That's good," Ciaran said. "I know they will do their best."

"Ciaran, are you okay? Did they feed you yet?" Grace asked.

Ciaran smiled. "I suspect they will soon. I'm fine, Mum. See? You know I've always been okay in the quiet. This is nothing new." He patted her hand reassuringly. "I do wish I had some clothes, though. Wearing the same thing for five days is going to suck. And stink."

Quentin asked the guard, "Will it be alright if I came back later with a change of clothes? Just me."

"If it's just you, alright," Williams said begrudgingly.

"Thank you. I will be back around the dinner hour," he told the guard and Ciaran. Before the guard could say it, Quentin said, "It's time to go."

Grace hugged her son as best as she could through the bars. Quentin and Hamish settled for handshakes. They stepped back. Ciaran gave them a small smile as Williams slid the metal door closed. The wall immediately appeared, and they were in the dimly lit stone hallway again. Grace couldn't help it; she choked out a sob and touched the stone wall, calling her son's name. Hamish had to pull her away. They went downstairs and left Claustra together, entering the biting cold and whipping winds on the island.

"Quentin, we'll follow you back to talk with Chris," Hamish said.

But Grace snapped, "I will do no such thing! It's his fault that Ciaran is in this position!"

"No, Grace," Hamish said lovingly. "It's no one's fault. Did you hear your son in there? He loves the boy."

"Yes, but does Chris love him the same? Would that Commoner risk his freedom if the shoe was on the other foot?" Grace asked.

"I believe he would, Mum," Quentin spoke up, making up for not calling her Mum earlier.

"And that's just it!" Grace cried. "We think, we believe, but we don't *know* anything about him! And I don't want to know anything about him either, not until my son is safely out of there. And if Ciaran stays in there, locked in that place, I will never forgive him!"

She stormed off in the cold and Wisp'd.

Hamish sighed. "She did not take kindly to the news at all. She wailed a bit, then demanded to come down and see him. I think she is worried about losing another son." He sniffed. "As am I." He sniffed again. "Come now, let's go talk to Christopher."

The door opened, and Quentin and Hamish came in. They were all still sitting at the kitchen table. Chris, Ted, and Diana had cups of tea, Rob was picking at his plate of leftovers, and Sean had his head down again. Everyone except Sean looked up expectantly for news.

"Ciaran is fine," Quentin started. "Seems in good spirits, especially after we told him the plan."

Ted noticed. "Where is Mum?"

Hamish answered. "She's not feeling well, so she decided to go home and lie down. I'm going to join her soon. But, Christopher, a word, please?"

Chris stood up. "Yes, sir." He followed Hamish into the parlor, which had been converted back to a sitting room.

He began, "Ciaran had a message for you. He wants you to leave London and return to Albania at once—"

"What!?" Chris cried. "No!"

"Listen," Hamish said with a touch on his shoulder. "Ciaran said that if it doesn't go his way, the Magi Enforcers will look to *abscondo* you, and I am afraid he is right. Ciaran couldn't live with himself if that happened to you. And for what it's worth, I agree with him. You must leave at once. I can arrange transport."

Chris walked away, farther into the parlor in thought, then walked quickly back to Hamish. "With all due respect, Mr. Beals, there is no way in hell that I'm leaving him. He's my whole life, my reason for getting up in the morning. As long as he's here, I'm here."

"And if he's here for the next five years, locked away in a cell?" Hamish asked plainly.

Chris looked him in the eyes and said strongly, "Then I guess I'm moving to London and waiting tables until he comes back to me. I'm not going. I'll never leave him."

Hamish touched his shoulder again. "Okay, son. Stay in the house; do not leave for any reason. If anyone outside of the family stops by, stay upstairs. Quentin has access to Ciaran and can bring you news. We'll figure it out together."

Chris nodded. Then he told him, "We really were going to tell you, today in fact. It was always the plan. I am deeply sorry for bringing all this trouble to your family."

Hamish shook his head. "No, son, no apologies necessary. Ciaran knew the risks and followed his heart, anyway.

Apparently, you are worth it to him. I hope you know that, that he feels the same about you."

Chris looked down, trying not to cry. Hamish lifted his head. "Chin up. It will all work out in the end." Chris nodded, unable to speak. Hamish patted his back and led him back into the kitchen.

"Listen up," said Hamish, getting everyone's attention. "Graham told me that Brickenhouse is going to try to destroy this family from the inside out. And we know why." He gave Quentin a knowing look. Quentin raised his chin. "But we are going to outsmart her. The purpose of bringing Magna and Lucy in is because they are close friends of Ciaran, and they plan to stack the jury with as many of Ciaran's supporters as possible. Alastair will be on the jury as well. We only need a majority vote, and with the four of them, that means they only need three more supporters. The hearing is set, and the plan is in place. Chris knows not to leave the house and to hide from visitors. No one except Graham knows anything about him, not even his whereabouts, and it's our job to keep it that way." They all nodded.

Ted stood up. "I'm going with you to see Mum. I have a feeling she is pissed off at me, too. Chris, I'll be back later to check on you."

"I don't need another nanny, Ted," Chris said, exasperated.

"No, you need your brothers around you, and you have that with us. Don't argue." He patted him on the back and headed out with Hamish.

"Chris, do you mind packing a bag of clothes for Ciaran?" Quentin asked. "I'm going to Wisp back up there in a few hours."

"Yes, that's a good idea," Diana said. "Then come down and help me with dinner."

Chris smiled. "Keeping me occupied, the two of you? Well, add in some after-dinner whiskey, and I won't mind at all." They smiled back at him, and watched him go upstairs.

After a few minutes Quentin, remembering the conversation they had earlier about his dark cloud, said, "Should one of us go with him?"

Rob nodded. "Yeah, Ted said he doesn't do well without Ciaran. One of us should be with him at all times."

Sean lifted his head and stood up. "I'll do it. First watch."

He started walking out of the kitchen as Diana looked at him suspiciously. "Why?" she asked.

"Because I'm just that kind of guy," he said innocently and started up the stairs.

Diana's eyes narrowed. "He's up to something."

CHAPTER 32

Adventures in Babysitting

Chris was sitting on the edge of the bed trying to calm his nerves when Sean knocked on the door. Chris stood up and began pretending to gather clothes. "Come in."

Sean opened the door and said, "Whatcha doing?"

"Just picking out clothes for Ciaran."

Sean took note that the curtains were still drawn, and the light was off. He raised an eyebrow and said, "Yeah? In the dark?"

Chris stopped pretending and looked up. "What do you want, Sean? Come to babysit me, too?"

Sean closed the door and waved his hand to pull back the curtains. "Nope. You have enough people doing that."

"You're not supposed to be doing magic around me any-more," Chris reminded him.

Sean ignored him and walked over to the nightstand. "You see, when I stay over here, this is my room. So..."

He tapped the bottom drawer three times with his *dulé* and muttered an incantation that Chris did not hear, then opened it. He pulled out a clear plastic bag of marijuana, held it up for Chris to see, and grinned.

"Aha! That's how I'm getting through the next four days. How about yourself?" He sat on the edge of the bed, took out joint paper, and started spreading the seeds.

Chris shook his head. "Ciaran wouldn't want you doing that right now," he scolded.

"Yes, well Ciaran isn't here right now, is he?" Sean said plainly.

Chris was taken aback. "I thought you Beals were supposed to be encouraging."

Sean chuckled. "You must be looking for Ted. He's the encouraging one. That's not me."

Chris sat on the bed next to him. "Then which brother are you?"

"I'm the..." He licked the rolled joint together and continued, "Used to be half of a funny duo twin that is now the dark-humored, sarcastic one. I could be funny or an arsehole. It really could go either way." He shrugged and started adding seeds to another one.

Chris smiled. "You sound like me."

"Guess that's why Ciaran likes you so much. I mean, think about it: He spends a year with me, goes back to Albania, and falls for the first person whose personality matches my own. I say you owe me a thank you. And to that I say, you're welcome," Sean said smugly.

Chris let out a laugh. "So Ted is the encouraging one, you're the cynical one, and Alastair is obviously the smart one. What is Ciaran?"

Sean paused rolling "Ciaran... He's the practical one. That's really why this whole thing is so surprising. Not the falling for a guy part, but the hiding and sneaking around part. The not *abscondo*-ing you right away part. That's not

Ciaran. He lives his life within the rules all the time." He finished rolling, licked it closed, and said, "Well, maybe the gay part is surprising, too. I don't know how much he told you about our trip, but we kind of went a little crazy with the birdies."

"Bits and pieces, but no details," Chris admitted.

"And he probably never will tell you because it's just not practical to do so. But now that I think of it, maybe it was always there, just under the surface. Sex for Ciaran seemed to be a practical move, as well. He was smashing women because I kept bringing them around for him to smash, and he wasn't going to tell me no about anything I wanted to do. It was practical to just go along with me. But even the act itself seemed like a means to an end, not a spiritual journey like how I was on. He never connected with any one of them. And when it was no longer practical for him, he just ... stopped fucking around." Sean shrugged. "Maybe he needed something different, to make sex less practical for him. He needed to connect with someone emotionally and fuck differently to feel alive again."

He finished rolling his third joint, then said, "This is really getting awkward talking to my brother's lover about his sex life, so let's not do it anymore, yeah?"

Chris laughed. "That's fine. You told me all I needed to know." He started shifting through Ciaran's clothes again on the bed, then began to toss them angrily. "I can't believe he told me to leave. Fucker! He knew I wouldn't. I should give him all my clothes as a sign that I'm not going anywhere."

"You should," said Sean. "With a big message like, 'fuck you, don't test me like that again.'" He reached over to the white sweater with the trees on it. "Yours or his? I don't remember."

"Mine."

"Good, good. Make sure this makes it in the bag to Ciaran. I have a little message for him of my own."

Chris sighed. "I don't know what I'm going to do if this all goes to shit. Maybe we should have run. That was always Plan B, to run and live in a place where the Council can't touch us. Now that option is gone," he finished sadly.

Sean said, "I'll tell you what: If Ciaran goes to prison, I'll get you out of the UK myself and take you. We'll be on the run together for the next five years or so."

"Yeah, back to the States?" Chris asked, amused.

"No. Europe and the North American Magi Councils have an extradition treaty," Sean informed him. "If we go to the Americas or Canada and get caught, they will absolutely erase your memory, and I will be sharing a cell with Ciaran. I thought you were well read on Magi stuff?" he said sarcastically.

"Well, I thought you were the dumb one," Chris said back.

"No, that's Rob; he's the stupid one," Sean said, making Chris laugh again.

"Are you serious, Sean?" Chris asked. "About us going on the run?"

"As a heart attack," he said automatically. "And I hear the Amazon is nice this time of year."

Sean rolled three more joints as Chris packed Ciaran's bag. Twenty minutes passed before Chris realized he never gave Sean an answer. "Okay. Deal. If Ciaran goes, we go. And we don't tell anyone, we just go."

"Right. But I would probably tell Ted. So he always knows where to find us. But no one else." Sean lifted his hand to shake Chris's to seal the deal. "Now. How many of these do you think I can get into the seams..." he pondered as he lifted the white sweater again.

Chris helped Diana make a turkey stew from the leftovers they had from Christmas. He handed Quentin the bag before he left and said, "Tell Ciaran I said, 'Forever, and three days after that.'" Quentin didn't know what it meant exactly, but he got the gist and smiled at Chris.

After dinner, Sean and Chris moved to the parlor to pour drinks. Sean had rolled ten joints, but only six were left with them. He sat on one end of the couch and puffed. Chris had a drink in one hand and held out his other for the joint.

Sean hesitated and asked, "You aren't going to get all high and emotional on me, are you? No singing Taylor Swift songs, yeah?"

Chris rolled his eyes. "No!" Sean handed it to him. Chris took two puffs and said, "I don't know. Maybe."

He chuckled as Sean groaned. They finished the first joint and lit a second, Chris already feeling less anxious.

Rob came into the room. "What are you doing?" he asked curiously.

"Making s'mores and telling bedtime stories," Sean answered.

"Come off it," Rob said, annoyed. He sat down in one of the single chairs and watched them pass the joint back and forth.

Chris watched him watch them. "Do you want a hit of this?" Chris asked.

"You know, in my twenty-two years on this earth, I've never done it," said Rob. "My dad doesn't like the smell of it. He's always yelling at Sean when he smokes behind the shop." Chris and Sean didn't answer him. "But maybe I should try one time, you reckon?"

"Rob, this isn't peer pressure hour," Sean said rudely. "If you want to do it, do it. If not, don't. Nobody here gives a toss anyway. That's the beauty of doing it, actually." He and Chris snickered while Rob sat there.

"Okay, I want to try it," Rob announced. Chris got off the couch to pass it to Rob. Sean quickly put his legs up to lie across it.

"Sorry, find another spot, mate," he said playfully.

Chris rolled his eyes and sat on the floor in front of the couch near Sean's feet. Rob took a big drag, then began choking. Sean howled with laughter while Chris got up to help.

"Stop it," he said to Sean. "Don't be an arsehole to your cousin, who is practically your little brother." Then his eyes went wide as he patted Rob's back. "Wow. I sounded just like Ciaran, didn't I?" He started snickering again.

When Rob had stopped coughing, he told him, "It's okay, Rob, everyone chokes the first time. Sometimes on their hundredth time."

Rob conjured himself a glass of water and drank. "Thanks. I'm fine."

Chris took the joint back and puffed, then said to Rob, "You should apologize to your lady."

"No bloody way!" said Rob stubbornly. "It's her fault your boyfriend is in there."

"No, it's my fault, mine and Ciaran's alone," Chris said. "We broke the law. And now she's working her arse off to get him out. She deserves your respect and your support."

He passed the joint to Sean, who puffed and said, "And we all know you will *neeeeever* do better than Chloé Abbottsford. She's beautiful and intelligent and you're you. So don't be a git."

Rob didn't respond to Sean's remark. Instead, he asked, "Can I try again?"

Sean passed it to him wordlessly. Rob took a very small puff and did not choke. Sean waved his *dulé* and put on some music, and they all relaxed. They talked about why Brickenhouse hated the Beals so much, past relationships, football, and other random topics.

Ciaran was trying to eat the slop they called dinner when his cell door opened, both the steel door and the bars. Quentin walked in with a duffle bag, and Williams closed the steel bars behind him and walked away. Quentin and Ciaran hugged, simply because Ciaran thought he would never get to hug another person for a long time.

Quentin handed him the bag. "Chris packed your clothes."

Ciaran opened the bag and was confused. "These are all his clothes in my bag. Why did he do that?"

"Well, he had a message," Quentin said. "Forever and three days. Something like that."

Ciaran smiled. "Forever and three days after that." He shook his head. "Stubborn arsehole."

He went through the bag and chose Chris's white Simpsons t-shirt and a pair of bright red sweatpants, something he would never wear, but it made him feel close to him. The shirt even smelled of his deodorant, and that made him happy.

He said to Quentin, "I'm going to change, mate, just so you know."

"Oh. Okay, yeah sure." Quentin sat in a chair and turned it away from Ciaran so he could change. When he was done, he sat on the bed and went through the rest of the bag.

He pulled out the white sweater Chris wore at Christmas. "I'm surprised he put this in here. Did he think I would get cold?"

"No. Sean handed that to me last minute," Quentin said. "He had a message, too. He said, 'I like how the weeds are growing in between the trees.'" Quentin tossed the lighter he had to Ciaran, who caught it with one hand. "Keep that hidden."

Ciaran's eyes squinted in confusion; then he lifted the sweater up. He smiled coyly and shook his head again. "Any news?" he asked Quentin.

"Not yet. I have no idea what Chloé is doing."

Ciaran nodded. "Is Chris okay then? Keeping busy?"

"Yeah, he and Sean have been hanging out, and he helped Diana make dinner tonight. They were eating when I left, his first meal all day."

"Him and Sean, you say? Hmm... Watch that closely for me, will you?"

Quentin nodded, then turned the tables on him. "Are you okay, Ciaran?"

Ciaran didn't answer at first; instead turned his face away and touched his pillow. He said quietly, "Sleep is going to be hard without him."

"It's only for a couple of days," Quentin said encouragingly.

"Unless it isn't," Ciaran said to the stone wall he was still staring at.

Quentin said, "I can stay as long as you need me to."

Ciaran smiled a sad smile and turned back to him. "I'll be fine. I just need you to take care of Chris for me, please. Even if he seems fine, he isn't."

"Yeah, I know. We got him. But we got you, too, Ciaran. Okay?"

"Right. Okay."

Ted walked into a room full of marijuana smoke and rock music blasting loudly. Chris was lying on the floor near the couch, and Rob was lying on the fireplace hearth. He sighed and waved his *dulé* to clear away the smoke and turn off the music.

"What the..." Sean lifted his head from the couch, saw Ted and groaned, then lay back down. "Party's over. Daddy's home."

"So this how we're passing time, gentlemen?" Ted chided.

"Hey, you told me to keep him occupied. I'm keeping him occupied," Sean said.

Chris sat up. "So you were babysitting me!" he said accusingly.

Sean did not deny it. "Hey, I'm the best nanny you'll have all weekend."

Ted looked over to Rob, whose eyes were closed and who had not moved. "Did you kill Robert, too?" he asked them. "ROB! ARE YOU DEAD, ROBBY?!" Ted yelled at him.

Rob said quietly, "No. Just ... thinking..."

Chris and Sean snickered as Ted shook his head. He sat in the one seat chair. "Ciaran would not approve of this."

Sean scoffed. "Ciaran is probably getting high as we speak. He'll be canned all weekend. I made sure of that."

"How?" Chris asked.

Sean smiled. "Magic." They looked at each other for a moment, then started laughing hysterically.

"Ah, shit," Ted said. "No more. This one's coming home with me." He took the last joint off the center table and stuck it in his ear as Diana came into the room.

"Oh, good. A sober adult has shown up." She sat on the floor next to Rob.

He opened his eyes and looked at her. "Any more pie?" he asked. Diana waved her *dulé* and conjured a tray of the dinner they made tonight and the desserts from Christmas the night before on the coffee table.

"Sweeeet!" Sean said. He rolled off the couch and over Chris to get to the tray and Chris following right behind him. Rob came last. The three of them sat around it and ate with their fingers.

Diana looked at Ted and said quietly, "At least he's eating."

Ted nodded. "Sean might not be as foolish as we thought. But let's not leave Sean alone with him anymore." Sean looked up and winked at Ted, then went back to eating.

"The 'he' you speak of can hear you," Chris said as he stuffed more pudding into his mouth, then licked his fingers. Ted and Diana smiled.

They ate until everything was gone, then went back to their respective places, with Sean on the couch stretched out and Chris sitting on the floor in front of Sean's feet. Rob made his way to the piano bench to sit down, but ended up lying across it. That was where Quentin found everyone when he came home. Diana was still on the floor by the fireplace, so he sat down next to her, and she laid her head in his lap while he stroked her hair.

"Ciaran is okay," he told everyone, but mostly Chris. "I gave him your message and your clothes, and I think he got it pretty clear."

"Good," Chris said. His face fell, and he let out a breathy sigh as he looked down, thinking of Ciaran.

"Oooh, somebody change the subject quick before Chris starts to cry," Sean teased. Chris swung his arm backward to hit Sean, but he lifted his leg quickly, anticipating his reaction. "Too slow!" he cackled.

"If I were a real Magus I would *silencio* your arse daily," said Chris. "How you do all put up with him?"

Sean stopped laughing and said, "Speaking of silencing spells, what was that crack you made earlier, Rob? About Ciaran using *silencio*?"

"*Arcanos susurrus*," Rob clarified from the bench.

"Yeah, what was that about?" Sean asked.

Diana chimed in. "Oh, you mean the spell that was *not* used last night?" she said, amused, and Quentin laughed heartily.

Ted was confused. "I don't get it."

Chris answered, "Well. Ciaran and I were very … *libidinous* with each other last night. And he didn't care to sound-proof the room."

Ted's mouth dropped open. Sean sat up saying, "Whaaaaaaaaat?"

"And it was loooooud," Rob bemoaned. "So, so loooooud."

Ted could not close his mouth. "Holy shit!"

"And it wasn't just loud, Ted," Diana said with her face still in Quentin's lap. "It went on and on for well over an hour, nonstop. Groaning and banging and hollering. It was passionate. And terrifying."

Quentin laughed again, and Sean fell back on the couch, cackling.

Chris was smiling. "It was not my idea, nor was it planned. I think he just stopped giving a toss about what anyone thought of him, of us."

"Holy shit," Ted said again. "Who has my brother become?"

"Poor Chloé must have heard it all," Rob said. "I slept right here. I only heard them muffled through the walls."

"Yeah, we heard more than enough from the second floor," Quentin said. "We had to *surdi* our ears to get some sleep."

Ted was still stunned. "Wow."

"Well, you know us libidinous Beals men!" Sean said. He laughed and made gyrating motions on the couch. "Sounds like Ciaran's inner dragon came out, and he tamed Chris all night." That made them all laugh.

Chris laughed too, then said, "Wait a minute. Why is the assumption that I was on the bottom?" No one spoke, and they looked at each other, then laughed again. "Seriously? I am not the girl in this relationship, dammit. I'm a man!" He deepened his voice.

"No one is denying your manliness," said Ted. "It's just that Ciaran seems like the more dominant one here."

"Well, he's not," said Chris defiantly. "It's more like 50/50."

Sean laughed out loud. "Get the fuck out of here! No one here believes that!" he yelled.

"Okay, maybe 60/40," Chris admitted.

Ted raised an eyebrow. "70/30?"

"90/10!" Sean yelled again, and everyone laughed.

Chris swung his hand back again and managed to actually hit Sean on the leg, who yelled in pain. "Ugh, I hate this bloke! Really, why do you keep him around?" Chris said playfully.

"Comic relief, apparently," Ted said, laughing.

As the laughter died down, Chris thought of Ciaran again. He drew his knees up to his chest and held himself close. "Guys, I don't know how I'm going to sleep tonight. Or what I'm going to do if he goes away. I don't think I can live without him. No, I know I can't," he said sadly.

"Don't talk like that," Ted said. "We're not there yet. Take it one day at a time. Get through tonight. Then the weekend. It will all sort itself out on Monday," he said encouragingly.

Sean playfully nudged Chris's shoulder with his foot. Chris looked up, and Sean gave him a look. Chris nodded back.

Ted noticed. "What was that about?" Neither responded. "Don't do anything stupid, Sean," he said to his brother.

Sean lifted up his right hand and said, "I solemnly swear we won't do anything stupid over the weekend."

Ted's eyes narrowed at him. Chris snorted, then unsuccessfully tried to stifle a laugh.

Ted stared at Sean a little longer before he turned to Quentin. "Can you go check on Ciaran tomorrow? Make sure he is okay?"

"Sure. I can go every day if you need me to and stay as long as I want," Quentin said.

"If you don't mind," Ted asked.

"Not at all," Quentin said. "He's my brother too now."

"Thank you," Ted said. "Indeed, he is." He looked at Diana, who was still in Quentin's lap, her eyes closed now as he continued to play in her hair. "You look happy, little sister." She opened her eyes and looked up at him, smiled, and then closed her eyes again.

Ted stood up and said, "Try to get some rest tonight, all of you. I'll be back in the morning. Sean, are you staying the night?"

"You know I don't like to Wisp when I'm high. I'm afraid half of me will be at my flat while the other half is in the Gran Canaria." They all chuckled. "But I'm not substituting for Ciaran, if that's what you're asking."

"And who says I want to spoon with a smelly bloke like you?" Chris responded.

Sean pushed his three first toes on Chris's cheek to hit him, then jumped up to run as Chris chased him around the house.

CHAPTER 33

Separated

Chris had terrible dreams all night about Ciaran being separated from him. He woke up before the sun and went downstairs to the kitchen. He made tea and stared out the back window into the garden, feeling heavy with sadness. Chris said a silent prayer, wishing he had thought to bring his rosary beads with him. His heart ached so much, but he refused to cry over it. He wanted to be strong and positive for Ciaran.

He turned around when he heard a noise behind him. Diana came into the kitchen and said, "I thought I heard someone stirring down here. Come, let's make breakfast for Ciaran. Quentin's going to bring it to him and keep him company today."

He smiled at her. "Thank you."

"Of course," she said kindly. "Now let's get to work."

Ciaran was lying in bed staring at the ceiling when his cell door opened a little before 9 a.m. Quentin walked in and said, "Morning, Ciaran."

"Hey!" Ciaran was surprised and happy.

Quentin handed him a wrapped package, then sat down in the chair. Ciaran knew what it was before he opened it. He tore the foil off and took a bite of Chris's homemade shawarma, and he melted. "Hmmmm, I could cry right now. Did you taste it?"

"I did. He made us all one. He has exceptional skills in the kitchen. I'll give him that."

Ciaran took another bite. "The first time he cooked for me, really cooked for me, was a few days after we made our relationship official. He said, 'We are not eating at the Atrium today; we're going grocery shopping.' Quentin, I didn't even know where the market was. I picked up things at the store to get me by and ate cooked meals from Mum and Phoebe. So we bought all this stuff and stacked my fridge and icebox; then he made me one of these. Now, I eat these a lot at the Atrium; Lewis is great, but something about the way his melt in your mouth, it's like heaven on earth. He definitely missed his calling." He took another bite, then asked, "Is he okay?"

"Yeah, seemed in good spirits today. Him and Sean are ... bonding. A bit of a bromance forming."

"I know what that means." Ciaran shook his head. Quentin chuckled. "I'm okay with him numbing himself for a bit, if that's what gets him through. Sean is going to do it, I'm sure of it, and pull Chris along."

He took another bite and talked about Chris and their first date at Nemo's. But he paused after they reached the bedroom and said, "You don't want to hear all about that."

Quentin couldn't help it. "Yeah, I think I heard enough the night before last." He grinned.

"Oh. Right. I'm sorry about that." Ciaran went a little pink with embarrassment.

"No, you're not, and that's okay," Quentin said.

Ciaran laughed. "Okay, you're right, I'm not that sorry," he said.

Quentin laughed. "It's good that he makes you happy. It means something."

Ciaran looked up at the wall over Quentin's head. "It means everything. He means everything to me."

—

Quentin left for work and came back at 6 p.m., and Ciaran was overjoyed to see him. He looked forward to Quentin's visits, especially since Williams did not hang around to listen anymore, and it gave him a break from the depressing thoughts in his head. Quentin handed him a bowl this time, and Ciaran knew it was Tavë Kosi, an Albanian dish. They ate together and talked.

"How is he?" Ciaran asked, as usual.

"Okay. Sean and Rob took him to the shop, so he spent the day with them. Then he came home and dived into cooking. He was quiet when I left. Nights are hard for him, I think."

"I know the feeling exactly. I'm glad you're all getting to know him, accept him. Maybe Mum and Dad will get close to him, too." Quentin made a face that Ciaran caught. "What? Tell me."

Quentin hesitated, but said, "Your dad's been around, but I haven't seen your mum since we all left Claustra together yesterday afternoon."

Ciaran leaned back against the stone wall. "She hasn't come by?" he asked quietly. "She hasn't talked to Chris at all?"

Quentin chose his words carefully. "No. I think she's really scared for you, and it's making it hard for her to connect with anything or anyone linked to this whole thing."

Ciaran read between the lines. "So she blames him for this and doesn't want to get to know him at all. She hates him," he said sadly.

"I don't think she hates him. I just think it's really hard for her," Quentin tried. Ciaran sighed and was quiet. "I'm sorry, Ciaran. Let's talk about something else."

"No, it's okay. I think I'm tired now. I appreciate the dinner. The food here is shit. Can't imagine eating it for the next ten years," he said, defeated.

"Well, I'll come back tomorrow, bring breakfast with me."

Ciaran was thoughtful. "Tell Chris not to make me food anymore. It's just torture..."

Ciaran felt his eyes begin to well up with tears and closed them. Thoughts of his mother rejecting Chris, thoughts of never seeing Chris again, and thoughts of being in the same cell for the next five years suddenly overwhelmed him.

His voice cracked as he asked Quentin, "Can you go?"

Quentin stood up and touched Ciaran's shoulder, then left.

Chris was sitting in the parlor with Ted, getting intoxicated to numb himself. "Would you believe me if I told you I could feel what Ciaran is feeling right now?"

Ted looked at him. "What do you mean?"

"I mean..." Chris closed his eyes and took a sip of his fourth drink of whiskey. "He's anxious. He's so afraid that it's going to be permanent. He doesn't like the feeling of not being in control of his own destiny. And it's tearing him apart inside. And he's so sad. He misses me."

"Hmmm... the *Ardenti* is getting stronger between the two of you. Do you think he could feel what you're feeling?"

"Not right now," said Chris. "It's too overwhelming for him, his own feelings, to sense mine. I just wish I could talk to him, you know? Tell him it will be okay. Tell him anything he needs to hear to reassure him. Even if I don't feel all the way reassured myself."

"Well. You could talk to him. He just can't talk back." Chris opened his eyes and looked at Ted, puzzled. Ted said simply, *"Aminas."*

"Oh, like his shadowy dragon, Kumoi," Chris understood. "Unfortunately, I haven't got one of those, have I?"

Ted smiled. "Obviously. You'll use mine."

Chris was surprised. "I didn't know you could do that. Actually, I don't think I've ever seen Ciaran create one. I just know it has to be about knowing your inner self or something."

"Well..." Ted stood up, waved his *dulé* and said, *"Nantius animam produceré."* A blast of silvery white came out of his *dulé* and formed a lion that roamed around the room, then stopped in front of him.

"That easy, huh?" Chris teased.

Ted smiled and said, "I know exactly who I am. The eldest son, which makes me a leader. A great husband to an amazing, beautiful wife who lives to make me happy. A great father to two wonderful children and another beautiful daughter on the way. Great job that I'm confident in." He paused, then said, "Ciaran makes them effortlessly, too, just so you know."

Chris smiled and watched Ted bend over and say to the lion, "*Nuntius* Christopher. Go on, boy."

He pointed to Chris, and the lion dutifully came over and stood in front of him. It began to glow blue and waited.

———◆———

Ciaran lay in the dark, staring at the ceiling again. He was reliving his time in the Amazon with Sean to avoid thinking of Chris. He thought he imagined the light until it got brighter. He turned around to see Ted's lion *Amina* sitting in the middle of the room.

He smiled. "Hey, Ted."

"Ciaran."

Ciaran stopped breathing for a moment hearing Chris's voice. "Chris..." he breathed out. He sat up to put his bare feet on the floor.

"Um... hi. Surprise! This is my new Amina!" the lion said.

Ciaran busted out laughing, then covered his mouth so as to not alert a guard.

"No, obviously I'm using Ted's. Because surprise, I'm not a Magus! Just a Commoner in love with one. I was thinking about the first few days and the weeks after..." [Chris looked at Ted who pretended not to listen, then resumed talking.] *...after the first time. I was so nervous about how things would go. Remember, you asked me that Sunday why I didn't touch you all night? I guess I was expecting things to be awkward between us, you know? But it wasn't. It was like we were the same, except we were fucking, too.* [He laughed, and Ciaran laughed again, softly this time.] *"It was so..."* ["Easy," Ciaran said for him during his pause.] *"...easy. I kept waiting for the drama, the getting tired of seeing each other every single day, or seeing your socks on my floor, anything. You really aren't a neat person*

without your Vis. But it just never happened, did it? In fact, the exact opposite did. I couldn't get enough of you; all I wanted to do was be with you all the time. Just be with you, like how we lie on the couch, head to foot, reading or watching Animal Planet or NatGeo Wild. Or lying in the bed looking at each other... I'm just rambling now. God, I wish I could just hear your voice, telling me in that calm way that it will be fine. I feel like someone put a crack in my glass heart. And any moment now it's going to shatter..."

Chris's voice broke, and he paused. Ciaran whispered, "I feel the same."

"I want you to know that I'm sticking with Plan A. But Plan B is still an option. Sean will see to that." [Ted looked up at Chris; Ciaran nodded in understanding.] *"Because no matter what happens, no matter how long it takes, we will be together. I told you that I'm going to love you forever, and I meant it then. I mean it now... Okay, I've talked enough. I don't even know if this thing comes with a cutoff recording time. Hope you get all of this. Sorry for the rambling."* [He sighed, and Ciaran sighed right with him.] *"I don't know if this is making you feel worse or better. Equally for me. God, I wish I could just hear your voice... End it, Ted. I can't—"*

The lion walked out the side wall. Ciaran was grateful for the darkness again, so no one could see the tears streaming down his face.

CHAPTER 34

Going Under

Chris did not get out of bed on Saturday morning. Diana knocked on the door, then opened it, and he pretended to be asleep. She went downstairs and told Quentin that Chris wasn't ready to come down. At a quarter to nine, everyone was downstairs except Chris, who still pretended to be sleeping.

"I'm going up," Quentin announced.

He went to the room, knocked once, then opened the door. "Chris, I'm going to leave soon to see Ciaran. Anything you want me to tell him?" Chris did not answer. Quentin tried again. "If I tell Ciaran you're not doing well, he's going to worry. You don't want him to worry about you, right?"

Chris shifted in the bed and put a pillow over his head. He said muffled, "Shut the door on your way out please, Quentin."

Quentin went back downstairs and told Rob, Sean, and Diana. "I think this is what Ciaran was afraid of."

"So what do we do?" asked Rob.

"I don't know," said Quentin.

"You can't tell Ciaran, Quentin; it will depress him," Diana pleaded.

"I know," said Quentin. "He will ask as he always does, and I have to figure out what to say."

"Alright, I'm going up," Sean announced. "I got it."

He did not knock; instead, Sean opened the door and pulled back the curtains with a wave of his hand again. Chris shifted away from the light and pulled the pillow tighter to his face.

"What are you doing, mate?" Sean said. "You gotta get up." Chris ignored him.

Sean walked over to pull the comforter off him, but Chris caught it and pulled it back, returning his head under the pillow. "Do you really want Ciaran to know that you are moping around and feeling shitty?"

"Well, Ciaran isn't here, is he?" he said plainly.

Sean groaned. "Okay, come on. I just said that to be an arsehole the other day. Remember, it could go either way with me." Chris didn't answer. Sean sat on the edge of the bed.

"Chris, I know it's hard. I miss him, too. But you can't fall apart right now." Chris didn't respond. "Dammit, Christopher, get the fuck up! I thought you were fighting. This isn't fighting; this is giving up. And if you give up on yourself, on what you and Ciaran have, then... then you don't deserve him in the first place!" Sean yelled angrily.

Chris didn't say anything for a moment, but then said under the pillow, "Sean, kindly fuck off, will you?"

Sean stormed out of the room, leaving the door and curtains open, and Chris did not get up to close them.

Quentin was at the bottom of the stairs. "I take it, it didn't go so well?"

"I might have just made it worse," Sean muttered sourly. "I'll call Ted when I get to work. He'll know what to do."

Quentin nodded. "I'm going to go see Ciaran and tell him as little as possible."

They left together, Rob and Sean to open up the shop and Quentin to go see Ciaran.

Diana went into the kitchen and made a cup of tea. She took it upstairs to the third-floor bedroom and placed it on the nightstand. Chris had his back turned away from her, with the pillow on his head covering his face. Diana touched the back of his head that she could see, gently running her hand through his curls once. She closed back the curtains so the room was dark and quietly closed the door.

Chris was in and out of consciousness. He let his mind take him back to moments with Ciaran, reliving them over and over again: the first time he gave Ciaran a ride home and watched him nervously play with the saltshaker at the Atrium, their first date, how they bonded over music the day after the first date, Ciaran's first blow job, the first I love you's under their tree, the last I love you's on Christmas morning, the first time they had sex, the first time they made love and Ciaran saying to him, "That's how you make love to your boyfriend"...

Every time he opened his eyes to the dark room and the empty bed, he wanted to die. So he would close them again and relive more moments: laughing about something on the bed in the Tank, Ciaran drunk off his ass for his birthday, then again that night they took Ted to the bar, then high as a kite for Chris's birthday... He heard Ciaran talking with him and laughing with him. He could feel Ciaran's mouth on his skin, hands entwined with his, the smell of his arm-pits, the smell of him.

Sean thought Chris was giving up, but he was doing the opposite; this was how he was holding on. Because if this was where Ciaran was going to be, right in his head, then this was where Chris would be as well. And as long as he could see and feel Ciaran, his dark cloud couldn't pull him under.

Quentin gave Ciaran a bowl of eggs, bacon, sausage, veggies, and black pudding. "Diana made you an English breakfast."

Ciaran thanked him. "You're late today. Everything okay?" he asked as he ate.

"Yeah, sure. Everyone slept in, so it was a late start," he said nonchalantly.

"Yeah? How is Chris doing?"

Quentin was waiting for the question and prepared his answer. "He was still asleep when I left, but I'm sure he's fine." Not exactly a lie, but Ciaran caught it anyway.

He stopped eating and gave Quentin a hard look. "Chris was sleeping soundly, was he?"

"Yeah." Quentin quickly averted his eyes. "So I brought a Commoner chess set. They wouldn't let me bring in Magi games, but this was okay. Let's play when you're done."

Ciaran knew he was being evasive, but decided to let it go for now. "Set it up."

Ted left Elodie with the kids and came over early afternoon. He went straight upstairs and opened the door. Chris lay unchanged from the morning with a pillow over his head. Ted sat on the edge of the bed and didn't say anything.

After five minutes of silence, Chris said, "Go home, Theodore."

"No," Ted said simply.

They sat in silence for another couple of minutes. Then Ted said, "Is this your plan for the next two days? To drown yourself in your sorrows? Because I have to tell you, no one here is going to let that happen." Chris didn't respond. "If I had known that sending him a message was going to do this to you, I would have never done it."

Chris was silent, then said in a broken voice, "I just want to see him. I can see him, hear him, talk to him, smell him right here. Just let me stay here with him."

Ted's heart was breaking for him. "Chris..." he began. But even he didn't have the words. If he were separated from Elodie, he would probably want to do the same. And they didn't have *Ardenti*. He couldn't even begin to imagine how Chris was feeling.

Chris spoke again, pleading, "Please ... just let me stay here with him... He's here with me... Just let me stay here..." He trailed off in a whisper.

Ted sighed. "Someone's going to check on you every hour. The curtains can stay drawn, but the door stays open. And try to eat or drink something. I'm right downstairs until Sean and Rob get home from work."

Chris didn't respond. Ted got up and left the door open a crack and went downstairs to talk to Diana. As soon as he left, Chris started sobbing under the pillow.

They were halfway through their chess game when Ciaran said without looking at Quentin, "I can feel it, you know. There is an air of depression I feel deep inside, and it's not my own. How bad is it?"

He made a chess move and sat back. Quentin didn't respond at first, pretending to be concentrating on his next move. When he finally moved a piece, he looked up, but Ciaran was not looking at the game. "How bad is it?" he asked again.

Quentin sat up straighter and put one foot over his knee. "It's nothing we can't handle. I think it's just hitting him hard today. He spent the first day high as a kite with Sean and the second day acting like he was okay."

"And day three he won't get out of bed," Ciaran finished for him. Quentin nodded.

Ciaran got off the bed and walked around, thoughtful. "Let him feel what he's feeling today. If he held it in, he was going to explode later, so maybe this is better. Tell him he has twenty-four hours to sulk; then he gets his shit together. Tell him I said it just like that. Twenty-four hours, then get the fuck up and deal with it. Because I can feel what he's feeling, and it sucks, and I won't make it if..." Ciaran stopped walking. "He has twenty-four hours." Ciaran sat back down.

Quentin watched him for a moment. "How are you doing, Ciaran? Has the reality of this whole thing hit you? Did you have your twenty-four hours yet?"

"I don't need twenty-four hours," he said strongly. "But yes, I had my pity party last night, and now I'm done. I've also been high every night to sleep so..." He shrugged.

"Okay. Just know that I'm here for you, too," Quentin said. "If you want to talk."

Ciaran gave him a genuine smile. "I know. And you've been brilliant, really. Thanks, little brother."

Quentin grinned at Ciaran calling him little brother. It was a Beals thing.

Chris did not come downstairs for dinner, and Quentin hadn't come back yet. When Diana checked on him last, she noticed he was not drinking the tea, but she kept replacing it with a fresh cup. She had been adding a few drops of Anxiety Ease elixir to each cup, hoping it was helping to ease his mind. After dinner she went upstairs with her fourth cup of tea, put it on the nightstand and saw his head was on the pillow instead of under it. She touched his hair gently as she did every time. But this time Chris reached up and grabbed it and kissed her palm. He opened his eyes and turned to her.

"Thank you," he said softly.

"You're welcome." She continued to play in his hair, and he closed his eyes, welcoming her soft touch. Then she started talking.

"Did you know that Quentin left England at fourteen? He just disappeared on us and popped up a year later to join the Magi military. He told Rob, Chloé, and I that he had to prove to himself that he was not a dark witch like the rest of his family. And then he just ... left. For four years. I was devastated to say the least. I didn't know if I would ever see him again. I got posts from him so sporadically, there were times when I didn't know if he was alive or dead. I would go days and pretend to be fine, and then it would hit me, and I wouldn't get out of bed, let alone go to any classes. I was walking around with half a heart. It was awful. Honestly, it was Chloé and Rob who pulled me out, stayed with me, understood me, and encouraged me. But then the war ended, and the first thing he did was show up at my door. And when he did, we both just knew we would spend the rest of our lives together.

"I don't know why I'm telling you this. Except to say, everything that we went through was all worth it in the end.

It solidified what we have. And I believe that this will be the same for you and Ciaran."

He looked at her, then slowly closed his eyes again. She ran through his curls a few more times and left.

Quentin came home about an hour later and gave Chris Ciaran's message. Chris sat up in the bed and looked at him. He opened his mouth to respond, but then threw the covers back over his head. Quentin sighed as he came back downstairs.

"Nothing?" Ted asked.

"No, not really," said Quentin. "What do we do, Ted?"

Ted sighed deeply. "I'll be back," he said.

Ted walked out the back door and Wisp'd on the spot, appearing on the back porch of his family home in Kingsbridge. He let himself in and found his mother knitting in the living room.

"Ted!" she said, surprised. Then her face turned scared. "Is Ciaran alright!?"

"Ciaran's fine, Mum. Quentin saw him today and spent the day with him."

"Oh, that's good." She went back to knitting. Ted took a seat on the couch and faced her.

"You need to talk to Christopher," he started.

"I will do no such thing," she said without looking up. "That boy—"

Ted cut her off. "That *boy* hasn't gotten out of bed all day. He is sinking right now, and no one can pull him up. Not even Ciaran's threats from Claustra."

"Well, if he's not listening to any of you, he's not going to listen to me." She kept knitting.

"But he will," Ted told her. "His mother was the closest thing to him before she died. Next to her is his eldest sister. Neither of them are here right now, but you are. He needs a mother, Mum. A mother to get him out of bed, cook him a hot meal, and tell him everything is going to be okay."

"I don't even know if everything is going to be okay, Ted," she snipped at him.

"And when has that ever stopped you from encouraging us to believe it? Why can't you do that now?"

Grace slammed her knitting tools in her lap in frustration. "Don't I get to be upset right now? I don't have anyone to tell me it's going to be okay either, apart from your father, because we just don't know." Her voice broke, and tears started falling.

Ted got off the couch and kneeled beside his mother. "Mum, Ciaran's not dying. And Chris didn't do anything to spite you. They fell in love! That's their entire crime. And if Ciaran does get sentenced to any amount of time, it will be up to us to keep them connected, for Ciaran's sake. Ciaran, who selflessly puts everything aside to be there for each of us when we need him to, who has never asked anything of us in return, is asking us to accept Christopher as not just a part of his life, but a part of ours. And if this was Quentin or Elodie sinking into despair, you would be there making sure they didn't fall into a depression, whatever it takes. Why can't you do the same for Chris?"

"I don't know," Grace said quietly. "I don't know if I can do that right now."

Ted stood up and spoke to his mother sternly. "Well, figure it out. Because I know you're the only one who can."

He kissed his mother on her cheek and said good night, Wisp'ing back to London.

Chris moved his foot sometime in the middle of the night and kicked something.

"OOWWW!" someone yelled.

Chris sat up in the dark. "Who the fuck is that!?"

"It's me. Rob."

Chris sighed and lay back on the bed. "And why are you in my bed, Robert?"

"Well. I know sleeping alone for the last three nights sucks. I figured you could use the company. I know I can." He rubbed his nose that Chris kicked, thankful it wasn't bleeding.

Chris was quiet for a moment, then said, "You are definitely not the stupid one."

"Who said I was the stupid one!? Sean, innit? What an arsehole!" Rob said angrily.

Chris smiled for the first time all day. "I'm sorry I kicked you, Rob."

"That's okay. You want me to go?"

"No. Stay. You're right. I could use the company."

"Okay." Rob rolled over and quickly fell back asleep.

Chris stayed up a little bit longer, thankful for Ciaran's cousin, brothers, and sister, who refused to leave him alone.

CHAPTER 35

Mum

Diana, Quentin, Rob, and Sean were sitting in the kitchen early Sunday morning trying to decide how to handle Chris when the front door busted open. They all looked as Grace came into the kitchen. She did not say hello.

"Is he still in bed?" she asked.

"Yes, Mum," Diana answered. She was about to say more, but her mother abruptly turned around and stormed up the stairs.

Grace swung open the bedroom door, and they could hear her yelling from upstairs.

"ENOUGH OF THIS! GET UP!"

Chris was startled awake and sat up quickly. Grace drew the curtains with her *dulé*, which made Chris's eyes hurt from all the sunlight as she talked, or rather, hollered.

"Do you *think* that YOOOOU are the only one who feels like crawling under the covers right now? Is it YOOOUR heart alone that's breaking? Do you *think* that you're special somehow, that YOOOUR feelings are more important than

Ted's or Diana's or Sean's or Rob's or Alastair's or Quentin's? More important than his DAD'S? THAN MINE?"

Chris was stunned. He opened his mouth to talk, then closed it.

"THAT WAS AN ACTUAL QUESTION, YOUNG MAN!"

"No, Mrs. Beals," he said automatically. "No, my feelings are not more important than yours, certainly not. Or anyone's really."

"Good. Now that we got that established, you're going to get up, take a shower, and wash that *stink* off you, and come help me in the garden," she demanded.

Chris opened his mouth again, then closed it. She walked over to the bed dangerously. "Excuse me? Am I to believe that you were about to refuse my nonrequest? Did you not say to me on Tuesday that you were going to help me in Diana's garden? DID YOU!??"

"Yes, Mrs. Beals. I did."

"Well!?"

Chris nodded. "I'll be down in an hour."

"THIRTY MINUTES!" she bellowed. "Do *not* keep me waiting."

She left the door open and went back downstairs to the four of them in the kitchen, looking stunned and amused.

"AND WHAT ARE YOU STILL SITTING AROUND FOR!? Don't you have a shop to run? Don't you have a prison to visit?"

Rob, Sean, and Quentin were up and out of the kitchen before she finished speaking. She turned to Diana and said calmly, "Diana, dear, pull out the deweeding tools, dragon dung, and two sets of dragon hide gloves. Leave them on the table; then you leave, too. You haven't left the house either; go find some friends to hang out with today."

Diana grinned and kissed her mother on the cheek before she too followed her mother's instructions.

——◆——

By the time Chris came downstairs, the house was quiet. The back door was open, and he went over to see Grace pulling up weeds. She barely looked at him when he came outside, but started giving him orders.

"We are going to clear the left side where the herbs are and the back side where the magical botany is, then add the dragon dung, and mix it with the natural soil. Watch out for gnomes; they bite."

"You don't use magic for that?" Chris asked.

Grace paused and looked at him. "Magic does not solve all of life's problems. Sometimes you need to just get in there with your hands and make something happen. To feel human. Now stop talking and get to work."

Chris grabbed the gloves on the back porch steps he knew were for him and joined her. They worked all morning, barely speaking except Grace giving out instructions, and only stopped when she announced that she was making lunch. Chris ate Grace's vegetable stew, which warmed and filled his belly, and realized how hungry he was. His heart still ached, but now his hands and arms did too, and he felt a little less empty, physically and emotionally. They resumed right after lunch.

As he was adding dragon dung to the back side of the garden, he heard Grace say, "Your mother died eight years ago, is that right?"

Chris gasped, not prepared to talk about his mother. "Yes."

"I'm sorry. I know it's still painful for you."

"Yes," Chris replied. "It is."

"Do you know that I lost a son? Almost four years ago?"

Chris stopped working altogether and sat down to face her. Grace had her back turned, still scraping at the dirt. "Yes, I know. Shane," Chris said.

"Well. The pain is different for me. Until you become a parent and lose one of your children, you will never understand that pain, that kind of hole that lives in you every day. Every day, Hamish and I wake up knowing that something is missing from our lives. And we make the decision to get up and go about our day, knowing it will always be there. I know you know what that feels like. But for a parent to come face-to-face with the real possibility of losing another... Well. You can't imagine."

Chris was quiet for a moment, then said, "No. I suspect I can't."

"I know he loves you," Grace acknowledged. "I know you love him. I am just not sure if it was worth all the risks you both took. And I'm angry. I'm angry at both of you for being so incredibly reckless and foolish and stupid. He could have just *abscondo* your memory that first day, literally found a reason to meet you the next day, and you would have been none the wiser. Because, obviously, it's not the magic that draws you to him, it's him. And when it became serious, he should have approached the Council at that point.

"And you! Once you realized that Ciaran had broken our most sacred law, you never encouraged him to come clean. Aren't you a lawman yourself? Where was his integrity? Where was yours!? No, you just ran around like two children in love without a thought to the consequences. And now we're all paying for it." She wiped tears with the back of her arm.

Chris hung his head down. "You're right. We should have handled it with more maturity. I'm so sorry, Mrs. Beals. You are a hundred percent right."

"I appreciate your apology," Grace said. "I am dreading losing another son; there is no mistaking that. But I've already lost a son, and I'm surviving it. I can walk around with a hole in my heart and still carry about my day. If Ciaran stays in Claustra, I will survive that, too, for Ciaran's sake. And so will you, right?"

Chris nodded. "Yes. I will survive it, too. For Ciaran."

"Then stop acting like you won't," she said sternly.

He nodded again. "Yes, Mrs. Beals."

She turned around. "Is there a reason you stopped working?" Her eyes narrowed. Chris smiled and started adding dung again.

Quentin came back late in the afternoon to Chris and Grace in the kitchen, cooking dinner. He went to hug Grace. "That's from Ciaran. I told him what you did this morning."

"Yeah? What did he have for me?" Chris asked, amused.

"Something that's never going to happen," Quentin said, and they both laughed. "Where's Diana?"

"I sent her to find some friends to play with," Grace said.

Chris laughed. "She's not seven years old, you know."

"Hold your tongue," Grace said playfully. "When you and Ciaran start having children, you'll see that they will always be seven years old in your eyes."

The thought of him and Ciaran having children together made him grin. Then he looked at Quentin. "Why are you back so early?"

"Ciaran told me to go. He said he wanted to do some thinking alone before tomorrow. The hearing is at 8 a.m., so I'm picking him up at 7:30 a.m. so we can get there early enough. Chloé sent me a message and said Magna got me assigned to that courtroom on Monday so I will be the official Magi enforcer on-site. And I will be with him the whole time."

Chris nodded but didn't say anything more.

CHAPTER 36

For Ciaran

Ted came by with Elodie, Victoré, and Teddy for Sunday dinner. Quentin went to play with the children as Elodie sat down at the kitchen table. She said to Chris, "So I hear you're experiencing *Ardenti* as a Commoner?"

Chris chuckled. "If it isn't a soul connection that Ciaran and I have, then I don't know what it is."

"*Oui,*" Elodie agreed. "Any magic that is created from love or blood is the strongest kind of magic. My grandparents have *Ardenti*. My *grandpère* saved my *grandmère's* life, and that is how it began for them. *Ardenti* is born out of care and passion and intensifies with love as time goes on until two souls are unrecognizable from the other. It occurs when there is an intense situation, life or death, and one soul will cling to another. The other soul receives it."

"Well, Ciaran saved my life, twice," said Chris. "So I know it was my soul that grabbed onto his."

"But his received yours, too," she said. "Don't forget that part; it's very important. True *Ardenti* is slow and gradual, but, eventually, they fuse into one the longer the souls are together. You slowly start to feel what the other feels; telepathy forms—"

"I can hear his thoughts!" Chris remembered. "Not all the time. Usually when we're in a ... passionate state," Chris said sheepishly. Elodie grinned. "But he can send his thoughts to me. I can't send them back, though."

"That's only because you aren't Magi," she said. "If you were, you could. My grandparents, to this day, will sit quietly for hours, only conversing with each other. It's beautiful and romantic—"

Suddenly, she lifted her eyes up as if she was thinking. Then she slowly turned around to Ted, who was not looking at her but had a grin on his face. *"Tu veux que je lui raconte les sales pensées qui viennent de te traverser la tête?"* she asked him.

But Chris said, "I do not want to hear about any dirty thoughts." Ted laughed out loud. Chris looked at Ted, then at Elodie. "So do you two have *Ardenti* too?"

"Sadly, no," said Elodie. "Ted and I met the regular way; he came to my Magi town in Marne for a case that Scholarly sent him on and charmed me. But some Magi are either born or can train themselves to be telepathic."

"I learned from a Chinese monk about twelve years ago, one of my first assignments," Ted said. "I used to freak my brothers out with it. Now, I just do it to my love." He grinned at her, and she grinned back.

Elodie and Chris continued talking, breaking into French in the midst of their English. Chris knew Ted brought her there to take his mind off of things, but he also knew she was happy to do it.

Sean, Rob, and Mr. Beals joined them by the time dinner was hitting the table. Sean sat next to Chris and said, "Oh, did we forget to tell you our mum is a madwoman?"

Chris smiled. "She's brilliant. You are all lucky to have her."

They ate dinner and shared stories of their day. Ciaran and the hearing were on everyone's mind, but no one mentioned his name until an argument broke out between Ted and Sean.

"Absolutely not. It's suicide," Ted said firmly.

"No, it's brilliant, and I already have all I need to—"

"Do you know what Ciaran would do to us if you got caught, or if something happened to Chris?"

Chris perked up at his name. "Come again?"

"Nothing. It's nothing at all," Ted murmured.

"Yes, nothing except we were discussing how to get you into the Council office building tomorrow," said Sean.

Everyone stopped talking as Ted said, "No. We're *not* discussing that because it's suicide. It puts Ciaran's whole case in danger, and it leaves Chris vulnerable to *abscondo*. It's all the risks and none of the rewards."

"Except for Ciaran to see him. For them to see each other! Because if this all goes to shit tomorrow, Ciaran will be grateful for the chance to say goodbye. And if it all goes well, then all the parties are present for a celebration." Sean smiled triumphantly.

Ted shook his head. "Dad, will you talk some sense into him, please?"

Grace answered first, "No, I don't like this plan at all. One of us will stay with Chris, and that's that."

But Rob said, "But how is that fair, Aunt Grace? Ciaran's our family, and we should all be there for him, including Chris." Rob feared, as the non-Beals and youngest member without ties to the Council, it would be him they would volunteer to stay, and that couldn't happen.

"You can't sneak Chris into the Magi Council!" Grace shrieked. "It's impossible!"

"Well…" Quentin said. "It's kind of … not. Others have done it, mostly Magi, but still. Not impossible to get in if you know the right guard."

"See, it's the getting out part that's going to be suicide," Ted lectured.

"And I got that covered too," Sean said.

"NO!" Grace yelled. "That's enough lawbreaking from the Beals for a lifetime. Tell them, Hamish!"

They all looked at Hamish, and he was quiet, thoughtful. They waited. He turned to Grace first and said, "It does seem like a huge risk to take. But I agree with Sean. At the very least Ciaran should be able to have a conversation with him, hopefully not their last."

Grace was horrified. "Hamish! NO! And we don't even know if he wants to go and take that risk to be caught and have his memory concealed instantly. Knowing that it could hurt Ciaran in the long run if he was caught." She tried to lay out all of the risks, just like Ted did.

"I didn't think I had to ask," her husband said to her. "I'm sure Chris made up his mind as soon as he heard about the possibility of being in the same room as Ciaran." Hamish looked at him, and Chris nodded. Hamish turned to Sean. "What's your plan, son?"

"Simple, really," said Sean. "Malcolm's Metamorphosis."

Rob gasped. "Really? We're going to use it?"

Sean smiled at him as Grace scowled. "What has my crazy brother cooked up now?"

Sean answered her. "It's a transformation elixir. It's only fifteen minutes tops, but he'll be me and go in with all of you at 7:30 a.m. Then when those fine Council folks start coming in droves for work around 8 a.m., I will blend in with them. And because I'm already in, the guard won't stop me; and if they do, my *dulé* will already be registered, and they'll just think I stepped out and now am stepping back in." Sean sat back and smiled.

"It's brilliant!" Rob said excitedly.

Diana asked, "But how will you get out? Good or bad outcome, he has to get back out of the Council building."

Sean said, "And that's why I will have a second vial of potion. We just need body secretion like spit or sweat. With all those fine Council folks milling about, he could be anyone. He could be Quentin James!"

"He cannot be Quentin," Quentin said, annoyed.

Chris said, amused, "I don't know, I think I'd make a great Quentin."

"I think so too; try it," Sean said.

Chris made a goofy face and mocked, "I'm Quentin James, and I'm actually Magi royalty!" Diana giggled.

"Oy, can you guys decide on someone else?" asked Quentin, rolling his eyes.

Sean ignored him. "That was fantastic, Chris, but try more confident and a little less awkward."

"HE CANNOT BE QUENTIN," Quentin said more loudly as Diana, Rob, Chris, and Sean cackled.

When it died down, Ted said, "I'm not convinced this is a good idea. But. Maybe the reward outweighs the risks. For Ciaran." He looked at his mother.

Grace finally resigned. "I don't like it. But Ciaran will be so happy. So for his sake... fine."

"Well," Hamish stood up. "I shan't hear any more of these plans. And Quentin and Diana, if you know what's good for you, you will leave as well."

He and Grace left, and Diana followed her father's advice, pulling Quentin upstairs with him. Chris listened to Sean, Rob, and Ted formulate the plan. Despite how terrible the circumstances were, a warm spot formed in his chest, replacing the last remnants of the dark cloud that tried to pull him under. Christopher was happy. He knew that no matter what happened next, he and Ciaran's story was far from over. He could feel it in his soul.

———————

Ciaran was sitting on the bed in the dark, trying not to freak out. He wished he had another joint to distract him, but he finished the final one last night. He told Quentin to go because the panic attacks kept happening, getting more intense. He would breathe through it, telling himself everything was going to be okay. That he wouldn't be separated from Chris. But the squeezing of his chest would start all over again.

He wondered if that was how Chris felt every time he went on a mission. The days apart were torture enough, but then not knowing whether he would see him again… That was the part that made him want to crumple up into a ball.

Suddenly the room brightened. He thought he was hallucinating when he saw the Barnaby lion *Amina* enter his cell again. He half expected to hear Chris's voice again, but Ted's instead came through.

"*Quentin said you sent him away tonight, saying you wanted to be alone to think. And we decided not to accept that, so we're going to keep you company until you fall asleep, aren't we?*"

Elodie's lioness found its way in. "*We are rooting for you and Chris's Ardenti, Ciaran.*"

Quentin's hawk came through the wall next. "*We got Chris back to it. He's fine. But remember, we're here for you too.*"

Diana's horse came galloping right behind and said, "*We love you, Ciaran!*"

Rob's Jack Russell terrier said, "*I'm here too!*"

A phoenix flew in. Ciaran was confused until it said in Sean's voice, *"Just because you don't see me, doesn't mean I'm not there."* He smiled at Sean's new *Amina*.

Chloé's rabbit came hopping in and said, *"I'm sorry I haven't come to see you. But I'm here for you, Ciaran. And we are going to win,"* she said confidently. *"Have faith. I will see you tomorrow."*

Alastair's possum said, *"Bordering on inappropriate since I am on the jury, but nevertheless you are my first cousin, and so I will also provide my full support."*

Hamish's fox said plainly, *"Son."*

Grace's minx said to him, *"Everything will be alright. You'll see."*

As the ten glowing animals milled around the small cell to find spots to fit, Ciaran was overwhelmed with love and happiness. He had never conjured one without his *rodulé* before, but somehow he knew he could do it. And he wouldn't need his wrists at all.

He stood up, stretched his arms wide, and closed his eyes, saying calmly, *"Nantius animam produceré."*

Kumoi, the tattoo, began to glow, and the dragon flew off his back in a silver form. It flew around the room for a moment before landing between the lion and the phoenix, joining the rest of his family.

"No," he told his dragon. "Go to him. Stay with him. All night."

He recorded a quick message. The dragon abruptly got up and flew out of the ceiling of the stone cell.

Ciaran lay on his side as the animals settled around him, watching him. Before he fell asleep, he thought to himself, *It's nice to cry happy tears for a change.*

It was well after midnight when Chris finally went upstairs to his room, finishing a cup of tea that Diana made especially for him. He opened the door, and the room was already bright. The dragon was perched on the top of the bedpost. Chris slowly closed the door and sat on the bed.

"Ciaran," he said softly.

The *Amina* flew down and also sat on the bed. "*No matter what happens, we will be together again,*" Ciaran's voice said. "*I love you forever...*"

Chris said the words along with him. "...and three days after that."

"*I'll see you soon. For now, rest. I am here with you,*" the dragon concluded.

Chris tucked himself in the bed and got comfortable. "Soon," he said in a whisper.

His eyes began to close. He knew Diana put something in the tea to put him in a deep sleep, and he welcomed it with a full heart, a connected soul, and Ciaran's spirit right beside him.

CHAPTER 37

Encouraged

Quentin showed up at Ciaran's cell at 7 a.m. in his soldier's uniform. Chloé had sent him a message letting him know that Quentin would be his personal officer and escort throughout the day and trial, and he was grateful for it. He knew that Chloé was doing everything in her power to get Ciaran through this even if she was the reason he ended up in Claustra in the first place.

When Quentin opened the gate, Ciaran was standing in the middle of the room with his head down, hands in his suit jacket pocket. "What are you doing?" Quentin asked curiously.

Ciaran was silent a few moments, then said, "Saying a prayer." He looked up. "Did you know Chris is Catholic? He doesn't go to Mass, but I caught him praying the rosary a time or two. And since our trip around the world, Sean follows this African ancestor spirituality that he learned in Cape Town, something that even I don't understand. Between the two of them, I might be a bit more spiritual. And if there was ever a day to pray, it would be today." Quentin grunted, but he understood. "Do you believe in God, Quentin?"

"I don't know," he said with a sigh. "The Jameses went to church every Sunday to keep up appearances, but as the whole Magi world knows, my mother's side of the family is Pure Evil, Incorporated. But I'm not an idiot; there has to be something out there somewhere, right? I would like to believe that a higher power was looking over me my whole life. Other than your parents, Rob's parents, the Livingstons, and Graham, the Grandminister. Maybe they are all my higher power. They saved me."

That made Ciaran smile. "Right."

Quentin asked, "Are you ready?"

"No," Ciaran admitted. "But here we go." He held out his hands for the invisible shackles.

Quentin shook his head. "No need for that. I'm assuming you aren't going to hop out of the transport and Wisp, right?"

Ciaran smiled. "It's definitely an option. But then what would Chris say?"

Quentin smiled back. "Come."

There were no other guards as Quentin stepped back out of the cell and Ciaran followed. He escorted him out of the cell unshackled and got looks from the guards at the front desk. But no one dared to say anything to Quentin James.

Quentin led him to the Claustra transport bus that had three prisoners and Magi officers on it, all others shackled. He sat down next to Ciaran, and they rode in silence. Then Ciaran asked quietly, "How was Chris this morning?"

"He is actually in really good spirits. Happy," Quentin said.

"Really? Why?" Ciaran asked. Ciaran was sure his message last night with his *Amina* wasn't enough for Chris to be happy on such a solemn day.

Quentin gave him a sly smile. Ciaran tried to catch what he was trying to tell him. "What's going on? Where is he?" he asked.

Quentin shrugged and spoke quietly. "He could be anywhere. Or anyone. Who knows? Maybe he'll appear where you least expect him to." He smirked at Ciaran again.

Ciaran was understanding, and his mouth formed an "o." "Seriously!?" he whispered. "You're not joking with me because I could not handle it right now." His heart started beating fast as the van went into a rock formation and appeared in the Blackwall Tunnel in London.

Quentin nodded slightly. Ciaran leaned back, closed his eyes, and sighed. He sent up another thank you to whatever divinity was listening. No matter what happened after, he was going to see his love again one more time.

The entire Beals clan—Hamish, Grace, Ted, Rob, Diana, and Fake Sean—arrived at the Magi Council building in Myrddin at 7:15 a.m. Pretend Sean, formally known as Christopher Jennings, presented Sean's *rodulé* for admittance. The guard barely looked at the Beals as he went through the six wands at the same time. Then he told them, "No *dulés* in the courtroom except for Council and Scholarly officials." He handed Hamish Beals and his eldest son, Ted Beals, back their wands.

The elixir that Chris took to transform him into Sean Beals was only good for fifteen minutes, enough time to get them inside, past the guards, and upstairs ten levels to the courthouse. Ciaran's trial was in courtroom number twelve, and there were two chambers attached to it, one for the accused and witnesses, the other for the jury, committee members, and officials. Hamish led them into the room on the right and not a moment too soon as Pretend Sean started changing back into Chris in the hallway, his skin getting darker, his body getting taller, his straight auburn hair becoming dark brown and kinky. They had to usher him into the room quickly to avoid suspicion.

Chris sat on the back bench and waited, staring at the door.

After ten minutes, the door opened, and Quentin walked in with Ciaran right behind him. He looked in the opposite direction of where Chris was. But Chris crossed the room in three long strides and wrapped his arms around Ciaran's neck, startling him. He turned around, and they hugged tightly for a while, whispering each other's name in their necks. There was no one else in the room that mattered but each other in that moment. Chris grabbed Ciaran's face with both hands and gently kissed him on the lips, once, twice, three times. They both chuckled and held back tears as they stared at each other.

Chris heard Ciaran in his head, still faintly but loud enough, say, <Are you okay?> Chris nodded. Ciaran nodded back. <Me, too.>

I missed you, Chris's brown eyes said, touching his face again. Ciaran did not need to hear Chris in his head to know how he felt.

<I missed you, too,> Ciaran returned in thoughts, leaning into Chris's hand.

They held onto each other again, tightly, Chris's arms around Ciaran's neck, Ciaran's arms around his waist.

Grace came over and said quietly, "I don't want to break up a happy reunion, but I could also use a hug from my son."

Chris moved back. "Of course, Mrs. Beals!"

Ciaran hugged his mother long as well as she wept on his chest. "I'm okay, Mum. I'm okay." When Grace finally let go, Ciaran went around and hugged the rest of his siblings and his cousin, Rob. But he noticed one of his siblings was missing. "Where's Sean?" he asked.

"Real Sean or Pretend Sean?" Diana asked slyly.

He looked around quizzically, and Chris explained how they got him in. "Malcolm's Metamorphosis," Chris said. "Rob's dad created this potion to transform someone into someone else. It doesn't last long and can only be used one vial at a time. Sean made two, just in case." He turned to Diana. "But now that you know the whole thing, you'll be forced to tell."

"And I will," Diana said. "I have twenty-four hours to tell either Graham or Magna, and I will do so. But for now, I'm just here as family."

Ciaran hugged her again. "I love you, little sister. Never change." Then said, "Wait a minute. If Sean doesn't arrive until after 8 a.m., I won't see him."

Chris nodded. "Yes, he knows. He thought it would be best to be the one to make the sacrifice. He said to tell you just because you don't see him doesn't mean he's not here with you."

Ciaran nodded, remembering his phoenix *Amina* from the night before. He went to sit on the long bench in the back and straddled it. Chris sat directly in front of him and straddled it as well, so their knees touched. They clasped their hands in the middle.

Chris smiled. "Hi."

Ciaran smiled back. "Hi."

"Are you okay, really?"

Ciaran shrugged. "Better now that I get to see you, touch you."

Chris smiled again. "Yeah. Me too." Ciaran looked down and played with Chris's fingers.

"So your family is wonderful," Chris began. "Your little brother got me high, your older brother told me I was the girl in our relationship, your dad called me son a few times, your little sister comforted me, and your cousin Rob slept in the same bed with me. Oh, and your mum yelled at me and made me work so hard my arms are still aching, then fed me. I think it's been a successful holiday. Who knew that admittance of our wrongdoings would lead to full acceptance of your family?"

Ciaran grinned. "Always looking to the bright side." Chris grinned back. Ciaran looked down at their fingers again. He started, "So, if this doesn't go our way—"

Chris cut him off. "It will."

"But if it doesn—"

Chris squeezed his hand. "Look at me." Ciaran looked up. "I hear you have the best Magi lawyer that ever lived, a couple of friends on the jury already rallying on your behalf, including your first cousin, and the actual top Council official is a close and personal friend of your dad's. So, no. It won't go to shit. It will be fine. We'll be fine. No matter what happens today, we'll survive it. Stop worrying."

Ciaran looked at him curiously. "Since when did you become the emotionally mature one of us?"

"Since your mum threatened to kick my arse if I didn't." They laughed together. "I'm just optimistic. I believe in our love."

Ciaran nodded, actually feeling positive. "I do too."

The door opened, and Chloé walked in. She wore a white Magi robe with three big stars on it: yellow, blue, and purple, with a matching pointy witch hat. Rob was frozen in place staring at his girlfriend, who he had admonished a few days ago for being the one forcing everyone to tell on Ciaran and

Chris's relationship. They had not seen or spoken to each other since. But he missed her tremendously.

She glanced at him, then walked over to Ciaran. The others gathered around her, with Rob staying in the rear.

"So the strategy is simple," Chloé said, getting right to it. "You answer the questions honestly, but briefly. Give brief answers whenever possible and do not elaborate. If you aren't sure, simply say, 'I do not recall' or 'I don't know.' Savannah Brickenhouse, the orchestrator of this charade, is going to weasel her way onto the jury, and if she does, she is going to try to trip you up. Don't let her antagonize you. Stay calm. Be emotional, but not angry or indignant. To everyone else, be very apologetic. I am going to ask about how you met and the nature of your relationship, then open up the questioning to the jurors. Alastair is on the jury and will keep everyone on task, which is to focus on whether or not you had malicious intent or reckless indifference of the law. Clearly, you didn't have either."

She turned to everyone else. "I am going to call two additional witnesses. Ted, who can attest to the nature of the relationship, and Diana, who will speak to the initial confession and your candor. They both already know, but any one of you should be ready to be called, including you, Quentin. They know the confession took place in your home. They will also want to know Chris's whereabouts. Everyone, be very vague. Don't lie; just be evasive. I'm going to wrap up with the sixteen statute breaches very similar to yours. Most got some level of probation; some got actual jail time, but less than a year, and that was because they told several others. I have read the investigative reports, and it works in your favor that no one can confirm they knew about Chris being an unregistered Commoner, from The Atrium or the

Dragon Reservation of Albania. And from Chris's circle, no one knew that Ciaran is a Magus or even believe magic exists."

She took a deep breath and looked at her watch. "It's five minutes to eight. You will be called in soon, so..." She looked at his parents. "Grace and Hamish, I got permission for you to sit in the courtroom in the stands and watch. Everyone else, unfortunately, will need to stay here." She glanced at Rob again, who met her gaze, then turned back to Ciaran. "Are you ready?"

"No. But I'm going anyway."

Chris squeezed his hand. "He's ready. He's got this." He squeezed his hand again. "We got this."

Chloé turned to Quentin. "Quentin, let's go. He'll be back to get you, Ciaran, when it's time."

She turned to walk out with Quentin behind her, but looked at Rob one more time before the door closed.

Ciaran and Chris looked at each other. They knew at any moment they would be separated, possibly forever.

CHAPTER 38

Magician and Man

Quentin and Chloé came into an uproar in the courtroom. Magna Keystone was sitting in the first chair seat right next to Grandminister Graham. Mistress Savannah was behind her yelling, "Step aside, girl! You will NOT be first chair here!"

Magna said strongly, "And why not? I am a top Council official, just like you."

"You think I don't know what you've been doing these last few days?" Savannah snarled. "Rallying all of Ciaran's old Campus chums for this hearing? Well, it won't work!"

"I've done no such thing!" Magna yelled back. "I have simply gone around asking people to come in on their *holiday* to sit in a hearing that *you* created. And the *only* person that has talked with Ciaran in the last couple of years outside of his cousin Alastair is Lucinda Chesterfield, and that's simply because Lucy is the Scholarly Director of Magi Anime and Wildlife in Europe and quite literally the head of the Dragon Reservation of Albania, making her Ciaran's boss's boss. This is a fair and just panel, unlike what you're trying to do!"

"Watch your mouth, little girl!"

Magna stood up slowly and raised her *dulé*. "Call me 'girl' again, and I will show you what this warlock can do!" she said dangerously.

Graham stood up. "Enough of this. Savannah, if you can make an accusation, you better be able to back it up. Now we'll go down the list of jurors and see if anyone actually has a relationship with Ciaran and who can be impartial. You can start, Savannah."

Savannah said, "I have never met Ciaran Beals before the day I arrested him. I am one of the few people who could say that here. I am completely impartial." She huffed.

Mia Santana, who was eight months pregnant, wobbled up as she stood. "It's true that Ciaran and I were in the same year at Campus. But we weren't friends; we did not run in the same circles, and honestly, I can't remember any classes we had together. Maybe Elixirs & Apothecary, and I think European Commoner History? But no, I don't know Ciaran. And I believe that makes me impartial."

Cecil Winger, who was next to her, helped her sit down, then stood up. "I don't know him. He was in the same year as my younger brother, or maybe he was a year younger, don't know for sure. There were so many Beals running around during that time, who knew which one of them was Ciaran? I can be impartial." He sat down.

Tova Price said, "I don't know Ciaran at all. I know his brother Ted; he has participated in the Magi Trading Task Force from time to time, giving some expertise as a Magi-chartered surveyor. I absolutely can be an impartial judge."

Larry Tolbert stood up. "I don't know Ciaran either. I know the twins, or rather knew Shane and know Sean. I shop at Malcolm Livingston's shop frequently with my daughters. I obviously know Hamish Beals. But I don't know Ciaran Beals. So yes, I can be impartial."

"I will admit that I was friends with Ciaran at Campus," Magna said as she stood up again. "But I haven't seen or spoken to Ciaran in over three years since the days of that last battle right on the streets of Myrddin. I have no idea if he is the same individual from the military that I knew, and for that, I can be as impartial as anyone else." She sat down with a huff.

Lucy stood up next. "Well, I do know Ciaran. And we last spoke earlier this year. He called me to discuss some Reservers wanting to start their dragonology studies early. I will be transparent and say that Ciaran and I are friends. But I never knew he was in a relationship. I am completely surprised at these charges as they are unlike his character. That being said, I can and will be an impartial judge. My record of integrity speaks for itself."

She sat down next to Magna but didn't look at her as Savannah made a sarcastic noise.

Moore Catrell stood up and said plainly, "I do not know Ciaran Beals or any of the Beals personally. I can be impartial."

"Well, obviously I know the Beals," said Joshua McFadden. "I've worked alongside his father Hamish for decades. Had dinner in their home. Our children played with theirs. But no, I don't know Ciaran very well, not since he was a boy."

Savannah interjected sarcastically, "I guess you too are saying you would be impartial?"

"Well, yes," Joshua said. "Hamish and I have done quite a number of these hearings against people I've known a lot more intimately than Ciaran. I will be impartial because it's my job. I know how these things go."

Rory Cropper said, "Ciaran and I were dorm mates at Campus for a short time. He was always a kind bloke, and I liked him. But I haven't seen or heard from him since he left England to join the dragon reservation at nineteen. So I don't know anything about Ciaran the man, as he is today. That makes me impartial."

Alastair cleared his throat and stood up to talk, but Savannah shut him down. "Don't you even try it! You are literally his first cousin. If there is one person here who is not impartial, it is you! You need to leave at once!"

"Excuse me, Mistress Brickenhouse. I take great offense to that statement," Alastair said coldly. "I have been nothing but a loyal Council official for the past twelve years, even to the detriment of my own family. Or did we forget that I sacrificed my relationships with my family members for the sake of standing on the side of the Council time and time again? I went a whole year without talking to my own mother during the war because I wholeheartedly believed in what we were doing here. So if there is one person who has proven impartiality and loyalty to the Magi Council on this panel, even above familial relationships, certainly it is me." He sat down and raised his chin up high.

"I am impartial," Graham said simply, knowing no one would dare challenge him. He asked her, "Are you satisfied now, Savannah?"

"No. But I am here to do my job. And I will sit first chair because I outrank all of you."

"You do realize that by you sitting on the jury, that makes the number an even twelve. So if there is a tie, as Grandminister, I alone will make the final decision," Graham stated.

"Unless you remove someone!" Savannah said angrily.

"And I'm not going to do that." the minister said definitively. "The fact is, you have a problem with the Beals because of how they took in and cared for your nephew, Quentin, all those years ago. And I would sooner remove you for coming in with a negative impression of Ciaran from his name alone than remove anyone else here that will give him the benefit of the doubt and see him as innocent until proven guilty. So you can decide to stay and make it an even number where the deciding vote is me, or you can go and let us proceed without you as impartial jurors, and let a jury of his peers decide."

Savannah scowled. "I will sit first chair."

"Agreed," he said politely.

She sat down as Chloé winked at Quentin and smiled. It was so far going according to plan.

Graham rose. "Quentin, please bring in the accused."

◆

It was after 8 a.m. when the door busted open and Sean wearing an identical black hooded sweater and blue jeans as Chris walked in. "Surprise!" he exclaimed.

Ciaran jumped up, excited to see his brother. "Sean!! You made it!" They hugged tightly.

"Yeah, I had to wait until a crowd of seven or more officials were piling in. Hey, what are you still doing here? I thought you'd be strapped, hogtied, and flown to Claustra by now," he teased.

"That's not funny, you nob!" Ciaran yelled at him. But they both laughed and hugged again.

Sean turned to Chris. "And you, you're not crying yet?"

Chris shook his head. "I really hate this guy." They laughed as Sean pushed him, then hugged Chris.

They barely noticed Quentin coming in. He cleared his throat. "It's time, Ciaran," he said softly.

Ciaran turned to Chris, and Chris immediately felt panic spread through him as if it were his own. Chris swallowed his own fear, took his hand gently, and gave him a reassuring squeeze. Sean hugged Ciaran again; then Ciaran turned to hug Diana, Rob, Ted, his father, and then his mother, who held him the longest.

Quentin said to his parents, "You two can head in there first. Ciaran and I will be right behind you." They both hugged Ciaran again.

"We'll see you in there, son," Hamish said. They left the room.

Ciaran turned to Chris again, lost for words. Chris pulled him close and wrapped his arms around his back. Ciaran did the same and put his head on his shoulder and closed his eyes. They stood that way for a moment. Then Chris started singing softly, the song he made for Ciaran a few months ago. Quentin casually closed the door and stood against it. They could take all the time they needed as far as he was concerned. No one spoke as Chris sang and held onto Ciaran.

"Me and you, time stands still.
Magic and man has no will.
When it's me and you, and no one else,
The heat that you feel, it's all so real between us.
You and me, fingers entwined,
You and me, hearts aligned.
When it's you and me, and no one else,
The heat you feel, it's all so real between us.
Ranger and Magi, magician and man,
Hold my hand, hold my hand.
Magi and ranger, your Commoner understands,

Just hold my hand, hold my hand.
When it's me and you, and no one else,
The heat that you feel, it's all so real between us."

Ciaran surprised them all by joining Chris in the last chorus of the song, and they sang to each other. Diana was visibly crying, and Rob was frozen in place again, watching their display of love. Ted was also watching, but mostly watching Chris, and so was Sean.

After the song faded from both their lips, they held each other a bit longer. Chris pulled away first. He kissed Ciaran lightly. "I'll see you soon, okay?"

Ciaran nodded, unable to speak with the lump in his throat so great. He walked to Quentin at the front door, then turned around again. Chris gave him another reassuring smile and head nod.

Love you, Chris mouthed.

Ciaran nodded back. <*I love you,*> he thought. <*Forever and...*>

The words echoed in Chris's head as they walked out and Quentin shut the door.

As soon as the door closed, Chris let out all the air in his lungs, wailed, and collapsed. Ted, anticipating his breakdown, reached out to grab him around his waist to prevent him from hitting the ground face first. Chris ended up on all fours and threw up his tea from this morning, then threw up a few more times until nothing but stomach bile came up, dry heaving. Ted and Sean were on both sides of him, rubbing and patting his back. Rob continued to be frozen in place.

Diana knelt on the floor in front of him, careful to move away from the throw up he just did and said calmly, "Christopher. Christopher, look at me. Look at me."

Chris raised his tear-streaked eyes at her. "Breath with me," she said.

She put her hand on his shoulder and held his eye contact. She breathed in and out slowly, and he tried to mimic her breaths. But Diana looked the most like Ciaran out of all his siblings. Staring into her face with the freckles around her nose and her bright blue eyes was torturous. His face grimaced, and he let out another long wail and tried to lie down in his vomit.

Sean said, "Oh no you don't!" He waved his hand, and Chris's vomit disappeared.

Ted was shocked. "How the bloody fuck did you do that? You don't have your *dulé*!"

"Not now, Theodore," Sean said as he held Chris up by his chest.

He pushed and pulled him into a kneeling position, and Ted held his back up while Sean held onto his arms. Chris continued to whimper and cry, tears, snot, and spit all over his face. Diana moved closer and kneeled directly before him. She took a tiny amber stone out of her pocket, took his hand and put it in the center of her chest, then placed the hand holding the stone flat against the center of his. Her palm against his chest began to glow orange.

"Breath with me, Christopher. Stay with me," she said softly. Chris heard her this time, and he could feel his chest began to loosen with the warmth of her hand. They began to breathe in sync while Sean and Ted encouraged him.

"You did brilliant," Sean told him. "Honestly, mate. Brilliant."

"Amazing," Ted said. "You were so strong for him. You're the fucking man, Chris."

"It was exactly what Ciaran needed to get through this. You were there for him, and that's all that matters," said Sean.

"We're so proud of you," said Ted. "None of us could have done that for him. It needed to be you."

"And you did it! You did it, mate," Sean said. "He's going in there with confidence, and he's going to ace this shit."

Chris nodded at their affirmations as Diana moved her hand. Ted handed him a tissue that was in his pocket. He wiped his eyes and face, then sat cross-legged on the floor, hands folded in his lap. Ted and Sean sat down on either side of him. Chris leaned his head on Ted's shoulder, and Sean reached over, took his hand, and held it between his two. Diana took off her shoes and sat down in front of Chris, practically curled up into his lap. Rob came over and sat on the floor next to Diana and held her hand.

They sat together on the tile floor and waited.

CHAPTER 39

The Hearing

Ciaran entered the courtroom to twelve unsmiling faces seated directly before him. He saw his friend and boss Lucinda, and Magna and Rory all grown up, neither he had seen in years. He saw his dad's work partner, Joshua. But other than those four, Graham, and his cousin, he did not know anyone else. He wanted to give Lucy a small smile, but her face was stoic, watching him. And so was Savannah, watching his reaction to the jurors. So he kept his face straight and walked farther into the room.

Graham motioned for Ciaran to sit in the high-back chair before them. As soon as he sat down and put his arms on the armrest, chains appeared and fastened themselves over his wrists. He jerked them and looked up, alarmed, as he heard his mother shriek behind him.

Graham looked at Savannah. "Mistress Brickenhouse, is that necessary?"

"He is accused of some very serious crimes," she said simply. "Do we not usually chain criminals during a hearing?"

"Actually, we don't," Joshua said. "Not crimes of breaches."

"And he's not a criminal yet, Savannah. He is the accused," Magna said hotly.

Savannah's eyes narrowed to say something, but Alastair said sternly, "Can we please get on with it?" Everyone turned to face Ciaran again.

Graham said, "We are here to determine the innocence or guilt of one Ciaran Archibald Beals, the severity of his crimes if so found guilty, and the sentencing. All will happen today. Please confirm you are, in fact, Ciaran Archibald Beals?"

"Yes, Grandminister, I am."

"Thank you," said Graham. "Do you have a Magi Council representative or will you be representing yourself?"

"Yes, Minister. Mage Chloé Abbottsford, the legal administrative coordinator for the Magi Council, has agreed to be my Councilor in this hearing."

"Excellent. Let the record reflect that Mage Abbottsford is the Councilor for Ciaran Archibald Beals. Mistress Abbottsford, please state your name and your relation to the accused."

Chloé stepped forward and began. "I, Mage Chloé Abbottsford, have known Ciaran many years through a close and personal relationship with members of the Beals family."

"State your case," said Graham.

"Ciaran Beals's crime was that he knowingly and willfully broke Magi's highest law of secrecy. You are correct, and he willfully and knowingly did so." She paused as the group murmured in front of her. "Ciaran also knowingly and willingly came to a Magi Council member and confessed his crimes. He was not caught. He was not arrogant, devious, spiteful, or had disregard for the Magi world and the laws we uphold to the highest standard. He simply fell in love with a Commoner."

She smiled at him kindly. Ciaran smiled back. "Many of you don't know Ciaran. So let me tell you who he is, at his core."

Chloé described Ciaran's background as a *Nigri Veneficus* and the work he did on the Reserve. She spent the next couple of hours reading statements of Ciaran's character from Campus professors; old Magi military commanders; Esme, Erle, and Phoebe from the Atrium; Dale, Sarah, Vlad, Sven, Felix, Jesse, Khalid, Sahid, Bruno, and Tommy from the Reserve; and other friends, such as Alexi, Chitra, and his neighbor Charlotte. They all testified to his ethics, integrity, model behavior, leadership, and moral character, and all left a plea for leniency.

She concluded, "Ciaran's crimes revolve around his love for another and wanting to share the deepest parts of himself with that person. I think we all can understand that if we've ever been in love at one time or another. But I wouldn't be able to do any justice in describing the love Ciaran has for his partner, so I am going to let Ciaran tell you himself, in his own words." She sat down on the side and looked at him.

Ciaran looked up again at the twelve unsmiling faces, but noticed that Lucy gave him a soft, reassuring nod. He took a deep breath and talked for the second time in a week of how he and Chris met and described their evolving relationship.

He told them, "We decided it would be best if I introduced him to my family first and then talk to my father, Minister Hamish Beals, a Magi official, on his Commoner status. I recognized that I had already breached the statute, and I wanted to come clean properly. I meant no harm or disrespect of the laws or our world. I fully understand why we have them and how we need to put ourselves and our livelihood before anything else, for the sake of Magi and Commoners everywhere. I believe in the Magi Council and what it stands for. And I am eternally sorry for how my actions have disgraced my family, especially the ones who count themselves as loyal Magi officials. I humbly apologize to Quentin James for bringing my indiscretion to his home and family. And my sincere apologies to everyone on this Council, who had to take time away from your families this holiday week because of my lapse of judgment." Ciaran kept his face and voice calm, but apologetic and candid.

Everyone just looked at him after he stopped speaking. Then Savannah loudly scoffed.

Graham asked, "Does anyone have questions for Ciaran?" Almost everyone raised their hands, except Alastair and Magna. Graham called on them one by one. "Lucy, you may start."

"Thank you, Grandminister," she said. She looked at Ciaran and spoke to him like she always did. "Okay, help me understand. You and I have been speaking often in the last year and a half. I'm a Magi official, too, and you never mentioned it to me. Why? I could have helped you before it reached this point. And you know I would have, Ciaran."

He heard the scolding in her voice, loud and clear. Ciaran valued their friendship and was completely honest with her. "Lucy, I considered telling you a thousand times. But I had already broken the law, so the damage was done. I know you to be a person of integrity, and I would have never wanted to put you in the position of having to choose between your friendship with me and your loyalty to the Council. I know I would have lost, hands down."

"But technically, you didn't break secrecy, Ciaran," Lucy said. "It was a fluke accident by a runaway dragon. You just failed to *abscondo* the Commoner once he saw the dragon on his own, but you didn't initially break secrecy, correct?"

"Correct," Ciaran said. If he could, he would have given her the biggest hug.

"So in that sense, if you would have told me from the beginning, 'Lucy, this is what happened; I failed to erase his memory; now I have feelings for him; and I want him to know me...' In that instance, I could have helped, especially since it was literally a mishap in my department and I'm head of MAWE. I would have absolutely assisted you with him becoming a part of our world." She wanted to add, "you dunghead," but didn't.

He smiled at her, hearing it in his head, anyway. "You're right, Lucy. I didn't think about it that way, but you're absolutely right. I should have trusted you."

"You should have," she agreed.

Savannah coughed for attention. "And now we're just playing around with words and circumstances."

"Wait your turn, Savannah," Graham said. "Mia? Your question?"

"Thank you, Minister," Mia said. "Yes, my only question is why didn't you just use *abscondo* on him immediately?"

Ciaran thought she looked familiar, most likely from Campus. He answered her honestly as well. "Everyone keeps asking me that, why didn't I just erase his memory right from the beginning. The truth is, I don't know. I honestly don't know why I didn't just point my *dulé* and *abscondo*. There was something about him. I remember how sincere and honest he was with me. I remember he made me laugh. And in those few short moments, we connected. He told me he wouldn't tell a soul about seeing a dragon, and I just ... believed him. It was like..." Ciaran couldn't find the words.

"Fate," Mia said, smiling at him, his first smile from any juror.

Ciaran found himself smiling again despite the situation. "Yes. Fate."

Larry spoke up, "So, when did you actually start using magic around him?"

Ciaran answered, "I would do things sparingly behind his back, but the first real bit of magic he saw was when I brought him a pack of Magi cards and taught him how to play Blow Fish—" But Ciaran was cut off by the murmur and laughter that erupted on the jury.

"Oh, my God, Ciaran," Lucy laughed, and Magna laughed with her.

"You still play that?" Rory asked incredulously.

Graham was confused. "Order! What is the meaning of this?"

Rory said, "I apologize, Minister, it's just that Ciaran and Blow Fish are so ... *him!*"

Lucy also answered, "It's like his favorite game ever. Of course he still plays!" They all laughed, and even Quentin smiled from the doorway.

"ORDER!" Savannah yelled, then said, "And see this, Minister, is why Ciaran's friends should not have been allowed to preside over this case. It is obvious that—"

"Let it go, Savannah," Graham said, cutting her off.

"Thank you, Minister," Larry continued. "So aside from card games, no magic tricks from your *rodulé?*"

Ciaran remembered Wisp'ing in front of Chris for fun, calling it a magic trick, but Larry's words specifically asked about magic from his wand. "Not in the beginning, no. He had seen my *dulé,* but the first time he saw me use it was when we were attacked by the dark warlock."

Alastair waved his *dulé* and passed around copies of the report. "Detailed notes from Inspector Arslan of the Albanian Magi Division in regard to the encounter with the *Caerulus Veneficus*."

Joshua said as he looked over the document, "So again, your breach of the use of the *Vis* in front of a Commoner both times wasn't a personal breach. The first was a Reserve accident where you saved his life, and the second was in protection and in defense of your partner, who was just a friend at the time, is that right?"

Ciaran sat up straighter in the chair, giving out another virtual hug. "Yes. I never planned to use magic in front of him, ever, after the first incident."

Joshua turned to the other jurors, "Which protection of life, Magi and Commoner, is an agreeable use of magic in Magi law, in case you younger Magi were not aware."

"Yes, thank you," Savannah said sarcastically. Joshua ignored her.

"But obviously the floodgates were opened, and you used magic liberally after that?" Cecil asked. Magna gave him a dirty look.

"Actually, no," said Ciaran, shaking his head. "I still didn't activate my *Vis* around him. I did at one point block the aversion incantation off him, the one around the Dragon Reserve, so we could patrol together. But he didn't see me do it; I did it behind his back."

"Wasn't that dangerous?" Rory asked.

"I mean, he had already come face-to-face with a dragon and a warlock, so nothing was more dangerous than what he had already encountered. Plus, we were together all the time by then. I would have never let anything happen to him."

Larry came back with, "I'm asking these questions for a reason, son. It goes to show your motive. So think carefully.

The first time you intentionally activated your *Vis* in front of him was...?"

Ciaran knew the answer, but had been trying to avoid it out of embarrassment. "Six months into our friendship, the weekend we became more than friends. I used the *arcanos susurrus* spell in front of him in his house. To block out ... sound ... from ... his bedroom." Ciaran went red immediately but kept a straight face. All Magi used it generally for one true purpose.

Larry went red as well and avoided his eyes. "Ah. I see."

Magna and Lucy smiled; Mia stifled a laugh through her hands.

Graham wiped his face with his hands and asked tiredly, "Any more questions?"

Magna composed herself and stepped in. "So, Ciaran, it's safe to say that after you were getting closer, you began talking to him about being a Magus and showing him parts of yourself."

Ciaran nodded. "Yes. He was spending more time at my place, which had some usual components in how we enter and exit that residence and magical garden. I had a library of books from Campus that he noticed. So subtly, but yes."

"Did you frequent any full Magi spaces in Albania?" Moore asked. "For example, has he been on the Reserve?"

Ciaran shook his head. "Absolutely not. The Atrium Restaurant is frequented by Commoners and Magi alike. The first time he was in a Magi Community was when I took him to Myrddin on Christmas Eve, and later on he was in a room of my family members on Christmas Eve and Christmas Day. I admitted my infraction on Christmas Day. This was always the plan: Meet my family, confess my infraction, accept the consequences, and give him the opportunity to be inducted into our society."

Graham asked, "Any other questions?" No one spoke. He turned to Chloé. "Please bring in your next witness."

She nodded to Quentin, who left. "The next witness is Ted Beals."

CHAPTER 40

Testimony

Quentin came back moments later with Ted, who took a seat in a chair that was conjured a few paces in front of Ciaran. He winked at Ciaran before he sat down, then waved, and smiled at the jury; some waved back. He crossed his legs and put his hands in his lap.

"I have called Ted Beals to attest to the nature of their relationship," said Chloé. She turned to him. "State your full name for the record and relationship with the accused."

"Theodore Marco Beals, older brother of Ciaran Beals, by three years."

"Thank you. Ted, it is my understanding that you were the first to meet Ciaran's partner."

Ted answered, "Yes. I went to visit Ciaran in Albania on my way to a mission in Somalia."

He explained how they met at the Atrium and how Ciaran later confessed the relationship to him. Ted purposely left out the parts of their conversation around Chris being a Commoner. Instead, he described his trepidation about telling him anything over the last six months because of the change in his sexuality and his fear of how he would be judged or perceived by his friends and family.

"I now understand that the fear was compounded by the breach. But I know my brother. For Ciaran, it was one of the same, and to reveal one was to reveal the other. He was struggling with his feelings, and that was why I believe he didn't come clean right away. He needed to know that we accepted him being with a man first, before bringing up his Commoner status. Because if I'm honest, while the breach was important, Ciaran falling in love with a man far outranked any other issue for him."

"So you never suspected the man was a Commoner?" Tova asked him.

"Actually, I did," Ted stated factually. "The truth is, I did suspect that the ranger was an unregistered Commoner."

A murmur went through the jury again. "And... and you did *nothing*!?" Rory asked incredulously.

"What was I supposed to do with a suspicion?" he asked, composed.

Savannah raised her voice. "You confront! You accuse! You don't just—"

Ted cut her off and raised his voice louder. "I just told you my little brother was struggling. He was pouring his heart out to me about feelings that he's never had before. Was I supposed to accuse him of breaking laws, interrogate him of how much information he let slip about who he was, make him feel even more judged and ostracized than he had already put on himself? I wasn't going to do that. No loving brother would do that. Besides, I have never known my brother to be anything but honest. I knew he would tell me if there was something to tell. And I left it at that."

No one spoke for a moment. Then Savannah said, "So you want us to believe that you never talked with Ciaran about your suspicion about him being a Commoner, especially on your trip to Somalia? That whole time you never discussed him it with him?"

Ciaran held his breath. Ted chose his words carefully. "If you recall, Ciaran fell victim to a curse on that trip and almost died. So, no, my concern wasn't whether or not he was with a Commoner, my concern was getting my little brother out of there alive and safely."

"Did you spend any time with Ciaran and the ranger at all?" Magna asked.

"Yes, the night Ciaran told me about the relationship, I asked him to bring Chris out to dinner the following evening so I could meet him properly."

"And what was your impression of him? Honest? Trustworthy?" she asked.

"All of those things. He's a standup bloke. He's funny, kind, loyal—"

"Aww. It sounds like you just described a dog," Savannah said sweetly. Ciaran and Ted glared at her.

Chloé redirected. "Ted, please continue."

He looked back at everyone else. "He's a good guy with a kind heart. And it's obvious how much he loves Ciaran. Anyone in a room with the two of them can see it."

"So the relationship is a solid one?" Mia asked.

"Absolutely. They move as one heart. And they are broken over being apart from one another right now. I am afraid to think what would happen if it were permanent."

Savannah chuckled. "Oh, don't worry about that. Neither of them would remember if they are."

Ted and Ciaran gave her death stares again as the other jurors tsked their disgust.

"Are you really this evil?" Lucy spatted.

"That was so unnecessary," Mia said.

"Wow. Just … wow," Moore said, shaking his head.

"I'm just stating a fact; it was not ill intended." Savannah smiled sweetly.

"Any more questions for the witness?" Graham asked. No one answered. "Ted, you are free to go."

"Actually, do you mind if I join my parents in the pew? Since I am a part of the hearing now, I think it's only fair I get to hear the outcome," Ted said.

Ted heard a lot of "sure's" and "it's fine" from the jurors and one loud, "No" from Savannah.

Graham ignored her. "Ted, please join your parents in the stands."

Ted stood up and smiled at Ciaran again, patted his shoulder as he walked past, and went to the left instead of the right to sit with Grace and Hamish.

"Please call your next witness, Chloé," Graham said.

Chloé looked to Quentin and nodded. He left the room as she said, "My next witness is Diana James."

Diana came in looking solemn and serious, reminding Ciaran of how grown up she was now. She hugged her brother even though he could not hug her back. She sat down on the chair in front of him as Ted had just done, putting her hands together on her three-quarter length green dress.

"Please state your full name and relationship with the accused."

"Diana Mercy James, the youngest sibling and only sister of Ciaran Beals, age twenty-two."

"Please describe the events that took place on Christmas day," said Chloé.

Diana relived Christmas evening after everyone had left and ended talking when Ciaran and Chris left the room. She did not think Rob and Chloé's fight was relevant. Instead, she described Ciaran's reaction, his confession, and his willingness to go to the Council first thing in the morning. She also described Chris's apology to the James household.

She concluded with, "Then they went upstairs and did what only could be described as passionate lovemaking. I turned to Quentin and said, 'They really are connected, mind, body, and soul.' And neither has been right since Ciaran was selfishly taken away. They are broken shells of themselves. It just breaks my heart to think of it."

Diana let the tears fall. Mia and Lucy wiped the tears from their eyes as well, as everyone else was silent.

Graham asked quietly, "Does anyone have any questions for the witness?"

"I do," Savannah said, breaking the silence. "Where is he now? The ranger?" Diana remained silent. Savannah's eyes narrowed. "Come now, girl. I know you are a Council official even if it is in secret. He's still at your flat, isn't he?! Harboring a known criminal, are we?"

"Stop it, Savannah!" yelled Lucy, done with Savannah's accusations. "He's not a criminal; he didn't break any laws. And neither is she."

"Ah, but he will be when Ciaran gets convicted, and they intend to give him safe refuge, don't you?" She turned to Quentin. "Tell the truth, boy! He's in your home right now, isn't he?"

Quentin spoke for the first time. "I can honestly say without a doubt that he is not at my flat right now."

"But he was!" Savannah piped.

"Yes. We hosted them both between Christmas Eve and Christmas Day. That's all part of the record."

"Ah!" Savannah yelled excitedly again. "You had a Commoner in your home for forty-eight hours and you performed magic in front of him. The whole lot of you should be rotting in Claustra right now!"

Alastair spoke up. "Excuse me, Savannah, but I personally wrote and passed around the transcript of what was relayed to the Minister on the day of Ciaran's arrest, and each family member confirmed when they found out about his Commoner status. We also have the affidavits of the other dinner guests that were present before the confession, and they also had no clue of his Commoner status, including myself. The law specifically states *knowingly* use of the *Vis* in front of a Commoner. I assume all magic ceased to be used after that, correct, Quentin? No one used magic in the house during the duration of his stay?"

"Not to my knowledge, no," Quentin stated.

"Well, that settles that," Alastair said definitively. "Do you need me to resend you the transcript, or are you having trouble reading?" he asked with a straight face. He waved his *dulé*, and a written piece of parchment appeared. She glared at him as it floated down to the table in front of her.

"Does anyone else have questions for Diana?" Graham asked. No one spoke. Graham looked around. "Does anyone have any question for anyone, for Ciaran, for Ted, for Chloé, even for Quentin? Cecil, you've been quiet this whole time. Do you have questions for anyone to help you make your decision?"

Cecil cleared his throat. "I've been taking in all the facts. Honestly, the only other person that I would personally like to hear from is the partner. I want to hear how committed he is in this relationship, what he understands of our world and does he want to actually be a part of it for Ciaran. But I suspect he's left the country by now, in hiding naturally."

Tova turned to him. "Yes, I agree. It would have been nice to hear his side; how he feels about all this."

Alastair gave Chloé a knowing look. She took a deep breath. "What if... what if I could... produce him—"

Ciaran yelled at her, "*What!? No!*"

"Why, Ciaran?" Savannah said to him. "Are you scared we'll find out how much you really told him?"

Chloé ignored her and spoke to the other jurors. "If it would help the court to see the other side of it, from the Commoner's side—"

"No, Chloé! I said NO!" Ciaran found himself struggling against the chains wrapped around his wrist. "I'm warning you!"

She spoke louder over Ciaran's protests. "—from the Commoner side to see how things came about, to show you that there was never any malicious intent—"

"SHE'S FIRED! I don't want her as my Councilor anymore!" Ciaran yelled, trying to rise.

"—to show you his character and integrity. Would it help to understand why Ciaran, and even Ted, found him trustworthy—"

"BLOODY HELL, CHLOÉ!"

"If I could... If I could get him here to testify, would that help?"

Ciaran was beside himself with fear and anger. "Chloé, what are you doing!? They will erase him! They will take him from me... No, Chloé! No!"

"Ciaran," Graham said calmly. Ciaran stopped squirming and looked up at him. "We would only use it on him if there is a conviction where the sentence calls for it. If we invite him into our courts, we will not conceal his memory just because he is here. He is obviously already familiar with our world, so there is no need for that. Now I would like to make allowances for an unregistered Commoner to enter into the

Council and these chambers, and no harm will come to him at my request. Are you okay with that?"

Ciaran wanted to tell him no, that he wouldn't allow it. But he looked at Alastair, who lifted his chin up, and slowly brought it back down. "Yes, Grandminister Graham," he breathed out.

"Thank you." Graham turned to the jury. "Are you all in agreement?" Everyone either said yes or nodded their heads, including Savannah. "Then it's settled. Chloé, do you think you can produce him in an hour?" He looked at his watch.

"I will do my best," she said. Ciaran stayed quiet, but he was fuming.

"Excellent. It is almost noon, so let's have an early lunch and reconvene at 1 p.m. Quentin, please escort Ciaran back to his chambers with his family." He motioned for Savannah to release the chains, which she reluctantly did.

Ciaran jumped up and went straight to Chloé. Before he could start yelling at her, she said quietly to him, "Do you trust me, Ciaran?"

"This isn't about trusting you!" he angrily whispered. "Whatever Graham just promised doesn't matter. Savannah will take him away from me for good!"

The rest of his family had made their way to him, along with Quentin. "I think it's brilliant, Ciaran," Quentin said. "It's the love story that they want to hear, and Christopher is pretty charismatic."

"I agree," said Ted. "If anyone can win them over, it's Chris. I'm watching them; no one up there really wants to convict you, except Bitchenhouse. Give them what they want, so they will let you ride off into the sunset with your man." He touched his shoulder.

"I don't like it either. It feels like it could be a trap," Grace said. "But it also might be your best shot."

Ciaran sighed in frustration. Then he whispered, "How the hell are we going to get him back out, then back in again?"

Ted said, "Let's talk to Sean. He always has a plan."

CHAPTER 41

Twin

The chamber door opened, and Chris got up off the floor; Sean and Rob followed.

"Is... is it over?" Chris asked in fear.

Ciaran came in last. Before Chris could talk, Ciaran went over to him and held him tightly. "What's wrong, Ciaran?" he asked, hugging him back.

"They want you to testify, Christopher," Chloé answered.

"Me?" Chris asked incredulously.

"Yes," she said. "They want to hear your firsthand account of the relationship."

Ciaran was still holding onto him, chin on his shoulder. Chris pulled back a bit and looked Ciaran in the eyes. "Do you want me to, Ciaran?" Chris asked.

"Honestly, no. But Chloé is convincing me, along with Ted and Quentin and even Mum... that it's worth a shot. Even Alastair gave me a look..."

Chris and Ciaran had a silent conversation with their eyes and their shared feelings, conveying their concern and fear around this decision. Then Chris said, "But how will

I get out? I can't just walk in there as if I've been here the whole time."

Rob said, "We'll just sneak you out with the second vial of transformation, and you'll walk back in as yourself."

"But..."

Chris looked at Sean, who stared back. They also had a silent conversation with their eyes. The plan was to sneak Chris out and keep going if Ciaran was convicted, get on the next plane to Italy, then sail to North Africa from there, and stay on the continent. If they used the potion now and Ciaran was convicted, Chris would have no way out.

Ciaran saw the look between them. "What? What were you planning?"

Sean put his hand on Chris's shoulder. "It's up to you. Fight or flight. Literally."

Chris looked at Ciaran, who was still holding onto him. "We stay and fight," Chris said. Ciaran nodded.

"Time is of the essence, so can we get you out of here, please?" Chloé said anxiously.

Sean took out the small vial he had in his pocket, opened it, spit in it, and then shook it. It turned reddish orange as he passed it to Chris. Chris drank it in a gulp, then bent over, and almost retched. "God, you taste awful."

"Bet Ciaran tastes better, innit?" Sean said with a wink.

"Oh, gross!" Diana yelled.

"Sean!" his mother scolded him.

"You're disgusting, mate," Ted said with a smile. Sean grinned and shrugged.

But Ciaran was not paying attention. He watched his boyfriend slowly turn into his brother right before his eyes. Chris shrank a few inches shorter, his skin got paler, and his hair grew straighter, then turned mahogany. When he stood up, he was next to Sean, just like Shane would have been.

Wearing the same outfit made it even more shocking, and Ciaran gasped as a hush fell over the room.

"Hello, twin," Sean said, smiling at Chris. "Where have you been?" Chris grinned back.

Tears fell from Grace's eyes before she could stop them. "Shane," she whispered, then put her hands over her mouth. It was like all her children in the same room once again.

Ciaran couldn't help it either. He grabbed Fake Sean/Pretend Shane/Chris around the neck and hugged him. He closed his eyes and remembered his brother.

Chris said in Sean/Shane's voice, "Whoa. I'm your brother, not your boyfriend, remember?"

"My God, you even sound like him," Ted breathed out.

"Grace, your brother is a fucking genius," said Hamish, his eyes also wide.

"I know," said Sean, staring at Chris/Shane with awe. "It's freakishly great and incredibly depressing."

Chloé was growing impatient. "Okay, let's move! You leave first, and one of you go with him."

"I'll go!" Rob volunteered.

Chloé looked at him and found herself speaking to her boyfriend for the first time in five days. "Take him to a safe location, and I'll meet you there."

Sean said, "Take him to Wanderlous. It's not too far from my apartment, and he'll need a change of clothes. Also, me popping in midday is not uncommon." Chris/Shane nodded.

"We'll meet you there," Ted said. "I'll go with Chloé."

"Okay," Rob said. Then turned to say something to Chloé, but the words were stuck.

"Go!" she cried.

"Okay, okay!" Rob exclaimed. He grabbed Chris/Shane's arm and left the room.

The first floor of the Council was mostly empty that time of day. The guard glanced up as they walked past and put his head back down again, disinterested in Rob and Fake Sean who had come in earlier in the day. They walked all the way down to the farthest revolving doors.

"I'll go first," Rob said. "Rotate three times, make a left, and keep walking like you know where you're going. Go five doors down and enter the pub. Watch out for the first step; it's a dip."

Rob stepped forward and circled the doors. After the second one, Rob didn't appear on his side anymore. Fake Sean took a deep breath and tried to repeat Rob's movements. The guard looked up, but the young men had already disappeared.

Fake Sean walked out onto the cold street, the sun bright in his eyes. He immediately turned left and kept going five doors down and saw the pub, but forgot about the dip. He opened the door and walked forward, falling right onto his face.

"Ooooh..." he groaned. Two pairs of shoes appeared before him, a pair of sneakers and steel-toed boots.

Rob and Marvin the barman looked down at him. "Are you drunk, or did you forget, mate?" Marvin asked curiously.

Fake Sean stood up quickly and mumbled, "Yeah, a little tanked right now."

Marvin scoffed. "How is that different from any other Monday?" He walked off.

Rob helped him up and led them to a table nearby. Fake Sean asked, "So what do we do now? Where do we go?"

Rob whispered, "Neither of us have our *rodulés*, so we just have to wait."

Five minutes later, Chloé and Ted rushed in through the doors. "I got the keys; let's go," Ted called out.

"Keys?" Fake Sean asked.

Ted's response was to walk back out of the bar. Rob got up, and Chris followed. They walked down three blocks and turned into an alley and through a set of doors into Sean's apartment on the third floor of the building. Chris had started turning back into himself during the walk and was back to his normal body and voice by the time they entered Sean's flat.

"I will be right back," Ted said. "I'm going to get some clothes for you. You're more my size than Sean's."

"Okay, but nothing fancy," Chloé warned. "It has to look like we didn't plan this."

Ted nodded and left. Rob and Chloé stared at each other. Chris watched them watch each other. "Do … you … two … want … to … be … alone?"

Rob opened his mouth to speak, but Chloé quickly left the room to enter Sean's bedroom. She came back with a brush and Sean's hair spray and told Chris to sit down so she could comb his hair. Rob sat down as well and watched. Everyone was silent.

Ted came back about twenty minutes later with a dark brown suede suit jacket with leather brown patches on it, an orange button-down shirt, and dark brown loafers. Chris went into the next room and put on the clothes, then came out with a grimace.

"Can you change the color of the shirt to tan or even a yellow? It's clashing a bit."

"You can't be serious," Ted said.

"If you want me to sell it, I have to look my best." He smiled.

Ted rolled his eyes as Chloé pointed her *dulé* at Chris to turn his shirt to a light tan.

"Better," Chris said.

The four of them walked back to the Council together and went through the same entrance they came out of. They walked up to the guard, and he gave Chris a suspicious look, forgetting that four Magi had left and only three had come back.

"I have special permission to bring in Christopher Jennings, Commoner from Albania, to bear witness in the testimony of Ciaran A. Beals," Chloé said importantly.

The guard's eyes went wide, and he started looking through the memos that had recently appeared on his desk. He found it, signed by the Grandminister himself.

"Hold out your right hand," he told Chris.

Chris did. The guard touched the inside of his palm, and a tattoo of a wand with a star above it appeared on the back of his hand, then disappeared. "This is good for six hours, starting..." He looked at his watch; it was 12:53 p.m. "Now." He waved them through to the lifts.

Ciaran stood up upon Chris entering the room and smiled. "You look like you smell good."

"Well, come on, smell me then!" Chris said cheerfully.

Ciaran laughed, walked over to lean on his neck, and sniffed. He closed his eyes and kissed him there. "Mmmm..." Chris said, as his eyes fluttered. "Your mum is watching."

Ciaran pulled back but kept his faces inches from Chris's. "So? I'm an adult. And you're my boyfriend." He kissed him lightly on the lips.

Chris smiled. "She told me we're like two horny teenagers."

Ciaran reached his hand up to the back of Chris's neck, rubbing it. "I never thanked you for the first time. From the first kiss to the next forty-eight hours after that. You changed my life."

Chris's smile faded a bit. "Ninety-six hours," he corrected Ciaran. "And you've changed mine, for the better. Now this sounds too much like goodbye, so stop talking."

Ciaran opened his mouth to say something else, but Quentin came into the room saying, "The jurors are back. We have to go." Ciaran inhaled deeply, then exhaled loudly.

Chris turned his face back to him. "Hey. I'll see you in there, love." He kissed him lightly on the lips, returning the kiss. Ciaran nodded and followed Quentin out with his parents and older brother.

Ciaran's mind was so foggy as he walked back into the chamber that he forgot to not put his arms on the armrest again. Once he did, he quickly tried to remove them, but his right arm was caught. "Fuck," he murmured. He saw Savannah smile.

"Call to order," Graham hit his gavel. "Chloé, please proceed with your next witness."

She nodded to Quentin, who went out of the room. "I call Commoner Ranger Christopher Jennings as the next witness." The jury murmured, but all went silent as Chris walked in.

Chris looked around. He saw Hamish, Grace, and Ted sitting in the stands first, then Ciaran in the middle of the room in a chair with one arm in restraints. He looked up and saw twelve people on a raised platform looking down at him. He relaxed and smiled at them. The two women in the middle, one white and one black, were the first ones to smile back at him. The pregnant woman on the end waved at him, and he waved back. He figured they must be Ciaran's friends and knew where to direct his words to.

He didn't realize he stopped walking to gawk around until Quentin moved closer to him. "Sit in the chair, mate. The one in front of Ciaran."

He glanced at Ciaran and gave him a reassuring smile as well before he sat in the chair, careful not to put his arms on the armrest. He folded his hands in his lap.

"Please state your name, title, and residency for the record," the large, black British man said.

Chris assumed that was Graham. "Ranger Christopher MacDougal Jennings, of Korçë, Albania, Grandminister, sir." The man nodded. Chris nodded back.

"Christopher, who is Ciaran Beals to you?" Chloé began.

Chris turned around to look at Ciaran, who was unsmiling, staring at him intently, nervously. "Ciaran... Ciaran is the love of my life," he said softly. "The other half of my soul. Literally."

But because the room was cavernous, his words echoed. Ciaran let a smile appear on his lips for Chris, and Chris smiled back.

"I am sorry, Christopher, you need to face the jury at all times," said Graham. "And all of your responses need to be directed to us. You cannot address the accused."

Chris turned back around. "Right. I apologize to the Council officials. It won't happen again," he said seriously.

Chloé continued, "Chris, can you please tell us a little about your relationship? Particularly how it began, the nature of the things you do and discuss as a couple, and what it has been like since you've been apart from each other." She sat down.

"Okay. That's a lot to cover," said Chris. "But Ciaran says I talk too much anyway, so here I go!"

He grinned, bringing the others on the jury to smile with him.

CHAPTER 42

Tell Me A Story

Chris told the jury of how they met and their journey together. But unlike Ciaran, who stuck to the facts, Chris described details as if he were telling a few friends while they were out having drinks.

"And then I called from the ground, 'Robetta!' I used to know a girl named Robetta, and I never heard another name like it, so I thought, hey, the beast needs a name, and I had one in my back pocket, so why not?

"And somehow I knew he was raising his wand to take the memory from me, so I just instinctively said, 'No!' and I reached up and grabbed his arm. We just locked eyes, you know? Have you ever just met someone, and you just … *know*? That this person was going to be in your life? The extent of it, who knows, but you just knew… you know?

"To be fair, he never actually told me he was wizard, or magician. To this day, I think he's never said the words to me, 'Chris, I'm a Magi.' I just sort of guess, you know? I read a lot of sci-fi and fantasy stuff for fun. I know what a wizard acts like, especially one who doesn't want to be noticed. So we made a deal: I don't ask about anything related to dragons—except our Betta, of course—or magic, or anything about him, and get to keep my memory of it all. I don't tell a soul about anything I've seen or heard, and Ciaran, my new best mate as I called him, will allow me to talk about it with him to keep me from talking about it with anyone else. We shook on it. Then we started hanging out almost every night after that. He kept his promise, and I kept mine.

"I think the dark warlock encounter changed things for us. Ciaran has never said this to me, but I think that's where he started realizing he had feelings for me. We had this moment, you know, when we were arguing about whether or not I was going to head into the woods, which by the way, was my job as a ranger and lawman. And the way he looked at me, yelled at me about how dangerous it all was; it was not like a friend trying to protect another friend, it was like a man trying to keep his love safe. I don't think he even realized it; we've never talked about it. But he's listening. So he knows now."

And Ciaran was. Like everyone in the room, Ciaran was hanging off of Chris's every word. Chris was animated, his hands moving as he talked, the inflection in his voice jovial and dramatic and dreamy when it called for it.

"You have to understand, I don't go after straight guys, ever. And Ciaran isn't exactly my type. He's more rugged than what I'm into, with his square jaw, amazing rock hard body, smooth skin, adorable freckles, hair longer than mine that flows in a wavy ponytail, sparkling bright blue eyes... Okay, so maybe he is my type a little." He laughed, and several members of the jury laughed with him as Ciaran smiled behind him, turning a little pink. "But again, he was straight, and we could never be more than friends, right?"

"So maybe I started it a little. Maybe I pushed him with the massage. But I couldn't help it. Here I had this beautiful specimen of a man in front of me, shirt off. I had to touch him. And keep touching him. He wasn't mine yet, you know, but he was mine at that moment. He was all mine." He looked down and smiled to himself as Lucy and Magna exchanged smiles.

"I realized I had real feelings for him. My best friend. And I suspected he had feelings for me too after that, the way he bolted out of there and the way he didn't show up to patrol with me the next day. Also weeks later when he sat at the table at The Atrium and played with the saltshaker to keep from blurting out how incredibly horny I was probably making him."

He laughed, and some jurors laughed loudly with him, except Savannah. He heard Ciaran groan behind him, but did not turn around. "I suspected he knew he had feelings, but I didn't really know until around this time last year."

Chris talked about how his mother died eight years ago and how it affected him, and the way Ciaran lay next to him and let him grieve, then hugged him in front of the Reserve. "It was the first time he touched me in that way, lovingly. I should have kissed him then. But it wasn't time yet. Our time would come."

Chris talked about the next couple of weeks of the "mental chess" they played and how Ciaran would disappear for days at a time when they got too close, then reappear again; that explosive argument they had right before Valentine's Day; Ciaran stalking him and Chris catching him, then finally confronting him.

"So then I kissed him under the lamppost," he concluded.

Mia squealed and asked the first question of all the jurors. "Waaait! You just ... *kissed* him?"

"I did," Chris said proudly.

"Just to see what he would do? What if he pulled away?"

"Then the question in my mind would have been answered, and I would have never tried again."

"But instead, what *did* he do?" Lucy said slyly, looking at Ciaran this time. Ciaran shook his head and smiled at her.

"He closed his eyes. He let me put my lips on him; then he opened his mouth and pulled my bottom lip with his two lips. I'll never forget that moment for as long as I live. Ciaran kissed me back," Chris said dreamily. He could not stop smiling, and Ciaran couldn't contain his smile either.

"Wow," Lucy said softly.

"So what happened next?" Magna asked excitedly.

"Well," Chris said, still smiling. "I went back to work, and he went back to the Reserve. Then he showed up a few hours later at the Tank, determination all in his eyes. And … let's just say the story gets a little graphic from here on, but it was the greatest ninety-six hours of my entire life. A whirlwind of a long weekend."

Mia began to fan herself and leaned back in her chair. "Whew!"

"Well, tell us—" Lucy started, but Savannah cut her off.

"Enough of this, Mages!" Savannah scolded. "Control yourselves! This is not cinema hour at teatime. This is a real trial with a real breach, and the evidence is right there in front of us!" She pointed at Chris.

Larry, who had also been enjoying Chris's version of the story, said, "She's right, let's move on to the actual breaches." He turned to Chris. "Now, Christopher, when do you recall the first time Ciaran used magic in front of you? Think hard now. We asked Ciaran this same question earlier. Let's see if your story matches up."

"Well," Chris said. "We played magical card games together, like *Flama Arca* and Blow Fish."

"Yes, yes, we know of those. I'm talking about the *Vis*. You do know what the *Vis* is, correct?"

"Yes, sir, the source of your magical bloodline," said Chris.

"Correct. Now, think hard. The first time Ciaran knowingly used his *Vis* in front of you, outside of containing the dragon and the dark Magi incident."

Chris was thoughtful. "I don't know how Ciaran answered you, but I definitely remember the first time I saw him use actual magic in front of me. See, I live in a duplex; my sister's flat is directly above mine. She has two children, but at the time she was pregnant and had the one. It was right after our first date, and we were in my bedroom. Ciaran lifted up his *dulé* in front of me and said, '*Arcanos susurrus.*' Yellow sparks shot upward to the ceiling and spread across, down the walls, and collected back under our feet. I asked him what that was, and he said to soundproof the room. And I thought how incredibly thoughtful for him to do that. And then we made love. Afterward, he called a glass from my dresser and used his finger to add water into it. We drank from the same cup; then he said, '*Expletus*' and the glass went back to my dresser. So if he said any one of those: *Arcanos susurrus, cedo, sitio,* or *expletus*, he would still be correct. Before that he never personally showed me his ability to do magic."

Lucy sat back happily. Magna kept a straight face but squeezed her leg in happiness, too. No one got embarrassed at the way Chris spoke about it, and Ciaran was once again grateful for him.

"And after that, did he use magic more freely around you, talked about being a Magus?" Tova asked.

"Some but not really," said Chris. "It was still only as a needed thing, doors to be opened or locked, rooms sound-proofed so we would not disturb anyone else. But really, our relationship didn't revolve around magic. In fact, I would argue that he did not reveal anything to me, but it was me finding out things for myself by hanging out at the Atrium or going through his library. Everything I know about the Magi world came from me reading about it. If I had a question, he would answer it, but not go into detail, except about the last battle in Myrddin, which affected him deeply, obviously.

"Our relationship is so much deeper than magic tricks. We hang out and listen to music or argue about football teams. We would take weekend getaways and go dancing, or get dinner and drinks at bars and lounges. Or we would stay home and cook dinner... Well, I would cook, and Ciaran would watch. We would go hiking in other woods other than our own or in the mountains, or swimming or to arcades and just have fun. Sometimes we would spend the whole day in bed, sleeping, making love, sleep some more, then go to work in the evenings. Or sometimes we would just talk. I told him things about myself and my past that I've never told anyone, and he likewise opened up to me in the same manner. Any breaches he has done was just a way to share more of himself with me. I knew he had a brother who died and how much it affected him. But how could he tell me about the despair of losing Shane and his best friend Darragh, without explaining to me the civil war and damage Talindra did to cause brother to turn against brother? Your world is a part of him, and now it's a part of me, too."

At the sound of Darragh's name, Magna reached out and grabbed Liz's hand who held it tightly. They both had tears in their eyes.

"I didn't know…" Magna said and sniffed. "I didn't know that you still cared about her as much as I did … to talk about her. You just left us in the middle of the war and went to the Reserve. We thought you turned your back on us, Ciaran. Until the day of the battle…" She sniffed again. "Here I was thinking we would absolutely get through this trial without this being brought up. Silly me." She sniffed a third time and conjured tissues.

"Magna, no," Ciaran spoke. "I left because I was tired of killing our own people. Yes, they were dark and doing evil things, but they were still Magi. I just… I wanted to be a dragon tamer, not a mercenary. But Darragh was a sister to me, you know, even after I left London. We spoke all the time until her duties took her farther away. I miss her every day, just as much as I miss Shane."

Magna was openly crying. "I miss her every day, too."

Savannah said sternly, "I hate to disrupt, but once again, I am reminding you all that is, in fact, a trial. And despite your best efforts, Mr. Jennings, you have not convinced me that this relationship warranted a breach. Furthermore, I know your type. Commoners are like leeches when it comes to the supernatural. We all know it's the magic you've been sniffing around for, and once Ciaran goes away for good, once it's gone, so will you."

Ciaran tore his eyes away from Magna to give Savannah a cold stare. Chris, on the other hand, smiled at her. "Hello, Savannah Brickenhouse. I have heard great things about you."

Savannah's eyes narrowed. "Charmed, I'm sure."

"To answer your question," Chris said, "which I thought I already did, but again, our relationship did not and still does not revolve around magic. If Ciaran were to lose his *Vis* today, it would devastate him, maybe change him, but there is nothing Ciaran could do, say, or become that would make me love him any less than I do right now, in this moment."

Mia snapped her fingers. "Well said!" Lucy giggled. Alastair gave a small head nod.

"I would really like to get us back on task," Graham said. "Does anyone have any other questions pertaining to the case and not just the play-by-play of their obvious romance?"

"I do, Minister," Joshua said. "Can you go over again any spells or incantations that Ciaran performed with you, outside of the first three? What was used regularly? And were you always alone when it was used, or were there others present?"

"No, no others were present," said Chris. "An as far as spells go… *Obex, Indocillis, Renodo, Colligere,* we *Wisp'd* once, *Quod electrica, Dilato…*

But Chris stopped, realizing he must have said something wrong as he felt the mood in the room change. Some jury members gasped or were open-mouthed, except Savannah, who sat back and smiled, and Alastair, who took notes furiously. Ciaran took a deep breath and closed his eyes, then exhaled, expecting the fallout.

Magna scolded him first. "Ciaran! You didn't!"

"You can't *Wisp* with a Commoner!" Rory cried.

"That was really, really dangerous," Cecil said, shaking his head.

"What do you have to say for yourself, young man?" Tova scolded as well.

Before Ciaran could respond, Chris answered, "Hey, okay, listen. I know that it sounds really bad, but in his defense, I was really, really drunk, and we were far from home, and obviously Ciaran doesn't drive. I trust him with everything, including my life. So when he said to think of the hotel we were staying at, to clear my head and let him guide me, I was able to do it. And it was okay because we did it together, like we do everything else. We're always of one mind, one soul now actually, so I knew if he believed I would be safe, then I would be safe with Ciaran. One mind, one heart, one soul, we are, always. Even now, I can tell you what he's thinking. He's thinking, 'Bloody hell, mate, the one thing no one asked you to bring up, you just volunteer that information. You really do talk too damn much, Chris.' But he is also sending me mental messages, saying it's fine, that I told the truth because that's what I came here to do. That it all needed to come out, and whatever happens, we will deal with it. Also, mentally he's hugging me and playing in my hair because he loves to do that."

Ciaran laughed out loud, in spite of himself and the seriousness of the situation.

Chris smiled at hearing his lover laugh behind him. "You have to understand something about us. We have always fed off each other's energy, even when we were just friends. We found each other at a time when we needed something in our lives, and we filled that void for one another and then some. We've created this unbreakable bond, the *Ardenti*, as my new sister-in-law has informed me."

"The *Ardenti?*" said Tova in disbelief. "Really?"

"Really," Chris said with a nod. "I'm in love with him, and he's my best friend, but it's so much deeper than that. Our souls are fusing together as one for life. I can hear his thoughts; I can feel his feelings. And we'll never truly be separated now. I feel it with everything in me every day. I trust him with my heart, my life, my soul. I don't just love him. I'd die for him if he asked me to today. And I know he feels the same way about me."

"I do," Ciaran said softly, as it still echoed. "And I would too."

Everyone was silent for a moment. Then Graham asked, "Any more questions for the witness? Or for Ciaran?"

Alastair spoke for the first time. "I have a question for Christopher."

Chris sat up straighter. "Yes, sir."

"Once you knew for sure that Ciaran had broken a serious Magi law and you understood how severe the breach this was, why didn't you convince him to come clean? Didn't it go against your moral code as an officer of the law to continue the lie and the breach? Where was your integrity in all this?"

Chris silently thanked Grace for this conversation yesterday and was ready to handle it. "You are absolutely correct, Alastair. We were being reckless and foolish, like two teenagers in love without a care in the world. As someone who upholds the law, I should have pushed harder for us to confess. I have no regrets regarding our entire relationship, except that we should have handled it with more maturity. We should have said something to someone sooner when we knew it was getting serious. We were caught up in ourselves and our love for each other, and while exhilarating and powerful, it wasn't right to hide in secret at all. We've made mistakes, and we humbly apologize for the disrespect and disregard for Magi laws."

"If you were a juror here, and you were just sticking with the facts of the law, what would you do?" Alastair asked. "How would you decide the fate of the accused?"

Chris took a moment to answer. "The truth is Ciaran is guilty and deserves to be punished."

Another series of gasps and open mouths erupted from the jurors, including Savannah.

Chris continued, "We all know it. Ciaran knows it, too. That's why he walked in here five days ago. Not to get away with it, but to face the consequences of his actions. That is where his integrity is, in always wanting to do the right thing. So here we both are, trying to do the right thing, ready to face the consequences. But, as a lawman and sticking to just the facts, I would also go for leniency. The accused has never been in trouble with the law, ever. He is an upstanding and valued member of the Magi Community. He has dedicated his life to preserving the lives of an endangered species. And let's not forget that through his leadership, he helped to end the civil war by bringing over eighty skilled Magus and one fierce Mage to the fight, giving the Magi Enforcers the chance they needed to end it once and for all. For all of these reasons, he deserves mercy. Speaking as a lawman of course." Chris saw Moore give him a full head nod.

"Speaking as his partner, Chloé asked me to tell you what life has been like without him. Since we came together, Ciaran and I have only been separated like this twice before: The first was his successful dragon mission in April and the second was his trip to Somalia with Ted in September. Both times I found myself having to find the will to get out of bed in the morning and go about my day, and that was with the knowledge that he would be coming back to me. Today I am … broken." Chris held back tears as he spoke.

"Until today I haven't seen him, touched him, kissed him, and it is ripping me apart inside. You can't imagine the level of pain that I feel, when it feels like my very soul is being separated. Whatever happens today, I'm going to survive it, because Ciaran needs me to, but that doesn't mean I won't be walking around every moment of every day with half my soul. Whatever decision is made, we'll both respect it. But I just ask one thing: Please do not take away the memory of him from me, or the memory of me from him. We can survive anything you throw at us, except that. Otherwise, you might as well kill us both."

There was silence again. "Any other questions for Christopher or Ciaran?" Graham asked. No one spoke. "Quentin, please escort Christopher to the chambers where the rest of Ciaran's family is. He can wait there with them. Chris, you are free to go."

Chris stood up and adjusted his jacket, but instead of walking toward the right to where Quentin was waiting, he walked straight toward Ciaran and grabbed his free hand. They held tight to each other. Ciaran put his head on Chris's body and closed his eyes. Chris looked down at Ciaran in the chair and used his other hand to gently stroke Ciaran's hair.

Ciaran looked up. <I love you,> he said in Chris's head. *I love you too*, Chris mouthed back to him.

The jurors exchanged looks of sadness, except for Savannah. "Oh, Christopher?" she said in false sweetness. "Please don't go far, in case we need to finalize things with you as well." She smiled.

Ciaran shook his head at Chris. <Don't do it.>

Chris winked at him and turned around. "And leave Ciaran? I thought you were paying attention, Mistress Brickenhouse. Even if I wanted to, my soul wouldn't allow it." He gave her his best smile.

Chris turned back to Ciaran, lifted up his chin, and kissed him on his lips, then let go. Ciaran watched him walk through the chamber doors and stared long after they closed. It took him a moment to realize Chloé had started her closing statements.

Ciaran turned back to hear her say, "The fact is of all of the sixteen breaches throughout history, all were caught, and only Ciaran willingly informed the Council of his breach." She went through each case and their sentencing, which was either probation or up to one year in Claustra. "In conclusion, since it has been noted that the breach began and ended with Ciaran and Chris, there was no harm done, no real risk to the Magi Community, and on the contrary an honest and full confession to the Grandminister himself. Therefore, I propose a full pardon for Ciaran A. Beals."

Cecil snorted a laugh.

"Are you out of your mind, girl?" Savannah said.

"You expect us to let this go completely unpunished?" Tova said.

"Yes," said Chloé confidently. "Ciaran came of his own volition, and the truth is this court would have never been aware of this breach, if he did not bring it to your attention. It's only fair that he should be rewarded for his honesty and bravery."

"Thank you, Chloé," said Graham. "We will take your recommendation under advisement. Ciaran, is there anything you want to say before we conclude this portion and begin deliberation?"

Ciaran was at a loss for words. At that point, he just wanted to get back in the room with Chris. At first, he shook his head no. But then said, "I just..." He looked at the closed door again, knowing Chris was behind it as Quentin was standing before it. Then he looked up at the jurors desperately.

"Please don't take him from me," he said just above a whisper, fighting back tears. Mia put her hand over her heart.

"Thank you, Ciaran. We will also take your plea under advisement," said Graham. "Quentin, please escort Ciaran back to his family. Chloé, you are fine to sit with them as well."

Chloé said, "No, I think I will wait in the adjacent chamber." She bowed respectfully to the Council officials and left.

The chain fell off Ciaran's wrist, and he walked to Quentin. Ted gave him a hug, and so did his parents. They all walked back to the chamber together where Rob, Sean, Diana, and Chris were waiting.

Chris walked right up to him cried, "I'm so stupid! So stupid! I'm so sorry!"

Ciaran grabbed his face. "No, you were brilliant! You did everything right. And yes, you talk too fucking much." He kissed him on the mouth again. "But it's alright. It's alright, my love." They held each other.

"Christ, how was I to know to Wisp with me would come off as the most dangerous thing we've ever done?" Chris said in disbelief.

"Because I told you that, you big horse's arse!" Ted yelled. "Remember, I told you both how completely stupid and dangerous it was and to never, ever do that again!?"

"Not really, mate. I was pretty tanked the night before," Chris said, and Ciaran laughed out loud.

"You two bloody idiots are made for each other." Ted shook his head.

Ciaran hugged the rest of his family again. Then he sat down on the floor in the corner of the chamber with Chris. They held hands.

"So what happens now?" Chris asked.

"We wait," Ciaran said. "And pray."

CHAPTER 43

Integrity

Graham began. "We are going to go around and reveal our initial thoughts around the accused and the charges; then we can debate the circumstances. Mia, you can start."

"Well," Mia began. "They certainly have an interesting dynamic. There is a connection there that is undeniable. And if they truly do have *Ardenti*, then I do understand why he did the things he did. His soul literally would not allow him to *abscondo* Christopher. How incredibly romantic. I am all for crime and punishment when it calls for it, but this is not a criminal matter, it's a heart matter."

Savannah scoffed. "Did you come here for a play about forbidden love, or did you come here to be a juror?"

Mia's eyes narrowed. "I am so glad we don't work together in any capacity, you miserable old—"

"Enough!" Graham cut her off. "Savannah, you will get our turn. Cecil?"

"Like Mia, I get it, too. Nothing was done intentionally, and it has not escaped me that the breach began and ended with one person. But as Magi officials, we have to uphold the law. Nothing severe, but there does need to be some consequences," Cecil said.

"I agree," said Tova. "I feel for them; I really do. But the fact is, a law was broken, and we must act accordingly."

"So you're going to send Ciaran to jail for the next ten years for revealing to his boyfriend who he really is?" Lucy cried out. "That's madness!"

"To be fair, he wasn't his boyfriend when the secrecy was broken," Rory said.

"Oh, shut up, Rory!" Lucy retorted.

Alastair interjected, "Arguing isn't helpful. Let's just stick to going around—"

Magna stood up, cutting him off. "I have something to say! Chloé was right. Ciaran came to us. That deserves some kind of leniency."

"Agreed," Tova said. "And for the record, I would never advocate for ten years in Claustra. That would be too extreme for this breach."

Joshua joined in. "Why are we talking about Claustra at all? A little probation is enough. Tracking and such should work fine."

"Probation!?" Savannah shrieked. "Well, why don't we just let him walk out of here holding hands with his lover and a pat on his back? Have you all forgotten yourselves? I will accept nothing less than the maximum amount of sentencing. We *must* set an example!"

"That's not setting an example. That's making him a scapegoat, and I will have no part of that," Larry said calmly.

"Then leave," Savannah said nastily.

Graham slammed his gavel. "Okay, that's enough. I'm taking ten years off the table. In fact, I'm taking five years off the table. And *abscondo* is completely off, for either of them. Nothing in the charges warrants any of those extreme sentences."

"And what of the Wisp'ing? Does that not warrant time in Claustra? Or would your best friend Hamish disapprove?" Savannah said coldly.

Everyone was quiet. "Careful there, Savannah," Graham said to her. "I take my position very seriously and do not use it as petty revenge schemes. If I did, you would have been out on your arse a long time ago. You will do well to remember who has the power to demote you to front desk guard duty."

He paused to let his words sink in. She shifted uncomfortably, pursed her lips together, and looked away.

"Now, I haven't heard from Moore, Rory, or Alastair," said Graham. "Let's continue with initial summations."

Chris and Ciaran talked and relived past moments they had together while Sean, Diana, and Rob listened. Ted and Hamish had left and came back with sandwiches for lunch, and they all nibbled a bit, but everyone was too nervous to be hungry. Ciaran left the group to sit with his mother, who was knitting on the other side of the room on the bench.

"Hi, Mum," he said as he sat next to her.

She smiled. "Hi, Ciaran."

"I just want to officially say, again, how sorry I am for all this. And I love you." She patted his leg in forgiveness and appreciation. "I also want to thank you for taking care of Christopher for me."

She put her needles down and looked over at him, laughing with the others. "Well, your siblings certainly like him."

"And you?" he asked. "Do you like him?"

"I like how dedicated he is to you," she responded. "I believe him when he says he loves you with all his heart. That he lives for you and would die for you. Can that be enough for now?"

Ciaran smiled at her. "Before we leave London, you will see what I see. And you'll love him, too."

Grace smiled. They both sat and watched Chris playfully talk with the others. Then Grace said, "Go to him. As he told the world today, he needs you. And you need him."

Ciaran kissed her on the cheek and went back over to sit with Chris, entwining his fingers with him.

"You're right, it's tricky for sure," Moore was saying, over an hour later. "But I do believe their account. I don't believe Ciaran was intentional, malicious, or had willful disregard for the law. He simply talked about himself as any one of us would do with a significant other. I don't want to punish him for that, so let's be fair about sentencing."

"And what is fair?" Savannah said. "Because without actual time in Claustra, there will be no real impact."

"But what would that do to this family? This poor family that has been through so much," Joshua said.

"And to their relationship," Mia said. "The *Ardenti*, remember? That is a powerful kind of love magic. One that cannot be unbound."

Tova said dismissively, "If the *Ardenti* is real, you heard him; they will survive it."

"What do you mean, if it's real? Did we not just see and hear how real it is?" Lucy asked angrily.

"It could all be an act, you know," Cecil said.

"For Houdini's sake, Cecil, you can't be serious!" Magna also said angrily. They all began arguing for the third time until Graham banged his gavel.

He turned to Alastair. "Alastair, you've spent time with them over Christmas. Is their relationship real?"

"Why yes, they seem very comfortable with each other," Alastair stated.

Joshua laughed. "That didn't sound convincing, son."

Alastair said, "Well, if I'm honest, I spent more time talking with my father about extending the Commoner aversion spell around Fairfield Park, where many Magi festivals happen than actually conversing with the man. It's an important—"

"Not now, Alastair!" Magna yelled at him. "Listen, Ted says it's real, Diana says it's real, that's all the witness accounts that we need, especially since not one investigative report contradicts what we have seen and heard today."

"Well, some of us might need more," said Tova.

As Magna and Tova started yelling at each other again, Graham looked over at Quentin, who was minding the door and pretending not to listen.

He called out loudly, "Magus Commander Quentin James! Please step forward."

Everyone stopped talking and watched a surprised Quentin come to the center of the room. "Quentin, you have spent time with them together and apart," Graham said. "Why don't you tell us your observations?"

Before he could speak, Savannah said, "And now I have seen it all. We're trusting the word of a Magi soldier, a boy who has close and personal ties with the accused, in a serious trial."

Moore scoffed. "Who's more trustworthy than Quentin James, son of the great Magus Quinn James? Grandson of the mighty Magus Quentin James the first? Great grandson of the majestic Magus Quigley James?" Moore asked, confused. "Quentin fought harder than us all during the years of the civil war, proving himself over and over again to be a dedicated member of the Magi Enforcers. Who is more trustworthy than that?"

"No one," Mia said, rolling her eyes. "Savannah is just being ... *Savannah.*"

"Don't worry, Aunt Savannah. I take after my father, not after dark Mages like Mother and Talindra, your two cousins. I do not manipulate or lie," Quentin said coldly. They glared at each other.

Then he turned to Graham. "To answer your question, yes, I have spent a lot of time with Ciaran and Christopher together in my home for two days, Christmas Eve and Christmas Day. If you weren't paying attention, you would think they were just the best of mates. They hang out, joke around, have fun together, and invite everyone around them to be a part of them, into their circle. Their affection for each other was very subtle, mostly in unspoken words and glances at each other, slight touches on the hand, arm, back, or shoulder. But after the confession and the breach was revealed, from the moment it all came out, their love and affection for each other expounded. It became overt, openly fearful of being separated and almost clinging to each other.

"Afterward, I spent the majority of my time with Ciaran at Claustra, while my wife spent more time with Chris. Apart from each other, they are shells of the men who came to us on Christmas Eve. Ciaran spent a lot of time talking about Chris, asking every day if he was okay, with no concern about himself. And he told me that he could feel what Chris was feeling from his cell in Claustra: the fear, the depression, the despair. That it was separate from his own feelings.

Personally, I don't think he can survive Claustra, no matter how strong he appears to be, even without *abscondo*. These last five days have been literal hell for him.

"And Chris—well, my wife tells me that he was literally wasting away. Not eating, spending all day in his head and in bed. Everyone has been really worried about him, and I don't think he could survive it either, despite what he said on the stand. I think they both believe they will, but none of us believes it. And I'm not talking about their relationship. I'm talking about literal, physical survival. They don't do well apart. So if you're asking for my opinion as an observant bystander, their love is real, the *Ardenti* bond is real, and Claustra is not the way to go."

"So probation then," Magna said definitively. "It's the best course of action."

"Preposterous! What's to stop him from committing more breaches?" Savannah said.

Tova said, "We'll add a trace, like Joshua suggested. To ensure we know when he is using his *Vis*."

"A trace on the partner as well," said Cecil.

"We can't put a magical tracking on a Commoner," Lucy reminded them.

"We can if he takes the Oath and joins our world," Mia chimed in. "Which I'm almost certain he will have no problem doing that."

"And if either does breach secrecy or does something dangerous again, like Wisp'ing—" Rory said.

Lucy dismissed him. "Oh, shut up about Wisp'ing."

Rory got angry. "No, you shut up, Lucy! I couldn't imagine risking someone else's life like that, especially an unregistered Commoner."

"We'll address the Wisp'ing, son," Larry said. "But for now, are you okay with probation with a trace? In fact, is everyone in agreement with that decision? I certainly am."

Everyone nodded except one. "I am not, but that doesn't matter much, does it?" Savannah said.

Magna answered her, "No, it doesn't." Then she turned to everyone else. "Now for how long? A year? Five years?"

"Five years, goodness that's too long," Joshua said.

"According to the bylaws," Alastair said, "the sentence must fit the duration and severity of the crime. The breach was sixteen months, so no longer than that if we are sticking to the regulations."

"Agreed," Tova nodded.

"Let's put it to a vote," Graham said. "All in favor of a sixteen-month probation with a trace for both Ciaran and Chris, raise your *rodulé*." Everyone raised their wand except Savannah, which was not surprising. "Thank you. We will get his confession again and plea of guilt on record for the charges and administer sentencing. As long as he pleads guilty, the sentence stands. Alastair, please bring Chloé into the room and reveal nothing regarding the sentencing. Quentin, please bring in the accused and his entire family."

Alastair and Quentin both left.

As soon as the door closed, Savannah said sweetly, "Minister Graham, there is a third charge. Willfully endangering the life of a Commoner. Rory is right, what he did was ... *very* dangerous."

"Well, Alastair just left, so we can't add on a third charge without a vote from the jury," Lucy said.

"I can." Savannah smiled. "The charges are brought down by the Office of Magical Law Enforcement. And I just did." She waved her *dulé,* and each person received a memo. They all glared at her.

Magna didn't even read it. "Fine, but it doesn't change the sentencing. It is still sixteen month's probation with a trace. I know what you're doing. He will not be put in Claustra for ten years, you hateful old witch."

Savannah remained so sweet it was sickening. "As long as he pleads guilty to all three charges, his sentence stands. But if he does not plead guilty to all three, an automatic sentence of ten years in Claustra is the law and will be carried out. With *abscondo*. For both of them." She sat back and smiled slyly.

"No fucking way!" Lucy said, horrified.

Moore as well was annoyed. "That's extreme, Savannah."

They began to argue with her when she lost her smile and started yelling, "No! I have had ENOUGH of this mockery of a trial! You want your prize Magus to get off with only probation, then he must plead guilty to all three. Otherwise, his integrity is not as intact as they tried to display it, and this was all for show. I will not stand idly by, and I will go to the radios and tell the Magi world how the Council and their band of friendly Magi let off guilty convicts with a slap on the wrist and a pat on the head. Let's see how you will lead then, with pitchforks at your back."

Everyone was silent. Graham was staring at Savannah as if he wanted to throttle her, but then his face changed. "Fine. Ciaran pleads guilty to all three and receives the agreed-upon sentence. If he doesn't … five years in Claustra."

"With *abscondo*," Savannah reminded him.

"With *abscondo*,"

"For both," Savannah said.

"Fine, Savannah. We will put Ciaran's integrity to the test."

CHAPTER 44

The Aftermath

Alastair opened the door to see Chloé with her head on the table. "Chloé Abbottsford," he called out. She lifted her head. "A verdict is reached." She exhaled, stood up, and started walking toward him.

As Chloé walked past him and out the door, Alastair whispered to her, "I believe, Ms. Abbottsford, that you have succeeded. He must plead guilty again. Make sure he pleads guilty, no matter what."

Chloé kept a straight face as well, but inside her heart leaped for joy.

Quentin opened the door to the chamber to an animated room of laughter. "Hey, everyone. A verdict has been reached. Will everyone follow me into the courtroom, please? Ciaran, you first."

Chris and Ciaran held hands tightly to walk out together. Quentin kept a straight face, but when Diana walked out last, she asked him the question with her eyes, and he winked at her. Her eyes went wide with relief as she followed her family into the courtroom.

As they entered, Chris walked Ciaran over to his chair. They embraced and kissed before Chris made his way to the stands. Ted left a seat open between him and Diana.

Chloé met Ciaran right before he sat down and said, "Plead guilty. No matter what they say, plead guilty."

"I already did," he whispered.

"Do it again," she said.

"Okay. Sure."

"Do you trust me?" she asked him for the second time today.

"Literally with my life right now, Chloé."

"Plead guilty," she said one more time and walked away. Ciaran sat down, careful not to put his arms on the armrest this time. His heart was pounding.

Graham banged his gavel. "Ciaran Archibald Beals, please stand."

Ciaran stood up slowly. There were no smiling faces on the jury, and his friends' faces were unreadable. That made him even more nervous. But he remembered Chloé's words and would trust her.

Graham stated, "Ciaran Beals, you have been accused of knowingly and willingly breaking the Magi Law of Secrecy and Concealment by revealing yourself as a Magus to a Commoner with no apparent ties to the Magi World and Community. How do you plead?"

"Guilty as charged," Ciaran said in a clear voice.

"Ciaran Beals, you have been accused of violating the reasonable restriction of the use of your *Vis* by knowingly and willingly using magic in front of an Unregistered Commoner on multiple occasions. How do you plead?"

"Guilty as charged," Ciaran said again.

"And a third charge has been added," he said, shocking everyone but the jurors, excluding Alastair. Alastair looked up, confused, but no one would look at him.

Graham stated, "Ciaran Beals, you have been accused of violating Clause 73: willfully endangering the life of a Commoner with the potential to cause harm or draw notice of the Commoner Community to the Magi Community by Wisp'ing with an Unregistered Commoner. How do you plead?"

Ciaran's mouth formed a full "o" in shock as he heard his mother shriek from behind him. Ted said quietly, "Holy shit." Diana gripped Chris's thigh next to her.

"What does that mean?" Chris whispered to Ted.

Ted whispered back, "A Clause 73 breach is an automatic minimum ten-year sentence."

Chris's mouth mimicked Ciaran's. "It's... it's all over. That's it then." He couldn't wrap his head around not seeing Ciaran for ten years.

No one made a sound. Ciaran was still standing there, mouth opened. He closed his mouth and swallowed. He turned to Chloé, but she was looking at Alastair, who was looking at Graham. No one was smiling, but Savannah had a small smirk she simply could not hide. And he took that as a sign. Ciaran took a deep breath and looked directly at Graham.

"Guilty ... as charged," he said, not as confidently as the first two times.

He heard his mother yelp again and wished he could turn around, but couldn't face Chris either. He had accepted his fate.

Graham stood up. "Ciaran Archibald Beals, by your own admission, you have been found guilty of all three charges.

Your sentence is as follows: You are hereby sentenced to sixteen months of probation with a magical trace—"

Graham could not finish because the Beals erupted into shouts and cheers.

Chris was still stunned. "Probation!??" he yelled. "Did he say probation? Not jail time! No Claustra!?"

"YES!" Ted yelled, and they stood up and hugged tightly.

Graham had to bang his gavel a few times and yell, "ORDER! I am not finished!"

He waited for them to sit down quietly. Ciaran had not moved a muscle since Graham started talking. He continued, "You are hereby ordered to sixteen months of probation with a magical trace for you and Ranger Jennings.

"Ranger Christopher Jennings, please stand." Chris slowly stood up. "You have some decisions to make. You are mandated to take the Magi Oath and receive your tracking or be *abscondo'd* forthwith. What say you?"

"Well, Grandminister, sir, I believe I made that decision a long time ago. Wherever Ciaran is, I am. So yes, I will take the Oath and join the Magi Community, without question. Just consider me an honorary Beals."

"HERE, HERE!" Sean said loudly. He stood up, reached over, and shook his hand. "Welcome, Mr. Beals!"

Chris shook his hand back. "Thank you, Mr. Beals."

He turned and shook Ted's hand, who stood up and also called him Mr. Beals. Rob stood up, and Chris shook his hand as Sean shook Ted's hand; they continued to switch and shake hands, comically calling each other Mr. Beals.

Graham banged his gavel again. "Thank you!" he said loudly to regain order. "And what of your family? Breaches occur not in huge ways, but in letting information out to family and loved ones, as you can see. And a breach, while on probation, will bring you both right back here with an automatic sentence in Claustra for five years for Ciaran, and concealment of memory for the both of you."

"Is there an option to bring them in as well?" Chris asked. "Not everyone, just my sisters. My mother is gone, and I'm not close with my father, so he doesn't need to know."

"Absolutely. I will personally escort you back home to explain the situation and administer the Oath. Hamish, will you escort me as a Council official?"

Hamish stood up. "Of course, Grandminister."

"It's settled then. Please come down and step forward to take the Oath and the trace."

But Chris said, "With the deepest respect, do you mind if we wait until we are back in Albania, and I take the Oath with my sisters? As much as I love Ciaran and would want to be by his side, I think it's important that we Jennings do this huge thing together as a family."

Graham turned back to the jurors. "Yay or nay vote on delaying the Oath and trace on Christopher Jennings until the identified family members can be included. Raise your *rodulé* for yay?" Almost all raised their wands except Savannah, which was again not surprising. "We have agreed to your stipulations, Christopher. Quentin, please administer the tracking on Ciaran."

Ciaran, who still had not spoken or moved since his sentence came down, turned to Quentin. Quentin smiled at him. "You alright there, Ciaran?"

"I... yes. Yes."

Quentin pointed his *rodulé* downward and moved it in a circular motion like he was mixing a cake. "Please lower your head or kneel so I can reach the center of your skull. This might hurt a bit."

Ciaran opted to kneel, and Quentin touched the center of his head with a red light stemming from the tip. *"Vis magicis vestigium,"* Quentin murmured.

As Ciaran stood back up, a warm sensation went through his head and down his body. He started to say, "This doesn't feel so ba—" when the sensation hit his wrists and hands, and it burned like fire, making him cry out, "Aaaaaah!!"

"Sorry, mate," Quentin said and meant it.

Ciaran was shaking. He looked down, and the black bands around his wrists that he received when he first entered Claustra were gone, replaced by a thin red one. It faded into his skin.

Graham spoke again, gathering his attention. "Ciaran, and eventually Christopher, you are hereby ordered to report to the Albanian Magi Division once a month for probationary check in until sixteen months from this date or until a time the Magi Enforcer over you decides appropriate, whichever comes sooner. Furthermore, these proceedings are closed and will not be a matter of Magi public record for the full duration of the probationary period of sixteen months. Ciaran and Chris, you are free to disclose your probation status and the circumstances as such, but we as members of the jury will be bound by magical law not to do so. Do either of you have any questions?"

Ciaran shook his head no; Chris said, "Just one. Can I take my man home now?"

Some jury members laughed. Ciaran shook his head and smiled. Graham found himself smiling as well. "Ciaran A. Beals, you are free to go. The hearing is concluded." He banged his gavel.

Ciaran walked over to Chloé and lifted her off her feet, kissed her on the check. "You did it! You did it!" he kept shouting.

But Chloé was crying. "I'm so sorry, Ciaran. I didn't mean for any of this to happen! I just thought—"

He put her down and held her. "It was perfect as it happened, and you were brilliant. Thank you so much!"

He felt hands and hugs grabbing him from behind as Diana, Ron, Sean, and Ted had come up, and they ended up in a group hug. They let go as Grace pushed her way through and hugged Ciaran, also crying; then Hamish, who had tears in his eyes but they did not fall, gave his son a hug. He turned around to find the face he was waiting for.

Chris, who had stood back a little bit, smiled. "I told you it would be fine."

Ciaran walked up and touched his face with both hands, then moved them to the nape of his neck. He kissed him passionately in front of his family, friends, and adversaries. Chris wrapped his hands around Ciaran's back and kissed him back.

Ciaran broke away first. "I love you so much."

Chris pulled him in for a hug, and they held each other tightly. "I love you, too, Ciaran."

Ciaran heard a familiar voice behind him. "One for me too?" He turned to see Lucy, Magna, and Mia behind him.

He grabbed Lucy first. "Lucinda!!" he yelled, lifted her off her feet, and spun her around twice, knocking her glasses off her face.

"Merlin's pants, Ciaran, put me down!" she said with a laugh. As he did, she said, "You should be spinning Magna around; she did all the work."

Ciaran walked up to his other friend. He was reminded how tall she was as he stood in front of her, almost his height as his nose reached her forehead. She said to him sternly, "Don't you even think about it."

He smiled at her, then went serious. "Thank you. It's not even enough to say, but thank you." He gave her a hug then kissed her on the cheek. She slowly lifted her hands to pat his back. "Also, Magna the Maleficent? I'm never calling you that."

Magna pulled back and glared at him. "If you're in this building, you will if you know what's good for you." But then she gave him another smile, and he hugged her again. This time, Magna grabbed him tightly.

"Really and truly, thank you, Magna," Ciaran said again.

She shrugged. "Darragh would have done it. I just did what she would have done."

"The truth is," Lucy began in a whisper as they pulled apart, "You had the votes. We just needed to make sure it didn't get derailed by Savannah Bitchenhouse."

Chris laughed. "Oh, God, that's good. Bitchenhouse." They all turned to look at her, scowling as she left the courtroom.

Magna approached Chris. To him, she was intimidatingly beautiful, with her jet black hair pulled in a tight bun, her silver eyes, and extremely pale skin with dark red lipstick on her pouty lips. "Mr. Jennings, the cause of all of this," she started. "I am very excited to meet you."

Before he could speak, Mia said with amusement in her eyes, "As am I! You are so handsome."

Chris smiled. "Thank you. Thank you both. And you are both stunningly beautiful. I know which witches will haunt my dreams from now on," he said slyly. They both blushed, and Mia giggled.

"I'm a warlock. And you're a sweet talker," Magna said. "Is that what he did, Ciaran? Talk his way into your britches?"

Both men laughed. But Ciaran turned to the smaller one. "Mia, right?" Ciaran said. "I feel like I know you, but can't remember from where. We were in the same year, but never hung out, yes?"

"Yes, I was at Campus with you," she said with a smile. "But you didn't notice me. While you were running around with the cool Magi, I was trying not to be noticed. I work in Artifacts now."

Ciaran remembered. "Yes, but of course I noticed you. Silver hair, pink *dulé*. Exceptional mind in potions and history."

"Oh, my gosh, you do remember," she said with a smile.

He shook her hand and said, "Thank you as well."

"Oh, you're so welcome. When Magna called for me to sit among the jurors, I honestly did not know what I was getting myself into. But now, hearing your story, I'm so glad I did."

Before he could respond, Moore had tapped his shoulder. "Ciaran Beals? I'm Moore Catrell."

Ciaran turned around and shook his hand. "Thank you too, Minister Catrell. I appreciate your measured judgment of me."

"It's me that should be thanking you, Ciaran," he said. "My younger brother was on the streets of Myrddin that day, a 16-year-old by the name of Tyson. He said you saved his life. In the middle of a duel right outside, he had lost his *dulé*, and a CV raised his to kill him, but you blocked it with a protection spell, then killed the warlock. You helped him up and asked him if was okay; then someone called your name, and you left to keep fighting. You may not remember him, but he certainly remembers you. And that's all that matters to me." He touched Ciaran's shoulder. "I know you lost your brother that day, and I'm so sorry. But I am so grateful that because of you, I didn't lose mine."

Ciaran was stunned. "I am sorry that I don't remember him. I protected a lot of people that day, young and old. But I, too, am grateful that your brother was one of them. Not because of today, but because no one deserved to die that day, especially not underaged Magi."

"I appreciate that," Moore said. "Just know that no matter what you did, if you had actually killed this miserable, love-sick bloke behind you, you would have had my vote for a full pardon, no question." Chris laughed, and Ciaran smiled. They shook hands again.

Rory came over to shake his hand as well. "Ciaran, still as popular as ever."

"And you, Rory, continue to be underestimated. I appreciate you on this panel and you judging me fairly." Rory nodded.

Chris was in conversation with Lucy, Magna, and Mia while Ciaran went to thank the rest of the jury members. Savannah had left as soon as the verdict was passed, so it was a cheery atmosphere. After talking with Larry, Tova, and Joshua, Ciaran spotted Alastair and Grace talking with Graham, and he went over to shake Graham's hand.

"Ah, the man of the hour," Graham said, shaking his hand back. "I was just hearing an interesting story about an unauthorized, unregistered Commoner sneaking into the Magi Council facility this morning."

Ciaran raised both palms. "I was in Claustra and had nothing to do with it."

"Not to worry, no more charges will be brought against you or your family today," Graham said with a smile.

"Thank you, Grandminister. I hope I didn't cause you too much trouble."

"No trouble at all. In fact, this was what I was going to recommend anyway, probation for you, the Oath for him, so it all worked out. I will set up transport to Albania on Saturday morning so you can spend the New Year with your family and friends. Stay out of trouble until then, will you?"

"Absolutely," Ciaran said.

Ciaran then turned to Alastair, who also put his hand out for a shake. Ciaran slapped his hand away and threw his arms around his neck. "I love you, cousin. I could not have done this without you. You saved my life."

"Well," Alastair said, uncomfortable in hugs as always. "I wasn't going to let you go to prison for falling in love. That would be ridiculous, wouldn't it?" Alastair patted his back with one hand.

"Ridiculous indeed." Ciaran smiled at him, and Alastair smiled back.

***

The Beals family and friends headed into the lift and piled in together. Chris and Ciaran entered last, holding hands, and faced the mirrored doors. They smiled at each other in the mirror. Chris didn't know how or why, but in his heart, he knew this was the moment.

Chris looked at Ciaran through the mirror and said, "Ciaran? Marry me."

Ciaran's smile faded into shock.

"*What!?*" Grace exclaimed. "What did he just say!?" Diana shushed her mother and grabbed her arm. Chloé grabbed Diana's hand, her eyes opened wide.

Ciaran turned to Chris to look at him, still looking at Ciaran in the mirror. "You ... are... Did you... Are you *serious*?" Ciaran asked, still in shock.

Chris nodded. "Marry me, Ciaran. Okay?"

Chris turned to look Ciaran in the eyes. They stared at each other. No one spoke.

Ciaran then said softly, "Okay."

"Okay," Chris said. Then he smiled sheepishly, and Ciaran returned his smile. The elevator dinged at the bottom floor.

Diana, Grace, and Chloé turned to each other, let out excited screams, and hugged each other. Ted, who was in the back of the elevator, pushed to the front to grab Ciaran and Chris by their shoulders, yelling, "Did that happen!? Did that really *just* happen!?"

In the tight elevator, they gave each other another a round of hugs, spilling out of the lift with all smiles.

Quentin handed Ciaran something and said, "Go back to the house with Christopher." Ciaran looked at it, and it was a tiny *rodulé*, like a key fob. He grinned at Quentin.

"Yes, let's all go back to the house and celebrate!" Grace said, overhearing.

But Diana said, "Actually, Mum, can we go shopping first? Now that this is all behind us, I would love to get some drapes for the parlor for the new year. And Quentin has to go back to the courts and work, and I'm sure Chloé, Alastair, and Dad have to work as well. And, Sean, aren't you still planning on going into the shop for a bit?"

Grace was confused. "Diana, what are you—"

Hamish cut his wife off. "Diana is right, dear, we all have things to take care of. Alastair and I are headed back up to talk with Graham. Why don't we reconvene at Quentin's for dinner?"

Rob turned to Sean. "I already told my dad we weren't going into the shop today."

"*We* are not," Sean told him. "*You* are going to follow your girl, apologize for being a toad, and grovel at her feet."

Chris overheard him and agreed. "Seriously. Chloé just pulled off a miracle. Go apologize for being an arse."

Instead of talking, Ciaran turned Rob around and pushed him toward Chloé, who was getting on the lift back to her office. She was startled to see Rob get on after her, but they saw him grab her hand right before the doors closed.

"They will be fine," Sean said.

Quentin kissed Diana and went to catch another lift back to the courtrooms as Hamish and Alastair went back to their offices. The rest headed through the revolving doors, with Grace, Diana, and Sean deeper into Myrddin and Chris and Ciaran catching a taxi back to the James residence.

CHAPTER 45

Ciaran's Release

Upon entering Quentin's home and taking off coats, Chris started walking toward the kitchen asking, "Do you want me to cook you something to eat—"

But Ciaran grabbed him and kissed him, bit his bottom lip, and started unbuckling his pants.

"Whoa, slow down. Dinner first," Chris joked.

"No," Ciaran said sternly. "And shut up. You talk too much."

Chris laughed in between Ciaran's kisses and allowed Ciaran to get his pants down to his knees. Chris could feel his passion for him, his desire, as Ciaran got on his knees and put Chris in his mouth, deep-throating him repeatedly. Chris had to hold on to the banister with Ciaran's intensity and groaned loudly.

After a few minutes of sucking the pre-cum out of Chris, Ciaran stood up. "Let's take this upstairs," he said, the fire in his bright blue eyes blazing like never before.

"Alright," Chris said as Ciaran took full control.

After removing Chris's pants and underwear, leaving them at the bottom of the stairs, Ciaran held onto Chris, moving him backward up the stairs. Halfway up the first staircase, Ciaran changed his mind and pushed Chris down on the stairs.

Chris laughed again. "I think you missed me."

Ciaran got on his knees and put Chris in his mouth again, who instantly moaned. After a few sucks he said, "Shut the fuck up, Christopher. Stop. Talking." He deep-throated him again.

Chris got the message and grabbed Ciaran's head with both hands, guiding him, moaning loudly. Ciaran stood up and unzipped his pants and took them off right there on the staircase. "Lube," he called out, holding one hand up and stroking himself, no *rodulé* in sight.

To Chris's surprise, the lube came out of their bedroom, down the stairs, right into Ciaran's hand. "I guess we aren't making it to the room," Chris said in awe.

Ciaran shook his head as he prepared Chris, saying, "You don't listen very well, do you? Shut. Up."

Ciaran entered Chris, making him groan and laugh at the same time. Ciaran moved slowly at first, then quickly sped up, pounding Chris on the stairs as Chris yelled out all kinds of obscenities while holding onto his thighs. "Shit! Fuck! Dammit! Fuck! Shit!"

At the point where he couldn't take it anymore, he said in between shouts and moans, "Ciaran, these stairs are killing my back."

Ciaran kissed him. "Okay. Let's go upstairs, for real this time."

He stood up and took off his shirt. He followed Chris up to the second set of stairs, and when he was a few steps away from the top of the third-floor landing, he pushed him down again so that his torso was on the floor but his legs were still on the steps. He entered Chris from behind a bit forcefully making Chris cry out, but not move. Ciaran kissed his neck, his shoulders, and his upper back softly, gently, lovingly. But then he began to move, burying himself in and out with speed. Ciaran fucked him until Chris felt Ciaran swell and heard Ciaran roar, the warmth of Ciaran's cum filling up his insides. Then his lover collapsed on him.

"Jesus, Ciaran, you didn't wanker off not one time in Claustra?" Chris said.

"No," Ciaran said. "I saved it all for you."

He pulled out and sat on a lower step. Chris crawled the rest of his body to the step right above Ciaran and sat down. He touched Ciaran's hair and the beard that was growing in. "You should keep it," he said. "It's sexy."

"No," Ciaran said abruptly. "I'm not going to keep anything that reminds me of that place." His face fell, and Chris noticed.

"C'mon. Let's really make it to our room." Chris took off his shirt, which was his last article of clothing left, and reached for Ciaran's hand.

Once they entered, Chris brought Ciaran to the bed and laid him on his stomach. He spread Ciaran's cheeks wide and put his long tongue inside, licking the rim, then down to his testicles and back again. Ciaran moaned and moved his bottom against him. After a thorough rim job, Chris lubed himself liberally. He then lay over him, entering him slowly. Turning him to the side, he wrapped his arms around Ciaran's midsection and gave him slow strokes. Ciaran moaned softly in his throat, while stroking himself.

After a while, Chris turned Ciaran's chin upward to him, and they kissed. Chris heard him, loud and clear, <*I love you, Christopher.*>

Chris came up for air. "I love you, too, Ciaran."

Chris started moving faster after that and thrusted in and out harder, giving Ciaran an unexpected orgasm. He let out of a long, loud, "Oooooh!" He held onto the sheets as he was hit with wave after wave of euphoria. Chris pulled all the way out, stopping himself from cumming. He turned Ciaran onto his back and crawled between his legs to enter him slowly once more, as they kissed and rubbed hair and bodies together until Chris's orgasm was begging to come out. He held on as Ciaran grabbed himself again and began stroking to match Chris's thrust. Ciaran came first, still thick and white, shooting out in four successions, coating his freckled chest and pecs. The sight of Ciaran cumming, coupled with the tightening of his anus, was enough for Chris to cum, and he silently emptied out as the orgasmic waves took over his mind.

Chris moved to the side of him. Even after he came, Ciaran's body spasmed twice, and he lay there trying to catch his breath and slow his heartbeat. When he finally did, Chris said, "I can't believe I get to do this for the rest of my life."

Ciaran turned to him. "So we're really doing this? Getting married."

"I wouldn't have asked you if I didn't want to. But if you don't..."

"I do!" Ciaran said automatically. "More than anything now. I want to be connected with you in all ways. I'll take your last name if you want me to."

Chris laughed. "We'll hyphenate names because I sure do want to be a Beals now." Ciaran chuckled. Then Chris said, "I'm sorry I didn't give you Paris."

Ciaran touched his face. "Don't be. This was perfect. We'll make it to France one day." Chris took his hand and kissed it as a response. "You were so brave and confident today," Ciaran said. "Even when I wasn't. It was amazing having you by my side. You are amazing."

But Chris was honest. "Well, to be fair, I kind of had a meltdown after you left the first time. I wasn't that brave."

"But so what about that? You were still braver than me." Ciaran closed his eyes. "It was awful in there. Not the quiet, or being alone with my thoughts, but the idea of being separated from you was torture enough. I really thought I was going to stay there, and every single day a piece of me died. I just wanted to touch you and taste you, feel you, and I couldn't do any of that. I was so scared I was going to be without you, never see you again. I was so scared..."

Ciaran's voice broke, and he started dissolving into tears and sobbing.

His emotions took Chris off guard; he had never seen Ciaran cry like that before. And Chris started to feel it, Ciaran's feelings beginning to overwhelm him as if they were his own. He pulled him close and held him tight, letting Ciaran sob uncontrollably in his arms. Chris held him and rocked him until he quieted down.

"Nothing will ever separate us. We'll never be apart, you and me, love," Chris said softly. "That is my oath to you, today and always." He kissed Ciaran on the head.

"And mine as well," Ciaran said, sniffling. "Nothing, and no one, will ever separate us again. This I promise you, today and always."

Chris held his face tightly to his chest as Ciaran wrapped his arms around him. As Ciaran was falling asleep, he heard Chris say, "I'm going to love you forever, Ciaran Beals. Forever and three days after that."

Ciaran smiled as he drifted off.

Grace and Diana came through the door with bags but were blocked by coats piled up. Grace took one look at the clothes thrown around about the stairs and said, "Diana, did your washing machine explode?"

Diana laughed. "No, Mum, but I'll gather them up." She waved her *dulé* at the clothes, and they came together, folding neatly at the bottom of the stairs.

As Grace watched, it dawned on her whose clothes they were, and her eyes went wide. "Is that why you wanted me to go shopping with you? So they could—" She cut herself off.

"Mum," Diana chided. "They haven't seen each other in almost a week. They needed time to be alone. Surely you understand."

Grace didn't say anything. She turned and walked to the kitchen. Diana took their clothes upstairs to their room and noticed that the door was left wide open. She placed the clothes at the bottom of the bed and lit the dim lamp by the door. Chris opened his eyes and looked at her. Ciaran was still across his chest fast asleep. Diana smiled, and he smiled back, then closed his eyes. She gently closed the door.

Chris rubbed Ciaran's back softly, feeling how calm he was. He let Ciaran's love for him and contentment overwhelm him and put him in a deep sleep.

Will Chris and his family join the Magi Community? Find out in book 3, The Oath!

BOOK CLUB QUESTIONS

1. In book two, Ciaran continues to wrestle with naming his sexuality. Are labels important? Why or why not?

2. What are your thoughts about Vlad and Alexi's relationship?

3. The Motus Willow helped Chris and Ciaran express their love for each other, finally. Have you ever hesitated to tell someone that you loved them?

4. Ted scolds Ciaran and Chris on how they had not been honest about Chris's Commoner status. Did you agree with him then? Now that you've read through the novel, did your opinion change?

5. As Chris realizes that he was groomed into a relationship with Rem, he also realizes the mistakes he made with his father, Collum. At the same time, Collum has expressed homophobic attitudes toward his own son. If

you were Chris, would you try to build a relationship with Collum?

6. Who was your favorite dinner guest at Christmas? What was your favorite part?

7. Diana kept her position with the Magi Council a secret from her family. Why do you think she joined the Magi Secrecy Enforcers?

8. Was Chloé right?

9. What do you think about Grace Beals and her struggle with her acceptance of Chris in her son's life?

10. The author uses more magical realism in book two. Did the author do a good job? Would you like to see more or less?

AUTHOR BIO

Wife, mother, partner, daughter, sister, friend, social worker, life skills coach, and part-time erotic romance novelist, Eskay Kabba finds the complexity of human nature and creates romantic and erotic love stories. The characters reflect the notion that no one is all good or all bad, but we are all just trying to find love in hard places. Eskay pens erotic romance novels that celebrate the LGBTQ community, people of color, and interracial relationships. When not writing about the throes of passion, Eskay finds joy in spending time with her family and loved ones, reading dystopia and fantasy series, and binging popular shows from a streaming app.

Eskay.Kabba@gmail.com

Discover more at
4HorsemenPublications.com

10% off using HORSEMEN10